CINDERELLA OF HARLEY STREET

BY
ANNE FRASER

MILLS & BOON

For Flora, with love and thanks.

First published in Great Britain 2013
by Mills & Boon, an imprint of Harlequin (UK) Limited.
Harlequin (UK) Limited, Eton House, 18-24 Paradise Road,
Richmond, Surrey TW9 1SR

© Anne Fraser 2013

ISBN: 978 0 263 89887 3

Harlequin (UK) policy is to use papers that are natural, renewable and recyclable products and made from wood grown in sustainable forests. The logging and manufacturing process conform to the legal environmental regulations of the country of origin.

Printed and bound in Spain
by Blackprint CPI, Barcelona

CINDERELLA OF HARLEY STREET

BY
ANNE FRASER

YOU, ME AND A FAMILY

BY
SUE MacKAY

Anne Fraser was born in Scotland, but brought up in South Africa. After she left school she returned to the birthplace of her parents, the remote Western Islands of Scotland. She left there to train as a nurse, before going on to university to study English Literature. After the birth of her first child she and her doctor husband travelled the world, working in rural Africa, Australia and Northern Canada. Anne still works in the health sector. To relax, she enjoys spending time with her family, reading, walking and travelling.

With a background of working in medical laboratories and a love of the romance genre, it is no surprise that **Sue MacKay** writes Mills & Boon® Medical Romance™ stories. An avid reader all her life, she wrote her first story at age eight—about a prince, of course. She lives with her own hero in the beautiful Marlborough Sounds, at the top of New Zealand's South Island, where she indulges her passions for the outdoors, the sea and cycling.

Dear Reader

As my readers will know, I've written about damaged heroes and heroines who find themselves in heartbreaking and traumatic medical situations. This time I wanted to write about a heroine who has post-traumatic stress disorder and her journey to happiness—and so Cassie was created.

Cassie has had a difficult childhood. Taken away at an early age from her drug-addicted mother and adopted by a couple who don't love her, she's grown up striving for perfection, doubting that anyone can love her for ever.

All that got her through her lonely childhood and teenage years was a burning desire to become a children's doctor.

When she meets Dr Leith Ballantyne, Cassie begins to dream that perhaps she can have her fairytale ending after all—until she discovers that the man she is falling in love with has a son. Not trusting that she can be a good mother to any child because of her own childhood experiences, she decides the best thing she can do for Leith and his son is walk away.

However it seems that fate has different plans for her when she finds herself working with Leith once more, and she is drawn not just to him but to his unhappy little boy.

I have indulged my love of travel in this book—the hero and heroine meet on the Mercy Ship in Africa, are reunited in London, visit Leith's childhood home on the Isle of Skye and fall in love all over again in the Caribbean.

I hope you enjoy Leith and Cassie's story.

Anne Fraser

Recent titles by Anne Fraser:

HER MOTHERHOOD WISH**
THE FIREBRAND WHO UNLOCKED HIS HEART
MISTLETOE, MIDWIFE…MIRACLE BABY
DOCTOR ON THE RED CARPET
THE PLAYBOY OF HARLEY STREET
THE DOCTOR AND THE DEBUTANTE
DAREDEVIL, DOCTOR…DAD!†
MIRACLE: MARRIAGE REUNITED
SPANISH DOCTOR, PREGNANT MIDWIFE*

**The Most Precious Bundle of All
†St. Piran's Hospital
*The Brides of Penhally Bay

**These books are also available in eBook format
from www.millsandboon.co.uk**

CHAPTER ONE

CASSIE HEAVED HER bag along the quayside, feeling unbearably hot in the midday African sun.

She stopped to rest her aching arms and glanced upwards. The boat was enormous—far bigger than she could ever have imagined. That was good. It would mean that there would be plenty of corners for her to hide in. Naturally she'd socialise whenever it was necessary, but she needed to know that there were places, apart from her cabin, where she could be alone. It wasn't that she didn't like people, she simply preferred her own company.

Her attention was caught by a man standing next to the rail, talking on his phone. Just as Cassie looked up at him he turned his head and for a moment their eyes locked. Her head spun as the strangest sensations twirled around her lower abdomen.

It wasn't as if he was particularly good-looking—God knew, she had been out with men better looking in her life—but it was the way he carried himself, the tilt of his head, the slight smile on his lips, the way his eyes creased at the corners. If she didn't know differently, she would have sworn she was experiencing simple, pure lust.

When he tipped his head to the side and raised one

eyebrow, she flushed, knowing she had been staring. Now a deeper shade of red would be added to the beetroot colour she must already be from heat and exertion. Great. In those few seconds they had held each other's gazes, all sorts of warning bells had gone off in her head. She decided instantly that whoever he was she'd do her best to ignore him in the coming weeks.

She was halfway up the gangway when disaster struck. Her over-filled, slightly battered and definitely seen-better-days suitcase decided it had had enough of being stuffed to the gills, and it exploded, showering her path with T-shirts, dresses and, most embarrassingly, her underwear. She watched with horror as a pair of her lace and silk panties, which had cost her more money than she cared to remember, flew over the handrail, snagged on a piece of metal and fluttered there like some sort of lacy flag of surrender.

Mortified, Cassie lunged for them and almost toppled into the sea. And that was exactly what would have happened had she not found herself caught and held fast against a broad, hard chest.

For the briefest of moments she stayed there. There was something achingly secure about being held in these particular arms.

Which was ridiculous. She didn't need a man—anyone—to make her feel safe.

Somehow she wasn't surprised when she reluctantly extricated herself from the stranger's arms to find that the man who had saved her from falling overboard was the same one who only moments earlier had caught her staring. So much for her promise to herself to avoid him.

'I know it's hot, but I wouldn't recommend the side of the ship for a dip.'

His accent was Scottish, warm and rich with a musical cadence of laughter.

When she looked up at him—he was a good few inches taller than she was—she was horrified to discover that he had rescued her panties and was now holding the flimsy piece of silk and lace in his hands.

'Yours, I believe?' he said with a cheeky grin.

Could her introduction to the ship and the staff get any worse than this? Cassie thought despairingly, noticing that several people were now lining the rails of the ship taking an unabashed interest in what was going on below them. To make matters worse, a group of locals had also stopped and were chattering away to one another in loud, cheerful voices while pointing to Cassie and giggling.

'Thank you,' she said stiffly, grabbing her panties. Really, was there any need for him to hold them up for all to see?

She crouched down and quickly scooped up her scattered belongings, shoving them into the suitcase. Normally, when she packed, everything was perfectly arranged, each item in its place, each T-shirt, skirt, dress and pair of trousers laid on top of each other in graduating colours. Although she knew it was a little obsessional, Cassie liked order—more than liked it, needed it. But unless she wanted to have every item of her wardrobe examined in minute detail there was nothing for it but to get the damn things back in the suitcase and out of sight as quickly as possible. She would have to wait until she reached her cabin before she could sort it all.

Her helper—she refused to think of him as rescuer; it wasn't really an appropriate term for a man who'd mostly retrieved her underwear—crouched down in the confined space of the gangway, so close she could feel the heat radiating from him. The sensation was so intense it robbed her of her breath. However, any attempt to move away would result in her going for the swim he'd joked about. Even if, right now, it was almost tempting.

'I can manage, thank you,' she said. 'I'm sure there are other places you need to be.'

'There are, but I'm pretty sure none of them are quite as entertaining.'

She glanced up at him and again there was that odd frisson running down her spine. She shoved the remaining clothes into her suitcase and almost immediately realised if she tried to close it, first, she would have to sit on it on the steep gangway and, second, even if she did get it closed there was every chance it would burst open again before she could reach her cabin.

It appeared as if the same thought had struck him. He picked up her suitcase, snapped it shut with a single easy movement and tucked it under his arm. 'Deck and cabin number?' he asked. 'At least, I'm assuming you are joining the ship as staff?'

Cassie studied him for a moment. He was tall, almost six-four, she guessed, with sun-lightened brown hair and a wide, full mouth that turned up more at one side than the other. But it was his eyes, an unusual shade of green that drew her. She had the uncanny feeling he could see right into her, see all her secrets, and the sensation wasn't a welcome one.

She became aware that he was waiting for her response with a quizzical smile on his face. 'Dr Ross. Cassie Ross,' she said, holding out her hand.

His smile widened. 'Dr Leith Ballantyne. Welcome to the African Mercy Ship.'

Damn—he was one of the doctors. That would make him difficult to avoid. But, with a bit of luck, he himself would be leaving soon. Cassie had been told that although the nurses tended to stay for a minimum of three months, most of the doctors held permanent jobs elsewhere and, like her, only usually managed to give a few weeks of their time in any one year.

At the top of the gangway she reached for her suitcase. 'I'll take it now, if you don't mind.'

'No. I insist. You must be tired from travelling.' He raised an eyebrow in question. 'London?'

'Yes,' she responded tersely. Then, realising she was being rude, she added, 'Seems days since I left England. I must have experienced every form of transport Africa has to offer over the last forty-eight hours. It's great to finally be here.'

'It's an excellent ship with an excellent team.'

'And I'm looking forward to getting stuck in this afternoon.'

'There'll be no work for you until tomorrow.' Without waiting for her reply, he headed off down a narrow corridor, still holding her suitcase, and she was forced to follow him.

'I'll be fine once I have a shower,' she said to his back.

He turned round. 'Believe me, you'll have enough to do while you're here. How long are you staying anyway?'

'Just over two weeks.'

'Then take the rest while you can. You're going to need it.' When he gave her a lopsided smile she had the crazy sensation of not being able to breathe. She dragged her eyes away from his, hoping he would put the heat in her cheeks down to the sun.

'Perhaps we could have dinner later and I could explain how it works around here?' he continued.

She hadn't been here five minutes and already he was hitting on her. Normally that wouldn't bother her—she'd dealt with men like him plenty of times before, usually brushing them off with a light-hearted quip—but there was something about Leith that disturbed her usual composure.

'I'd like to get to work straight away,' she replied stiffly.

Immediately the laconic manner was gone. 'It's not going to happen. A tired doctor is a dangerous doctor. You are forbidden from working until you've had a good night's sleep.' Then he smiled again. 'So, dinner? It's not haute cuisine, I'm afraid, but it serves its purpose.'

Just who did he think he was, telling her what she could and could not do? She was about to open her mouth to say as much when he swung round and carried on walking. He opened the door to her tiny cabin and dropped her bag on the narrow bunk. There was barely room to swing a cat and she was acutely aware of him standing just a few feet from her.

'I can take it from here,' she said quickly. 'If I can't work, I think I'll skip dinner and have an early night. Now, if you'll excuse me, I think I should find the showers.'

'They're at the end of the corridor.' As he stepped towards her she backed away. She didn't want to be any closer to him than she was already. Annoyingly her pulse was still beating a tattoo in her temples. It had to be the heat.

He grinned again, amusement glinting in his deep green eyes as if he'd noticed her instant reaction to him and it hadn't surprised him. 'If you change your mind about dinner, I'll be in the canteen about seven.'

When he left, Cassie closed the door of her cabin and sank down on the bed. If at all possible, she was going to avoid Dr Leith Ballantyne.

Leith was whistling as he made his way to his cabin. From the moment he'd first clapped eyes on her, he'd known that life was going to get way more interesting. He normally preferred women with long hair but Cassie's short silky black bob suited her heart-shaped, delicate features, making her eyes appear almost too large for her face.

Up until her suitcase had spewed her belongings over the gangway she'd looked impossibly cool and sexy in her white blouse and light cotton trousers that clung to her curvy figure. And as for those eyes! The icy look she'd given him when he'd caught her staring could have destroyed a lesser man, so the way she'd blushed when he'd retrieved her underwear had been a surprise—a good one.

She intrigued the hell out of him. Cool, almost shy one minute—and in Leith's experience women who looked like Cassie weren't in the least bit shy—sparky and determined the next.

Pity she was only here for a couple of weeks. He would have liked to take his time getting to know Dr Cassie Ross and, if she was only here for a couple of weeks, time was one thing he didn't have.

Cassie wiped the sweat from her forehead with the back of her arm and looked down at her line of patients, stretching along the dusty road and way into the distance. There wasn't room on the Mercy Ship to see outpatients, all the space being needed for the wards and theatres.

She'd seen more kids already than she could count and there were more still to be seen—most waiting patiently with their mothers, some playing in the dust and others tucked up in shawls on their mothers' backs.

It was the quiet ones you had to worry about most. Children who cried or played had to be fit enough to react to their environment. Those who lay limply in their mothers' arms were almost always the most in need of urgent attention.

On her first morning, she'd been allocated her duties by the medical officer in charge and she'd had her nose to the grindstone ever since. As the only paediatrician, Cassie was responsible for all the children the nurses referred to her at the daily morning outpatient clinic. She also had charge of the small but well-equipped children's ward and special-care facility on board and, in addition, she would assist with paediatric cases in Theatre whenever her help was required.

None of it fazed her in the slightest. She'd done a year as a surgical resident as part of her paediatric training and although didn't want to specialise in surgery had enjoyed her time in Theatre. In fact, the more challenges, the harder the work, the better.

She stopped for a moment to drink some water. In this heat it was important to keep hydrated. Suddenly, she heard a commotion in one of the other lines. Although the patients had to wait for hours in the burning sun they rarely complained so any disturbance had to mean something was wrong. With a quick word to the nurse who was assisting her, she went to see what it was about.

When she reached the point in the line where the

cries had been coming from, the patients stood back. A young woman, perhaps no more than seventeen, was lying on the ground, clutching her swollen stomach and moaning with pain. Cassie dropped to her knees. Judging by the size of her abdomen, the woman was close to giving birth. Then Cassie saw something that instantly put her on red alert. There was a pool of blood soaking the woman's dress.

'Get help!' she shouted to the chattering bystanders. She instructed some of the women to form a shield and lifted the woman's dress. Her thighs were covered in blood. This was a possible placental abruption—an obstetric emergency—and not Cassie's area of expertise. Unless the woman had a Caesarean in the next few minutes and was transfused, she would die.

As Cassie lifted her head to shout for a stretcher, someone crouched down next to her. It was the man from the gangway—Dr Ballantyne. Apart from that first day, four days ago, she hadn't spoken to him. She'd seen him about, of course, he wasn't exactly the kind of man that blended into his surroundings, but, as she'd promised herself, she'd gone out of her way to avoid him. Why that was she wasn't quite sure. Only that he unsettled her—and she didn't like being unsettled.

'Hello again,' he said quietly. Without Cassie having to say anything, he took in the situation at a glance. 'Looks like a possible placenta abruption,' he said grimly. 'There's no time to take her to Theatre on board. We'll have to get her inside and operate here.'

Cassie looked around. They could do with some help—a nurse and an anaesthetist for a start. But most of the doctors and nurses had stopped for lunch and retreated to the shady, cool dining room on the ship.

'We need a stretcher over here,' Leith called out.

Cassie breathed a sigh of relief when two nurses emerged from the interior of one of the huts. One of the local volunteers brought a stretcher and working together they loaded the stricken woman onto it.

'I need an anaesthetist,' Leith said. 'Like now.'

'They're all on board,' the nurse said. 'Do you want me to send for one of them?'

'Yes. Go!' As soon as the nurse had taken off, Leith looked at Cassie. 'Even if she finds someone straight away, by the time they get here it will be too late. Have you ever given a spinal?'

Cassie nodded. She brought up a mental image of a medical textbook. Luckily she had an almost encyclopaedic memory, one of the few benefits of a childhood spent mostly with books.

Although she'd been warned that working on the Mercy Ship might mean stepping out of her own area of expertise, she hadn't expected to be assisting with a case of placental abruption quite so soon after her arrival. She was glad that Leith was there and appeared to be taking it all in his stride.

As he prepped the patient's abdomen, Cassie loaded a syringe with local anaesthetic. Then they turned the woman on her side and Leith held her firmly while Cassie cupped the expectant mother's hips, feeling for the bones of the pelvis. Bringing her thumbs towards the middle line and on either side of the spine, she found the space between the L3 and L4 vertebrae. She moved up to the next space. It was important to take her time. If she gave it in the wrong place, the woman could be paralysed, but in the end the spinal went every bit as smoothly as she'd anticipated.

While they waited for the anaesthetic to take effect Leith took blood for cross-matching and gave the sample to the nurse to take to the ship's laboratory. Waiting for the results would take time—when every minute could mean the difference between life and survival.

In the meantime, the midwife had returned, bringing some bags of saline back with her, and Leith immediately set about putting up a drip.

'They are preparing a theatre for you,' the midwife said.

'It's too late,' Leith replied. Cassie ignored the flutter of anxiety in her abdomen and made sure to keep her expression noncommittal. Another skill she had mastered in her childhood.

As soon as she was satisfied that the woman couldn't feel anything below her waist, she nodded to Leith, who started to operate. With Cassie keeping an eye on the woman's breathing, he sliced into the abdomen and a few minutes later pulled out a small, perfectly formed baby, who was, however, disturbingly limp and still. Cassie stepped forward and as soon as she had checked that there were no secretions blocking the airway of the baby girl, she immediately began to breathe into the newborn's mouth. *Go on, little one. Breathe for me. If not for me, for your mummy. Come on, you can do it.*

To her relief, after a few breaths the child gave a gasp and a cry. When she glanced at Leith he grinned and gave her a thumbs-up. She smiled back at him. They'd saved this baby.

They weren't out of the woods yet. The neonate needed to be taken on board the Mercy Ship and straight to the special-care nursery.

Thankfully, just at that moment another two nurses, pushing a portable incubator, rushed into the room. Now the baby would get the mechanical support she required and once she got to the ship she would have the all help

the singing and dancing tiny special-care unit could
give her. As the midwives transferred the baby to the
incubator, Cassie glanced back at the baby's mother
and was alarmed to see that blood had pooled in her
abdomen.

'Damn. I'm going to have to do a hysterectomy,'
Leith said. 'But she'll need to be fully anaesthetised
first. That isn't something I can do here. We need to
get her to Theatre.'

As Leith started to pack the pelvis with swabs, one of
the other doctors hurried into the room. Knowing that
she would only get in the way if she stayed, Cassie left
the mother in their hands and accompanied the baby
and incubator back on board.

Once the baby was settled, Cassie handed over her
care to the neonatal nurse. Although the baby was
slightly smaller than Cassie would have liked, she was
breathing well on her own. As soon as the mother had
recovered from her anaesthetic, a nurse would bring
baby to her to have a feed.

By now it was after one and Cassie had to return to
her clinic to see the patients still waiting, and after she'd
finished there she was due in Theatre to assist with an
operation. Knowing it was unlikely that she would have
time for a sit-down lunch, she grabbed a sandwich from
the hospital canteen before making her way on deck for
a five-minute break.

She closed her eyes and let the sea breeze cool her
cheeks. Immediately an image of Leith filled her head.
Whenever she'd seen him on the ship, he'd been playing
cards or teasing the nurses, as if medicine was the last
thing on his mind. Occasionally, he'd glance her way,
but she avoided his eyes and always found a seat as far
away from him as possible.

Which one was the real Leith? The flirtatious, I-know-I'm-sexy-doctor of their first meeting or the one who'd been so focussed on his patient he'd barely noticed her? She shook her head. Why was she even thinking like this? She wasn't beyond having an affair, especially with someone she was unlikely to ever see again, but not with a co-worker. That, she knew, could get uncomfortable when it came to the parting of ways, which it inevitably did, as soon as they tried to turn the relationship into something it wasn't.

She took a last bite from her sandwich and chucked the remains into the bin.

No, she decided, it was better to trust her first instinct and keep well away from Dr Leith Ballantyne.

Just over five hours later Cassie was still in Theatre. The surgeon she was assisting was operating on a patient Cassie had examined at her first clinic and put forward for surgery. The teen had the biggest tumour Cassie had ever seen. Untreated, it had swollen to the size of a football, pushing the boy's features out of alignment so that his nose and mouth were grotesquely out of place. It wasn't that the benign tumour was life-threatening, but his unusual appearance had meant that he was ostracised in his village. Her heart went out to him. She knew what it felt like to feel as if you didn't fit in, and it had to be a hundred times worse for him.

Cassie stretched to ease the kinks from her back. The operation had been fascinating. The surgeon—Dr Blunt, who had worked on the Mercy Ship for the five years since she'd retired from a hospital in Boston, had told Cassie that she'd had more experience of dealing with this kind of tumour than she liked. However, she'd removed the growth with the minimum of bleeding and damage to healthy tissue.

There had been a scary moment when one of the blood vessels had started bleeding but Cassie had kept calm and managed to clamp it off without too much difficulty.

They stood back for a moment and surveyed their work. Even with the swelling, the boy looked much more normal. He'd never be a pin-up, but he wouldn't look out of place.

'Good job, Dr Ross,' Dr Blunt said. Although the operation had been a success, Cassie couldn't help but wonder if they could have made a better job of putting the boy's face back together. That was the problem. She was never satisfied. Only perfection would suffice.

She let the theatre nurse remove her gown and dropped her gloves into the bin. The thought of still having to pound the decks for her nightly run made her feel even more exhausted, but the habit was ingrained and she knew she would sleep better for it afterwards. First, though, she needed a few minutes to unwind.

She stepped out on the deck of the ship and drew in deep lungfuls of fresh air. Although the sun had dipped below the horizon, the air was still muggy and almost immediately she felt perspiration trickle down her back under her scrubs. She would wait until it was cooler to have her run and besides she wanted to check on her patient when he'd recovered from the anaesthetic.

A spurt of laughter came from below her. The staff not in Theatre or on the wards had gathered for dinner and were no doubt sharing their stories of the day. Cassie moved away, seeking the quieter starboard side—the one that faced the sea. There was a spot there behind the lifeboats where she often went when she wanted to be alone—no easy feat when there were four hundred staff on board.

To her dismay, someone had got there before her. A tall figure was leaning against one of the struts, staring out over the ocean. She was about to tiptoe away when he turned. She recognised him immediately.

He smiled at her. 'Dr Ross.' She had to admit she liked his voice with its attractive Scottish burr. 'I didn't get the chance to thank you for your help earlier today.'

'I didn't do much.' Cassie shrugged. 'How is your patient?'

'I had to do a complete hysterectomy. She won't be having any more children.'

'Perhaps that's for the best.' The area was so drought-stricken that despite everything the Mercy Ship and aid workers were doing, too many children were dying from starvation and, with clean water still a scarce resource, disease.

Leith looked at her in surprise. 'I doubt she'll see it that way.'

'At least she has a living child. I saw the baby earlier and she's going to be fine. Surely it is better for a mother to have one healthy child than several sick children?'

'I don't think we can apply our Western standards here, at least not without understanding more about the culture.'

Feeling as if she was being lectured, Cassie bristled. But before she could respond he went on.

'I watched you while you were assisting in Theatre earlier. You have deft hands.'

She hadn't noticed him among the observers in the gallery.

'Thank you—er—Dr Ballantyne. '

Amusement glinted in his jade-green eyes. 'How very formal. Call me Leith.'

'Very well. Thank you, Leith.' God, she sounded as if she was an awkward teen being introduced to her first boy. 'If you'll excuse me, I have to go and check on my patient.' She didn't really want to get into a conversation. Quite the opposite. For some reason she wanted to run away from this man as fast as she could.

He looked into her eyes for a second longer than was strictly professional before giving her a grin that sent her heart spinning.

Most days, as soon as she'd finished her early morning ward rounds, Cassie would make her way on shore and over to the school. Since their brief encounter on deck, Cassie found herself searching more often than she cared to admit for glimpses of Leith, but although they'd exchanged nods and smiles of greeting, to her relief—at least she told herself it was relief—he hadn't sought her out.

As often happened, the sun was beginning to set by the time the last patient had been seen. Cassie was taking a few moments to admire the reddening sky when she sensed, rather than saw, Leith come to stand next to her. To her dismay, her heart rate went into overdrive.

'Finished for the day?' he asked with a smile. His white, short-sleeved cotton shirt emphasised the dark hairs on his chest and his muscular forearms. Why on earth was she even noticing?

'Yes. Apart from ward rounds before bed.' Cassie turned her face upwards, enjoying the feel of the early evening breeze on her overheated skin. 'What about you?'

He rubbed his stubbly chin. 'Me too.' They stood together in silence as the sun flared, turning the soil pink.

'Such a beautiful country,' Cassie said softly, 'despite its problems.'

When he looked at her, her pulse upped yet another notch. His eyes were the colour of summer grass, she thought distractedly. She gave herself a mental shake and glanced away. What was wrong with her, for heaven's sake? Never before had she felt such instant attraction and it scared her.

Just then she noticed that a woman from the village was standing a couple of feet away, waiting patiently.

'Doctor—come with me. Please?' she said.

'What is it?' Leith asked. 'Is someone in trouble?'

The woman glanced around anxiously. 'Please. Just come. You both.'

Leith raised an eyebrow at Cassie. 'Are you up for it?'

It was as if every nerve in her body was screeching at her to run—to keep her distance from this man. Which was ridiculous. Someone needed their help and of course she wouldn't—couldn't—say no.

When she nodded the woman smiled with relief. 'My name is Precious,' she said. 'It is my sister, Maria, I want you to see.'

They followed Precious in the failing light along a narrow track. The cicadas had started chirping and the sounds of Africa permeated the night air. As the path entered a small stretch of trees the sun disappeared completely. Soon it was too dark to see properly, although the woman leading the way appeared to have no difficulty. Cassie stumbled over the root of a tree and Leith caught her hand. A spark shot up her arm and she had to resist the urge to pull away.

Still holding her hand and close on the heels of Precious, he guided Cassie along the path, pointing out intruding thorns from acacia trees and other obstacles for her to avoid.

A short while later they came to a cluster of huts. The villagers, lit only by the glow of the evening meal fires, were making preparations for the night.

But instead of stopping at one of the huts, the woman led them through the village and back into the darkness. Cassie had a moment's doubt. This was a poor country and it was possible that the woman was leading them into a trap. But they couldn't turn away now.

The thought clearly hadn't crossed Leith's mind as his footsteps never faltered. About two kilometres further on, with the village left far behind them, the woman stopped. At first Cassie could see nothing but then, as the woman pointed, she could make out a small hut in the shadows. This was unexpected. The villagers lived in close proximity to one another. Who could be living so far away from the comfort and help of others?

Precious led them inside. A young woman was crouched over a small fire, mixing a pot of mielie meal with a stick while a small child, no more than two, sat on the bed, watching her.

'This is Maria,' Precious said, before turning back to the woman and speaking rapidly in the vernacular.

Cassie couldn't understand a word but it sounded reassuring. When Precious had finished talking, the mother looked at them with a mixture of hope and despair.

'Maria has been sent away from the village.' Precious said.

'Why?' Cassie asked.

When Precious hesitated, Leith's brow knotted. 'I

suspect I know the reason.' He turned to their guide. 'Has Maria been wetting herself?'

'Will she allow me to examine her?' Leith asked.

Precious translated and, blushing deeply, Maria lay down on top of the bed after lifting the child and placing him on a rush mat. He stared silently with big, brown eyes.

'I will go and fetch some water,' Precious said, and slipped outside.

In the silence the little boy continued to watch them. Then he slid off the mat and toddled over to Cassie, lifting his hands. Instinctively Cassie reached down and picked him up. The child snuggled into her, peeping out at his mother.

'Seems he's taken a liking to you,' Leith said with a smile.

'Children seem to like me—which is an advantage given my line of work,' she responded lightly. Without warning an image flashed into her head. She couldn't have been very much older than this child—perhaps three or four. She'd fallen over and scraped her knee and had gone crying to her mother and held up her hands, wanting to be lifted, to have her hurt made better.

To her bewilderment her mother had turned away, saying it was only a scrape and not to make a fuss. But before she'd turned away, Cassie had seen something in her eyes that had made her forget about the pain in her knee and feel pain in her chest instead. Later she'd come to realise it had been dislike she'd seen.

When the time had come to choose which medical speciality to pursue, she'd been drawn to paediatrics. Perhaps because she wanted to rescue all the little Cassies out there. But she would never risk becoming a mother herself—experience had taught her that too often the worst parents were those who had been badly, or inadequately, parented themselves. Nevertheless, just because she wasn't going to have children herself, it didn't mean she didn't love having them as her patients.

'Cassie? You okay?' Leith's voice pulled her back to the present. She forced a smile and tightened her hold on the little boy in her arms. 'Sure. A little hot—that's all.'

Looking puzzled, Leith continued to hold her gaze, but when she returned his stare steadily he gave his head a little shake and focussed his attention back on Maria.

Leith examined the woman discreetly and gently, before straightening. 'As I thought, she has a fistula from her bowel into her vagina, which has led to her being incontinent. I've treated a few women with this condition since I've been here. They tend to be ostracised by their fellow villagers and rarely come for help, although I suspect that finally word is getting around that we can often do something for them.'

'Poor thing,' Cassie said. 'And can you? Help her?'

He smiled. 'Yes, I'm confident I can fix her problem.' He turned to Precious. 'She must come to the hospital ship. Tomorrow. Tell her I will have to operate, but it is a simple procedure and after she will be much better.'

Precious broke into a wide smile. 'She will be so happy. It has been hard for her here, all alone with her child. I can only help a little—I have my own family to care for.' She turned to her sister and spoke rapidly. With tears in her eyes, Maria reached out for Cassie's hand and said something Cassie couldn't understand.

'She asks if you will be there. She says you have a kind face. Like the other doctor.' Precious glanced at Leith and smiled shyly. 'But she will feel better if there is another woman.'

Cassie thought rapidly. She had a full clinic in the morning and was scheduled to assist with a couple of operations before then. Then she looked at the small child and the mother and knew that, whatever it took, she would find a way to be present. How could she deny Maria this one small thing?

Precious led them back to the village but once there Leith assured her that he and Cassie would find their own way back to the ship. Cassie wasn't so sure. The night was dark beyond the village and without so much as a torch to light their way it would be difficult to find the path. But as Precious clearly wanted to return to her sister, Cassie swallowed her anxiety and followed Leith. As he strode confidently into the bush, it seemed as if he had no problem seeing in the dark.

She kept her eyes on his broad back, pausing when he did and stepping over the roots of trees that he pointed out. They must have been almost halfway back to where the ship was docked when suddenly Leith stood stock still as if listening for something. Then he let out a yell and hit something from the back of his neck. It fell to the ground and Cassie heard the rustle of leaves as it scuttled away.

'God! What the hell was that?' Leith said, his face pale in the light of the moon.

'A bird or a spider, I suspect,' she said, trying not to laugh.

'If it was a spider it must have been a bloody huge one.'

'Whatever it was, it's gone. You're safe now. I promise I won't let that horrible beastie get you.'

He must have heard the amusement in her voice as he looked sheepish. 'Not very macho, was it? Jumping four feet in the air.' He grinned, his teeth flashing whitely in the dark. 'Spiders and I don't go together very well.'

Cassie smiled back. 'Don't worry, your secret is safe with me. I won't tell anyone.' And then, just like that, she knew that whatever she'd been telling herself about staying away from this man, it was too late.

CHAPTER TWO

AS SHE PROMISED, the next day Cassie joined Leith in Theatre once her own session had finished. His patient hadn't been put under yet so Cassie went over to her and squeezed her hand. Maria smiled tremulously.

'It's going to be okay,' Cassie whispered, knowing that the woman probably couldn't understand her but hoping she found her tone reassuring.

She stood back while Leith repaired the tear, which, judging by the image on the monitor, was significant. Happily, the Mercy Ship had many generous donors and was equipped with the best and latest high-tech equipment.

'She must have torn during labour—I'm pretty sure it must have been a breech delivery, 'Leith said as he worked. 'She's probably lucky to have survived. I'm guessing there was a great deal of bleeding.'

Cassie admired his surgical technique. He wasted no time and his stitching was neat. As he operated he explained to the nurses what he was doing. When he'd finished he looked up with a satisfied smile. 'I don't think she'll have any more problems.' He peeled off his gloves and chucked them in the bin. 'She'll need to stay in for a few days.'

Cassie walked with him to the door, glancing at her

watch. She had thirty minutes—just enough time for a quick shower and change of scrubs before she was due at her outpatient clinic.

'Meet me later?' Leith asked quietly.

Cassie's heart thumped. She already knew she wasn't going to say no. Last night she'd tossed and turned, thinking about Leith and wondering what she would do if he sought her out. She'd managed to convince herself that it could do no harm to spend time with him. She was tired of her own company and Leith was, well, interesting to say the least. It wasn't as if there was any danger of them having more than a short while together. Pretty soon they'd be going their separate ways.

'Why not? Let's meet at the harbour wall. Say, around seven-thirty?'

Leith grinned and her heart did a little somersault. Good God, it was like being a teenager again, except no one had ever made her feel like this. Not as a teenager, not as an adult, not ever. Determined to ignore the warning bells in her head, she gave him one last smile and headed to the changing rooms.

Over the next week they spent almost all their off-duty hours together and Cassie found herself constantly looking out for him as she worked. She was happy—yet terrified. In the past, whenever she had found herself getting too close to a man, she'd simply backed away before the relationship had got too serious, and every day she told herself to walk away from Leith while she could.

But her resolve melted away as soon as she saw him. Why not enjoy what they had while she could? It wasn't as if Leith made demands on her, simply seeming to enjoy her company, although she suspected, from the way he looked at her, that he wasn't immune either.

Was it possible that finally she'd met someone she could love and, even more importantly, who could love her in return? She groaned inwardly. What was the use in even thinking like that? She had her future all mapped out and it didn't—couldn't—include long-term relationships.

'Where will you go when you're finished here?' Leith asked one evening as they walked along the beach.

'I have a job with the United Nations—in their International Medical Corps.'

He whistled. 'The United Nations! A high-flyer, then?'

She smiled up at him. 'That's one way of putting it.' She had certainly worked hard enough to achieve her dreams. Always refusing to go out with her fellow medical students, although that hadn't simply been down to work, being the first on the wards and last off as a trainee, doing anything and everything that had been asked of her. After all, she of all people knew how to please.

But she didn't want to think about that. It was the present she cared about right now. 'My first posting is to Sudan. I go straight there from here.'

He frowned. 'Why Sudan?'

'I can't think of a more worthwhile use of my skills. I like the feeling I'm helping children in real need.' She breathed in the scent of sea and spice that she'd come to associate with Africa. 'And I've always wanted to travel,' she added. *Because no place felt like home.* 'I think it will be a real test of my skills. What about you?'

'I worked as a consultant in Glasgow for years and spent a long time abroad—mainly Africa but other countries too. I moved to London a couple of years ago. I work in Harley Street now.'

'Harley Street?' Cassie said, surprised. 'Bit of a shift from Africa to Harley Street, isn't it?'

'Hey, don't mock what you don't know. The practice I work for only employs the best—its patients won't tolerate anything else.' He grinned at her. 'If you're ever looking for a job, I know they'd like to have a top-class doctor on the team.'

Warmth spread through her at the compliment. Although she knew she was a good doctor, she wasn't used to praise. It felt good, especially so, she had to admit, coming from Leith. But of course what he was suggesting was impossible.

'Thanks, but, no, thanks. London in the rain? The crowds? Battling the Underground? Give me blue skies and sun any time,' she responded, knowing it was only a version of the truth. 'I've had my career all mapped out ever since I went into medicine. That's the way I like my life. It keeps me focussed.'

'What about the personal one?'

The look in his eyes made her bones melt and once again she found herself wondering if there could be room in her life for spontaneity. Did everything have to be planned down to the last hour? On the other hand, that *was* how she liked it. It was far safer.

'My work gives me everything I need—or want.'

He raised his eyebrow. 'Everything? You don't intend to get married? Have children?'

She stiffened. 'Not every woman is born to be a mother.'

'No,' he replied, looking surprised, 'but I've seen the way you are with the children. You're a natural.'

'Why does everyone think that every woman should

want to have a child? In my experience, some women should be positively banned from having kids. After all, no one seems to think it unnatural if a man doesn't want to have children. What about you, for example? Are they in your future?'

'One day perhaps.' His eyes crinkled at the corners. 'In a few years' time. In the meantime, I plan to have as much fun as I can.'

Her heart sank. His reply wasn't what she'd wanted to hear.

'And your parents? Are they in London?' he continued after a moment's silence.

Suddenly chilled, despite the muggy evening, she wrapped her arms around herself. 'Some of the time. They spend a lot of time abroad now. One way or another, I don't see much of them. What about yours?' She wasn't about to tell him that a bonus of going to work in Sudan was its distance from her adoptive parents.

He studied her for a moment as if he was about to press her further but then he seemed to change his mind. 'They live on Skye. They've been married for forty years and still crazily in love with each other. That's the way I want it to be if ever I get married.'

A familiar ache in her chest made her catch her breath. Wouldn't it be wonderful to believe love could last? They halted under an acacia tree. In the distance, small fishing boats lit by glowing lanterns bobbed about the waters of the Atlantic Ocean and the smell of jasmine hung on the heavy night air.

Leith tipped her chin so she was looking up at him. 'God, you're beautiful.' The world stopped turning as he brought his mouth down on hers. For a moment she felt as if she could hardly breathe. His kiss was gentle at first, his lips warm and questioning. But as she melted into him, his kiss became deeper, more demanding, and she wrapped her arms around his neck, wanting more of him.

She could feel his desire for her against her pelvis and an answering warmth flooded through her. She wanted him. She wanted to feel his naked skin on hers, to have his hands all over her body and hers on his. She didn't even care that after she'd left here she would never see him again—all she needed right now was this.

When they pulled away they were both breathing deeply.

'Come back to the ship with me,' he said simply.

When she nodded, he took her hand.

Cassie woke to bright sunshine streaming in through the porthole. At first she didn't know where she was, but as the fog of sleep lifted she remembered. She smiled and stretched as a warm peace filled her. She couldn't remember the last time she felt this good.

She propped herself up on her elbow and studied Leith. Even in his sleep his mouth turned up at the corners. She trailed her fingertips over the hard contours of his chest and as she did so his eyes snapped open and he caught her hand in his.

'Morning,' he said with a smile.

'Morning,' she whispered back.

He ran his hand along her shoulder and down the curve of her waist and every nerve in her body tingled. They had made love twice last night, but now she wanted him again with a need that shocked her.

She moulded the length of her body against his so that it seemed as if every inch of her skin was in contact with his.

He pulled her tighter. 'I can't seem to get enough of you,' he groaned.

Or her him. They didn't have long, but why think about the future and what couldn't be? Why not just be happy while she could?

It was her last coherent thought before she gave herself up to him.

Leith found himself humming under his breath at the oddest moments and when he wasn't with Cassie he was thinking about her. He constantly sought her out and loved to catch even the briefest glimpses of her, squatting on her heels in the dust, talking to a group of women, or distracting a child while carrying out some unpleasant procedure by making funny faces or dangling a colourful toy just out of reach before relinquishing it to them.

Sometimes he would find her on her own on the deck of the ship, staring out to sea with a wistful, almost sad expression on her face. But then she would catch sight of him and her face would be transformed by the smile he'd grown to love. It felt as if their coming together had been inevitable. Which was strange—very strange. He wasn't a man who believed in fate.

However, it felt good. It felt right.

But he still knew little more about her than he'd known at the start. Normally that would be good but with Cassie he wanted to know it all. In the past he'd always kept his relationships light-hearted and stayed away from the heavy stuff, but no one had made him feel the way he had since the first moment he'd spotted her lugging her suitcase along the quay.

However, he wasn't going to think about what might

or might not be. He was going to make the most of being with Cassie while he could.

He was smiling as he opened the email he'd received that morning.

He read it through and clicked on the attachment. It was a photograph of a boy of around four with large green eyes. He stared disbelievingly at an image that could have been him as a child.

An hour later, Leith was still trying to come to terms with what he'd learned. He had a son. He was a father. It just didn't compute. Okay, so he'd always thought that he might, one day, have children, but 'one day' were the two key words. One day in the future. So far in the future he couldn't even really imagine it.

But he'd better start imagining it.

He had a child.

He wasn't ready to be a father. Not yet. He liked his life just the way it was. No ties, no obligations. Doing what he wanted. Work, women and travel—that's what he liked. A child would put a stop to that. He'd have to be responsible, for God's sake. Cut down on his working hours, reduce his travel commitments, be selective about the women he dated.

He examined the picture for the umpteenth time. The child was clearly bright—anyone could see that. And he had the same set to his jaw that Leith recognised from his own childhood pictures, which his mother brought out every time he was at home; hundreds of him as a baby naked on a blanket, as a toddler standing proudly next to his father with his own child-sized fishing rod, on his mother's lap as she read him a story, all depicting the years until his graduation photograph and beyond. As his racing mind conjured up an image of him taking his son fishing or out on the boat, just as his father had taken him, something shifted inside his chest.

He studied the photograph again. In his childhood photographs he was always smiling—he might look the worse for wear, with patches on his knees and a dirt-smeared face, but he always looked blissfully happy.

He drew closer to the screen and his skin chilled. His son didn't look happy—he didn't look happy at all.

No child of his should look like that.

Cassie was happier than she could ever remember being. After the night she'd spent with Leith, they took every moment they could to be together. As soon as their medical duties were over they'd slip away, either to walk into the African veld or sometimes take a blanket down to the beach where they'd sit and talk about their day as the waves lapped against the shore.

Her heart cracked a little every time she thought about it ending. Leaving wasn't supposed to be this hard. Wasn't this the reason she'd always promised herself never to care too much?

Tonight they were sitting on their favourite spot by the shore. Leith was behind her with his legs and arms wrapped around her as she rested against his chest.

'Do you have to go to Sudan?' he asked suddenly.

The question caught her unawares and silence hung heavily before she answered. 'Why? What else would you have me do?' she asked lightly.

'Come to London. You could get a job with the practice or in one of the teaching hospitals. Someone with your credentials should find it easy to get a job anywhere.'

She doodled a picture in the sand, stalling for time. 'Now, why should I do that?'

His arms tightened around her. 'I'm not ready to let you go.'

Her breath stopped in her throat. For a moment her carefully constructed future held no allure, her need and want of him overriding every rational thought. Perhaps it needn't end? The thought shook her. Was she really thinking that this could last? What he was asking was impossible—she couldn't let her employers down at this late stage. Especially not for a dream that might not come to anything. 'I can't not go to Sudan, Leith. I've made a commitment.'

She felt his sigh. 'Damn it.'

Wriggling out of his arms, she turned to face him.

'You could come with me. They're always looking for people.'

'I can't.' His voice was flat, his expression unreadable.

The light inside her flickered and died. She had read too much into his words. He wanted her to come to him but he wasn't prepared to do the same for her.

'But we could meet again when you to return to London,' he added. 'Until then, we could write, email, phone even. I'm sure they have phones in Sudan.' His eyes glittered in the moonlight as he searched her face. She could almost hear the thudding of her own heart.

Why not? Perhaps it was time she trusted her heart to someone. To Leith. Take a chance. The thought was hammering around inside her head. Go on, take a chance. This man could love you—really love you.

But would he love her for ever? Could love ever be for ever? Could fairy-tales come true?

She leaned towards him and pulled his head towards hers. 'Enough of the talking,' she said lightly. 'Do you know it's been at least twenty minutes since you last kissed me?'

* * *

All too soon it was their last night together. The boat was setting sail at dawn to go further up the coast and it would be leaving her behind to catch her flight to Sudan. Leith still had a few days left before he too would be returning to his job in London.

Sometimes Cassie fantasised about the life they could have together but deep down she knew it was only that—a fantasy. Despite the passion they had for one another's bodies, they hardly knew each other. She had her life to lead, one that didn't include children— or a permanent relationship.

But there were still a few hours left for them to be together and she was determined to make the most of every second.

She was lying in the crook of Leith's arm as one of his hands brushed lazily along her shoulder. Over the last couple of days he'd seemed preoccupied. She'd often catch him looking into the distance as if he were miles away, but she didn't ask. If he had something to tell her, let it be in his own time. She hated people's questions too much to ever pry.

But tonight he seemed particularly distracted. Normally when they were together he focussed his full attention on her. She'd noticed that he did the same whatever he was doing, working, eating—or making love. At the memory of just how thoroughly he'd made love to her only moments before, her whole body tingled. She stretched languorously.

'Penny for them,' she said, wondering if he was thinking about a patient.

'I'm not sure you'd want to hear them.'

A shiver ran down her spine. There was something ominous about the tone of his voice.

'As long as you're not going to tell me you're married after all.' She laughed nervously.

His hand stilled on her shoulder. 'No,' he said. 'Of course it's not that.' He paused for a moment. 'I had an email a couple of days ago.'

She propped herself onto her elbow and looked down at him. Anxiety fluttered when she saw he was frowning. 'Bad news?'

'No. Yes. Damn it. I don't know. A bit of both.' He swung his legs out of bed and pulled on his jeans. The only light came from the moon shining through the open curtains. Even in the half-light, he was unbelievably gorgeous with his hair tousled by their lovemaking, his skin golden from the African sun and his broad shoulders that tapered to slim hips and long legs. When he turned his intense green eyes on her, her heart lurched at the thought that soon she would lose him.

Since the night he'd suggested they keep in touch, he'd been strangely silent on the subject. Had he changed his mind? Or had she simply read more into his words than he'd meant? Had it been no more than a casual throw-away comment and was this the part when he told her it had been great but…?

She plucked nervously at the trimming of the sheets. 'I'm afraid you're going to have to explain.'

He sank down on the bed and pulled her against his bare chest. She lay there for a moment, listening to the beating of his heart.

'I had a one-night stand a few years ago,' he said finally. 'Until recently I had forgotten about it.'

Cassie stiffened in his arms. She shouldn't be surprised he had a past.

'Her name was Jude. To be honest, I barely even remembered that. Anyway, her sister, Bella, wrote to me.

It seems Jude had a child—about nine months after we had our—er—thing.'

A chill ran up Cassie's spine. 'You didn't take precautions?'

He rubbed his hand across the rough stubble of his face. 'It had been a tough day. She told me she was on the Pill. I chose to believe her.'

Cassie guessed what was coming next. 'She had your baby.'

'Apparently,' he said dryly.

'She didn't tell you? So why has the sister written now?' The hollow feeling in her stomach was getting worse. She wriggled out of his arms.

'Because she's worried. Bella's been trying to persuade Jude to tell me that I have a son ever since Jude told her she was pregnant, but she wouldn't.'

'So what's changed now?'

'Bella doesn't think Jude is coping with him. She's even hinted that Jude's been taking drugs.' He raked his hand through his hair. 'God, Cassie, what kind of mother would do that when she has a small child to take care of?'

Cassie hugged her knees to her chest. She knew only too well what kind of woman. Someone like her own birth mother for a start.

She felt horribly disappointed. Had she misjudged him completely? Had she been too quick to put him on a pedestal? Of course it was ridiculous to think anyone was without flaws—she of all people should know that.

'I'm pretty sure she wasn't on any drugs when we met. According to the family her drug taking only started a couple of years ago. And as to why she should feel it necessary not to tell me she was expecting our child, Lord knows, I haven't all the details yet. Possibly because there was a man in her life, someone she was engaged to, when she and I had our—er—thing, and before you say anything I swear I didn't know. Anyway, he left her when he found out the baby wasn't his. Apparently that's when Jude started behaving erratically.'

Poor Jude. But it was the little boy that Cassie's heart went out to. Why did people have children if they weren't capable of looking after them? When she felt all the old anger boil up inside her, she pushed it away before it could take hold.

'Although he's only four, Jude's sister thinks that the boy is being badly affected by his mother's behaviour.' Leith rose from their narrow bed and started pacing up and down the small cabin.

'What are you going to do?'

'If he's my child, and I have no doubt he is judging by the photo the sister emailed me, then I'm going to do whatever it takes to get access to him—fight for sole custody even if need be.'

He strode over to his laptop and flipped the lid. He typed something into the browser and turned the monitor so Cassie could see. 'The sister sent me this picture of him.'

Cassie wrapped herself in a sheet and went to stand next to Leith. Immediately, just by looking at the little boy's eyes, Cassie knew without doubt he was Leith's son. The circumference of Leith's iris was slightly irregular—barely noticeable unless, like Cassie, a person had spent a lot of time looking into his green eyes. This little boy had exactly the same irregularity in the same eye. But it wasn't just the family resemblance that drew Cassie. In the child's eyes she recognised the same bewilderment and pain that she'd seen in the rare photos of herself at the same age. She sucked in a breath, conscious of a knot in her stomach. An image rushed back of her as a little girl, having woken from a bad dream, sitting on the top of the stairs, praying that her mum would come and carry her back to bed, kiss her, say or do anything to make the ghosts and demons of the night go away. But when Mum hadn't answered her calls, she had got cold and had eventually crept back to bed alone and miserable.

'What's his name?' she asked, swallowing hard.

'Peter.'

'Where do they live?'

'In Bristol.'

'So what next?'

Leith raked a hand through his hair again and stared back at the computer screen, his expression bleak. 'As soon as I get back to London, I'm going to consult a lawyer. If necessary, I'll have him removed from his mother's care.'

'Perhaps you should meet Peter and his mother first? Talk to her. Maybe there will be no need for lawyers. If you involve them now, it's possible Peter will be taken into care while access is sorted. Is that what you want? Think of him. Sometimes any sort of mother—if she loves the child—is better than a substitute.'

Leith narrowed his eyes. 'I want my son. And if Jude isn't able to look after him, then I want him away from her.'

This steel was a side to the normally easygoing Leith she hadn't seen before. Chilled, she went back to bed and huddled under the thin duvet.

Leith's pager buzzed. He cursed as he looked at the message that had come up. 'There's an emergency in Theatre and they need my help. Can we talk about this later?'

'I'm leaving before the ship sails,' she reminded him.

'I'll be back as soon as I can.' He tugged on his shirt. 'Damn the timing. I haven't even got your address or phone number,' he groaned, tossing his mobile to her. 'Could you put it in for me?' He glanced at his watch, hopping on one foot as he pulled his left shoe on. 'But be sure to come and find me if I get held up.' Then he gathered her against him and kissed her hungrily.

Despite everything, Cassie melted into him and responded with a passion that, until she'd met Leith, she hadn't known she was capable of.

He released her reluctantly. 'God, I would give anything to be back in bed with you, woman, but I have to go. I'll see you later.' And with that he was gone.

For a long time after Leith had left Cassie lay on the bed, wrestling with her thoughts.

Leith had a child and that changed everything.

When she'd agreed to keep in touch that had been before…before she'd known he had a child.

She couldn't be with Leith if he had a child. Particularly one who was bound to be needy. The parallels between her life and Peter's were uncanny and she couldn't, just couldn't, risk becoming even slightly involved in the life of a vulnerable child and riding the emotional roller-coaster along with him and his father.

But, a little voice whispered, *it's not as if he's asking you to be a mother to his child.*

It didn't matter if he was asking or not. He wasn't the kind of man who would put his child aside for anyone. If he had been, she couldn't love him the way she did.

And she did. Love him. With all her heart and soul, and would for the rest of her days.

But be a mother to his child? If it ever came to that? No.

She didn't know how.

She wasn't up to the task. She couldn't be objective enough, and soon, in all likelihood, she and Leith would end up disagreeing about what was best for Peter and he would be caught in the middle, her own objectivity compromised by a lifetime of hurt. Of course it was impossible.

She couldn't be with Leith. Her throat closed. All her dreams of a fairy-tale ending had been just that— a dream.

Flinging back the covers, Cassie dragged herself out of bed and started getting dressed. There was still the rest of her packing and a thousand other things to do and she didn't want to be here when he returned. Better to end it now, quickly and as pain-free as possible. Leith and his son deserved better. They deserved someone who could be part of their family, not a damaged woman who had no intention of being a mother—not even a stepmother—*particularly* not a stepmother. If she couldn't risk not loving a child of her own enough, how could she risk not loving Leith's son? And Leith would demand it. If she were in his shoes, she would feel the same.

As for Peter… The little boy had enough to cope with without a new woman in his father's life—one who might be there one minute and gone the next.

She tasted the salt of her tears. She loved Leith too much to get in the way of a life with his son. He would forget about her soon enough. But just in case she had to make sure he wouldn't come after her.

The tightness in her chest hurt.

She scrawled a few lines on a piece of paper she found next to his computer. Then she opened the door and slipped outside.

CHAPTER THREE

Eighteen months later

LEITH FLICKED THROUGH the CV of the applicant he and
Rose were going to interview in a few minutes' time. He
should have looked over it sooner, but his colleague had
been particularly excited about this candidate, listing
her credentials and experience, almost gloating about
the number of heartfelt letters of commendation, and he
hadn't felt the need to study the application until now.
But he should have. Damn it, he should have. It had to be
her. How many Cassie Rosses could there be who were
paediatricians and who had worked on the Mercy Ship?

Only one.

Resisting the temptation to screw her CV into a ball
and drop it in the wastepaper basket, he flung the application on his desk.

Why had she applied for the temporary position?
She must know it was where he worked. He clearly
remembered telling her he was a partner in a Harley
Street practice.

But there were hundreds of practices on Harley
Street and he couldn't remember if he'd actually told
her which one he was a partner of. On the other hand,

if she'd done her homework, she'd have seen his name listed as one of the partners.

What was she up to?

Eighteen months since he'd last seen her and she still haunted him.

She'd left without coming to find him, leaving only a note. That was all their relationship had meant to her.

That last night, the ship had sailed by the time he'd returned to his cabin. What had seemed to be a straightforward obstetric emergency had gone badly wrong when they hadn't been able to stop the woman bleeding. It had taken hours before he'd been happy to leave the labour ward. He'd known he wouldn't find Cassie, but to discover that she hadn't left her number in his phone—only a short note—had floored him. They hadn't made firm plans for the future, apart from agreeing to keep in touch, but he'd been so certain that she'd felt the same as he had that he'd imagined that one day they'd be together.

So much for his usually reliable radar when it came to women—although he would have bet his life back then that she had fallen for him as hard as he'd fallen for her.

So you got her wrong. Move on. You have enough on your plate with Peter. Let it go. Tell Rose and the others that you worked with her and you don't think she's up to it.

But he couldn't bring himself to lie. Whatever else she was, she had been a fine doctor.

And he was over her. Way over her.

He picked up the application form again. She'd spent six months in Sudan before taking a posting in Afghanistan. That had ended three months ago. What had she been doing since then?

An extended holiday? Marriage? Time off to have a child?

His stomach knotted.

What did it matter? He and Cassie Ross were history.

And the practice needed an experienced locum to stand in for Fabio. It was only for a couple of months. Eight weeks. Possibly less.

So what harm could it do to interview her? At the very least he could finally prove to himself she meant nothing to him now.

The nightmare woke her from sleep as it had for the last three months.

Her heart still pounding, Cassie tossed the covers aside and slipped out of bed. Today of all days she had to keep it together. Crossing to the window, she threw open the curtains, wincing as bright sunlight flooded into the room. The mini heat wave that had hit London showed no signs of abating.

She showered quickly and dressed. Wiping the condensation from the bathroom mirror, she studied her reflection and sighed. She barely recognised the pale face with the dull eyes that stared back at her.

After applying foundation and blusher, she thought she looked better. She wouldn't be winning any beauty competitions in the near future, but she looked passable—professional at least.

Today she'd be seeing Leith again. Her heart thumped painfully against her chest. Would he be married? Eighteen months was a long time and someone like Leith could never live like a monk. And as for his son, had he gained access to him?

Her hands were trembling as she applied her mascara. Was she out of her mind applying for a job at the practice where he was a partner? But what other choice did she have? Any more time cooped up in this flat on her own and she'd surely go crazy—if she wasn't already.

Stepping into the small sitting room, she glanced around. Most of what had once belonged to her beloved Nanny had been packed and donated to charity shops. The flat was bare, except for the few items of furniture Cassie couldn't bear to part with—and Martha's necklace, the one Cassie remembered her former nanny always wearing. She picked up the string of pearls, turning the cool gems between her fingers, and felt herself relax. She slipped it on and fastened it at the back.

'Wish me luck, Martha,' she whispered. 'I'm going to need it.'

The room felt as if it were closing in on Cassie. She tried to look composed, although it was almost impossible with Leith sitting opposite her and studying her through narrow, speculative eyes. She fingered the necklace around her neck for courage.

Although it had not been much more than a year and a half since she'd last seen Leith, it felt much longer. So much had happened. Physically he hadn't changed, but dressed as he was in a dark grey suit, white shirt and maroon tie, his formal appearance and cool greeting made him seem virtually a stranger to her.

No doubt he was curious as to what had brought her to apply for a job here. When she'd seen the advert in a medical journal she'd immediately wondered if it was his practice. So she'd done an internet search and, sure enough, his name had appeared as one of the partners. She'd hesitated but after waking to yet another day filled with nothing but emptiness she'd plucked up the courage to apply. Just because Leith worked there it didn't mean she couldn't apply for the temporary position they were advertising. Whatever had been between them was in the past.

But to her dismay the connection was still there— at least on her side. The air seemed to pulse between them, her body on red alert. With him so close it was impossible to suppress the images that flashed into her head; the two of them down by the shore or arms and legs entwined as they lay in bed together. She closed her eyes to shut them out. Damn.

'Are you all right?' Rose asked. 'Would you like some water?'

She needed to get a grip. She forced herself to focus on the kindly face of Rose Cavendish, the practice manager, sitting across from her. She twisted her hands together to stop them trembling and shook her head. 'No, thank you.'

Leith turned to Rose. 'Dr Ross and I worked together briefly some time ago.'

Rose's eyes widened. 'You didn't mention you'd met Cassie before.'

'Yup. Should have read the application sooner. But no matter, her referees confirmed my own impressions. No one can question her competency.' His lip curled slightly as cool green eyes swept over her.

Oh, God! He hadn't known. If he had, would she have been invited for an interview? Somehow she suspected not. Dismay washed over her. This was going from bad to worse.

'The Dr Ross I remember was about to take up a position with the United Nations,' he continued, holding her gaze. 'But I see from your CV that you stopped working with them—what, three months ago?'

Cassie chewed her lip. She'd been dreading this question.

She forced a smile. 'I had to come back to London for a while. This job was advertised as being for up to two months, which suits my current plans.' She hoped they didn't notice that she hadn't really answered their question. She didn't want to tell them that she'd spent the time in hospital, then recuperating while trying to decide what to do with the rest of her life.

Leith looked doubtful, as well he might. When she'd known him she'd been so insistent that her future was planned down to the last T. Well, let him speculate. Although there had been other jobs she could have applied for, they were either outside London or permanent posts and until she decided whether or not to return to her post with the UN, she needed to get back to work. Any more time with nothing to do but think and she'd go crazy.

'If we take you on we will want you to see the children who come to the practice,' Rose continued. 'At the moment Dr Lineham—Fabio—sees most of them but his wife is expecting and he's hoping to take some time off to be with her and the baby so you'd have sole responsibility for all our younger patients. How does that sound?'

'Perfect.'

'And you will be content to work in what essentially is a general practice?' Leith said, still looking puzzled. 'Apart from one or two of the children who have chronic or complex conditions—and Dr Lineham will still follow them up—you'll mainly be seeing the children of over-anxious parents with not much wrong with them.'

It seemed that he wasn't going to be satisfied with anything other than a full explanation. And could she blame him? She'd be asking the same questions if she were in his shoes. He wasn't to know how much she hated talking about the reasons she'd left her post with the United Nations. Everything they needed to know about her was all there in her CV.

Except it wasn't. Not everything. Not the stuff that kept her from sleeping at night.

'As I said, I need to be in London for a few months and your practice has a great reputation.'

Despite her racing heart, she held Leith's steady gaze. He was bound to question her motives for applying for this job, either suspecting her of exploiting their past relationship in order to secure a position in the well-respected, lucrative practice or—her colour deepened—to see him again. Neither could be further from the truth.

It was just one of those unfortunate coincidences that the only job on offer within the particular timeframe she wanted was this one, and she desperately, *desperately*, needed it. So it didn't matter what the hell he thought. He'd find out soon enough that she had no intention of picking up where they'd left off.

If only he would stop looking at her the way she remembered so well—his emerald-green eyes unreadable and searching at the same time. It still felt as if he could see into her head.

Judging by Leith's frown, he wanted a better explanation than the one she'd given. Just in time she stopped herself from rubbing the scar on the inside of her arm.

'My friend died recently and left me her London flat. I need time to sort it out before I put it on the market.' How easily the words slipped out. Nanny *had* been a friend—more than a friend. She'd given her the only consistent mothering Cassie had ever known, and the

flat she'd left her the only place that had felt like home.
Her death a year ago had been almost too much to bear.

Still Leith said nothing. His silence was beginning
to irk her. She was qualified for the job—more than
qualified—so what more did he need to know? Was the
thought of working with her so distasteful to him? She
rose to her feet. 'I'm sorry. Maybe this job isn't right
for me after all. I suspect you are looking for someone
with more general practice experience. Thank you for
your time.'

'Please, sit down, Dr Ross,' Leith drawled, sound-
ing almost bored. 'In a practice such as this it is important that we are all clear where individual skills lie.
Your references are all first class. And I remember your
work on board the Mercy Ship. It couldn't be faulted.'

Cassie took a breath and sat back down. Perhaps she
was being overly sensitive? Seeing Leith again had been
a bigger shock than she'd expected.

'I see your last posting was in Afghanistan,' Rose
said. 'Could you tell us a little about that?'

Cassie's heart thumped sickeningly.

'I went out there on my second secondment with
the UN. My job was to treat the children of the civilian population as part of the initiative to win hearts and
minds. Medical services for the civilian population are
suffering badly and it is the children who suffer most.'

Both Rose and Leith were listening attentively.

'I was there for nine months,' she said, choosing her
words carefully. This part was easy. She forced herself
to look at Leith. 'In many ways it wasn't very different to working on the Mercy Ship—or in Sudan. We
held clinics where we could and even went into the
hospitals to see patients if we were asked.' She didn't
mention that each visit had required the presence of

soldiers in order to protect her and the other members of the medical team.

'If we found a child who required surgery beyond what we could offer locally—as you can imagine, equipment was pretty basic if it existed at all—we sent the children to the UK or the US for treatment. Sadly there is often a far greater demand than can be provided.'

Rose turned to Leith. 'There must be something we could do to help.' Rose must have noticed Cassie's confusion as she smiled. 'We all feel incredibly fortunate to lead the lives we do so it's the ethos of our practice that we all do voluntary work for two to three weeks every year—either locally or abroad. And it's possible we could find surgeons here in Britain who would be prepared to help the children you talk about.' She smiled. 'My husband has many contacts and he's not beyond twisting an arm if he needs to.'

Cassie smiled back. She liked Rose already. 'That would be fantastic.'

'I must tell you that our doctors are required to travel occasionally. Will that be a problem?' Rose continued.

'Not at all,' Cassie replied. 'I don't have ties to keep me in London.' She was acutely aware of Leith's silence.

Rose beamed at her, looking relieved. 'That is good news. We all try to do our fair share of the trips abroad but as some of us have children...' she glanced at Leith before sending Cassie another smile '...we prefer to stay at home if we can.'

So it seemed Leith had managed to gain access to his child. She wasn't surprised.

'I don't care what I do or where I go as long as I'm working.' When Rose and Leith exchanged another glance she rushed on. 'I like to work.'

'And what do you do in your spare time?' Rose

asked. Leith leaned forward, staring at her intently. She shifted under his gaze.

'I run. I...' She hesitated, lifting the hair from the back of her neck. 'I like the theatre, going out to dinner, that sort of thing.' It wasn't altogether a lie. That *was* what she used to like to do.

'The practice is expanding almost faster than we can cope with,' Rose said. 'When I first came here there was only my husband and a couple of nurses. But in the last two years we have taken over the building next door and installed a minor surgery unit as well as full X-ray facilities. We have grown from a single-handed practice to three doctors and are continuing to expand. With Fabio planning to take time off, we badly need another doctor to see the children. By most standards we're a small practice but we're a happy one and we want to keep it that way. Everyone has to get on. And if our questions seem a little—er—searching that's because it's important that we all get along.' She smiled again.

'The other reason our questions might seem intrusive is because of the patients we deal with. They can be anyone from royalty to politicians, people in the media and sports stars. All of them rely on our absolute discretion. So our checks have to be thorough. I'm sure you understand.'

Cassie let her breath out slowly. Until now she hadn't been aware of how tense she'd been. Tiredness was making her defensive. Of course they were only doing what anyone would do when they were looking to take on new staff. They weren't to know how much she hated answering personal questions. And she did need this job. Even if the thought of working alongside Leith, who appeared to have turned into Dr See-Right-Through-You-and-Not-Sure-I-Approve, worried her.

'Dr Ballantyne and the other doctors also spend some time at the local hospital,' Rose said. 'You would have access to the facilities there if needed.'

'Sounds perfect,' Cassie replied. At least, the job *would* be perfect if it weren't for the fact that she'd be working with Leith.

This time it was Rose who stood and held out her hand. 'We have a couple of other applicants to consider and naturally any decisions we make will be made after discussions with the rest of the team.'

'When will you let me know?' Cassie was relieved to find her voice was steady, betraying none of the anxiety she felt at being turned down. She simply could not spend any more time not working. She would truly go mad.

'By tomorrow evening at the latest,' Rose promised.

'So, what do you think?' Rose asked when Cassie had left the room. Leith wasn't sure how to answer. Cassie was a top-class doctor. Almost too qualified for the job on offer. And what had really made her apply for this post? He didn't find her explanations totally convincing.

Seeing Cassie again had been like a punch in his solar plexus. So much for thinking he was completely over her.

Yet she'd changed. She was still beautiful, perhaps even more than he'd remembered, but distant—as if she wasn't really connecting. Her hair was longer, at times hiding her face, and she was thin, almost to the point of gauntness. And it wasn't just her physical appearance that had altered. Somewhere along the way she'd lost the fire in her eyes and she seemed almost… lost. At least, that's what he would have said if it didn't seem fanciful.

What had changed her? The death of someone close to her would account for some of the sadness but this seemed deeper than normal grief. Had something happened while she'd been working in Afghanistan? Had she seen things that had eaten away at her? Or was he reading too much into her manner towards him? Perhaps she was simply uncomfortable coming face to face with him? She needn't worry. He had no intention of resurrecting a past affair. An affair that had clearly meant little to her.

But hell. Despite everything, she still made him want to hold her. He couldn't stop himself from thinking of her naked body moving beneath his; the way she'd cried out when they'd made love; the way she'd felt in his arms. And not just that. He wanted to banish the aching sadness from her eyes—see her face light up with a smile and hear her laugh again.

Was he nuts? Completely out of his mind? He'd been mistaken about her before and his life was too complicated now to want her back in it again.

He became aware that Rose was looking at him, expecting an answer.

'I wonder about her commitment. This job doesn't seem to fit with what I know of her. Not that I knew her that well,' he added quickly. Hadn't known her at all, if the truth be told. He'd never thought she'd leave the way she had, with a casualness that had stunned him and making it abundantly clear she'd had no desire to pursue their relationship. But he'd been so focussed on getting his son that he hadn't thought about her—at least, not that much.

'Well, I liked her,' Rose said. 'I think she's perfect for the job.'

Could he work with Cassie again? They were both

adults and, as he kept telling himself, whatever had been between them was in the past. So why was he hesitating? Cassie *was* well qualified, far more than any of the other applicants they had interviewed, and if Rose had taken a shine to her, he trusted her judgement completely.

'If you like her, I'm sure Jonathan will,' Leith replied. 'And we do need someone to take over the paediatric side for a bit. But let's wait until we hear what the others have to say. And we also have the other applicants to consider.'

'Yes, but neither of us were really taken with them, were we?' Rose chewed on her lower lip. 'I think we should offer her the job. I've a good feeling about her.'

Leith shrugged. 'Fine by me, as long as Jonathan agrees.'

Rose slid him a mischievous look. 'You know Jonathan trusts my judgement completely. And you're happy with her medical qualifications. Surely that counts more than anything?'

If Rose knew the true extent of his relationship with Cassie perhaps she'd understand his reluctance. However, that had nothing to do with whether she was qualified for this position. This was, he reminded himself, a purely professional decision. 'Okay, you win,' he said with as much nonchalance as he could muster. 'Dr Ross it is.'

'I've just had the most perfect idea,' Rose said as she gathered up her papers. 'Why don't I invite Cassie to our gathering at Cavendish Hall at the weekend? It will be so much more relaxing for her to meet everyone when they're off duty and we can all get a chance to know her. What do think, Leith?'

Seeing Rose's delighted face, Leith didn't have the

heart to tell her that he very much doubted that Cassie would find being sized up over a weekend at Cavendish Hall relaxing. It was a sensible plan, though. 'I think it's a great idea, although you should ring her as soon as possible to give her some warning.'

So it seemed that, whether he liked it or not, Cassie was back in his life.

CHAPTER FOUR

CASSIE WOKE HERSELF up with her cries. Praying that the sound hadn't carried through the walls of her flat and disturbed her neighbours, she waited in the darkness until her heart rate slowed and she was able to breathe normally.

It was the same nightmare she had every night. She'd be walking along when suddenly a fireball would come from nowhere. She would fall to the ground and listen to the calls for help. But when she tried to move she couldn't. Then she'd look down and notice that her right side was on fire. It was horrible. Even worse in some respects than the reality.

Although it was only just after six a.m., it was already light outside. Slipping on her sweats and a T-shirt, she let herself out of her flat and started running in the direction of Hyde Park.

Would the practice phone today and offer her the job? And if they did, was she seriously going to say yes? She'd been dismayed—more than dismayed, horrified—at the way her heart had thumped when she'd seen Leith again. Maybe working with him wasn't such a good idea. On the other hand, perhaps she should think of her reaction to him as a good sign. It meant she wasn't totally dead inside.

He, to her chagrin, hadn't looked fazed in the slightest. Had he met someone else? He hadn't been wearing a ring, but many men didn't. The thought of him being married made her insides churn and she picked up speed, pushing herself to go faster—almost as if she could outrun her thoughts. And what about his son? Was he living with Leith? She shook her head. Leith and his child were none of her business. It was as much as she could manage to get herself through each day.

The unaccustomed exertion was making her chest ache. Once she could have done twice this distance without any difficulty but weeks of inactivity following her hospital stay had made her muscles lazy and her lungs underperform.

She was gasping for breath by the time she returned to her flat. She pulled the T-shirt over her head and stepped out of her jogging pants before throwing them in the laundry bin. She looked around the flat. Everything was in its place—just the way she liked it. She ignored the niggling unease in the back of her mind that her preferred level of tidiness was not normal. But, she told herself, it wasn't doing any harm and it made her feel in control.

On her way to the bathroom she noticed the red light of her answering-machine flashing. She hadn't checked for messages before going to bed last night. She picked up the phone and pressed the 'retrieve messages' symbol. She recognised the voice straight away. It was Rose Cavendish, asking her if she could ring her back as soon as she got a chance.

Cavendish Hall was a ninety-minute drive from London and Cassie left her arrival as late as she dared. She really didn't know how she was going to manage to get through the next twenty-four hours. Rose had been vague about what she should bring—some stout boots and a waterproof, otherwise just the usual.

From the rare times her adoptive parents had taken her with them when they'd gone to stay with their friends, Cassie knew that guests at house parties in grand houses normally dressed for dinner, so she had packed the one evening dress she had with long enough sleeves to cover the scars on her arms. If it wasn't fancy enough for dinner, that was too bad. There was no time to go shopping for another one. Once upon a time she had enjoyed scouring the shops for the latest fashions but these days she had little energy or interest for it.

The same could be said for a lot of things she'd once enjoyed. She gave herself a mental shake. Hadn't she promised herself that, instead of letting what had happened to her ruin her life, she was going to make the most of this second chance she'd been given? She had made a start by applying for this job. And if her head couldn't quite shake off the past, she would simply have to try harder.

As she turned into the long, sweeping drive, passing a gatehouse on her right, Cavendish Hall appeared before her. The double-storey, honey-coloured sandstone building was much larger than Cassie had expected, with what had to be at least a dozen Georgian windows facing out over a sizeable manicured lawn.

Rose was waiting at the bottom of steps, watching a little girl dousing some flowers with a watering-can almost as large as herself, with the affection that only a mother could have. Some things would never change, Cassie thought ruefully, though she still couldn't see herself with children.

Rose's face broke into a wide smile when Cassie

brought her rental car to a halt. She'd hardly had a chance to take her overnight case from the boot when Rose hurried towards her with her arms held wide, enveloped her in a hug and kissed her warmly on the cheeks. The little girl came to stand next to her mother, studying Cassie with wide eyes.

'Welcome to Cavendish Hall,' Rose said. 'I'm so glad you could make it on such short notice. The others have all arrived and are looking forward to meeting you. I hope you don't mind being dragged out here to meet everyone.'

Cassie's head was beginning to ache. 'No, of course not.'

'Now, we're quite informal here. Not like in Jonathan's father's day. Poor man passed away two years ago—he was a darling when you got to know him, although he was a bit fierce to me at first. Once Daisy came along, he melted like a marshmallow. Oh, forgive me—I always talk too much.' She bent her head to whisper in Cassie's ear, 'I still get nervous when I have to be hostess.'

For the first time in as long as she could remember, Cassie laughed. There was something so straightforward and down to earth about Rose Cavendish that Cassie couldn't help but warm to her.

'Katie, the practice physio, is inside and dying to meet you. Poor thing is huge and feels the heat. She's thirty-six weeks pregnant with her first child, you know. Oh, of course you don't. Well, she is.' As Rose had been talking she'd taken Cassie by the arm and was leading her up the stone steps.

'Jonathan and Fabio—that's the doctor you'll be covering for and Katie's husband—and Leith are out in the grounds somewhere, looking at fences or whatever it is that men do. They'll be back shortly, no doubt, in search of tea and some of Mary's home baking.' She looked down at her child, who was tugging at her dress.

'This little scamp is Daisy.'

Daisy held out a small, plump hand and Cassie shook it solemnly.

'And this is Benton—without whom Cavendish Hall would likely fall to the ground.'

Benton, clearly well past the first bloom of youth, harrumphed dismissively but the look he gave Rose was one of pure adoration.

'Actually, Benton, could you go and find Jonathan and let him know Dr Ross has arrived?' Rose asked.

Cassie looked around for her bag but Benton had already picked it up and was following them up the steps. He stooped to pick up the little girl and with the ease of a man half his age swung her onto his shoulders. Then, before Cassie could wonder if she'd stepped into a children's story book, she was in the drawing room and being introduced to Katie—a striking woman with thick blonde hair and large grey eyes.

'Please don't get up,' Cassie said hastily, as Katie struggled to ease her bulk from the deep, overstuffed arm chair.

'Thanks. I won't then. Particularly as it takes me about ten minutes to get on my feet. Rose, couldn't you find one chair that doesn't feel as if it is swallowing me whole?' The last was said with an affectionate grin at their hostess and Cassie relaxed a little more.

'Rose tells me you're around thirty-six weeks,' Cassie said. 'You must be excited.'

'Excited?' Katie widened her eyes and gave Cassie a mischievous grin. 'More like bored, fed up, huge, terrified, I'm afraid. Nobody warned me I'd feel like a beached whale at this point.' Katie cradled her stomach with her hands. 'And look like one too.'

'But, my darling, you look as beautiful as ever. Even more beautiful if that's possible.' A good-looking man with an olive complexion strode into the room and dropped a kiss on Katie's cheek.

The gesture was so full of love and affection that Cassie felt her throat tighten. What would it be like to be loved like that? She glanced over to the door and her heart banged painfully. Leith was leaning against the doorjamb, watching her, sexy as hell in dark jeans and a muscle-defining sage-green T-shirt. Damn. Whatever she told herself, she was still in lust. Quickly she composed her features and looked away. She didn't want him to see her reaction.

Katie swatted her husband playfully. 'Cassie, this is my husband, Fabio.'

Next to Fabio was another dark-haired man who, judging by his resemblance to Daisy, had to be Jonathan.

Was Leith on his own? No girlfriend? And where was his little boy? Hadn't he managed to get access after all—or had he just given up?

'Welcome to Cavendish Hall,' Jonathan echoed his wife's greeting, although his voice was much more public school than Rose's. 'I hope you have everything you need.'

'I haven't had the chance to show her to her room, darling. I'll do that after we've had some tea. I've put you in the west wing next to Leith. I thought you might like to be out of hearing of Daisy, who can make quite a racket when she's excited, I'm afraid. I hope that's okay?'

Despite her promise to herself not to, Cassie couldn't

help glancing at Leith. For a moment their eyes locked. When he grinned, her stomach lurched. Curse her libido to have chosen this time to resurface.

'Anywhere is fine. And I'm happy to wait until later to unpack—although I wouldn't mind a chance to freshen up.' The truth was she wanted a few minutes away from Leith to collect herself.

When Rose showed her to the downstairs bathroom, Cassie leaned against the door and took deep breaths before crossing over to the sink and splashing cool water on her neck. For heaven's sake, she chided herself, get a grip.

By the time she returned to the drawing room, tea was being poured and the room was filled with the sound of lively chatter. She paused just inside the doorway, feeling isolated. How would it be to feel a sense of belonging instead of always feeling like an outsider? To laugh and chat as if nothing else mattered but being in the moment—at ease with people who accepted you for who you were, and without judgement.

'Are you all right?'

She jumped. She hadn't been aware of Leith coming to stand next to her.

'Of course,' she replied. 'Why shouldn't I be?'

He looked down at her, his dark green eyes puzzled. 'I don't know. But something tells me you're not comfortable. I imagine as a group we can be a little overwhelming at first.'

'I'm not very good with large numbers of people if you remember,' she said at last.

A strange look crossed his face. 'I remember everything, Cassie. Trust me, there was nothing forgettable about you.' Her nerve endings thrummed like a still-vibrating guitar string.

'Why don't we get out of here for a bit?' He nodded towards the group of her soon-to-be colleagues. Rose and Jonathan were reading to Daisy, and Katie and Fabio had their heads close together as they shared a joke 'They won't mind.' There was a faint glimmer of a smile in his eyes. 'I doubt they'll even notice. Besides…' he lowered his voice '…we should talk.'

'I don't think there's anything to talk about,' Cassie whispered back. Thankfully, the others didn't appear to be paying them any attention. 'We worked together some months ago. Had a short shipboard romance. Isn't that all there is to say on the matter?' She shrugged, hoping she looked and sounded way more blasé than she was feeling.

He studied her through narrowed eyes. Then he took her by the elbow and steered her though the open French windows and out to the patio. There was little she could do about it without drawing the attention of everyone in the room. Besides, sooner or later they would have to talk so she might as well get it over with. And she was curious to know about his son.

As soon as they were outside she shook his arm from her elbow. They walked in silence for a while, following a path that led towards a small copse on the edge of the estate. The air between them shivered with tension.

'Why did you come back to London?' Leith asked abruptly. 'It must have been a blow to give up your position with the United Nations. If I remember correctly, you were determined to stay with them for the foreseeable future. So determined you didn't even leave me your contact number. Only a note. And a brief one at that.'

'I'm sorry. I thought it was better that way.'

'Hell, Cassie, I thought we meant more to each other

than that. I couldn't believe you left without coming to find me.'

'And as I said in my letter, I hate goodbyes. We both knew there wasn't a future in it. You had your son and I…well, I had my job with the UN.'

'The job you've now given up. And, if I remember correctly, we agreed to keep in touch. What changed?' His voice was ominously quiet.

She pretended to misunderstand him. 'As I mentioned at the interview, someone close to me died and left me her flat. I needed to sort it before I put it on the market.'

'You haven't answered my question, Cassie.'

'It was pointless to keep in touch. Surely you could see that? We were only together for a short while, Leith. You had your life and I had mine.' She dragged in a breath. 'I didn't want to be held to vague promises that we both knew would be difficult to keep.' She forced lightness into her voice she was far from feeling. 'I wanted to go to Sudan as a free agent. Months apart was never going to work—for either of us.'

'You never gave it a try, Cassie.' He shook his head. 'Of course, now I can see you were right. What we had was…good, but it seems neither of us was the person the other one thought we were. As you say, what happened back in Africa is in the past.' His eyes were guarded.

'But to give up your career with the United Nations? Surely you could have sorted the flat during your leave? Or handed it to someone else to do? Or was there another reason you left?' He looked her in the eyes. 'Or someone else?'

Her heart was beating so fast she felt nauseous. 'No, there's been no one…' She swallowed. 'It was just time for me to move on. As far as leaving Martha's flat for someone else to sort out…' When her voice hitched, she took a deep breath. 'She was someone I cared deeply about. I owed it to her to do this one last thing for her.'

'I'm sorry. I didn't realise…Was she a good friend?' The sympathy in his voice made her throat tighten.

'You could say that. But she was getting on in years and in the end, although her death was sudden, at least she didn't suffer. She would have hated to have become dependent on anyone.' She needed to change the subject. Martha was part of the life she didn't want Leith to know about. She took a breath to steady her voice. 'But what about you? Are you with someone? Married? And what happened with Peter?'

Her chest tightened as Leith continued to study her for a long moment. He shook his head. 'No, I'm not married.'

A wave of relief washed over her. Even if they couldn't be together, she hated the thought of him being with anyone else.

'As for gaining access to Peter,' he continued, 'that hasn't gone quite as smoothly as I thought. First I had to prove I was his biological father. Then I had to get Social Services involved.' His expression darkened. 'To be honest, it's been a mess. I've met him once or twice at his grandmother's house. I can't say it was a huge success. My son seems to hate me.'

Cassie was appalled. The very thing she had warned Leith about had happened. Poor mite. However bad his mother, it would have been a wrench to be taken from her.

And as for Leith, his son's rejection must have been a blow.

She touched his arm. 'I'm sure he just needs time to get to know you.'

'Jude's mother and sister keep in touch with me and are the only way I know what's happening with him. Not having him with me, I can't help worrying whether he's okay. They say Jude's behaviour is getting more erratic. Her mother has him living with her now, with Jude having supervised access. At least until custody's decided.' Leith's eyes were bleak. 'Damn a system that takes so long to decide a child's future.'

The system hadn't worked for her either. The poor little boy. He'd never know how his mother would behave from one day to the next. Cassie's heart ached for him—and Leith. 'It's good that Peter has people who love him and are watching out for him. Perhaps Jude could be persuaded to go to rehab? Wouldn't that be best for everyone?'

'Jude has been to rehab before—without success. I have just about persuaded her mother and sister to go to court and admit that Jude has a drug problem,' Leith said tightly. 'Understandably they are worried that if they do, Jude will lose access to Peter altogether and they'll lose touch with her. Personally I don't care. I just want my son here with me, where he'll be safe.'

Unfortunately, there was more to it than that. Cassie often wondered what would have happened if her mother hadn't died and she hadn't been taken into foster-care. Perhaps her mother would have found some way of getting back control of her life and with it her daughter. At least, for all her mother's faults she had loved her. It had been an erratic, careless love, but at the end of the day it had been more than her adoptive mother had been able to give.

'Isn't it better that he maintains some contact with his mother?' she ventured tentatively. 'With the grandmother and sister keeping an eye on things?'

Leith looked incredulous. 'You can't mean that!'

'It can't be doing your son any good to be fought over.'

'I want sole custody. I won't stop him from seeing his mother, I just want to make sure that my son is safe and that whenever he's with his mother it's under supervision. By her actions, Jude has given up the right to care for Peter. Surely, as a paediatrician, you must agree that being with me would be best for him?'

It might have been her professional opinion, but it would never be her personal one. Her head was beginning to ache again. Wasn't this one of the reasons she'd decided she and Leith could never be together? She'd spent too much time getting herself together to risk becoming involved in someone else's life—particularly his.

'If you don't mind,' she said, 'I think I'll go back to the house and unpack.'

As she turned, he gripped her by the arm. 'Why *did* you apply for the job, Cassie? With your track record you could have taken a job anywhere.'

She looked at him steadily. 'It wasn't anything to do with you, in case you're wondering. As I said before, this job suits me. I'm a good doctor, Leith. Patients like me. I'll do anything and go anywhere. As far as I'm concerned, that's all that matters.' She raised an eyebrow and smiled again. 'I promise I won't let you down. At least—' she dropped her voice '—I'll do my damnedest not to.'

Cassie was grateful to reach the privacy of her room without encountering the others. Leith was far too perceptive for her liking. He'd guessed she'd hadn't been telling the whole truth about why she'd left the United

Nations but, thank God, she'd managed to divert him. However, she suspected that one way or another he wouldn't be satisfied until he knew everything. Damn. He had no right to probe into her life. Whatever there had been between them was over.

At least they had talked. Even if it had been like two casual acquaintances. That was good. It kept everything on a professional footing and would make working together easier.

She unpacked the few items she'd brought with her and hung her clothes in the ornate mahogany wardrobe. She had to admit she loved the room she'd been given. It was distinctly old-fashioned but she liked the high double bed and slightly worn carpet. This house had history and she could almost sense the presence of generations who had lived here. What would it be like to know who your family was, going back through time?

Slipping out of her dress and into her dressing gown, she went in search of the bathroom. Rose had apologised when she'd pointed it out at the end of the corridor. They had, she'd said, hoped to upgrade Cavendish Hall, but were tackling major jobs—like a new roof for one of the wings first. And with a smile she'd added that with a small, lively child and a job, it wasn't high on her list of priorities.

Cassie liked Rose and Jonathan Cavendish as well as what she'd seen of the Linehams. If things had been different, perhaps she could even have been friends with Rose and Katie. But she didn't do friends.

She immersed herself in the enormous claw-foot bath and closed her eyes. It all felt like such an effort. It was as if lately she'd had a shell around her that muffled everything. She suspected she was probably suffering from a mild form of post-traumatic stress disorder, but that didn't make any of it easier to bear.

She'd considered going to a psychologist but the thought of having to talk to someone about what had happened—about her life—made her feel nauseous. No, she would get through this by herself. One day at a time. Keep busy. And work—caring for others—and not having time to think about her past was the best remedy.

She eased herself out of the bath and once she was dry she wrapped herself in her dressing gown.

Halfway down the corridor she was alarmed to see Leith walking towards her. He was naked, apart from a towel knotted loosely around his hips. Immediately the memory of his naked chest under her fingertips flooded back and the nerve endings on her skin tingled. She averted her gaze, but not before she'd seen the gleam of amusement in his eyes.

'The bathroom is that way,' she said, pointing behind her.

'Thank you. I have been here before.'

As the corridor was narrow she had to slide past him. She pressed herself so hard against the wall she could have made a dent. She raised her hand, almost as if she would push him away, but as she did so the sleeve of her dressing gown rode up.

'What the hell…?' Leith took her arm and turned it to catch the light.

'It's nothing…an accident.' When she tried to pull away he tightened his grip.

'It must have been some accident!' He ran the pad of his thumb over the scars. 'This would have taken months to heal.'

She wrenched her arm away. 'Please, Leith, it's not something I want to talk about. Let me past.'

'Damn it, Cassie, what is it you're not telling me?' he growled. When she shook her head he lowered his voice. 'You know you can trust me. I'm still your friend.'

'Really, there's nothing I need—or want—to talk about.'

He hesitated, before reaching up to push a lock of wet hair from her eyes. 'You know where to find me when you're ready,' he said softly, before stepping aside to let her pass.

As she fumbled with the handle of the door to her room Cassie was uncomfortably aware that his puzzled gaze had followed her down the corridor.

By the time she had dressed and come downstairs, everyone had assembled in the drawing room. To her mortification she was overdressed in her floor-length, long-sleeved blue gown. The heat rose in her cheeks as everyone turned to look at her.

'Cassie, how lovely you look,' said Rose, hurrying forward and taking her by the hands. 'My goodness, you're freezing and we haven't lit a fire.'

'It *is* the middle of summer,' Cassie responded lightly. Indeed, the late evening sunshine was flooding the room, making the dust motes dance. Leith was standing on the other side of the room, his hands wrapped around his drink. For a second their gazes locked and once again she had the sensation of the ground shifting beneath her. Quickly she glanced away, focussing her attention instead on the glass of champagne Jonathan pressed into her hands.

Katie was ensconced in an armchair, with Fabio sitting on the arm next to her. Daisy was nowhere to be seen. She would, no doubt, be tucked up in bed for the night.

'What shall we do tomorrow, darling?' Jonathan asked his wife. 'I thought I might take Leith and Fabio out on the estate and do some clay-pigeon shooting.' He looked at Cassie. 'Would you like to join us, Cassie? Katie doesn't care to be on her feet, and Rose will want to be with Daisy, but you might like to come along.'

'I was intending to come, too,' Rose protested. 'Vicki and Julie—our nurses—will be joining us, and Jenny, our receptionist, too. Unfortunately, none of them could manage tonight. I thought we could all picnic down by the lake.'

'That's settled, then,' Jonathan said.

'I'm sorry,' Cassie said. 'I meant to let you know sooner but I have to leave early tomorrow. A previous arrangement in London I forgot to mention.' She simply could not go through a whole day in Leith's company. Working with him would be bad enough.

'That's too bad,' Rose said. 'But we're all so glad you managed to come for the night. Particularly on such short notice.'

From somewhere deep in the house a gong rang. 'That's Mrs Hammond, our housekeeper, letting us know dinner is ready. Shall we go through? Leith, per-haps you'll escort Cassie?'

Her heart rate upped another notch when Leith took her arm. It was as if she'd been catapulted into another time, Cassie thought distractedly as Jonathan led the way into an enormous dining room. The table, lit by several candles, was laid with sparkling crystal and fine china.

Rose, noting her look, smiled wryly. 'Jonathan's fa-ther liked to keep dinner the way it always was in his time. Since his death, we've kept up the practice.'

'I've never socialised with a lord and lady before,'

Cassie replied, completely unable to think of anything else to say. She could still feel the warmth of Leith's fingertips through the sleeve of her dress and it had taken all her self-control not to yank it from his grip. But when he relinquished her arm to pull out a chair for her, she felt almost bereft.

Everyone laughed. 'You'll find that Rose and Jonathan don't care for their titles,' Katie said. 'I've never met anyone less like the lady of the manor than Rose!'

'Katie!' Rose responded. 'You've hurt me to the quick.' But her eyes were dancing. She turned to Cassie, who had been seated, to her consternation, directly opposite Leith. Now there would be no escape from his piercing gaze. 'I was born to loving but very ordinary parents. I grew up on a council estate outside London. I can't quite believe that I am Lady Cavendish. What about you, Cassie? Where do you come from?'

Cassie almost groaned. She should have refused the invitation to the weekend. She was certain to have found another job somewhere else. But she was here now and Rose was only being polite after all. Nevertheless, she had to force herself not to look at Leith.

'My father works for a bank and my mother—she's in the media.'

'A journalist?' Fabio asked.

'Not exactly,' Cassie admitted. 'She is—was—a war correspondent.'

'Good grief,' Jonathan said. 'What's her name?'

'Lily,' Cassie admitted. 'She uses her maiden name—Savage.' Savage by name. Savage by nature.

'You're Lily Savage's daughter?' Rose said, her eyes wide. 'I had no idea she even had children.'

That was hardly surprising.

'She doesn't cover war zones any more,' Cassie said. 'She mainly does documentaries.'

'Oh, what a coincidence,' Katie said. 'Fabio's mother is also in the media. He knows all about being the child of famous parents—don't you, darling?'

Fabio glanced at Cassie and smiled wryly. 'I know it's not always easy.'

The sympathy in his eyes made her throat tighten. She'd only been around these people for a few hours and already they were treating her as if she was some-one they cared about. The thought panicked her. She took a deep breath.

'No, it's not always easy.' She lifted her eyes to Leith, unsurprised to find his gaze on her. She couldn't read the expression in his eyes. 'How are your parents, Leith?'

'The same as always. And I'm glad that no one can say that my upbringing was anything but ordinary. I was brought up on a small croft on Skye by two loving but relatively skint parents.'

'Didn't hold you back, did it?' Katie said with a smile.

'Quite the opposite,' Leith said. 'They taught me to believe that a person can be whatever he or she wants to be—as long as they have self-belief.'

Rose raised her glass. 'I'll drink to that. I also have a great deal to thank my parents for.'

Cassie's heart squeezed. At that moment she envied Rose—and Leith—with all her being.

'What about you, Katie?'

'Nope. No famous parents either. Fabio has it all on his side.' She closed her eyes for a moment and Cassie saw pain wash across her face. 'I did have a brother.

He was a doctor in the army. He was killed in Iraq just over a year ago.'

Nausea swelled in Cassie's abdomen. In her head she heard explosions—saw flying dirt—and then that eerie silence that was almost worse than anything that had gone before.

'Are you okay, Cassie?' She was aware of Leith's voice coming as if from a distance. She gave herself a mental shake. She simply couldn't lose it! Not here. She looked at Katie, noticing that Fabio had reached over to take his wife's hand. 'I'm so sorry, Katie,' Cassie said. She forced herself to take a mouthful of whatever was on her plate. What was it anyway? She couldn't tell. Her mouth was so dry she doubted she'd manage to swallow.

'Perhaps we should talk about something else,' Leith said quickly, and to her relief they moved on to discussing patients. Cassie concentrated on trying to get her heart rate down, nodding and smiling in what she hoped were the right places.

Eventually dinner came to an end and they rose from the table.

'Would you think me very rude if I went to bed?' Cassie asked. 'I'm afraid I have a bit of a headache.'

Five pairs of concerned eyes turned her way, but before they could say anything, Cassie smiled vaguely at no one in particular and fled.

Safely back in her room, Cassie paced the floor. Of all the people she could have chosen to look for a job alongside, it had to be this lot. It wasn't that they were unkind—quite the opposite. Their friendliness was genuine and that was the problem.

Cassie didn't want to form attachments. She remembered leaving the Mercy Ship. It hadn't been just leav-

ing without saying goodbye to Leith that had been a
wrench. She had tried to slip away but some of the
nurses had got up early so that they could see her off
and their hugs and entreaties to stay in touch had moved
her. She'd only been there for two short weeks yet they'd
made it clear that they saw her as part of their 'family'.

And then there were the staff she'd worked with in
Afghanistan. She'd allowed herself to get close to them
too—and that had brought her nothing but agony. No.
It was far better not to get involved. That way no one
got hurt—at least, not emotionally.

As for Leith, almost eighteen months had passed and
he still made her heart pound. Now he looked at her as
if he had never made love to her with an intensity that
had taken both their breaths away.

But if she wouldn't let him love her back then she
was even less likely to let him love her now. The woman
he'd thought he'd cared for no longer existed—if she
ever did—and he would find that out soon enough. She
rubbed her aching temples. The headache hadn't been
a lie.

No doubt the team would be thinking she had a screw
loose and perhaps they were right. Perhaps they were
even having second thoughts about hiring her. She could
still turn the position down and sign up with a locum
agency instead. Almost as soon as the thought came into
her head, she dismissed it. Hadn't she promised herself
she'd get on with her life? If the practice was happy to
have her, she would make sure they never regretted it.

'So what do we think?' Rose said. 'Have we done the
right thing in offering Cassie the job? Oh, do stop pacing, Leith, and come and sit down.'

Leith did as she asked. Cassie was behaving oddly,

there was no doubt. He'd noticed her reaction when Katie had talked about her brother's death. Then there were those scars on the inside of her arm. Those were the result of a serious accident. Exactly what secrets did Cassie have? What was she not telling him? And, more importantly, why?

'I think we have,' Jonathan said, looking puzzled. 'We need another doctor and she's more than qualified.'

'I'm happy,' Fabio said. 'I'll be taking paternity leave in a week or two and we'll be short-staffed. We need someone with her skills and experience to take on the paediatric side.'

'No second thoughts, Leith?' Rose looked at him and raised an eyebrow. 'You know her best.'

'As I've said, she was a fine doctor when I knew her on the Mercy Ship,' he said honestly. 'One of the best. No one had anything but praise for her.' He pushed his doubts aside. Whatever alarm bells were going off in his head about Cassie had nothing to do with her medical ability and he shouldn't let his personal feelings cloud his judgement. They did need someone to take over from Fabio and it would only be for a few weeks. 'I voted yes and I'm sticking to it.'

Jonathan got to his feet. 'In that case, we're agreed. Ask her to start on Monday. That way she can get to know some of my patients before I have to hand over their care.'

As everyone trooped out of the room on their way to bed, Leith remained standing by the window. Cassie was back in his life and he wasn't at all sure that was a good thing.

Cassie was dreaming again. This time she was standing in a field. At first she thought she was all alone. She knew there were bombs and that she couldn't move right or left. She would have to stay exactly where she was until someone rescued her.

Then she heard it. The sound of someone sobbing. It was coming from her left. It looked like a pile of rags but she knew it wasn't. It was Linda. She was hurt and Cassie had to get to her. But her legs wouldn't obey her.

Linda got to her feet and staggered. Cassie tried to call out to her—to tell her to stay where she was, that help was on the way—but the words wouldn't come. Almost in slow motion Cassie saw Linda turn. A smile of relief crossed her face and she lifted her foot and started to walk towards Cassie.

Cassie found her voice. 'No!' she screamed.

Leith jumped out of bed, unsure of what he'd heard. Had it been the cry of a fox or an owl? He wandered over to the window and looked out, his ears straining for the sound.

The large gardens of Cavendish Hall were in semi-darkness. At this time of year it didn't get truly dark until much later and then only for a brief time.

He thought of the evening that had passed. It had been strange spending time in Cassie's company after all these months. Strange—and unsettling.

It wasn't as if he hadn't thought of her since they'd parted. He had, and too often for his peace of mind. He'd thought of trying to track her down several times, but at the last minute he'd always changed his mind. Between the court case and work there had been little time for anything else—even if Cassie hadn't made it clear that whatever had happened between them on the Mercy Ship had just been a way of passing time.

And—speak of the devil—there she was. At first

she'd been just a shape in the moonlit night until his eyes had adjusted to the darkness and she'd moved.

What was she doing outside and at this time of night?

Despite the way she seemed to have changed, she still had the same effect on him. His senses still came alert whenever she was near. His stomach clenched as images of her in his arms forced their way into his head.

Back on the Mercy Ship he'd started to believe he'd found the only woman he could even imagine having a future with and then...well, if she hadn't made it clear she didn't feel the same, there was Peter. But now she was back in his life and although he wasn't at all sure that that was a good thing, he had to deal with it.

He narrowed his eyes to see better. She was leaning against a tree, the back of her head pressed against the trunk. There was something in the slump of her shoulders, the despair in the tilt of her neck that sent a flicker of alarm up his spine.

Quickly he stepped into his jeans and pulled a thin sweater over his head. Not bothering with shoes, he ran quietly down the stairs, took a torch from the table in the hall and let himself out of the heavy front door.

His bare feet made no sound on the grass and he was almost upon her when she looked up. Her eyes widened for a moment and even in the dim light he thought he saw relief and something else he couldn't name in her expression, but then she straightened and blinked and he knew he must have been mistaken.

'Oh, it's you,' she said flatly. 'What are you doing out at this time?'

'I could ask the same of you,' he murmured.

'I couldn't sleep,' she said. 'I thought a walk might help.'

He showed her the torch. 'A walk sounds good.

There's a path that leads around to the summer pavilion. Unless you knew it was there, you'd never suspect there was one.'

She hesitated and looked towards the house as if about to refuse, but then she smiled faintly. 'We always did seem to meet more often in the dark,' she said finally. Then her smile grew broader and he caught a glimpse of the Cassie he'd once known—or thought he'd known. 'Been attacked by any more giant spiders recently?' she teased.

He grinned back. 'No, but I'd be grateful if you didn't let the rest know about my failing.'

'My lips are sealed,' she replied, falling into step beside him.

'I hope this evening wasn't too nerve-racking,' he said. Although the Cassie he'd known wouldn't have let meeting a few strangers affect her, she'd always seemed to prefer her own company or—on the Mercy Ship—his.

'Everyone was lovely,' Cassie replied. 'I don't imagine anyone would mind working with them.'

Then what? Leith wondered. Something had upset her at dinner. He would have bet his life on it. She had been like a cat on a hot tin roof all evening—oh, she'd disguised it well but he had sensed her unease and then, when Katie had spoken about her brother, Cassie had paled. And there were the scars. Something had happened in Afghanistan. Something bad. His stomach clenched. He bit back the temptation to quiz her further. He would find out. In time.

'We want you to start on Monday,' he said instead, watching her expression closely. 'Is that too soon for you? Or have you changed your mind about joining us?'

She was quiet for a few moments. 'Monday's fine.'

She slid a glance in his direction. 'And I wouldn't have applied for the job, far less come here for the night, if I had any intention of changing my mind about accepting it.'

She didn't sound convinced.

'Will it be a problem us working together?' he said. It was the only reason he could think of for her hesitation.

'Now, why would you think that?' she said lightly. 'We had a brief—er—thing months ago. Hardly a reason to avoid one another.'

'Was that all it was, Cassie? A thing? I could have sworn there was more.'

He thought he saw a flash of pain in her eyes, but then she smiled sadly. 'It was good, really good, and I don't regret a moment of it, but neither of us were looking for something permanent, were we?'

What could he say to that? That he had thought that there could be something, and he'd been sure she had felt the same? But he'd been wrong and she was right. What was the point in raking over something that had happened so many months ago?

Cassie shivered. 'I think I'll go back to my room now.'

He pulled his sweater off and, ignoring her protests, tugged it over her head, amused to see it reached to well below her knees.

She looked him directly in the eyes and for a second he saw something flare in their depths. And he knew then that whatever she said, whatever had been between them, had never truly gone. For either of them.

CHAPTER FIVE

CASSIE PERCHED ON the edge of her chair, holding onto her mug of coffee as if it were a life jacket and she was about to be tossed into a stormy sea. She took a deep, surreptitious breath and forced herself to relax. Today would be the first time she'd be seeing patients since Afghanistan. Although she felt anxious, her longing to get back to work was greater. Everyone was smiling at her, doing their best to make her feel welcome—Jenny, the receptionist, and the nurses, Vicki and Julie.

Even the cleaner, a stout lady called Gladys, had been introduced earlier. 'Keep on the right side of Gladys,' Rose had whispered, 'and she'll see you right. She's been here since Jonathan's uncle's time and will probably see us all out.'

'Now you've met everyone,' Jonathan said when they were all gathered in the elegant, high-ceilinged staff meeting room, 'let's discuss what we have on.'

'We have six coming in to see Vicki, the same number to see Julie, around a dozen over the course of the day on Jonathan and Leith's clinics, and I've taken the liberty of booking in a couple of new patients for you, Cassie, as well as the drop-ins, if that's okay?' Rose said.

'The more the better,' Cassie replied.

'Don't worry, we'll have you working at full pelt in no time at all. It's just that our regulars like to see their usual doctors if at all possible.' She turned to Leith. 'Speaking of which, the Duchess of Fotheringham is coming incognito for her antenatal visit with you, Leith. I've put her at the end of the list when most of the others have left. Apart from that we have a request from her that you and another doctor go to their Caribbean island next month with them as part of their house party. That would be for a few days. They wanted Fabio but as he's not available, could I put you down for that trip, Cassie?'

Cassie's head jerked up. She glanced over at Leith, who was looking at her with his head cocked to one side and a small smile on his face. She wished the other doctor could be anyone but him. She wasn't quite ready to spend time with him outside work, but she could hardly refuse to go.

'Sure,' she said. 'That would be fine. But does she really need a paediatrician?'

'The Duchess was born prematurely and her mother had a couple of miscarriages before her, so she's understandably a little anxious,' Leith said. 'She'll be thirty weeks at the time of the trip and as their home on the Caribbean is a little way from a major hospital, she's asked for both a paediatrician and an obstetrician to accompany her. It's only for a week and, of course, if I had any high-risk pregnancies that were due to deliver around that time, I would have had to say no.' He shrugged. 'But as I don't...'

Cassie wondered again if she'd made a mistake, taking this job. It all sounded very different from the work she'd been doing in Afghanistan and Sudan. Would she cope with looking after patients who weren't really ill, just demanding?

She quickly realised that not all her patients were coming to see her with colds and vague aches and pains. Her second patient was a teenage girl with swollen glands who Cassie thought might have glandular fever. Not sure how to go about ordering more tests, she went in search of advice. As luck would have it, the first person she came across was Leith, who was chatting with Jenny about fitting in a patient as an emergency.

He explained who she needed to call to rush the results, but despite his usual politeness he seemed distracted—almost offhand.

It was on the tip of Cassie's tongue to ask him if something was wrong but she bit back the words. Hadn't she promised herself that she wouldn't let herself become involved in his life? She had to keep their relationship on a professional footing.

As soon as she'd taken blood from the teenager and advised her to go home to rest, Cassie went back to Reception to find out whether there was anything else she could do. She'd go stir crazy if she wasn't kept busy.

The waiting room was half-full, but when she checked the diary, none of the patients were scheduled to see her. Jenny was on the phone, looking excited.

As she was about to turn away, the receptionist signalled to her to wait. 'That was Fabio on the phone. Katie is having some mild contractions so he's asking if you would cover for him. He says to call him if you have any questions. Or to ask Leith.'

Leith was at the desk, filling out some blood-test forms. He glanced up. 'Just yell if you need me.'

'Sure,' Cassie replied, glad that she would have something to do that didn't involve studying her fingertips.

'If you could take Mrs Mohammed there? The lady with the young girl? That would be a help.'

Mrs Mohammed was an anxious-looking woman holding a child of around three in her lap. The little girl clung to her mother, darting anxious glances in Cassie's direction. Cassie crossed over to them.

'I'm Dr Ross,' she introduced herself. 'Would you like to come through to my consulting room?'

'No!' the little girl cried. 'Not going! Take me home, Mummy. Want to go now!'

'Come now, darling, the doctor's not going to hurt you. She wants to make you better.'

But the child wrapped her arms around her mother's neck and hung on even more tightly.

'Jasmine's your name, isn't it?' Cassie asked. 'It's a pretty name.'

The little girl released her hold on her mother's neck and regarded Cassie with steady brown eyes. 'My mummy's called Imani. That's a pretty name too.'

'Yes, it is. And my name's Cassie.'

'Are you a doctor?'

'Yes. But not a scary one.'

'Don't like doctors.'

'It's okay, Jasmine,' Cassie said gently. 'I'm not going to hurt you, but I need to look in your throat and listen to your chest.'

Jasmine shook her head before burying her face in her mother's chest.

'Tell you what, Jasmine, why don't I listen to Teddy's chest first?' She picked up a teddy from the pile of toys next to the chair. 'He's not been feeling very well either, and I need you to help me find out why not.'

The child slowly released her grip on her mother and turned to look at the teddy. Cassie made a big show of listening to his chest and nodding. 'Mmm. Nothing a day in bed won't cure, and possibly some ice cream might help too, if his throat his sore,' she said. 'Would you like to listen through my special hearing thing?'

When Jasmine nodded, Cassie placed the stethoscope in the girl's ears and let her listen to Teddy's chest. Then Jasmine listened to her mother's chest too.

'Now, can I listen to yours?' Cassie said before Jasmine asked to listen to hers. 'We can stay here, but it would be better to do it in my room.' She held out her hand. 'Would you bring Teddy for me?'

The little girl thought about it for a few moments before making up her mind. She slid from her mother's lap and, still holding Teddy, held out her hand to Cassie.

As they passed the reception desk on their way to Cassie's room, Leith, out of sight of the mother, smiled at Cassie. 'Good job,' he murmured.

Jasmine, having decided to trust Cassie, allowed herself to be examined—as long as Teddy was subjected to the same treatment. As Cassie had suspected, she had little wrong with her that a couple of days in bed wouldn't put right.

But when her relieved mother stood up, she cried out in pain and pressed her hands to her abdomen.

'What is it?' Cassie asked.

'Mummy's tummy sore,' Jasmine said. 'Mummy's tummy sore *a lot*.'

'Is that right?'

Imani shook her head dismissively. 'It's nothing. It comes and goes. It's not too bad.'

'Jasmine, would you wait outside with one of the nurses while I talk to your mummy?'

When Jasmine shook her head and stuck her thumb in her mouth, Cassie knew there was no chance of separating the child from her mother.

'Jasmine, could you go to the window and show Teddy the garden?' Cassie requested, and to her relief the little girl did as she was asked, talking to the soft toy as she pointed out different birds in the garden.

While Jasmine was occupied, Cassie took a brief history from her mother. Apart from this pain, which had started a few months ago, she wasn't on any medication and didn't have any other symptoms.

'Is it okay if Jasmine stays while I examine you? I just want to feel your abdomen.'

Imani nodded.

When Imani was settled on the examination couch, Cassie palpated her abdomen. There was definitely something there that shouldn't be.

'I think it would be useful for Dr Ballantyne to see you. He's the practice gynaecologist/obstetrician and I think he'd have a better idea about what's causing you pain than I do.'

Imani shook her head. 'I don't wish to see a male doctor.'

Cassie lowered her voice. 'Then I should refer you to hospital. You can see a female obstetrician there.'

'Really, no thank you. It is nothing. So much fuss for nothing.'

But Cassie knew it wasn't nothing.

'Would you object to my having a quick talk with Dr Ballantyne while you wait?'

'If you must.'

Cassie left her, and after checking that Leith had no

one with him knocked on his consulting-room door. When he saw it was her, he gave a distracted smile. As his green eyes locked onto hers, her heart did an annoying hippity-hop and she had to force herself not to look away.

'Cassie! Something up?'

'I need advice.' Quickly she outlined everything Imani had told her. 'Naturally I took a full history. The only thing of note is that she's experiencing intermittent pain in her lower abdomen. On examination I felt something—but I'm not sure what. I plan to do a full blood screen, of course.'

Leith was immediately on his feet. 'You want me to see her?'

'Ideally yes, but she won't hear of it.'

'Why not?'

'I'm not sure. I suspect she only wants to be examined by a female doctor.'

'I see.' He sat back down and narrowed his eyes as he thought. It was the same thing he'd always done when he was concentrating, whether on patients—or on her.

As the memory of how thoroughly he'd concentrated on her on those last days on the Mercy Ship, heat rushed to her cheeks. Cassie forced the image away.

'Nothing's likely to change in the next twenty-four hours,' Leith said after a moment. 'In addition to the bloods, I suggest you do a pelvic scan—ask if she'll allow Vicki to help you. Once we have the results we can speak again.'

He swivelled his chair so that his back was towards her and started drumming his pen on his knee. There was something about the set of his shoulders that bothered her.

'Is everything all right?' she asked.

He was silent for so long she wondered if he'd even heard her question.

'I'm expecting a call from my solicitor this afternoon,' he said finally, his mouth set in a grim line. 'About Peter and whether I'm going to be granted greater access rights or—even better—shared custody. The decision will be made later today.'

Before she realised what she was doing she had crossed the room and taken his hand. 'I hope everything works out, Leith. I'm sure you'll make a good dad.'

She caught her breath as he looked deep into her eyes. He squeezed her fingers briefly before letting go. 'I'm going to do my best for my son. He deserves that.'

After she'd finished seeing to Imani, who had reluctantly promised to return in a couple of days to get the results of the tests, Cassie was kept busy for the rest of the afternoon with a number of patients who had dropped in unexpectedly.

When she'd seen everyone, she went to the staff kitchen to make herself a cup of coffee. Rose was there before her. 'How's it going?' she asked. 'Settling in?'

'It's busier than I thought,' Cassie admitted. 'But I like that.'

'We try to keep the afternoons free for drop-ins or home visits,' Rose said, filling their mugs with hot water from the kettle. 'Organising the day can take a lot of juggling—particularly when we're asked to accompany patients abroad.'

'It must be difficult. I have to say I didn't expect to have my first trip scheduled so quickly. Not that I'm complaining,' she added quickly. 'Who wouldn't want to visit the Caribbean?'

'Jonathan and I can't really do trips any longer because of Daisy—or at least I can't, although Jonathan has to when no one else is available or when a patient asks for him particularly. Fabio obviously doesn't want to travel right now, so I'm afraid you and Leith will be our first port of call if we get any more requests. Of course, if Leith gets shared custody of his son he'll be more restricted too.

'We really need more doctors and nurses on a permanent basis. The practice is growing so fast it's hard to keep up. Jonathan would prefer to keep it small, but unless he starts turning patients away we're going to have no choice but to take on more staff.' She eyed Cassie speculatively. 'Do you like living in London? Could you see yourself back here permanently?'

'I do like London, but I'm not ready to put down roots. Sometimes I wonder if I ever will,' Cassie replied, taking her mug from Rose.

'No one special then?' Rose asked, tipping her head to one side. 'I would have thought someone like you would have them queuing up at the door.'

Cassie grimaced. 'I really don't do the whole relationship thing. I like my independence too much to give it up.'

Rose raised an eyebrow. 'Marriage doesn't necessarily mean giving up your independence. Quite the opposite.' She smiled dreamily.

Cassie looked at her askance. In her book there was nothing to recommend marriage. As far as she knew, her biological father had abandoned her mother the second he'd found out she was pregnant and, as far as she could tell, her adoptive parents had only stayed together because of appearances—the same reason they had adopted a child whom they'd never been able to love.

She remembered the day she'd found out that the Rosses were not her real parents.

She hadn't been able to sleep so she'd got out of bed, intending to go downstairs and ask her mother for a glass of milk.

But when she'd got to the top of the stairs she'd heard her parents talking in angry voices. So she'd sat down and listened.

'I don't think I can continue like this,' Mummy had been saying. 'I simply can't manage her.'

Cassie hadn't been able to hear what her father had said in reply. He always spoke more softly than her mother.

'I don't care what the social workers say. I won't have a child in this house that won't do as she's told. Cassie will find new parents, I'm sure. A couple who are more suited to deal with a child with her needs.'

Cassie was puzzled. What needs? She didn't want new parents. What could they mean?

'Give her time, Lily. At least she's well behaved. A little stubborn perhaps, but she's a pretty child and any tendency to her becoming like her birth mother can be moulded out of her.'

Cassie's heart felt like it was about to explode. She didn't know what a birth mother was, but suddenly the memory of a woman she'd once called Mummy too—a different mummy, one who was loving most times except when she was sick—rushed back into her head. But that mummy had sent her away. And now it seemed her new mummy wanted to do the same. She ran back to her bed and hid under the covers. Was there a place naughty children were sent? Was it hell? She shivered all through the night, but at the end of it she resolved to be as good as gold. So good that she would never get sent away. Again. Nanny arrived soon after that day.

'Are you all right?' Rose's voice pulled her back to the present.

Cassie forced a smile. 'I'm fine.'

'Are you sure? You looked so sad there for a moment,' Rose persisted.

'Now, what would I have to be sad about?' she replied lightly. 'I have everything anyone could ever want.'

Leith tossed his pen onto the table and slumped back in his chair. Perhaps he should have gone home to wait for the call, but he would have driven himself crazy without something to distract him. Besides, with Fabio on alert in case the Braxton-Hicks contractions Katie was having turned into full-blown labour, the practice was even more short-staffed than usual.

The court battle had been an excruciating process with brief flurries of activity followed by long delays as his solicitors waited for reports from what seemed to be hundreds of different professionals—half of whom seemed to be on holiday exactly when they were needed. But none of that would matter as long as he got decent access to his son.

At times he'd wondered if he was doing the right thing to persist with the court case. Had Cassie been right? Was it fair to uproot a child from everything he knew? But he didn't think like that for long. Perhaps if Jude had been a better mother he would have left things the way they were. Peter had the right to know his father. To know that there was someone in his life who would move heaven and hell to be with him.

Just when he thought he could stand the suspense no longer, the phone rang. He snatched at it. He listened for a few minutes then sank back down on the chair. It was over. Or almost.

CHAPTER SIX

'I THINK YOU should let Leith have a look at these,' Jonathan said to Cassie a few days later, handing her Imani's notes. The results of the blood tests had been normal but the pelvic scan was a different story. Sure enough, there was something on one of her ovaries that didn't look normal. Frustratingly, Imani still refused to let Cassie refer her to hospital.

'I would if Leith was here,' Cassie said.

'Damn, I'd forgotten he isn't coming in today. He has his son for the first time, doesn't he?'

'So I understand.'

The staff at the practice had been buzzing with the news that, finally, although he hadn't won sole custody, he had been awarded regular access to Peter, including weekends and school holidays. Today was to be the first day father and son would meet without either Jude's mother or sister being present. Cassie wondered how it was going.

'I think you should pop over to his flat and show him her notes.' Jonathan handed back the results.

'I don't think it's fair to disrupt his day,' Cassie protested.

'I'm sure he won't mind. His flat is only a short distance from here. Let me check if he's in.' Before Cassie could protest, Jonathan had lifted the phone and was dialling. 'Do you have anyone waiting to see you?' he asked Cassie as he waited for his call to be answered.

Cassie shook her head. But she didn't want to meet up with Leith—especially not when he was with Peter. It was difficult enough working alongside him.

To her dismay, judging by the side of the conversation she could hear, it seemed as if she was going to have to do just that.

'He's at home. Apparently he tried to get Peter to go to the park but he didn't want to. To be honest, he sounded relieved to have an interruption.'

That didn't bode too well.

A short while later, Cassie found herself outside the door of a smart Edwardian tenement.

And, sure enough, as Jonathan suspected, Leith looked relieved to see her.

'Come in, Cassie.'

'I'm not staying. Jonathan thought I should bring you Imani's results to look at.' She passed him the paper.

'At least come and say hello to Peter while I have a look.' He didn't just sound relieved, he sounded desperate.

Cassie followed him down a long corridor with a highly polished floor into an open-plan sitting room, dining room and kitchen, furnished in heavy dark wood and leather, warmed by bright rugs, cushions and bookshelves crammed with books. Colourful abstract paintings hung alongside or above African masks and artefacts. Not quite the minimalist bachelor pad she'd imagined but a lived-in home that, she realised, reflected what she knew of Leith.

The little boy was sitting on the edge of a leather sofa, ignoring the cartoon on the wide-screen TV and instead staring blankly at the floor. His olive complexion must have been inherited from his mother, although he had Leith's unusual green eyes and light brown hair. It was a striking combination.

'Peter, this is one of my colleagues, Dr Ross,' Leith said.

The boy slid his eyes towards them and then returned to staring at the floor.

But in that short glance Cassie saw again the same lost and lonely look she'd seen in his photo, and her heart ached for him. She went to sit next to him.

'Hello, Peter. You can call me Cassie, if you like.'

There was no reaction from the little boy.

Leith rubbed a hand across his face. 'Say hello, Peter.' He looked at Cassie. 'He hasn't said a word since he arrived, except "no". I tried to give him a snack but he wouldn't take it. He doesn't want to go to the park or to the library.'

The library! It wasn't the first place she would have thought of taking a little boy of six. She noticed Peter had a soft toy gripped in his fingers.

'Who's that you have there?' she asked softly.

'Mr Mouse.' The words were softly spoken. Still, he didn't look at her.

'And is Mr Mouse feeling okay?' Cassie asked.

'He doesn't like it here.'

'Now, why can that be? Is he a bit scared because everything is different? Or is he missing his mummy?'

'He's worried about *my* mummy. He knows she doesn't like being on her own.'

Leith seemed utterly bewildered.

'Well, she won't be alone for long, will she? Not when she has your aunty and your gran to keep her company,' Leith said.

'Mummy likes *me* to keep her company,' Peter replied sullenly.

'I can see why your mummy would like to have you to keep her company,' Cassie said.

This time, Peter did look up. 'I make her tea,' he said proudly. 'She says I'm big enough to be the man of the house.' He flicked his eyes towards Leith. 'We don't need him. Mummy says he wants to take me away from her.'

The look of bewilderment on Leith's face changed to one of fury and Cassie shook her head in warning. Now was not the time to challenge Jude's obvious manipulation of her son.

'I'm sure your mummy loves you very much, but so does your daddy. That's why he wants to spend time with you. He doesn't want to take you away from your mummy. He just wants to share you.'

'I don't want to be shared.' Peter hugged Mr Mouse tighter.

Cassie held out her hand. 'I can see you're not interested in watching television. Why don't you, me and Daddy go to the park for a little while? I passed it on the way here and it has all sorts of fun things in it. Perhaps we can all get a burger after? What do you say?'

Peter studied her for a long moment. 'I'll go if you go,' he said finally.

Cassie smiled. 'Didn't I just say I would? Now, I need to speak to your daddy about something very quickly. Then we'll go.'

When she stood up, Leith indicated with his head that she should follow him into the kitchen. It looked as if a tornado had hit it. There were dishes piled in the sink and pink milk spilled on the black granite countertop.

'What happened here?' she asked.

'I tried to make him a milkshake. Seems like I forgot to put the lid of the blender on. Took me half an hour to hunt the damn thing down in the first place. In the end I only managed to make enough for half a glass. He wouldn't even take a sip.'

Cassie hid a smile. 'Give him time, Leith. Think of it from his point of view. He barely knows you and from what you told me on the ship—and from what he's saying—his mother has him very confused.'

'How dare she tell him that I want to take him from her?' A muscle in his jaw twitched. 'I'm more sure than ever she's not fit to look after him.'

'Perhaps she fears losing him to you? But Peter loves her, Leith. She must be doing something right.'

'I don't want good-enough-some-of-the-time for my son.'

Cassie flinched inwardly.

'Of course you don't,' she replied. *Which is why I can never be a part of your life—and Peter's,* she finished silently, aware of the familiar ache lodging itself in her chest.

Leith picked up the notes Cassie had brought and flicked through them.

'Remind me about this lady. She's a previously fit and healthy twenty-five-year-old with recent onset of abdominal pain and on examination you felt a mass?'

'Correct.'

'And if I remember correctly, she reported that the lower abdominal pain she was experiencing intermittently would go away on its own after a few hours. So you decided to do a pelvic scan.'

'It was you who suggested it. All the routine bloods are normal but the scan shows an abnormality. I'm not sure what I'm seeing, so Jonathan suggested I bring it to you to have a look.'

Leith studied the pelvic scan. 'These images almost certainly show a dermoid cyst.'

'And the prognosis?'

'Not good generally but we may have caught her in the earliest stages of the illness. She'll have to have the cyst removed first—hopefully without having to remove the ovary at the same time.'

Poor Imani. Although Cassie had no intention of having children, she knew most women were devastated when the option was taken away from them. 'As long as she has one ovary, she'll still be able to have more children.'

'But if we don't get to the primary cause, her condition will get worse. Do you have her mobile number?'

'No, but it should be on her notes. I'll give her a ring right now, shall I?'

By the time Cassie had called Imani and persuaded her to come in the next morning, Peter was waiting at the door.

'Is it time for me to go home now?' he asked hopefully.

'No, sweetie. We're going to go to the park first, remember? Your daddy will take you back to your gran's after that.'

Peter slipped his hand into hers. 'You'll stay till then?'

Over the top of Peter's head Cassie caught Leith's eyes and she saw the desperation in them. Then she knew. Like it or not, it was too late to back out now. She was already involved with Leith and his son.

CHAPTER SEVEN

CASSIE FINISHED WRITING her notes and leaned back in her chair. Leith had been correct in his diagnosis. He'd removed the cyst and Imani was home once again and recovering. It had been a good call. There was a knock on the door and without waiting for an invitation to enter, Leith strode in.

It had been a couple of weeks since she'd gone to his flat and since then she'd been with Leith and Peter to the movies and on the London Eye on both Saturdays—Leith's usual access day. The little boy still barely acknowledged his father, but he was beginning to relax with Cassie. However, if she tried to leave him alone with his father, Peter would panic and grab her.

'I need to speak to you,' Leith said. His usual calm, easygoing manner was absent. Instead, he looked like someone near the end of his tether.

'Okay,' Cassie replied calmly. 'Coffee?'

Leith shook his head. 'I need you to come to Skye with me for a few days. Can you do it?'

Cassie frowned. 'A patient?'

'No. Nothing like that,' Leith replied. 'I have Peter for the whole long weekend and I want to take him to meet his grandparents. I need you to come with me.'

'Why me?' Cassie asked after a long pause.

'I doubt Peter will be happy to spend four days with me unless you're there.' He paused. 'Please, Cassie. I just don't know how to win him over.' He pulled a hand across his face. 'It will be easier for him to have you there. You've seen how he is with me.'

'He'll warm to you eventually. Give him time.'

'Eventually isn't soon enough, Cassie. Right now it's you he feels comfortable with. He trusts you. You have a way with children. They're instinctively drawn to you. It doesn't matter where in the world they are. Here. Africa. Remember Maria's little boy? You couldn't even speak his language, yet it didn't matter.'

As soon as he mentioned Africa, Cassie was back there. She could almost hear the cicadas, smell the sea, feel Leith's arms around her, his lips on hers.

She shook her head in an attempt to clear it. What were they talking about? Oh, yes, some crazy suggestion that she go with him and Peter to Skye.

It was impossible. Go away with Leith? To his family home? When she'd promised herself she would keep her distance as much as possible?

So why then had she spent those couple of days with Peter and Leith? Now, see what it had started. But that was different. That was a matter of a few hours, not days.

An image of the timid little boy flashed into her head and she tried to push it away.

'Do you think it's fair to take him away at this stage?' she said.

Leith's face darkened. 'Do you have any idea how long I've fought for this? Finally I have the moral—and legal—right to be with him and I need—want—to spend time with him. I want him to meet my parents and I know he'll love Skye once he gets there. It's a wonderful place for children.'

'Put yourself in his shoes,' Cassie said gently. 'As you say, he doesn't really know you yet. Skye will seem a very strange and alien place to him—and you'll be introducing him to more strange people.'

'I realise that,' Leith admitted. 'But it's the first time I have access for the whole weekend and if I don't take him to Skye I don't know how the two of us would manage on our own.' He looked so anguished that Cassie's heart went out to him. 'Maybe I am expecting too much too soon,' Leith continued after a moment. 'God, Cassie, do you have any idea how it feels to have your child look at you as if you were some sort of monster?'

'You love him. In the end that's all that really matters. He'll come to believe that in time.'

'I'm not giving up until he does. So, will you come? I need you as a buffer—just until he comes to trust me.'

He seemed so woebegone, she felt herself melt. He was so competent in every other area of his life yet a six-year-old had him beaten. 'I don't know, Leith. Isn't there anyone else you could ask?'

'It's you he wants. You're the only one familiar to him. And, as you just said, more strangers aren't what he needs right now.'

Damn! Hoisted by her own petard! 'But the whole weekend, Leith? Can the practice do without us both?' She knew as she said the words that she was caving in.

'We'll leave on Saturday morning. It's a public holiday on Monday and Tuesday, remember? There's only ever one of us on call at a time and it's scheduled to be Jonathan's turn. We'll fly to Glasgow or Inverness and drive from there' His expression cleared. 'We'll be back by Tuesday evening.'

She still wanted to say no—she really didn't want to spend time with Leith or get more involved in his life—but how could she refuse? It wasn't as if she had anything lined up for the weekend. And it wasn't Leith she'd be doing it for—it was Peter.

'Okay, you've convinced me,' she said. 'I'll do it this once, but after that you're on your own. Agreed?'

He grinned at her and it was as if all the tiny hairs on the back of her neck were standing to attention. 'Thanks, Cassie. I owe you.'

The next day, Cassie was asked to see a child in his home.

The address of her patient was in Kensington and Cassie found herself outside a grand Edwardian town house.

Wealth and a title didn't stop you from having a sick child, she thought as she ran up the steps. But surely it made things easier? However, in Cassie's experience, rich or poor, the mothers—and fathers—with a sick child were all the same. Scared and worried.

From the notes she'd read she didn't think the girl she was to see was ill—at least, not physically. It sounded as if she was a little slow with her development markers, but Cassie had met enough anxious parents to know that they often grossly over-estimated where their child should be.

The door was opened by the housekeeper. Cassie hid a smile. Really, did people still live like that in this day and age? 'Madam will be with you shortly,' the housekeeper said. 'If you could wait here?' She pointed to a chair in the large reception hall.

After ten minutes Cassie was getting irritated. Even if she was being paid for her services it really was unforgivably rude of Mrs Forsythe to keep her waiting like this. However, it was possible she was with her daughter and of course Cassie wouldn't want her to rush her.

More time passed and, frustrated, she got to her feet. She'd already studied every portrait and painting that adorned the walls and she should get back to the practice.

She decided to have a peek into the rooms that led off the hall to see if she could find the missing mother. The first room on the left was an enormous dining room, set with sparkling crystal and fine china, as if Mrs Forsythe was expecting guests for lunch at any moment.

The room next door was equally grand with its high ceiling and ornate cornicing. The brilliant white linen upholstery looked elegant but uninviting. It was a lovely room, but Cassie wouldn't describe it as homely or welcoming.

But it was the last door she opened that shocked Cassie. At first she thought she'd stumbled into a storage room, but then at the opposite end of the room she noticed a playpen.

The room was probably where Mrs Forsythe kept her daughter's toys and equipment out of sight when she was expecting guests. It would save carting it all back up to the playroom, which she guessed would be on one of the upper floors.

Just as she was about to turn away a sound startled her. There in the playpen was a girl of around three, standing gripping the edge of the playpen and watching Cassie with large mournful eyes. This had to be Letitia.

What was the child doing here on her own? Perhaps the mother had left her sleeping? Or had a baby monitor in the room where Cassie couldn't see it?

Nevertheless, Cassie had an uneasy feeling. A child of this age shouldn't be left in a playpen.

'Hello,' she said quietly.

There was no response.

'What's your name?' Cassie tried again. The child continued to look at her with blank eyes. Then the little girl sat down and, thumb in her mouth, opened a book and began to flick through the pages. At least she wasn't without stimulation altogether.

'Oh, you must forgive me for keeping you.' The voice came from the door and Cassie whirled round to find a woman, skinny almost to the point of gauntness, in the doorway. 'Has Letitia been keeping you company?'

It seemed an odd thing to say.

'Is it Letitia who I've come to see?' Cassie asked.

'Yes.'

Cassie noticed that Mrs Forsythe had made no move towards her daughter or even looked in her direction. There really was something odd going on here.

'And what seems to be the matter?'

'You can see for yourself. She doesn't seem to take any real interest in what's going on around her.'

Cassie was beginning to suspect where the problem lay.

'Perhaps you could lift Letitia out of the playpen?' she suggested, 'so I can have a look at her.'

Mrs Forsythe lifted her daughter up but it was clear that it wasn't something she was comfortable doing.

'I did have a nanny to help in the beginning,' Mrs Forsythe said, 'until Letitia was six months old. But then she left and I haven't quite managed to sort anyone else out. My husband isn't really keen on my hiring a new nanny. He says I should look after Letitia myself. He was brought up by nannies and hated it. But, frankly,

I don't see how he can expect me to be with Letitia all day.' She lowered her voice. 'It's so boring. It's not as if I can take her with me to lunch or to the gym.'

Cassie was horrified. This woman was talking about her daughter as if she were an unwanted Christmas present.

She gritted her teeth and, ignoring the impatient glances Mrs Forsythe was giving her watch, examined the child.

'I'd like you to bring her down to the practice for some more tests,' she said eventually, striving to keep her voice matter-of–fact, although inside she was seething.

She was pretty certain that all that was wrong with Letitia was lack of stimulation and parental attention. Why did some women have children when it was clear that they were not cut out for motherhood? Was the stigma against childless women still so strong? She was certain it was the only reason Lily had adopted her, but surely times had changed?

'Could you bring Letitia in tomorrow?' She wasn't even sure why she was suggesting it, but she wanted the opportunity to discuss the little girl with her colleagues—perhaps even have Fabio come in to assess her. She needed to be certain her own prejudices weren't clouding her judgement.

'I'm not sure about tomorrow,' Mrs Forsythe said. 'Is it really urgent?'

'It's not life-threatening, no. But I would like to see her again as soon as possible so I can carry out some more tests.'

Mrs Forsythe looked thoughtful. 'I suppose I might be able to bring her in next week. I'll have to check my diary first, though.'

'Oh, for heaven's sake, Mrs Forsythe.' Cassie couldn't help it any more. This woman had no right to call herself a mother. 'Nothing—I repeat, nothing—is more important than the welfare of your child. Why the hell did you have her if you can't be bothered with her?' It was as if all the years of frustration had built up inside her and was going to erupt. She had to get out of here before she really told this woman exactly what she thought of her.

Mrs Forsythe paled. 'Well,' she said, 'I really don't think there's any need…'

But Cassie wasn't listening. She closed her medical bag with a snap and before Mrs Forsythe could say any more, she let herself out of the house.

She was still breathing deeply when she arrived back at Harley Street. All she wanted was to get to the privacy of her consulting room before anyone noticed her agitation.

But to her dismay the first person she bumped into was Leith.

He tipped his head at her. 'Walked it off yet?'

'And what is that supposed to mean?' she demanded.

Leith took her by the arm and led her into his room. 'Mrs Forsythe has been on the phone. What on earth did you say to upset her? She's refusing to bring her child to see you. Says you were unforgivably rude and unprofessional.'

'*I* was rude?'

'Why don't you tell me about it?' Leith said calmly.

'The woman is a monster. She keeps her child isolated in a playpen because she can't be bothered with her. She wonders why her little girl seems to be slower than her friends' children and can't seem to understand that it's probably to do with the lack of stimulation and love from her mother.'

Cassie was pacing up and down. The tension was continuing to build inside her and she knew she should take some time out to get herself back together but somehow now that she'd started she couldn't stop. 'I'll never understand why some women have children. There should be a test.'

Leith said nothing, just raised one eyebrow.

'Mrs Forsythe has everything money can buy and access to all the help she needs, yet, as a mother, she's not a patch on those women we saw in Africa.'

'Have you considered the possibility that she's depressed?' Leith asked.

'That woman is no more depressed than I am!'

'Are you sure?' He sat down and hooked his arms behind his head. 'Cassie, what's going on? You must have come across women like Mrs Forsythe before!'

All of a sudden the fury leaked away and Cassie was horrified. What on earth had all that been about? Leith was right. She *had* come across women like Mrs Forsythe before—not often but a few times in her career— and she'd never reacted like this. It had been completely and utterly unprofessional. For the first time she could ever remember she had lost her professional objectivity—something she prided herself on. She sank down in the chair opposite Leith.

'My God,' she whispered. Using every ounce of self-control in her, she forced herself to breathe deeply. 'I've never reacted that way before.'

'It happens to most of us at some time,' Leith said. Cassie doubted that. 'Luckily, I was the one who took her call and I think I managed to persuade her to come in and see Fabio. But she might still complain to Jona-

than, I'm afraid. Not that Jonathan will necessarily believe everything she says, but this practice takes patient
complaints very seriously.'

Cassie closed her eyes. She had never, ever had anyone complain about her and yet here she was less than
three weeks into a job and she had upset a patient.

'What makes it worse,' she said, 'was that Letitia
might be the one to suffer from my conduct. Her mother
might decide not to seek any further professional help
at all.'

'I think you should go to Jonathan and let him know
what happened.'

Cassie stumbled to her feet, bright red with mortification. 'Of course,' she said. 'I'll go now.'

To her surprise, Jonathan wasn't annoyed in the
slightest.

'I doubt I would have reacted very differently,' he
said. 'But...' he held up a finger '...we cannot let personal feelings get in the way of doing the right thing
by our patients. And it is Letitia who is our patient, not
the mother.'

Cassie sank down into the armchair. 'I know. I'm
sorry. I really don't know what got into me.' But Jonathan deserved more than that.

'I...' She licked her lips. 'I was brought up by a
woman—my adoptive mother—who couldn't bear the
sight of me. I'm sorry...little Letitia brought it all back.
And I've not been the same since...'

Jonathan leant forward and studied her intently.
'Since?'

But she couldn't bring herself to continue. She was
too afraid she'd break down and it was all too humili-
ating as it was. She stumbled to her feet. 'I let my own
experiences cloud my judgement. I'm sorry. It won't

happen again.' And leaving an astonished Jonathan staring after her, she made her exit with what little dignity she had left.

Later that afternoon there was a soft tap on the door and Rose popped her head in.

'Are you free for a coffee?' she asked.

Without waiting for a reply, Rose pushed the door open with her hip and placed a mug down on the desk.

'Black, isn't it?'

Cassie nodded. She had a good idea what had brought Rose to her office and she didn't know how she felt about it. Embarrassed? Certainly. And also anxious. She had apologised and Jonathan had seemed to accept her apology with good grace. But what if they decided that she wasn't a good fit for their practice? All these years she had managed to present a cool, unruffled façade to everyone, yet she'd barely been here a month and she'd allowed her guard to slip in the most unprofessional way possible.

She took a sip of coffee before placing it back down on the table.

'It's okay,' she said to Rose, 'if you want to let me go. I perfectly understand.'

Rose's eyes widened. 'Whatever do you mean?'

'If you and Jonathan have decided that I'm not a good match for the practice because of what happened with Mrs Forsythe…'

'Goodness me, Cassie,' Rose said with a laugh. 'Whatever must you think of us? There isn't one of us who hasn't had a moment with a patient and had to rely on one of the other staff to smooth things over. And for the record, I've never liked Mrs Forsythe anyway. She's one of those women who think that we should drop whatever we're doing to run and see her every time she has a sniffle. Not even our richest or most influential patients expect that—except perhaps for the sheikh. If it wasn't for little Letitia we would have taken Mrs Forsythe off our list months ago.

'No, it was you Jonathan was worried about.' She set her own mug down and leaned back in the chair. 'He had a pretty cold and unloving upbringing too. He only told me what you told him because he wanted to make sure you were all right.'

Rose leaned over and took Cassie's hand. 'We like to think of everyone in this practice as part of our family—and that means accepting there will be differences of opinion, even the occasional fallout. We all make mistakes, but in the end we all have to support each other. Do you understand?'

There was a lump in Cassie's throat the size of a golf ball. She didn't know if she could speak so she simply nodded.

'Is there anything you'd like to talk about?' Rose asked. 'I'm good at keeping things to myself.'

There was genuine concern in her voice and Cassie smiled, remembering that Leith had said the same thing. 'No, really. I'm okay now. But thanks.'

'I won't probe,' Rose said, getting to her feet, 'but if you ever need to chat, I'm your woman. Wild horses— or even Gladys—won't drag your secrets from me.'

When the door closed behind Rose, Cassie felt touched. These people hardly knew her and she'd acted in a way that could have brought their practice into disrepute, yet all their concern was for her.

Some of the tightness in her chest eased. For once she hadn't been perfect, yet no one had turned away.

* * *

Leith pushed away from his desk.

He couldn't concentrate. Every time he tried to write a report his mind kept wandering back to Cassie.

It was strange seeing her every day. Strange but good. He found himself looking out for her, smiling when he caught glimpses of her as she went about her work. The same way he had constantly looked out for her on the Mercy Ship.

Everything about her reminded him of their time in Africa. He just had to catch sight of her and he was transported back there to the feel of her in his arms, the way she'd laughed up at him, the way his heart had lifted, still lifted, whenever he saw her.

He picked up his pen then threw it back down. It was no use. Who was he trying to kid? The last weeks had shown him that his feelings for her weren't in the past. They were still there. Deeper than ever.

But he still didn't have a clue what was going on under that calm, distant exterior she liked to show the world—the world with the exception of Peter. She was different with him. Funny, teasing, affectionate. If he was honest with himself, he envied her for her natural way with Peter—something he was still trying to emulate and was failing miserably at.

It was a cop-out to ask her to go with him. Surely he should be able to manage his son by himself by now? But Peter still made it clear he hated being with him— yet he had formed an attachment to Cassie and she hadn't even appeared to be trying.

She was the same with Peter as she was with all her patients, relentlessly kind, patient, caring. He hadn't been wrong about that side of her, so perhaps he hadn't been wrong at all?

So what had that issue with Mrs Forsythe been about? He'd never seen Cassie lose her cool, not even when confronted with the most testing situations on board the ship, and there had been plenty of them.

He was more certain than ever that she was keeping something from him. What was the real reason she'd left him with only that damned note? Whatever it was, he was going to find out. Perhaps when they were on Skye?

He turned to stare out the window. It was hot and there was a hint of thunder in the air. The weather matched his mood.

She had run from him once and he wasn't going to let her run again. At least until he was sure that she was running for the right reasons.

CHAPTER EIGHT

CASSIE WAS ANXIOUS as she packed for the weekend away in Skye with Leith. Whatever he thought about her having a way with children, those children were her patients. How could anyone not be kind to a child who was ill?

But this was different. Peter was Leith's son and he was expecting her to interact with him without the safety barrier of her profession. One of the reasons she'd walked away from Leith was that she didn't want to get too involved. Yet here she was, doing exactly what she'd promised herself she'd never do.

However, it was too late to back out now. She could hardly send Leith a text to say she'd changed her mind at this late stage. What had possessed her to agree?

She knew why. A little boy with the saddest eyes she had ever seen.

She folded a dress into her small carry-on bag with an impatient sigh and followed it with a pair of sandals and then, as an afterthought, a pair of wellington boots.

One long weekend. Four days. After that Leith was on his own.

They took a flight to Glasgow, where Leith hired a car to drive the rest of the way. Peter sat in the back, either playing on his games console or watching DVDs on the portable player Leith had bought for him.

He still didn't talk much, but when he did he was polite. Hopefully, soon he would come to trust Leith the way he seemed to trust her.

When they got to Loch Lomond they stopped so they could show Peter the boats on the water.

Peter got out of the car, gave the loch a dutiful look as if to say, So what? and turned to Cassie. 'Can we go?'

Cassie saw the look of despair on Leith's face but to his credit he quickly masked it and just held open the back door for his son before strapping him into his car seat.

It was the same when they stopped in Glencoe. Despite the creepy grandeur of the mountains, Peter only glanced up once before returning his attention back to his games console.

'Do you know there was a very famous battle here?' Cassie said, twisting around in her seat. 'Between two famous Scottish clans—the Campbells and the MacDonalds.'

He raised his head with the first sign of interest Cassie had seen. 'Did people get killed?'

She suppressed a smile as she slid a glance at Leith. This probably wasn't the kind of stuff one told timid six-year-olds but at least she had his attention.

'Quite a few,' she said. 'You see, what happened was...' And she went on to relay a very much censored story of the Campbells' perfidy towards the MacDonalds. 'You know, Peter, even these days some MacDonalds won't speak to a Campbell.'

Peter looked thoughtful. 'That's just silly,' he scoffed. 'People shouldn't be angry about something that happened before they were even born.'

'Which is why you shouldn't be angry about things that happened between Mummy and Daddy before you were born,' Leith said.

Cassie closed her eyes and suppressed a groan. Just when she thought they were getting somewhere, along came Leith, putting his foot in it.

'And when we get to Skye,' Cassie said hastily, noticing that Peter's mouth had turned down at the corners and he was glaring at his father, 'I shall tell you stories about the fairy people who some people believe live there.'

Leith shot her a surprised look. 'I didn't realise you'd been to Skye.'

'I haven't. I read a couple of books as soon as I knew I was coming with you. I like to know my way around a country before I get there. I like to be prepared. No nasty surprises.'

Leith's eyes were dancing. 'Another country,' he repeated. 'Aye, well, I suppose many of the English do think of Scotland as being another country.'

'That's not what I meant,' Cassie retorted. Then she smiled. 'Admittedly, what I read about Skye does make it sound almost like another country. I'm looking forward to seeing it.' She turned back to Peter, who'd clearly been listening intently to the conversation. He dropped his gaze back to his game, but not quite soon enough—she'd seen the glint of interest in his eyes.

She widened her own in mock horror. 'There's a castle with a horrible dungeon and its very own fairy flag. I don't know about you, but I'd like to see that. But if we do, I'm going to need a brave boy to stop me from being scared. Do you know where I could find such a boy?'

Peter studied her for a moment. Then he nodded

slowly and she caught a glimmer of a smile. 'I'll look after you. I'm not scared of *anything.*'

'Then you must be very brave because I'm scared of lots of things and so is your daddy.'

Peter stared at her in disbelief.

'He's terrified of spiders. Once one jumped on his shoulder and your dad nearly jumped out of his skin.'

'Hey,' Leith protested, 'you promised not to tell anyone about that.'

But Peter seemed pleased. 'Can we go to see the dungeon?' he asked.

'Sure. Perhaps tomorrow. You, me and your dad.'

Peter pursed his lips. 'Just you.'

Before Leith could say anything, Cassie jumped in. 'If that's what you want, that's fine by me. But let's see how we feel tomorrow, okay?'

When they arrived in Staffin, Peter was fast asleep.

The journey across Skye, from the point they'd crossed the bridge that joined the island to the mainland, had been breathtaking. There was something almost other-worldly about the deep glens surrounded by high mountains with their ridges like the spines of prehistoric animals. Cassie had the immediate impression of lives being lived here for generations and a sense of how life went on. The thought was comforting.

Leith slid her a look almost as if he could read her mind. 'Makes you feel small and immortal at the same time, doesn't it?' he said.

'Almost as if you could believe in magic and fairies.'

It was the first time in a long time that she'd seen Leith look so relaxed. Perhaps it was having his son with him, or perhaps it was coming home to the place he'd known all his life. Whatever it was, it was good for him.

What would it be like to feel that sense of belonging? To feel connected to a place? To know that, wherever you were in the world, there were people who longed to see you?

It had to feel wonderful.

Leith's parents were waiting for them at the door of their house and Cassie could see the family resemblance immediately. Although his father was developing a slight stoop, he was, or had been, as tall as Leith and had the same deep green eyes.

And when his mother came forward, holding out her hand and introducing herself as Maggie and her husband as Robbie, Cassie instantly recognised the smile she'd seen so often on Leith's face.

Leith shook hands with his father then picked his mother up, swinging her round and making her giggle.

'Oh, son,' she said, 'you've no idea how wonderful it is to have you home with us. Now, where's the little lad we've been hearing so much about?'

'He's asleep in the car,' Leith said. 'He's been asleep since we hit Kyle of Lochalsh. I suspect that's him out for the night.'

'I think it's better if we take him upstairs to his room without waking him,' Cassie suggested. 'He'll probably find all the new faces a little overwhelming. And if he's tired, he's bound to get cranky.'

'Good idea,' Maggie said straight away. 'I've made a bed up for him in the room next to yours, Leith. You're opposite, Cassie, if that's all right. I did wonder if you and Leith wanted to be together. If so, I can sort that out easily enough.'

Cassie sent Leith a startled look. When he raised an eyebrow and grinned she shook her head and frowned at him. He'd no right to even hint to his parents that they were a couple. Happily, his parents were peering through the car window, trying to get a glimpse of Peter, and didn't notice.

Leith's grin grew wider. 'No, Mother, Cassie will be fine where she is. We're just colleagues.' He wriggled his raised eyebrow. 'And friends?' It was more of a question than a statement and Cassie nodded. They were friends, she acknowledged. At least, as much friends as she ever allowed anyone to be.

Leith opened the car door and gently scooped his son into his arms. 'Let me get Peter upstairs and settled and then we can catch up properly.'

Cassie followed Leith up the staircase to the first floor, noticing as they climbed that each window had spectacular views out to the sea and cliffs. The moon was high in the sky, casting a silvery glow.

'It doesn't quite get dark at this time of year,' Leith said. 'We have blackout curtains in most of the bedrooms so the light doesn't wake folk up too early.'

In that case, Cassie wouldn't be drawing hers. She hated waking from one of her nightmares in the dark.

'It will be better to leave the curtains open for Peter too,' she said. She paused. She remembered once, when she'd been sent away by her adoptive parents for some imagined misdemeanour, waking up in a strange bedroom with children she didn't know and adults who, although not unkind, had frightened her.

Actually, frightened was too weak a word. Terrified was closer to it. She'd been petrified of making a mistake or saying the wrong thing—anything that might prevent her from being sent home. Because whatever and however her parents behaved towards her, it had been home and she would have done anything to get back there. 'I think I should stay with him. At least for tonight. He might be frightened if he wakes up and doesn't know where he is.'

Leith looked at her strangely. 'He only has to call and I'll hear him. I'm right next door.'

But Cassie shook her head. 'I'd rather stay with him—honestly.'

'You care about him, don't you?'

Cassie pulled the duvet over Peter's shoulders and bent to kiss him on the temple. 'No child should ever be frightened,' she murmured.

'Cassie…' Leith's voice was low.

She kept her back to him. 'Goodnight, Leith. I'll see you in the morning.'

CHAPTER NINE

When Cassie awoke it was still very early—not quite six. Yet the sun was streaming in through the opened curtains, the rays settling on Peter's bed.

Quietly she checked to see whether he was still sleeping. He was staring up at the ceiling with his troubled green eyes, Mr Mouse clutched firmly in the crook of his arm.

'Morning, sweetheart,' Cassie whispered. 'Are you ready to get up now?'

Peter held out his arms and she scooped the warm and sweet-smelling body onto her lap. She hugged him tightly as he snuggled closer. 'This is your daddy's house. Do you remember us telling you?'

He nodded.

'And you remember we told you Daddy's own mummy and daddy—your grandparents—live here? They're really looking forward to seeing you. Is that okay?'

Peter nodded again.

'Now, why don't we get you dressed and then we'll go and explore. We can see the sea from the garden. Would you like to have a look?'

Another nod. More vigorous this time.

'Daddy?' Peter said. Cassie smiled. It was good he

was finally willing to ask about his father. Now, if only she could stop Leith from expecting too much from his son, they might even get somewhere before the long weekend was over.

She helped Peter dress quickly and then took him through to her room while she did the same. He climbed up on the window seat and knelt, fists pressed into his neck, to stare out the window.

As soon as Cassie had pulled on her jeans and T-shirt she joined him. The gardens stretched into the distance—the sea glinting sapphire blue in the early morning sun.

'Are you ready?' she asked. When Peter nodded she took him by the hand. 'Shall we see if Daddy wants to come too?'

Peter looked at her for a long moment before shaking his head.

Cassie sighed inwardly. Perhaps by being here she was preventing Peter from bonding with his father? She reminded herself what it would be like to be a little child in an alien place surrounded by strangers. It was quite possible that he thought he was being punished. It's what she would have thought at the same age. No, if Leith wanted a relationship with his son and she had no reason to doubt that he did, it was up to him to find a way to his child. In the meantime, she couldn't—not in a million years—abandon the little boy.

They tiptoed downstairs and left by the unlocked front door. The moment they stepped outside the salt air hit Cassie and she closed her eyes. After the heat and traffic fumes of London, it felt fabulous. Above them an eagle stooped and swirled. Peter watched with his thumb in his mouth and then suddenly he smiled. He looked so like Leith it made her heart splinter.

'Come on, then, Peter, let's see what else we can discover before breakfast.'

From his bedroom window, Leith watched his son look up at Cassie and smile. Would his child ever feel half as easy with him as he did with Cassie? It was as if they'd recognised something in each other from the moment they'd met.

Just as he'd felt the first time he'd met her. How he still felt.

He was in love with her.

He had always been in love with her.

Hell.

Holding hands, Cassie and Peter were racing towards the sea. Instantly, Leith was out of the door. He should have warned Cassie last night. How could he have been so stupid?

As they got closer to the bit where the land seemed to disappear, Cassie stopped running.

'We have to be very careful,' she said to Peter. 'I think there's a very steep cliff here. You must never come here on your own. Okay?'

''Kay.' As a bird hopped over the grass, searching for worms, Peter let go of her hand and scampered after it.

'Stop!'

The shout came from behind them and Cassie whirled round to find Leith running towards them. Peter stopped chasing the bird, looked at his father and stuck his thumb back in his mouth. He started walking back to Cassie.

'Don't go any further,' Leith shouted. 'Not a step.'

Cassie's head swirled and all of a sudden she was standing miles away on a dusty road in Afghanistan, in the middle of a nightmare.

Leith moved as carefully as he could. Since he'd called out, Cassie had remained rooted to the spot, her eyes staring blankly somewhere beyond his right shoulder. Why didn't she walk towards him? Or reach for Peter?

A few steps away from her, his son had stopped in his tracks and was looking at Cassie, as if expecting her to tell him what to do. Why didn't she react?

If Peter continued towards her, his added weight could send the piece of overhanging cliff she was standing on plummeting down.

He forced away the image of the two people he loved most in the world falling to their deaths. He couldn't show his panic. It would only make Peter run for the shelter of Cassie's arms. And if he ran towards his child, intercepting his son's path to Cassie, Peter might turn and run towards the cliff.

Leith hunkered down and held out his hand to his son. 'Peter, could you come to me?' he said, forcing his voice to sound calm.

Peter shook his head and took a step towards Cassie.

'Please, Peter. You need to walk to me. I have something I'd like you to see.'

For a moment he thought his ruse had worked and that Peter's natural curiosity would get the better of his reluctance to come to him, but in the next second, when Peter started running towards Cassie, he knew he'd failed.

He hurled himself towards them.

Suddenly Cassie felt herself being picked up and carried before she was unceremoniously dropped to the ground.

She screamed in terror, vaguely aware of another cry that seemed to be coming from far away.

She was lying in a tangled heap of arms and legs.

Peter was crying, his squirming body trapped underneath hers. Leith was sprawled next to them, breathing deeply, his face white.

She wasn't in Afghanistan. She was in Skye. With Leith. She was safe.

'What the hell?' she said as soon as she got her breath back. She sat up and held out her arms for Peter, who came willingly. 'Shh, Peter. It's okay.' She turned back to Leith. 'What on earth did you do that for? You terrified us both.'

She looked around. They were a good bit away from where they'd been standing. At least fifty yards. He must have carried them both all that way.

'You were standing on an overhang. We expect it to fall into the sea any time. I should have warned you. If I hadn't seen you…' Leith got to his feet. 'I called out. Why didn't you answer me?'

She scrambled to her feet with Peter still in her arms. 'I have no idea what you're talking about,' she said, trying not to flinch under his blistering gaze.

'You went as white as a sheet. I thought Peter was going to go to you and his weight, along with yours, would make the cliff crumble.'

She should have stopped Peter. Gone to him. And she hadn't.

Because she'd been transported back to Afghanistan and she'd frozen. Again.

Her teeth were chattering, her legs felt boneless. She needed to get away before she lost it. Leith looked down at her, clearly puzzled.

'I...I had no idea we were in danger,' Cassie said. To her mortification her voice was shaking.

'I'm going to have to get that part of the croft fenced off. I grew up with it so it didn't even occur to me to warn you about it.' He frowned. 'How am I supposed to remember all of it? Isn't there a damn book I can buy? Some sort of manual that tells you what to do and what not to do—something that reminds you what to watch out for?'

He looked so bewildered that Cassie's heart went out to him. 'You're doing just fine,' she said softly. 'You weren't to know I would take Peter for a walk.'

'No, but I should have warned you anyway. Next time check with one of us before you take off. Skye is full of steep cliffs that fall away suddenly and without warning.'

Cassie really, really needed to be on her own. She placed Peter on the ground, took his hand and Leith's and joined them.

'Perhaps it's time you started learning. I'm going for a walk. You should take Peter back inside.'

Before Leith could protest, she'd turned on her heel and was striding away across the moors.

Leith took Peter back to the house, the little boy trotting uncomplainingly by his side. Strange that his son should choose this time to trust his father.

'Is Cassie angry with me?' Peter asked quietly.

Leith stopped and crouched next to his son. 'Cassie would never be angry with you. She just got a fright.'

'You rescued me from the sea... And Cassie.'

'You...' He was about to lie to Peter—tell him that he'd been in no danger—but he decided against it. That wasn't the way it was going to be between him and his child. 'I wasn't going to let anything happen to you. I love you. I promise to keep you safe. It's my job. Do you understand?'

Peter nodded. 'You, me and Cassie. We keep each other safe.'

Leith's chest felt tight. He resisted the urge to crush his child to him. 'Yes, son. Now I'll take you to meet your grandmother. When I'm sure you're okay, I'm going to see if Cassie is all right.'

'I told you. I'm a big boy. You can leave me alone. Mummy used to leave me alone sometimes and nothing ever happened. I don't get scared. Not even when it's dark.'

Leith's anger towards Jude rose. How could she leave a child of six on his own? He forced a smile. 'You know what, Peter? Even though you are a big, brave boy, I'm never going to leave you on your own. Not until you're as tall as me anyway.'

Peter took his hand. 'I grow fast. I'm almost up to your waist already.'

'So you are. But don't grow too fast, son.'

Back at the house his mother was up and in the kitchen.

'You two must have been up early.' She smiled at them. 'Hello, Peter. I'm your daddy's mum. I know you have another granny so you can call me Granny Skye if you like.'

Peter studied her for a few moments. 'You've got white hair.'

'So I have,' she agreed. 'Are you ready for some breakfast?'

Peter nodded.

'Then why don't you take a seat at the table and

after breakfast we can go and fetch some more eggs
for baking?'

To Leith's relief, Peter did as she asked. He wanted
to go in search of Cassie. Something was very wrong—
she would never have left Peter after what had happened if it wasn't. But he didn't want to leave his son.
Especially not now.

'Where's Cassie?' His mother asked. 'Still in bed?'

'No, she's up too. She's out on the croft.'

'She got a fright,' Peter said. He looked at Leith. 'You
better find her in case she gets lost.'

'Will you be all right here with Granny Skye?'

Peter hesitated. He looked at his grandmother then
back to Leith. He popped his thumb in his mouth then
took it out again. 'I'll be good. You need to go and get
Cassie.'

Cassie stared out at the waves crashing onto the rocks.
Although she'd walked the terror out of her head, she
wasn't ready to return to the house.

She should have gone back with Leith and Peter. The
little boy had just had a scare. He'd needed her. Yet she
hadn't been able to do it. Her need to be on her own had
been too overwhelming.

If ever she needed evidence that she wasn't up to the
job of parenting, even on a minor scale, she'd just had it.

When she heard a footfall behind her, she knew it
was Leith. It was as if her body had its own radar as
far as he was concerned. Reluctantly she turned to face
him.

'You okay?' he asked.

'Why do you keep asking me that?' she replied.

'Because clearly you're not. Something isn't right.
You seem different from the Cassie I knew on the ship.'

'We all change, Leith. It wouldn't say much about us if we didn't.' But she hadn't changed. She was still the not-quite-up-to-it Cassie she'd always been. Surely Leith could see that now?

'It's not just that,' he said. 'Sometimes you look so sad. Lost even.'

Sad? Lost? She couldn't bear it if that's how he saw her.

'I can't make you out, Cassie.' He touched her on the shoulder, his warm hands sliding up towards her neck. 'You're still trembling.'

It took every ounce of her willpower not to bolt from the intimacy of his touch. Confusingly, at the same time she wanted to throw herself into his arms and rest against him for a while.

She sucked in a breath. 'Being here,' she began, 'brings back memories, and not pleasant ones.'

'I'm not sure I understand. You've never been here before.'

'Oh, it's not the place,' Cassie admitted. 'It's your family—the way you obviously all love each other and are desperate for Peter to know that he is loved too. I suspect you would walk to the ends of the earth if you thought it would make him happy.'

Her team in Afghanistan had been like her family.

'Your parents don't love you?'

Cassie laughed—but even to her own ears it wasn't a happy sound. 'Not every family is like yours, you know.'

'Come on, Cassie. That's not good enough. Talk to me. Tell me about them. We're friends, aren't we?'

Friends? Friends! Was the man completely oblivious to the way she felt about him?

He folded his arms. 'I'm not going anywhere until you talk to me.'

She wrapped her arms around herself. 'There's nothing really to tell. I was adopted. I never really got on with my adoptive parents. They spend half the year in South Africa so I don't see much of them.' Didn't see them at all, if she was honest. She shrugged. 'That's all there is to it. At least you want to be a good father to Peter. You want him to be happy.'

'Of course I do,' Leith said. 'But wanting to make him happy isn't the same thing as knowing how to. Cassie, this dad stuff is harder, much harder, than my own dad made—makes it look. Perhaps you should cut your adoptive parents some slack?'

Cassie had to smile. 'You'll learn,' she said dryly. 'And no one can say you're not trying.'

Leith's eyes searched her face and she turned away. Like always, it was as if he were looking right into her soul. She didn't want him to see what was really there. That would have been too much.

'Look, could we leave it?' she said before he could probe further.

She felt his hands on her shoulders and he turned her so she was facing him. The world stopped turning as he placed his hands on either side of her face.

'Talk to me, Cassie.'

She shook her head, unable to speak.

He lowered his head and his lips were on hers. She clung to him, unable to stop herself giving in to the oblivion of his kiss.

When she pulled away, his eyes were glinting. 'I knew I wasn't wrong back on the Mercy Ship and I'm not wrong now. There was something between us then and it's still there. I know you feel it too. For God's sake, Cassie, don't keep pushing me away.'

It was as if someone had pierced her heart with a shard of glass. He had no idea how much she wanted to go back to the way it had been. How it had been when she'd thought there might be a future for them. The time before Peter.

She stepped away. 'We're colleagues. That's all. I shouldn't have kissed you. You caught me off guard, that's all.' She forced a smile. 'Now I think I'll go to my room.'

His dark, questioning eyes were still on her. The last time he'd looked at her like that had been eighteen months ago—just before they'd made love for the first time. Her chest tightened and she spun on her heel and hurried back to the house as fast as she could. But not before she thought she heard him call her name.

Leith watched as Cassie disappeared behind the trees that shielded the house from the main road.

He frowned. She'd been fast but not fast enough to hide the desire in her eyes when he'd touched her. It was the same look he'd seen all those months ago, the same longing he was sure had been reflected in his own eyes. He'd bet his life that she cared for him. But, then, he would have said the same thing eighteen months ago, and he'd been wrong.

He'd seen the desire, but he'd also seen the pain and heard it in her voice. What had happened to her in the time since they'd seen each other? If she'd been reserved when they'd first met, she was even more shut off now. Something—or someone—had hurt Cassie, and badly.

And one way or another he was going to find out what—or who—it had been.

* * *

After the excitement of earlier, breakfast was a reassuringly casual and relaxed affair. To Cassie's surprise and relief, Peter seemed unaffected by what had happened earlier. When she'd returned, he'd run to her and wrapped his arms around her knees but then he'd gone back to helping Maggie lay the table.

After they finished eating, Maggie invited her grandson to go and look for some fresh eggs with her, and after only the smallest hesitation the little boy took her hand and allowed himself to be led from the room.

It was going better than she'd hoped. Peter seemed more comfortable around women, which was probably only to be expected, but he was clearly beginning to relax with Leith's family. It was just a pity that Leith couldn't always bring him to Skye—at least, until the child had familiarised himself with his father. Then she wouldn't be needed.

The thought didn't give her as much pleasure as she'd imagined it would.

Peter was smiling proudly when he returned with three brown eggs in his basket. Solemnly he lifted one from his basket and handed it to Cassie. Then he gave another one to his grandmother. Finally he turned to his father and everyone in the room held their breath. Cassie prayed that Leith wouldn't do anything that would startle the boy.

When Peter reached into his basket for the only remaining egg and held it out to Leith, Cassie let her breath out—she hadn't even realised she'd been holding it.

'Is that for me?' Leith asked quietly.

Peter seemed uncertain for a moment, as if thinking of changing his mind. Then he nodded and Leith accepted the egg with the same gravity he gave to his patients when they were telling him their symptoms.

'Shall I keep it? Or have it for my breakfast?' he asked.

'Keep it,' Peter said, 'until it hatches.'

Cassie hid a smile at the look of consternation on Leith's face. But then, even before he opened his mouth to reply, she just knew he was about to say the wrong thing.

'I don't think it will hatch, son. You see, an egg needs to be kept warm by its mother before it can become a chicken.' Oops. That was so not the right thing to say. As Peter thrust out his lower lip, Cassie shot Leith a warning glance and said quickly, 'We'll get you a box to keep it in—for a few days.'

It seemed from the dawning realisation on Leith's face that he was beginning to catch on. 'But when we go, perhaps we'd better leave it with the mother hen? They might miss one another.' Leith shot Cassie a triumphant smile.

Peter's face crumpled and he threw Cassie an anguished look before bolting from the room. As Leith's mother went to follow, Cassie got to her feet too. She shook her head at Leith.

'Not your smartest move,' she said wryly, 'reminding him that he's not with his mother.' And leaving a bewildered Leith staring at his father, Cassie hurried after Peter and his grandmother.

It was the nightmare again. It was never quite the same. She'd be walking along, laughing at something her companion had said. Sometimes it would be Angela, sometimes Linda—it changed from night to night.

Then suddenly there would be a blinding flash, a shock of heat and she'd be thrown up in the air.

When she came to all she heard was an eerie stillness where only minutes before there had been the sound of children's laughter and mothers' scolding.

She'd tried to move, but couldn't. She tried to talk but her mouth was caked with dust.

She looked over to where Angela should be and when she saw the crumpled, still form, she tried again to make her limbs move. She rolled over on her stomach—a feat requiring a gargantuan effort. She had to take a few moments to rest before, using her elbows, she crawled inch by painful inch towards her injured colleague.

And then...

'Cassie, what is it?'

She struggled to open her eyes. Where was she? There was something she had to do but she couldn't think what it was.

She tried to get out of bed but strong arms held her back.

'I have to help...' Cassie shouted, trying to push the arms away. Her heart pounded harder. She thought she could hear the sound of it beating.

'Cassie, you're dreaming. You're in Skye. Come on, wake up.' The arms held her loosely, as if knowing that pulling her closer would only make her feel more frightened. 'It's Leith, Cassie.'

Her heart was beginning to slow down. 'Leith?' What was he doing here?

'You're okay. You've just had a bad dream. You're safe now.'

Although her heart was still pounding painfully, the nightmare was beginning to recede. She wasn't in Afghanistan. There was no one calling for her. She wasn't too frightened to move.

But Linda was still dead.

She gave a little moan and this time Leith's arms did tighten around her. She let herself lean into him. Just for a moment. All of a sudden the feeling of his arms around her—the same, safe feeling she'd always had when with him—triggered something in her and she found herself sobbing against his chest, deep, racking sobs that seemed to come from a place so deep inside that she hadn't known it existed. Hot tears coursed down her face, filling her mouth with salty wetness. She hadn't known it was even possible to cry like this. But she couldn't stop herself.

He didn't say anything. Apart from a hand that came up to stroke her hair, he hardly seemed to move a muscle.

Eventually she managed to get herself under control. She pulled away from him, grabbed a bunch of tissues from the bedside table and hid her face in them.

What on earth had come over her? She'd never lost it like this before and certainly not in front of anyone. And that it should be Leith made it worse.

'Do you want to tell me what that was about?' he asked gently once she'd blown her nose.

She was glad that the room was dark so he couldn't see her face. 'I was shouting in my sleep, huh?' she said. 'Sorry if I woke you.'

'I'm a light sleeper.'

He would have had to be a very light sleeper to have heard her through the thick walls—or she'd been crying out louder than usual.

'It's time you talked to me.'

Cassie shook her head. She drew her knees up to her chest and suppressed a shiver.

'I'm not leaving until you do,' Leith said quietly. She felt the bed shift under his weight as he stretched himself out next to her. The length of his body was immediately familiar—almost as if the intervening time hadn't passed. 'Talking about it might help chase the demons away.'

Cassie doubted that any amount of talking could chase away her particular demons, but maybe it was the darkness of the room with only a sliver of light from the moon, perhaps it was the warmth of Leith's body next to hers and the fact that he didn't try to touch her, but without even knowing she was going to do it, she started talking.

'It was a normal day. Hot. But it was always hot in Afghanistan. We were based at a camp where the army has a medical facility. We weren't treating soldiers—just using it as a base.'

'Go on,' he said.

'There were five of us. Me, a paediatric surgeon, two nurses and an interpreter. Our remit was to carry out clinics and surgery if necessary at the local hospital. Although it sounds dangerous, we didn't think it would be. We were civilians and doctors and nurses. The hospital was well protected too. Just in case. I wasn't at all frightened. I was excited.'

'Cassie, I had no idea you were planning to go there. The last time we spoke you said the UN was sending you to Sudan.'

'They did and I went. But when the opportunity came to go out to Afghanistan I jumped at the chance.' She paused. 'I guess part of me wanted to prove that I was at least as brave as my adoptive mother.' She managed a smile. 'In my thirties and still trying to impress parents who I didn't even see.'

She felt Leith take her hand. He gave it a gentle squeeze.

'But it wasn't just that. I'd read how much the civilians needed medical help.' She sucked in a breath. She wasn't quite ready to tell him that the time she'd spent working on the Mercy Ship had been the happiest of her life—mainly because of him, but also because she'd found that what she'd been doing had made her feel truly good about herself.

For the first time she hadn't been trying to be what she thought her adopted parents wanted her to be—she hadn't been trying to be the best, the best in her class, the best in her year, the student and trainee who impressed everyone she came across. She had just tried to do the best job she could with what she'd had. Could Leith even begin to understand what it was like to be her? She was sure he'd never doubted himself in his life—or felt the need to prove himself.

'Anyway, we went out. We received some training from the army—what to do if we were attacked, or kidnapped, that sort of thing. But they made it clear that we would only be allowed to go to the hospital if they were certain it was safe.'

'Go on.' His voice was quiet but she was intensely aware of him. Although, apart from his hand, his body wasn't touching hers, she felt heat and energy radiating from him.

'The first few weeks were fine. The five of us made a good team.' Her voice cracked. The truth was she'd become closer to them than she'd ever been to her own family—apart from Martha, of course. 'Then one day, when we only had a couple of weeks left…' her breath hitched '…everything went wrong.'

As she thought back to that day her heartbeat quickened. 'As usual, we'd been taken to right outside the hospital by an armoured vehicle. They always dropped us off then patrolled outside until we were ready to leave. One of our regular escorts was a young captain called Linda. It was her last tour. She was going back to get married. She was so much in love.'

Cassie closed her eyes. It was unbelievable to recall now the envy she'd felt for Linda—to have found her soul mate and to be so certain that their future together would be for ever…

'Anyway, one of the nurses, Angela, hated the fact that there were always scrawny, half-starved dogs outside the hospital. She must have seen one she wanted to give a titbit to as she wandered off—at least, I think that's what happened. I heard Linda call out to her, telling her to come back, and the next thing I knew there was this almighty explosion. It was as if the world had stopped turning. For what seemed like hours but could have only been seconds there was this deathly silence. I didn't even feel any pain until much later. Some small pieces of shrapnel had lodged in my side. All I could see was a bundle of what looked like rags. There was a whimpering noise and I knew that Angela had been badly injured.'

Her throat tightened, making it difficult to speak. But Leith said nothing, simply increasing the pressure on her hand.

'To cut a long story short, I wanted to go to her, but Linda shouted at me to stay where I was. And then…' She didn't know if she could finish. In her mind she saw again the crumpled body on the ground, the shocked and empty silence, a bird hovering overhead. 'And then Linda took a step towards Angela and there was another explosion. And that's all I remember until I woke up back in the hospital at camp.'

'The nurse, did she make it?' Leith asked softly.

'Yes she did, thank goodness. It turned out that the dog she'd been following had set off the first IED. But there was another one and Linda…' She drew a deep, shuddering breath. 'She didn't stand a chance.'

This time she allowed Leith to take her into his arms and as the tears came she let herself relax against his chest. 'Why did it have to be her? She had everything to look forward to.'

Leith's hands were in her hair and he was murmuring words of comfort. Cassie pulled away from him. 'Don't you see?' she burst out. 'It should have been me.'

'But that's ridiculous,' Leith said. 'It wasn't your fault.'

'I can't help feeling guilty. If I had moved first Linda wouldn't have stood on the mine.'

'That's crazy thinking, Cassie! There could have been other mines. Linda was a trained soldier. She would have been trained to act instinctively and would have known the risks. On the other hand, you were a civilian. You did the right thing by listening to her instructions.'

'Linda was only there because she was protecting us,' Cassie replied bitterly. 'Why did she die and we survive?'

There was a silence for a while. 'I never thought I'd hear Cassie Ross feeling sorry for herself. I never put self-pity and you together somehow.'

Cassie felt as if she'd been slapped. What did he mean? She was only telling him how she saw it.

'I'm not looking for your sympathy,' she said stiffly.

'Just as well because you're not going to get it. At least, not for the reasons you think. You deserve sympathy for what happened out there. It was a horrific experience for anyone to go through and I can't even begin to imagine what it must have been like for you. But to hold yourself responsible… No, Cassie, that smacks of self-pity and I suspect Linda deserves more than that from you.'

'But if it weren't for us…if I hadn't ignored her warning and moved towards the nurse, Linda wouldn't have felt she had to intervene. She wouldn't have died.'

'It sounds to me that Linda was a very brave woman who was doing the job she'd signed up for. I don't think you are doing her memory any favours by rewriting the whole episode from your point of view.'

'Is that what you think I'm doing?' Fury bubbled up inside her. 'Do you know what it's like to relive something in your head every day, knowing that if only you could have sixty seconds over again it could all be different? Do you know what it's like to dream about it, night after night? To wake yourself up screaming with terror?'

'No, I don't. But it will pass, Cassie. Trust me, it will pass.'

He tucked the blanket under her chin, much the same way she'd seen him do with Peter. Then he pulled her against him and she could hear the beating of his heart.

'Go back to sleep,' he said softly.

'You don't have to stay.'

'Don't argue, woman. I'm not going anywhere.' And as she drifted off to sleep she thought she heard him murmur, 'Not ever again.'

* * *

Leith held Cassie as her breathing deepened and she fell into what he hoped was a dreamless sleep.

At least she was beginning to talk to him. What had happened to her in Afghanistan explained a lot—her haunted look, the way she'd frozen that morning on the cliff. But that didn't explain everything. There was more she was hiding from him. Stuff he needed to discover about her if there was the remotest chance for them to have a future together.

God, he loved this woman—this complicated, prickly, defensive, proud woman. The thought that she'd been hurt, inside and out, and he hadn't been there for her churned him up inside and he vowed that she would never have to face anything alone again. Not while there was breath in his body.

Without really knowing it, he had been waiting for her to come back to him. And if he had to wait another eighteen months, or even eighteen years, so be it.

Cassie slept deeply and dreamlessly for the rest of that night and awoke feeling refreshed and at peace. It seemed Leith had been right. Talking about what had happened had helped.

Or was it just that being around Leith made her feel safe? As if nothing bad could ever happen to her again?

He was still stretched out beside her. Quietly, so as not to wake him, she propped herself on her elbow and studied him. Even in sleep there was a small smile tugging at the corners of his mouth.

He opened one eye. 'Morning.'

She blushed, embarrassed that he'd caught her staring. 'You didn't have to stay the whole night.'

'I wanted to be here in case you woke up again,' he said.

She threw the blankets aside and jumped out of bed. He stared at her for a few moments through narrowed eyes. 'Cute,' he said. 'Very cute. Aren't those panties you're wearing the same ones you almost lost the day you arrived at the ship?'

'Of course they aren't,' she retorted, knowing her face had to be scarlet. She almost leaped to the end of the bed where she'd left her dressing gown. Indeed, a world-class sprinter couldn't have left the starting blocks as fast as she'd just moved.

Leith eased his long legs over the side of the bed and came to stand beside her. Still grinning, he tied the belt of her dressing gown for her. 'Feel better now?'

Damn the man for knowing exactly the way he was making her feel. He could at least have the decency to pretend.

'I'm perfectly fine,' she said through stiff lips. As his smile broadened she had to laugh. She pulled her hair into a ponytail and smiled up at him. 'You know, Leith, I actually think I might be.'

When he left, she dressed, suffused with an energy she hadn't felt for a long time, grabbed some fruit from a bowl and let herself out of the house.

She walked until her legs ached. Up steep hills from where she could see the ocean stretching into the distance and then down into hidden valleys where she discovered small whitewashed cottages huddled against the hills. Thoughts of Leith filled her head. She could imagine them here together, living in one of the small croft houses, going for long walks along the shore before returning to their bed to make love.

Of course, her fantasies were just that. She was still in love with Leith, of course she was, she had never stopped loving him, but there was still the matter of Peter. She still couldn't see herself as a mother—not even a stepmother. As for Leith... The time hadn't been right for them when they'd first met, and it wasn't right now—even if she knew she could never love anyone the way she loved him.

Nevertheless, by the time she'd returned to the house, she felt happier than she could remember. Certainly since the weeks on board ship.

She sniffed the air. Something smelled delicious. Following the aromas to the kitchen, she found Leith in the armchair by the Aga, reading a book to Peter, who was perched somewhat precariously on the arm. Leith's father was doing a crossword while his mother was kneading something in a large bowl.

'I wish I could bake,' Cassie said.

'You can't bake?' Maggie asked incredulously.

'Never learned. I suspect it's too late now.'

'Wheesh. Away with you! It's never too late,' Maggie replied. 'I was just about to start a batch of scones. Why don't you help me and I'll show you it's not as difficult as you think?' She glanced around and finding an apron handed it to Cassie.

Peter, she noticed, had slid down the arm of the chair and was now half on and half off Leith's lap. Leith shifted slightly to let his son make himself more comfortable.

Leith's mother showed her how to rub butter into flour before mixing it with milk to form a dough.

'Now we roll it out lightly and cut it into rounds.' Maggie looked over at Peter. 'Would you like to help?'

But to Cassie's delight Peter shook his head and snuggled deeper into Leith.

When Leith glanced up, her heart shifted as she read the pleasure in his eyes. He and his son were going to be all right.

After the scones were in the oven, Maggie started teaching Cassie how to make a clootie dumpling.

'It's called clootie because it's cooked in a cloth—a clootie. It takes a few hours of steaming but it's worth it.'

Leith had finished the story by this time and Peter had slipped off his lap. Peter came across to the table, sat down and propped his chin on his hands.

Cassie carried on stirring fruit into the flour mixture. The first batch of scones was ready and Maggie took them out of the oven.

'What about you, Peter? Do you want a go at mixing?' Cassie asked.

Peter nodded and Cassie handed him a wooden spoon. He stood in the space between her arms and the table and began to mix. When Cassie looked up it was to find Leith's eyes on her and the look of love she saw there took her breath away.

But it was Peter who he was looking at, wasn't it? Not her.

That afternoon they took Peter to the castle to see the dungeon and Cassie made sure she appeared sufficiently frightened to make the little boy feel he was protecting her. When they'd finished at the castle, they went for a walk to the coral beach. The next day they walked to the Fairy Glen. As it was a beautiful, clear day, Maggie had packed a picnic for them.

After their walk Cassie unpacked the picnic basket while Leith threaded some worms onto a fishing rod.

'I don't believe in fairies,' Peter said suddenly. 'I'm too big a boy.'

'You're certainly a brave boy,' Cassie agreed.

Peter crept closer to her until he was leaning his head against her arm. 'I used to believe in Santa when I was little,' he confided.

Cassie hid a smile. 'You don't any more?'

'Last year he didn't come to my house.'

'He didn't?'

Cassie looked across at Leith, who had stopped what he was doing and was watching Peter intently.

'Why do you think that was?' she asked the little boy.

''Cos I wasn't a good enough boy to get presents. But the next day Mummy bought me a whole pile. So I knew then it wasn't Santa who brought the presents.'

Cassie's heart ached for him. This trying-to-be-good-but-never-believing-he-could-be-good-enough behaviour she recognised only too well.

Leith growled something under his breath and scowled.

'You know something, Peter,' Cassie said carefully. 'I don't think there's a better boy in the whole wide world than you.'

Peter huddled closer to Cassie. 'Do you believe in Santa?' he asked.

A lump formed in Cassie's throat. 'I believe magic can happen sometimes.' She picked a dandelion 'clock' from the long grass. 'Do you know, if you close your eyes and blow, you can make a wish? Some people believe the seeds are little fairies who then scatter to make your wish come true.'

Peter looked up at her. 'I told you I'm too big to believe in fairies.'

Cassie smiled at him. 'Then there's nothing to lose, is there? Why don't we give it a go?'

Peter hesitated before taking the dandelion from Cassie. He closed his eyes, pursed his lips and blew hard. The seeds, each with its own 'parachute', danced in the sunshine before dispersing in all directions.

'You know what I wished,' he said, opening his eyes and looking down at the ground. 'I wished you could always be with me.'

The lump in Cassie's throat made it difficult to speak. She forced herself not to look at Leith.

'Oh, Peter,' she said hoarsely, 'if you ever need me, close your eyes and think of me. That way, if I can't be with you in person, I'll be in your mind.'

That night, Cassie lay in bed, tossing and turning.

Peter's wish troubled her. At least the little boy was coming to trust his father; no longer demanding Cassie or his grandmother's presence at all times. That was the way it should be. It wasn't as if Cassie was going to be anything but a temporary figure in his life—whatever she'd promised.

Her heart stumbled. She was going to do to Peter what had been done to her so many times; dance in and out of his life when what he really needed was constancy. Already the little boy was forming an attachment to her. It was one thing to care for the child over a few days, quite another being a stable, loving presence in his life day after day, year after year.

She wouldn't be around for very much longer. All too soon she'd be leaving. How could she bear to leave Leith again when the merest glimpse of him still sent shooting stars of desire along her nerve endings? When her nightmares had been replaced by fairy-tale dreams of the two of them in a cottage in a place pretty much like this—miles away from everywhere and everyone.

She pushed the images away. They'd be returning to London tomorrow. Leith was due to take Peter back to his maternal grandmother the following morning and soon her time at the practice would be coming to end. She closed her eyes as a shard of pain pierced her heart.

She thought back to the last few days. Leith and his family in the kitchen—the warmth, the love and the sheer enjoyment they had in each other's company. Being around Peter, Leith and his family made her feel good.

But it wasn't about her. It was about them.

CHAPTER TEN

A COUPLE OF weeks after their return from Skye, Cassie was in her consulting room, studying the blood-test results of one of her patients when there was a tap on the door and Leith walked in.

Cassie resented the way her heart flipped whenever she saw him. She repeatedly told herself that she would learn to live without him, and when the thought came into her head that she hadn't got over him in eighteen months, she ignored it. Being in love with someone was not the same as doing anything about it.

'Just to let you know everything is sorted for Friday. The duchess's secretary has emailed us both an itinerary. We fly out on a scheduled flight.'

'Sounds fine,' Cassie said. 'How's Peter?'

Leith smiled. 'He's great. His grandmother and aunt have noticed a difference in him. They say he's behaving more like the little boy he is rather than a miniature adult.' He perched on the edge of her desk. 'What's more, Jude's volunteered to go into rehab. Her mother and sister think she means to get off the drugs for good. Jude's told them it's time she sorted her life out so she can be a proper mother to Peter'

'But that's great, Leith! Peter deserves a mother in his life. A mother who loves him.'

Leith's expression turned serious. 'Have I said thank you?'

'What for?'

'For helping me with him. For making him feel safe to be with me. You'd make a great mother, Cassie.'

Would she? She'd never know. She averted her eyes. 'So what about these plans for the trip, then?'

On Friday morning Cassie was showered and dressed by six a.m. Leith hadn't mentioned her nightmare, but sometimes she would catch him looking at her, the expression in his eyes unreadable. Since that night she hadn't had the dream again. Instead, she fell asleep almost instantly, waking late and feeling refreshed and at peace. However, last night she'd hardly slept. In the end she'd given up, pulled on her sweats and running shoes and let herself out into the drizzly London streets.

Why was she getting herself worked up about this trip anyway? They'd fly in, be around if they were needed and fly back on Tuesday. She didn't see what she and Leith were actually going to do for the four days they'd be there. The duchess's pregnancy was going well and given that she was only thirty-two weeks it was unlikely she'd be going into labour any time soon. It was also unlikely that the duchess would wish or expect Leith and Cassie to be with her every moment.

But it wasn't as if she would have to be with Leith all the time either. At least, she hoped not. These last few weeks had made one thing abundantly clear. She was in love with Leith and would be until the end of her days.

When she returned from her run, she showered and changed into her favourite sundress. As she applied her lipstick she studied herself in the mirror. She'd gained weight and the shadows under her eyes had all but disappeared. Being in love had something going for it.

Her packing finished, she snapped her bag shut and paused for a moment. She had everything. Her bikini, a good book to read and her guide book to the Caribbean. There were several things she wanted to see while she was there if she got the time. She really had no idea how these trips worked. Were they treated as guests or as the hired help? Frankly, she hoped it was the latter. The thought of having to make small talk with the duchess and her party horrified her.

Nevertheless, the knowledge that she would be the guest of a duchess gave her some kind of perverse pleasure. Her adoptive mother would have been thrilled to know that Cassie had anything to do with such exalted company.

A car hooted below and she picked up her case, locked the door behind her and ran downstairs. Leith was waiting for her in a black sports car. He leaped out and opened the boot, which was minuscule. When he saw her bag he grinned. 'I see you've learnt your lesson about packing—no chance of this suitcase spewing its contents all over the street.'

She laughed. 'It wasn't my most sophisticated moment, was it?'

'No one could say you didn't make a grand entrance.' He lowered his voice. 'Not that you needed to throw your underwear around to get my attention. You had it from the first moment I saw you.'

The world seemed to stop spinning. Cassie sucked in a breath. She wished he hadn't said that. She wished he wouldn't look at her as if she mattered. She wished— God, she wished she could be in his arms again. Safe and loved. She gave herself a mental shake, hoping that she didn't look as hot and bothered as she felt.

'Hadn't we better get going?' She was glad that her voice sounded normal—cool and amused even. She was damned if she was going to give him the slightest indication that he affected her the way he did. These next few days were going to be tough if every time she saw him or he spoke to her she was going to react like a school girl.

'All set?' he asked as he accelerated the car. She was unbearably conscious of his proximity, his thigh inches away from hers, the faint smell of his aftershave.

'This is a Lamborghini, isn't it?' Cassie asked. 'Four hundred horsepower, I'm guessing.' She had mastered the art of small talk. Keep conversation away from the personal and everything would be all right.

'You know your cars?' Leith asked.

'Always been a hobby of mine,' Cassie replied with a smile. 'I used to rally drive at one time.'

Leith whistled. 'Any other hidden talents you've kept from me?'

Cassie darted him a look. On the Mercy Ship she'd always turned the questions away from her—usually by diverting him with a touch of her fingertips or her lips or… Now she was getting hot and bothered again.

Wasn't the plan to keep the discussion away from her? She shook her head.

'No. I lead a dull life really.'

His mouth lifted at the corners. 'I'd hardly say that. The Mercy Ship then Sudan, followed by a near-death experience in Afghanistan. Most people don't experience what you have in a lifetime, let alone a couple of years.'

She flushed under the admiration in his dark eyes.

Then it struck her. Leith knew more about her than any other person on the planet—and somehow that didn't scare her at all.

The island was beautiful with its whitewashed houses crammed up against the hill. The smell of olives and spices drifted on the heavy night air.

The duchess—'you must call me Veronica'—was relaxed and had an impish sense of humour.

'I do hope you won't be bored,' she said. 'I wouldn't have dragged you all the way out here if it hadn't been for my mother. She's so protective. But aren't mothers always?' Veronica looked at Cassie and she managed a smile in return.

'Now, I don't want you to feel tied to me. As long as I can get in touch with you by phone at any time, that's good enough for me. It's not as if this island is so huge you could ever be more than a few miles away anyway. On the other hand, you are most welcome to spend time with my party. It's just a few close friends. Mummy is here for a couple of days but she has to go back the day after tomorrow.'

'I wouldn't like to intrude,' Cassie murmured. 'To tell you the truth, I'm looking forward to catching up on some reading and doing some exploring.'

'I thought you might feel that way,' Veronica said, 'so I have arranged for you to stay in the Captain's Lookout—it's just a little distance from the main house but it has the most amazing views. It has everything you need—and someone to cook and clean—but if you'd rather stay at the main house, just say the word. And please come for dinner or lunch any time you wish. We are quite informal here.'

Staying somewhere with Leith wouldn't have been

Cassie's choice but before she could say anything, Leith replied for them both.

'That sounds good to me. What about you, Cassie?' She could have sworn there was laughter in his eyes. Did he have any idea how much he unsettled her?

She feigned indifference. 'Whatever is easiest.' Despite Veronica's words, there was no way she could invite herself to stay at the main house. 'And please don't worry about entertaining us. I'm sure we will manage to look after ourselves.'

'Very well, but at least come for dinner on our last night. Everyone will be there and we hope to make quite a party of it.'

'I'll be down to the house twice a day,' Leith said, 'to check up on you. Although I have to say I have no worries or concerns at all about the baby at the moment.'

Veronica flashed a smile. 'I feel like such a fraud. But having you here is reassuring for me as well as Mummy.'

If Veronica felt a fraud, where did that leave Cassie? The chances of her paediatric skills being needed were a thousand to one. Still, she was here and she might as well make the most of it.

Cassie was enchanted with the Captain's Lookout. It was built, a bit like the top of a lighthouse, with floor-to-ceiling windows. As Veronica had said, it was perched on top of a hill with a three-hundred-and-sixty degree view of the island—beaches on one side, forest on the other. The main house was fifty metres below, only a short walk away should they be needed, and was screened from view by a small wood.

Just behind their temporary home was a small building.

'That's where my wife and daughter, Tess, stay,' their

driver said. 'My wife, Josie, is the cook and house-keeper. And whenever you want to go somewhere it will be my pleasure to take you. There isn't much to see, apart from the beaches, but there is one bar and a good restaurant down by the pier.'

'It sounds heavenly,' Cassie said.

'How long you here?'

'Just a few nights.'

'That is a shame. You should stay for at least two weeks. You tourists need time to relax, become like us islanders. You are always rushing, rushing.'

Cassie and Leith shared a smile. Cassie supposed the chauffeur was right. They were always rushing, rushing. At least, she was. Whenever she didn't have anything planned, a horrible restless energy would build up inside her. It was one of the reasons she sometimes ran until she was so exhausted she could hardly put one foot in front of the other.

Inside, the Captain's Lookout was even more breathtaking. Someone had kept the inside plain, with scrubbed wooden floors and simple leather furniture, the only colour coming from bright rugs strewn on the floor.

But it was the view from the bedroom that made Cassie gasp. Jutting out slightly on a small promontory and facing the sea, almost two-thirds of her bedroom walls were windows that framed the view. Apart from the boats bobbing in the bay, the sea, lit by a full moon, was a mass of aquamarine blue tipped with white. It wasn't difficult to imagine a sea captain looking out from here, watching for pirates. Cassie smiled. Now, where had that thought come from? Before she'd met Leith she hadn't been prone to romantic thoughts yet here she was daydreaming again.

'You can have this room if you like,' Leith was saying. 'I'll take the cupboard at the back.'

Cassie whirled round. 'I'm sorry. I just assumed all the rooms would be like this.' She grinned back. 'I could toss you for it.'

Leith raised an eyebrow, his eyes glinting in the semi-darkness. 'I couldn't possibly deprive you,' he said. 'Not when you like it so much. I don't care where I sleep.'

Immediately the atmosphere between them thickened and Cassie's pulse started beating a rapid tattoo against her temples. She knew he was thinking of the nights they had shared, squashed together in either her or his single bunk. Not that their surroundings would have changed anything. They had been too obsessed with one another's bodies to care.

'Would you like to take a walk down to the beach before dinner?' Leith asked.

Not really, was the first reply that came to mind—*at least, not with you.* But that response would be childish at best and rude at worst. It wasn't his fault he made her feel like a girl with her first real crush.

'Give me a moment to unpack and freshen up, and I'll meet you in the sitting room. Say, in ten minutes?'

As it was, she was back in five and Leith was already waiting for her.

As they walked down to the powdery white sand and along the shore, Cassie was acutely conscious of Leith walking next to her.

Leith picked up a flat stone and sent it hopping along the water. 'Remind you of anywhere?' he asked.

'Yes,' she whispered. 'Africa.'

'Do you miss it?'

'Yes.' *I miss you, was what she wanted to say.*

'Do you think you'll go back? You haven't said what your plans are when you finish at the practice.'

'The UN is keeping my job open for me. They gave me six months to decide if I could work with them.'

Leith sent a final stone skipping across the water and turned to face her. 'And will you?'

'I—I don't know. I'm not sure if I have the courage.'

He stepped towards her and framed her face with his hands. 'I don't want you to go back, Cassie.'

She almost stopped breathing. She lifted her chin and closed her eyes, expecting, longing to feel his mouth on hers.

But his hands dropped and she felt him step away from her. 'I don't want you to go anywhere I can't be sure you'll be safe, Cassie. No one can say you haven't done your bit.'

Disappointment made her reel. But what had she been expecting? That Leith would kiss her as if she hadn't run away from him once?

Especially when she knew she was going to run away again.

Back at the house Josie had set a table for two on the deck overlooking the sea. Sadness washed over Cassie. If she were a different person, if she wasn't so scared all the time of being let down, of Leith finding that the person he thought she was didn't really exist, what then? Perhaps there could be a future with Leith? Not that he'd hinted that he still cared. But...but... The way he'd looked at her down on the beach—that wasn't the way a man looked at a friend.

Cassie almost fled to her room in a panic. Could she really spend the next few days with Leith pretending that he didn't set every nerve ending alight?

He pulled her chair out with a flourish. 'Your table awaits, milady.' Judging by his casual manner, he wasn't the least bit affected by her.

Later Cassie couldn't remember what they ate. The sound of the waves against the rocks echoed the beating of her heart. It was as if her world had narrowed until it contained just the two of them. Leith and herself. The way it was meant to be, the way it could never be.

But just for these few nights she was going to push all thoughts of the future away. She would forget about the past, not think of the future. Simply enjoy this short, precious time together.

The next day they were both up early.

Josie had left out a breakfast of fresh fruit and pastries and there was the rich aroma from coffee on the stove.

They sat at the scrubbed kitchen table. Cassie was ravenous. It had to be the sea air, she thought. But there was also this wonderful sense of peace. She hadn't intended to tell Leith about Afghanistan but now that she had she felt lighter than she had in months.

And because he had seen her scars and there was no need to hide her arms from him, she revelled in being able to wear a skimpy halter-neck dress over her bikini without feeling self-conscious.

'What are your plans?' Leith said, as he peeled an orange.

'I'm going for a swim,' she said. 'What about you?'

'I think I'll join you,' he said lazily. 'Once I've seen Veronica.'

'I'll wait here for you, if you like. I can't imagine you'll be long.' She swatted a bee away with her hand. 'There's so many of them there must be a nest nearby.'

'Then no doubt we'll be having home-made honey for breakfast some time.'

'So no spiders in your room last night?' she teased. 'I have to admit there was the largest and hairiest one I have ever seen on my ceiling.'

Leith grimaced. 'In that case, I'm very glad I gave you that room. Remind me to send you in tonight to do a recce of mine.'

They grinned at each other and Cassie's heart flipped. She couldn't help it. Everything he said made her remember having sex with him. Whatever else was wrong with her there was clearly nothing wrong with her libido. At least, not since she'd met Leith again.

He gave her another enigmatic smile before excusing himself. Were her lustful thoughts clearly there for him to see?

Leith had been gone for about half an hour when Cassie heard screaming coming from outside.

She rushed out to find Josie bending over the inert form of a little girl.

'My baby. Tess! Oh, God. Help me,' Josie screamed.

Cassie's heart banged against her ribs. She bent and felt for a pulse. Nothing.

'What happened?' she asked Josie. 'Did she fall? Has she been complaining of feeling unwell?'

'She said a bee stung her. I was just taking the sting out when she said she was itchy all over.' Sure enough, there was a rash on the little girl's body. Cassie hadn't noticed it at first against her darker skin.

Focussed as she was on Josie's daughter, she was only dimly aware of Leith crouching next to her.

'What happened here?' he asked.

'Bee sting. She doesn't have a pulse. I'm assuming

anaphylactic shock. Could you fetch my medical bag from my room?'

Leith was on his feet again and within moments he was back. He laid the bag down, opened it and started attaching a bag of fluids to a giving set.

Thank goodness she had brought her emergency paediatric kit with her.

She tried to find a vein, but to her horror they'd collapsed. It sometimes happened when a child's system shut down. It was bad enough in a hospital setting but here, without the right equipment, it could be fatal.

Leith had seen her difficulty and was searching for a vein too but if Cassie with all her experience of children wasn't able to find one then it was unlikely he would fare any better.

Josie was watching them in horrified silence, her little girl's head cradled in her lap.

Everything slowed down again. Just like that day in Afghanistan, Cassie became aware of the sound of crickets, the heat of the sun on her arms, every movement of hers and Leith's happening in slow motion.

Anxiety rose in her throat like bile. She took a deep breath. She had to do something. She simply would not let anyone die because she didn't act soon enough.

Then it came to her. There was another way to get the fluid into the little girl's veins. Thank God she'd added a couple to her kit.

As Leith monitored Tess's vitals, she rummaged in her medical bag. Right at the bottom was what she was looking for.

'I'm going to use an intraosseous needle to get fluid directly into her circulation,' she told Leith.

'I've heard it can be done,' Leith said quietly, 'although I've never seen it before.'

'It might be better if Mum doesn't stay,' Cassie murmured.

'I'm not leaving my baby,' Josie said fiercely.

'Okay. You need to hold her firmly then, Josie. I'm going to have to push this quite hard—it will look painful—but she won't feel it. Just keep her as still as you can.'

She glanced up and Josie nodded.

Cassie took the needle and using all the strength she could muster forced it directly into the marrow in Tess's bone. When Josie cried out, Cassie was only dimly aware of Leith's voice reassuring her. The procedure looked painful but the child was unconscious and wouldn't feel a thing. As soon as she was certain the needle was in place she started running the saline. A few seconds later, the child stirred.

Cassie felt dizzy with relief. Thank God she hadn't frozen. It was the thing she'd feared most since Afghanistan—that in moments of high stress she'd find herself unable to act. But she'd acted instinctively and had been able to think just as clearly as she'd ever needed to in an emergency. She looked up to find Leith's eyes on her. He nodded slightly. 'Good job,' he said.

'Thanks.' Cassie wanted to appear casual but she couldn't stop smiling. Only another doctor could understand the satisfaction that came with saving a life.

'Now, Josie, Tess is going to be fine. She'll need to be very careful around bees in future and she'll need to carry an EpiPen with adrenaline in it probably for the rest of her life but at least you'll know what to do next time.'

Josie, still pale with shock, nodded. Her little girl opened her eyes and blinked. When she noticed that her mother was crying she started to cry too. It was the sweetest sound. Tess would probably be running around in an hour or two.

'As a precaution, I think we should get her to the hospital and have her checked out though. They'll also be able to give you a supply of EpiPens and show you how to use them.'

'There is one on the next island. We will have to get a boat.' Josie looked around distractedly. 'My husband is down at the big house.'

Leith was on his feet. 'I'll see what I can organise.'

'I'll go with you to the hospital,' Cassie said to Josie.

'Do you want me to come too?' Leith asked.

'No, thanks. I can take it from here.'

Their eyes caught and held. In his she saw warmth and approval—and something else, something she dare not let herself believe but that made her catch her breath.

'Josie has a lot to thank you for,' he said. 'As soon as I've sorted transport, I'll be right back.'

Veronica offered her small private plane the family used for island hopping to take Cassie, Josie and Tess to the small hospital on the next island. The staff there checked Tess over again, pronounced themselves happy and gave Josie a number of EpiPens to take home with her.

By the time they returned home, most of the adrenaline from earlier had seeped away, but Cassie was still feeling charged up. Leith was waiting for her. At the sight of him, her heart leaped.

'Everything okay?'

She grinned at him. 'Yes.'

In fact, everything was more than okay—everything was perfect. She would have even gone as far as to say she was happy. Somehow over the last few weeks the

weight and the darkness that had surrounded her like
a fine mist had lifted.

And most of that was down to the man standing in
front of her. He was looking particularly pleased about
something.

'Veronica and the baby are doing fine,' he said. 'She
invited us to lunch, but I took the liberty of declining
for both of us. So she suggested we take one of the boats
over to one of the uninhabited islands and have lunch
there. She asked her cook to pack a picnic lunch for us.
What do you say?'

'I say, lead me to it.' Hadn't she decided she was
going to throw caution to the wind? So what if there
couldn't be a future for her and Leith? So what if there
was going to be no happy-ever-after in their story?

They had four days. Soon she'd be leaving the practice and Leith would be out of her life for good. And
if she got hurt? That was part of life and suddenly she
wanted to feel again, even if feeling meant hurting.

'I'll just grab my stuff,' she said.

The sky was a perfect blue with only wisps of cloud, and
the sea was almost translucent. Cassie watched multi-
coloured fish dart around the boat.

'Veronica's house manager gave me some snorkel-
ling gear,' Leith said. 'I thought we could have a go
before lunch.'

'Whatever,' Cassie said, lazily trailing her hand in
the cool water. She studied Leith through her lashes.
He was bare-chested and his muscles bunched every
time he pulled the oars through the water. 'I have to
say you row well.'

He grinned back. 'It's not often I get my rowing
prowess remarked on. It comes from being brought up

on an island. I can't remember a time when I wasn't in, or around, boats. My father took me sailing for the first time when I was five. My mother wouldn't let him take me before that. The seas around Skye can be treacherous if you don't know what you're doing. My father was prone to taking risks, in my mother's opinion. Not that he took too many of those when I was with him. His father was a fisherman and Dad taught me to respect the sea.'

'I can't imagine that we're in much danger here. Even if we do get tipped up, we can practically wade to land.'

Moments later that was what they did. Leith brought the boat as close to the shore as he could, rolled up his cotton trousers to the knee and jumped out. He reached out to Cassie and before she could react had lifted her out of the boat.

As he held her against him she felt the heat radiating from his body, smelled the faint scent of his aftershave, each muscle of his hard body achingly familiar. It felt as if she'd come home. She fought the impulse to wriggle out of his arms with some light remark and instead relaxed as he waded to the beach.

Once there he let her slide to the ground. As she did she felt the whole length of his body along hers and every cell and synapse seemed to snap to attention.

She laughed shakily and stepped back. She knew what was going to happen, but she wanted to prolong every delicious moment. She wanted to make him want her so much he couldn't think. She cupped his face with her hands and looked into his eyes. His desire for her was plain to see and she revelled in it. This day was hers. Nothing and no one could take it from her.

'What about lunch?' she said huskily.

'Lunch?' He sounded dazed and she suppressed a

smile. When he reached out to pull her towards him, she stepped away.

'I think we should eat first and then perhaps a snorkel.'

'You're hungry?' he said disbelievingly.

'Not so much,' she admitted, flicking him a look. Ignoring the way her heart was pounding, she spread the tablecloth on the white sand.

This island, if it were possible, was even more beautiful than the one they'd left. Behind them was a small copse of trees shielding them from view of the other islands and in front fine white sand stretched as far as the eye could see.

Cassie opened the basket as Leith stretched out on the blanket. She remembered every line of his body, every ridge, every muscle, the dark hair on his lower abdomen, the line of his hips. Lust shot through her as she remembered the feel of his hands on her body. She wanted more. She wanted him to be with her for ever. But if she couldn't have that, she wanted this single perfect day.

She laid the fruit out first, acutely aware of Leith's eyes watching her every move. Grapes, Oranges, Mangoes. There was freshly baked bread and salad as well as a bottle of wine. She held it up to Leith with a questioning glance, but he shook his head.

She plucked some grapes from a bunch and, leaning towards him, held them to his mouth. As he caught one between his teeth he reached out for her, but she laughed and moved away.

Keeping her eyes on him, she rolled her hair into a knot on the top of her head and slipped out of her sundress. She was wearing her bikini underneath.

Leith's eyes glinted in the sun and a smile hovered

on his lips. 'Do you have any idea what you're doing to me, woman?' he growled.

'Doing to you?' She raised her eyebrows in apparent innocence. 'I'm simply getting ready for a swim.' But she knew her eyes were sparkling. It was good to make him suffer for a while and she wanted to make him suffer for a little longer. Never before had she thought of herself as a seductress but she had to admit she was enjoying the role. Perhaps it was because, just by looking at her, he was making her body feel as if it were on fire. The tension was unbearable.

She stretched, knowing her itsy-bitsy bikini was revealing more than it was concealing. The Brazilian bottom, at which she had baulked at first, somehow now felt so incredibly sexy, so incredibly right. As she bent to pick up her sunscreen she didn't have to hear his muffled groan to know she was turning the screw one more inch. She felt deliciously powerful.

She held out the bottle of sunscreen. 'Would you mind putting some on my shoulders?'

'Come and sit here then,' he said. When he sat up, she positioned herself between his legs with her back towards him. His hands on her skin were cool at first with the cream and she shivered, although she wasn't entirely sure her reaction had anything to do with the temperature of the lotion. He slipped down one strap and then another to expose her shoulders and she sucked in a breath. She didn't know how long she could continue playing this game. The need to feel his hands all over her was so intense she thought she might spontaneously combust there and then.

'Is this okay?' he asked.

She couldn't trust herself to speak so she simply nodded. His hands moved down her back and she trem-

bled under the feel of his strong fingertips. Before she
could stop herself she gasped.

'I need to undo the strap at the back if I'm to do the
job properly.' His voice had dropped an octave and this
time she heard the laughter in *his* voice. She knew he
had felt her reaction—heard her small gasp of need
and desire—and now he'd turned the tables. He was
playing her.

All she could do was nod again and immediately the
strap at the back of her bikini was undone and her top
was lifted from her shoulders and tossed to one side.

His thumbs traced the ridges of her spine, swept over
her shoulders and down along the insides of her arms.
His hands stilled where she was scarred. For a moment
she wanted to cover herself with her hands but he bent
her forward and gently touched each scar with his lips.

She wanted to cry out with the exquisite heat racing along her body but forced herself to stay quiet. Not
yet. Not quite yet. She had to hold him away as long as
possible. Make the moments last.

Then his hands moved back to her shoulders and he
pulled her back until she was leaning against him, the
naked skin of her back against his bare chest. Every cen-
timetre of her skin seemed to sizzle where it touched
his.

His hands swept up the length of her neck and she
had to bite harder on her lip to stop herself from begging him to put an end to her agony. She desperately
wanted to turn in his arms so that she could straddle
him and have him inside her. But she used every ounce
of her resolve to stay where she was. She wasn't going
to be the one to break first. She had no doubt that it
had turned into a game now and he was much better at
it than she was. He was as determined to tease her, to

bring her as tantalisingly close to breaking point as she had been to bring him there, and although she no longer believed she was going to win this game, she was determined to hold out as long as possible.

His hands were on her stomach now, his fingertips exploring, touching lightly then harder, swooping down to the top of her bikini bottoms then back to just below her breasts. She couldn't stop herself. She leaned against him and arched her back to encourage him to touch her. She didn't care any more who won this game. She wanted his hands on her—all over her. And she wanted him inside her. Before she exploded.

Then his hands were on her breasts, his thumb and forefinger gently teasing at her nipples. It was no use. She couldn't hold on any longer. She would have to turn and face him. She would have to get him out of his trousers, and the thought of having to wait…

Before she could move, his hands were moving downwards again—across her stomach, gliding gently over the top of her bikini bottom, brushing between her legs and moving on to the tops of her thighs. Instinctively, she parted her legs and his fingers were touching her, gently at first and then with sure, rhythmic strokes. Unable to bear it for one more second, she swivelled round until she was facing him. She unbuttoned his trousers and eased them over his hips, holding his gaze all the while.

Then she reached for him and guided him inside her, where she desperately needed him to be.

Cassie looked up at the clear sky and wondered if she'd ever felt so peaceful—even though soon she and Leith would be parting again.

On the surface, nothing had really changed—Leith

had his life and she had hers. But inside everything had changed. Where she'd felt nothing before, now she felt it all, and the pain of loving Leith was the price she was willing pay. But she refused to think about any of that.

They had three days left to be together. Three days that she could pretend were never going to pass. She propped herself up on her elbow and lightly brushed her fingertips across Leith's chest. He opened his eyes and grinned.

When he reached for her she shook her head. 'No,' she whispered, 'this time I'm in control. And I'm going to do to you what you did to me—tease you until you beg.' She climbed on his chest, pinning his arms with her knees. She smiled into his eyes. 'So lie there and let me do the work.'

They'd spent the last three days making love and exploring the island and every night in Cassie's room, their limbs entangled in the sheets, the perspiration on their bodies mingling. It was as if they couldn't get enough of each other. She knew his body now almost as well as she did her own. She loved the feel of his skin under her fingertips, she loved to run her hands over the hard planes of his body and revelled in his response to her.

All too soon it was their last night on the island and, agonisingly, when she wanted to make the most of the last few hours she had with him, they'd had to have dinner with Veronica and her friends—it would have been rude to refuse.

Cassie had been acutely conscious of Leith throughout—without having to look, she would know where he was in the room. Often she would glance up from whoever she'd been talking to and find his eyes on her. And they would share a smile of anticipation, before returning their attention to their hosts. At the first opportunity they got they excused themselves. But to Cassie's surprise—and disappointment—instead of turning up the hill towards their temporary home, Leith suggested a drink down at the pier.

They took a seat at the smallest bar she'd ever seen. It was perched on a jetty, overlooking the crashing waves of the ocean. There was only the barman and one other paying customer, apart from Leith and herself.

The barman poured them their drinks and they took their glasses over to the single table on the edge of the pier.

Cassie leaned back and smiled, enjoying the sensation of the cooling spray from the waves, crashing against the rocks, on her bare legs.

Leith leaned forward and took her hands. 'Do you have any idea how beautiful you are?'

'You're not so bad yourself,' she replied. In fact, he had never seemed more sexy to her. Even in the few days that they had been here, his skin had darkened, emphasising his green eyes and even white teeth.

He looked at her intently. 'We should get married.'

Cassie sucked in her breath. Whatever she'd expected Leith to say, it wasn't this.

'Married?'

'Yes.' He placed his thumb and forefinger under her chin. 'I think we'd be good together.'

'Good together?' Cassie echoed.

'Yes. And Peter likes you. We could be a family.' He grinned. 'Never thought I'd say those words.'

'You think we should get married because Peter likes me?' she said incredulously.

'Well, that and the small matter that I love you and I think you love me.'

Cassie closed her eyes as a wave of happiness washed over her. Did he love her? Truly?

The six-year-old Cassie reared her head. Unlovable. Naughty. Send back. No good.

What did he really know of her now? Almost nothing. But she believed him when he said he loved her. He would never pretend to feel something he didn't.

'We could have more children,' Leith was continuing. 'Brothers and sisters for Peter.'

A shadow fell over her heart.

'But I don't want children, Leith. I can't even see myself as stepmother to Peter.'

As soon as he'd mentioned children, she'd known. Nothing had changed. Children meant pain and sacrifice. And what was worse, she didn't know if she could love a child enough or whether she would love it too much. She might feel better about herself now than she had for as long as she could remember, but that didn't mean she was ready for marriage and children, and deep down she doubted she would ever be.

He frowned. 'I thought you cared about Peter?'

'I do. He's an amazing little boy. But caring for him doesn't mean I could look after him full time. It's different being with a child some of the time to doing the whole mother thing. I don't think I'd be any good at it.'

Leith shook his head. 'I've never met anyone who would make a better mother. I've rushed you. Perhaps you'll change your mind about having children. There's plenty of time.'

'Not so much, Leith. I'm thirty-four, almost thirty-five. You know more than most what that means for my fertility.'

He came round to her side of the table and pulled her to her feet and into his arms. 'I don't care about your fertility. Just as long as you can love Peter. Whatever fears you have about your ability to mother him, I have none. I want us to be together. For the rest of our lives. Simple.'

'Oh, Leith, it isn't simple at all. Why can't we stay the way we are? We don't need to get married to share our lives.'

'I need us to get married, Cassie,' he murmured into her hair. 'I need to know that you love me and trust me and can't live without me. Or are you saying you don't love me?' He laughed harshly. 'I can't believe that.'

She pulled away until she could look into his eyes. 'Yes, I love you. I never thought I'd ever say those words, but I love you with my heart, my soul, with everything I have.'

'But you won't marry me? At least tell me why.'

She wriggled out of his arms and went to stand at the end of the pier, looking out to sea. Leith came to stand behind her and wrapped his arms around her, holding her so hard she could feel every muscle of his chest against her back. Her heart beat in time with the waves crashing on the shore.

She sighed. 'Remember I told you that I was adopted.'

'Didn't I tell you I remember everything you've ever said? But you didn't tell me much more than that you weren't close to your adoptive parents.'

'It's not something I talk about. I don't see either of my adoptive parents any more. The woman who left me the flat in London was my nanny. She was the person who mothered me in my childhood.'

'Go on,' he said quietly.

'I was removed from my birth mother when I was five—a little younger than Peter is now. Just like Jude with Peter, my mother wasn't able to look after me because she had an addiction problem.' She swallowed.

'It killed her and I was put into care. The woman who eventually adopted me was very like Mrs Forsythe—remember the woman I fell out with? I suspect Lily—my adoptive mother—although I can't think of her as my mother, not even to myself—only adopted me so that she wouldn't stand out as being different from the others in the world she moved in.

'At that time there was such a thing as open adoption, but somehow, I'm not sure how, she must have found out about my birth mother and I think that spoiled me for her. From then on she wanted nothing to do with me. In fact, she made it clear that she would send me back to Social Services if I didn't behave myself. That meant keeping my room immaculate, never questioning her, never speaking unless I was spoken to.

'From the age of eight I was left entirely in the hands of Nanny. Which wasn't so bad. I loved Nanny and I knew she loved me. She tried to explain that it wasn't my fault that Lily didn't love me. She said it was a fault with her own upbringing and not with me and I should always remember that. But children can't really understand. They always think that the fault is with them.

'I tried to be good. So good that she couldn't help but love me, or at least good enough that she wouldn't send me away. Perhaps it would have been better if she had. One good thing came of it, though. Medicine. I studied hard—at first as a way to please Lily and then, when my teachers praised me for always coming top of the class, as a way to feel good about myself.

'School work was never a problem and I suspect the only time Lily was ever proud of me was when I won a place to study medicine at Oxford. She couldn't wait to show me off to her friends then.' She smiled weakly. 'And at least I had Nanny—until I was sent to boarding school when I was eleven.'

Leith growled something under his breath and made to turn her round but she stayed rigid. 'Don't, Leith. If you look at me now I don't know if I'll find it in me to finish my story. And I want you to know everything.

'There was a dreadful fight one day,' she continued. 'I wasn't supposed to hear it, but I always was an inquisitive child. I must have been ten, I think. Nanny and Lily were in the drawing room. I was to go to boarding school, Lily was saying, and Nanny's services would no longer be required.

'Nanny said something about while she didn't approve of boarding school, perhaps in my case it was for the best as I wouldn't have to cope with being brought up by a mother who could hardly look at me and a father who barely seemed to notice I was even part of the household.

'Naturally, that didn't go down very well and Nanny was dismissed.' Cassie blinked. 'But not until I had left for boarding school a couple of months later. It seemed Lily would rather have Nanny and her outspoken views in the house for two more months than have to look after me herself.'

'And your father—Lily's husband?'

'I don't think he was a bad man—just a weak one. I suspect he only agreed to adopt me to keep on the right side of Lily. He was never cruel or unkind to me—but neither did he intervene when Lily was.'

'So that's why you don't see them much?'

'They seem happy not to see me either. They were always finding some reason not to have me home for the school holidays. Nanny—Martha—ended up taking me, which of course suited me just fine. I had become used to Lily's lack of interest in me by this time and to be honest I was happier with Martha.

'Boarding school wasn't really a problem. I didn't make many friends—I guess I thought there had to be something wrong, something unlovable about me—but I made sure I was well behaved. You won't be surprised to know I continued to do well in all my subjects. I was also head girl. Lily did attend the school functions, however. She liked to be seen by the other parents.

'Anyway, while at university I spent as many summers as I could abroad, either doing locums or any sort of voluntary job I could find. Lily wasn't mean when it came to money. When I wasn't away, I spent time with Nanny. Sometimes Lily didn't even know when I was in London. Then, as soon as I was financially independent, contact tailed off with my adoptive family completely.'

This time he did turn her so she was facing him. 'I have never met anyone more lovable than you. God, Cassie, you're as beautiful on the inside as you are on the outside. Don't you know that?'

'I'm coming to believe it,' she said. 'Being with you…makes me feel good. You make me feel whole in a way I've never felt before. But I'm still scared I would be useless as a mother. I'm scared I wouldn't be able to love my children enough, or I'd love them too much—in which case I'll probably suffocate them with my love. I know what I'm saying is difficult for you to understand—I don't know if I understand it myself.'

His eyes flickered and she watched his dawning realisation. 'That's why you left me in Africa with only that note, isn't it? Everything was good between us until you found out I had a child.'

She nodded. 'I knew it wouldn't be fair to let you be-

lieve there could be a future for us. Not when you had
Peter in your life.'

'But that's crazy. He loves you. And you love him.
You're not Lily. You could never be her.'

'I know. At least, I know in my head that the way
I feel isn't rational, but I can't seem to talk myself out
of it.'

'So what are you saying, Cassie?' A muscle twitched
in his jaw. 'Don't ask me to choose between you and
Peter, because I won't. No matter how much I love you,
I won't give up my son.'

She touched his face with her fingers, imprinting the
memory of him into her pores. 'I know. You wouldn't
be the man I love if you did.'

He placed his hands on either side of her face and
smiled wryly. 'I've waited this long to find the woman
I want to spend the rest of my life with, so I guess I can
wait a bit longer.'

He rubbed his thumb along the line of her jaw. 'But,
my darling love, please don't make me wait too long.'

That night, as he lay with Cassie in his arms, Leith
thought about what she'd told him. It explained so
much—her fear of loving and being loved, of becoming a mother, her lack of trust.

Of course he wasn't looking for a mother for Peter—
he just wanted Peter's natural mother to be well enough
to care for their son the way he needed to be cared for.
But whatever Cassie thought, she would make an out-
standing, loving mother. Peter, as he'd told her, had already fallen under her spell.

He gazed down at her. His chest tightened as he saw
that in sleep she had a smile on her lips. Over the last
weeks the bruise-like shadows under her eyes had dis-

appeared and more and more often he'd see her eyes light up and hear the laugh he loved so much.

It would take time to peel back all the layers that made up the woman he adored. If only she could believe that her heart was good. The lines of a poem came back to him. Didn't she know he would never tread on her heart?

But he wouldn't abandon his child. Not even for her. He loved them both and he had to believe that Cassie would come to trust his love for her.

Until then, he would wait.

The next morning, Cassie woke to an empty bed. Knowing that Leith was probably down at the main house, seeing Veronica, she went into the garden to pick some oranges to squeeze for breakfast. She'd only been there for a few minutes when Josie came in search of her.

'Dr Leith wants you at the house.'

Immediately Cassie knew there was something wrong. She picked up her bag and hurried down the narrow path to where Veronica and her party were staying.

A grim-looking Leith met her in the hall. 'I checked the baby's heartbeat as usual. Up until today it's been fine, but I think you should check it too. It seems to be really slow—about sixty beats per minute. I checked Veronica's pulse in case that's what I was hearing, but hers is a bit faster than usual—probably from anxiety.'

'Sure,' said Cassie, mentally running through the reasons the baby's heart rate could have dipped. None, in her experience, was likely to be good news.

'I've put Veronica's pilot on alert,' Leith said. 'We should get her to hospital in case I have to deliver her.'

'God, Leith, she's only just thirty-two weeks.'

He rubbed his chin. 'I know. It's only a precaution at the moment.'

Veronica was waiting for them in her bedroom.

'Hi, Veronica,' Cassie greeted the anxious-looking woman calmly. 'Leith has asked me to listen to the baby's heart. Would that be okay?'

As soon as she heard the slow beating of the baby's heart she knew Leith had been right to call her. The baby was still moving so that was good but, nevertheless, they had to get Veronica to hospital—and as soon as possible.

A few hours later Veronica was lying in a hospital bed looking pale and frightened. Leith and Cassie had consulted with the local doctors and following several scans and tests now had their diagnosis. It had been agreed that Leith and Cassie would be the ones to tell Veronica their diagnosis.

Cassie sat down next to Veronica and took her hand while Leith remained standing at the foot of the bed.

'The first thing you need to know is that there is every chance your baby is going to be fine, Veronica,' Cassie began. 'So you mustn't panic when you hear what we have to say.'

'But something is wrong, isn't it?' Veronica's voice was thin with fear.

'Yes. Your baby's heart rate slowed suddenly. This can be caused by a number of things, which is why we wanted you in hospital.'

'Is she going to be all right?'

'We think she has a heart condition—that's why we've been doing all these scans. But looking at the scan, your baby's heart looks normal—she has all the usual chambers and connections to all the important blood vessels—and we can't see any holes in her heart or other abnormalities. So we wondered if the problem could be a heart block—that's where the electrical signals through the heart aren't being conducted as usual, causing the heart to pump more slowly than usual.

'We've also ordered some more blood tests in case there are antibodies in your blood that is causing heart block in the baby.'

'What does all that mean?' Veronica cried. 'I don't understand.'

'It means it's likely that she will have to be delivered early by Caesarean and may need an operation, but…' Cassie rushed on as Veronica blanched, 'I have seen many babies with the same condition grow into healthy children and know of many more that have grown into healthy adults. I know all this sounds scary but we will make sure that you have the best cardiologists looking after you.

'You'll need regular scans to check that the baby is still growing and you'll need to be delivered in a hospital where there are specialist paediatric heart surgeons. At delivery we'll check that baby is okay and she'll be monitored closely until we can tell whether she'll need a pacemaker.

'If the baby appears unwell at birth, we may put in a pacemaker as an emergency just to be on the safe side. Sometimes it's not possible to tell until some time after the baby is born. I know this is a lot to take in, but we'll go over it as many times as you need. In the meantime—although I know it's hard—try not to worry.'

'Why wasn't this picked up before? You did my last scan, Leith, and you said everything was normal.'

'It was, Veronica,' Leith replied. 'These things often only become apparent later on in pregnancy.'

'So what now?'

Cassie could see that Veronica was determined not to cry.

'There's nothing that can be done until your baby is big enough to be safe to deliver her.'

'I want to go home to England. I want my mother. I need her with me.' Frightened eyes held Cassie's. 'Please let me go to her.'

Leith and Cassie looked at one another. Cassie nodded. While she wouldn't usually recommend travelling, it couldn't hurt the baby and it could only help Veronica if she was close to home. Her heart tightened as she recognised Veronica's desperate need to be with her mother. That's what a mother and daughter relationship should be like.

'I could try and organise an air ambulance to take you,' she offered.

Veronica sagged against the pillow, as relief replaced the anxiety in her eyes. She shook her head. 'No need. My husband will organise our private plane for me.' She looked at Cassie and Leith and her mouth trembled. 'You'll both stay with me until I get home?'

'Of course,' Cassie said. 'We'll be with you every step of the way.'

CHAPTER ELEVEN

CASSIE STOOD NEXT to Leith looking down at the tiny newborn. Veronica was sitting beside the incubator, her face white with anxiety.

'She's so small to be needing an operation,' she whispered.

'They're very good here,' Cassie said. 'She couldn't be in safer hands.' As they'd suspected, Veronica's daughter did need a pacemaker. However, the paediatric heart surgeons were optimistic that the little girl would go on to lead a happy and productive life.

But looking down at the tiny form, Cassie was reminded once more why she couldn't bear to have children. Loving brought nothing but pain and terror.

They left the new mother with her baby and stepped outside. Summer was almost over and soon Cassie would be leaving the practice.

It was as if Leith had read her thoughts. 'Would you come with Peter and I to Skye after you finish here?' he asked.

Leith and Peter were to spend the last couple of weeks of the school holidays on Skye. Apparently Peter was desperate to go back.

'I'm not sure that's a good idea.'

He cupped her chin with the palm of his hand. 'Say yes. Please.'

She shook her head as tiny shards of ice pierced her heart. Nothing had changed. She loved Leith but she couldn't be the woman he wanted—the woman he and little Peter deserved.

'For God's sake, Cassie, what do I have to do to convince you that I love you? That you'll be safe with me? That I'll never stop loving you?' He placed his hands on either side of her face and she couldn't stop herself from kissing the soft pad of his hand.

Her throat was tight and she knew tears weren't far away. 'There's nothing you can say or do. Forget about me, Leith.'

As she turned to leave he grabbed her by the arm. His eyes had softened. 'You know that's not going to happen. I know you love me. And Peter. All I need is for you to trust me.' He touched her lips with his fingertips. 'Trust me, Cassie. Trust my love. We can be a family—the three of us.' He dropped a kiss on her forehead. 'And when you come to believe that, I'll be waiting. However long it takes.'

In the days that followed, Cassie couldn't stop thinking about Leith and his proposal. Why couldn't she trust him enough to believe that he would never stop loving her? Why couldn't she trust herself enough to believe she could be a good wife and mother? Why couldn't she trust him enough to believe him when he said she and Peter were enough for him?

What was wrong with her? She knew that her adoptive parents' attitude towards her had been wrong. Hundreds of children grew up unloved yet managed to make loving, supportive parents. At least, she knew that on an intellectual level. Deep inside she still felt like the same unlovable child.

But Leith had said he would give her time. There was no hurry. They could carry on as they were. Katie had given birth to a baby boy two weeks ago while Leith and Cassie had been in the Caribbean. Fabio would be coming back from leave soon and she'd no longer be needed.

She finished her morning clinic. There was nothing too worrying, just the usual sore throats and immunisations. She had a home visit that afternoon to a little boy who wasn't developing as fast as his mother thought he should be. The mother had offered to bring the child to the practice, but Cassie thought it would be better to see him in his home environment.

In the meantime, she needed some coffee and a sandwich. And, she admitted to herself with a smile, if she caught sight of Leith, that would be a bonus.

Katie was in Reception, showing off Marcus, her new baby, to Rose and the nurses. The new mother was glowing as she basked in the admiration of the staff.

Knowing it was expected of her, Cassie stepped forward to add her congratulations.

She had to admit he really was the cutest baby with his button nose and shock of dark brown hair.

'Would you mind holding him for me?' Katie asked as the others melted away. 'I need to visit the ladies.'

Before Cassie could say anything, Katie had passed her the small bundle wrapped tightly in his blanket.

A pair of brown eyes stared up into hers.

'Hello,' Cassie whispered.

Marcus brought a tiny fist up towards Cassie's face and the little fingers grasped her finger with surprising strength. Something inside her shifted.

What would it be like to be responsible for this

life for the rest of your own life? To know that whatever happened your life was inextricably linked with another's? To live in fear every day that you might not be a good enough mother—that because of you your child might grow up broken inside? It was such a responsibility. Little Marcus yawned and burped. Just then a warmth spread through her, bringing with it a longing so intense it almost made her cry out loud.

Katie came back from the ladies. 'Let me take him.' When she passed Marcus across Cassie felt bereft. Dear God, what was she going to do?

CHAPTER TWELVE

LEITH AND PETER left for Skye the next day. Their leaving hurt more than she could have ever thought possible. By the time they returned she'd be gone.

Leith's goodbye was cool, almost as if he was taking his leave of a stranger. And who could blame him?

Before he left he'd slipped a note into her hand. She hadn't read it yet. What was the point? Unexpectedly, the thought of never seeing Peter again made her heart splinter into tiny pieces. It was almost as bad as knowing that she wouldn't see Leith again. Her days would be so dark without him. Without them both.

She stared out of the window of the flat. Summer was all but over and the new owners would be moving in at the end of the month. Turning the note over in her hand, she noticed for the first time that the writing of her name on the front of the envelope wasn't in Leith's hand. The large block letters, along with the misspelling of her name, could only belong to one person.

She tore open the envelope and read.

Dear Casy
Please come to sky. I miss you. I made a wish.
You promised.
Peter.

The letter fell from her fingers. What an idiot she'd been. As Leith had said, Peter already loved her. How could she walk away from him now? How could that be better for him?

She loved Peter. She would never stop loving the little boy, just as she would never stop loving Leith. She might not always be a perfect mother, but didn't she owe it to them—to herself—to try?

And if she stumbled along the way, Leith would be ready to catch her. Catch them both. Keep them safe. Love them. No matter what.

It was Saturday morning by the time Cassie made it to Staffin. She would have tried to make it last night but she'd been held up. The practice had thrown her a small party. The gesture had touched her more than she would have thought possible. Once more she'd allowed herself to get close to people. They had become her family, but this time it was different. She didn't feel that she had to keep up a façade. They knew her and still cared about her.

Now it was time to see Leith and Peter. How could she have almost let her chance of happiness slip away? She didn't have to be the best wife and mother in the world. All she had to do was the best she could. And to love. And, God, did she love.

As her car pulled up at Leith's parents' house she saw he was digging in the garden, a small figure beside him mimicking every move. They both had their shirts off and were wearing jeans. There couldn't be any doubt whose child Peter was.

Behind them, Leith's mother was feeding the chickens.

When Leith looked up his face broke into a wide

smile and her heart leaped. She would never love anyone the way she loved this man. Peter threw down his spade and ran towards her, flinging his small arms around her legs and almost knocking her off her feet with the ferocity of his grip. 'You came! My wish came true!'

'Hey, Peter,' she said, hunkering down. 'It's great to see you.' She loved Leith's son as much as she loved Leith. With Leith by her side, how could she fail? How had it taken all this time for her to realise that she wasn't like Lily? Leith and Peter wouldn't stop loving her if she wasn't perfect.

'Come and see my chickens,' Peter said, taking her by the hand. 'My dad says they're mine to keep. All mine.'

He beamed up at her and there was no sign of the pale, troubled boy she'd first met. When she looked at Leith, his grin got wider. She knew what having Peter's trust and love meant to him.

Taking Peter by the hand, she let him drag her over to where his chickens were. Five tiny yellow chicks were huddled together in a little nest made of straw. Peter pointed out each one by name, although Cassie had to wonder how he could tell any of the identical chicks apart.

'I wanted to take them home to our house in London with me,' Peter said, 'but Daddy says it's cruel to take them away from their mum until they get older.' He looked up at Cassie. 'He says they only took me away from my mum until she gets better and can look after me again. Soon, if I want, I can go and live with her when I'm not with him.'

Cassie looked up at Leith in surprise and raised one eyebrow in a silent question.

She moved away from Peter, who was crouched next

to his little chicks and watching over them like any proud father.

'Apparently she's doing well,' Leith said. 'Bella says that Jude'll be leaving the clinic soon and she plans to move in with her and Peter. So I don't see any reason why he can't go back to live with Jude some of the time. As long as she keeps well, that is.' He looked over at his son. 'She's determined to stay well for Peter and I believe her. In the end, only time will tell, but I'm optimistic.'

'That's wonderful news. And to see Peter so content... It must make you so relieved.'

Leith grinned. 'I never thought I'd enjoy being a dad so much. Now there's only one thing missing from my life.'

As he looked into her eyes, Cassie thought her heart would leap out of her chest. 'Cassie...' But before he could say anything more, Peter had run over to them and flung himself into his arms.

'Now Cassie is here, can we go back to the Fairy Glen, Dad? I want to see if there are any fairies about.'

'I don't think the fairies like to be seen, son, but, yes, of course we can go. That is, if Cassie would like to...?'

From the look in his eyes Cassie suspected that wasn't all he was asking. She held her breath. How could she have ever believed that she could live without this man for the rest of her life? A man who had waited, with the patience of a saint, for her to trust him. Finally she knew without a shadow of a doubt that she would love him and his son the way they deserved to be loved, just as she knew they would always love her.

With Leith by her side she could do anything. At last she was ready to take a chance on love. As her heart swelled, she smiled. 'Silly Daddy, doesn't he know that fairy-tales can come true?'

Leith looked at her and she read the question in his eyes. She held the gaze of the man who had become her life. 'Wherever you and your dad go, Peter,' she promised softly, 'I'm coming too.'

Six months later Cassie stood next to Leith outside Dunvegan Castle. It had seemed the natural spot for their wedding. Peter was running around in his smart new suit that had been made especially for him to wear as pageboy. No doubt it would be ruined. But Cassie didn't care. She adored her stepson and, in eight months, he would have a little brother or sister. Although she was looking forward to the baby, she wouldn't love Peter any less. He was as much her child now as he was Leith's.

Sometimes in the night she still woke up feeling anxious and panicky, but Leith was always there to hold her and to hush her back to sleep. He knew that her fears and anxieties were part of her and he had promised to spend the rest of his life making sure she knew that she was loved and treasured.

She looked into the eyes of the man she loved more than life itself. She had nearly lost him twice but she would never, ever lose him again. Whatever happened, Leith, her darling husband, would be there by her side, and she by his.

She had her fairy-tale ending after all.

* * * * *

YOU, ME AND A FAMILY

BY

SUE MacKAY

MILLS & BOON®

*To Dad and Mum. No matter what, you were always there
for us as we grew from little hellions to adults. I miss you.*

First published in Great Britain 2013
by Mills & Boon, an imprint of Harlequin (UK) Limited.
Harlequin (UK) Limited, Eton House, 18-24 Paradise Road,
Richmond, Surrey TW9 1SR

© Sue MacKay 2013

ISBN: 978 0 263 89887 3

Harlequin (UK) policy is to use papers that are natural, renewable
and recyclable products and made from wood grown in sustainable
forests. The logging and manufacturing process conform to the
legal environmental regulations of the country of origin.

Printed and bound in Spain
by Blackprint CPI, Barcelona

Dear Reader

I'm often asked where the ideas for my stories come from and I have to say I haven't got a clue. They just arrive in my head. Yes, it's chaos in there sometimes.

So where did Mario and Alexandra come from? In the sunshine by the marina at a restaurant in Nelson, celebrating a friend's birthday earlier this year, I found my story. Sitting at another table was a very big, gorgeous, Italian-looking guy.

And that's how it began. What if this man was a doctor? What if he were bringing up a child alone? Why? What kind of woman would take his heart? It was easy to visualise a tiny but strong woman with him. And how perfect it would be to make her his boss.

We had a great lunch that day, and I didn't spend all my time on the story, preferring to enjoy the celebrations. But during the hour and a half drive home my mind worked overtime. I hope you like the result.

Cheers!

Sue MacKay

www.suemackay.co.nz

sue.mackay56@yahoo.com

Also by Sue MacKay:

EVERY BOY'S DREAM DAD
THE DANGERS OF DATING YOUR BOSS
SURGEON IN A WEDDING DRESS
RETURN OF THE MAVERICK
PLAYBOY DOCTOR TO DOTING DAD
THEIR MARRIAGE MIRACLE

**These books are also available in eBook format
from www.millsandboon.co.uk**

CHAPTER ONE

'ALEXANDRA KATHERINE PRENDERGAST, how do you plead? Guilty…?'

The judge paused, drawing out the excruciating moment, forcing her heart to clench with pain.

Just when Alex thought she'd scream with frustration and humiliation, he added in a disbelieving taunt, 'Or not guilty?'

Her mouth was drier than a hot summer's day. Her tongue felt twice its normal size. Tears oozed from the corners of her eyes to track down her sallow cheeks. 'Guilty,' she tried to whisper. *Guilty, guilty, guilty,* cried her brain, agreed her knotted belly.

'Speak up, Alexandra,' the man standing on the opposite side of the operating theatre table growled. His eyes, staring out at her from under his cap, were cold, hard and demanding. Their hue matched the no-nonsense blue of the scrubs they both wore. 'Did this child die in your care or not?'

'I did everything within my power to keep him alive, your honour. The other doctors told me there was nothing I could've done, that I did nothing wrong. I wanted to believe them, but how could I? He was totally reliant on me and I failed him.' The familiar, gut-twisting mantra spilled over her sore, cracked lips. The old pain and despair roiled up her throat. 'I failed Jordan.' The words flailed her brain.

'Jordan died because of you. Have you done everything within your power to prevent the same thing happening again?'

'Yes,' she croaked. 'Every day I try to save other babies.'

'I sentence you to a lifetime of looking after other people's ill children.' Her judge's eyes were icy, his voice a perfect match.

Alex gasped, shoved up from her pillow and clamped her hand over her mouth. Sweat soaked her nightgown, plastering it to her breasts and shoulders, making it pull tight against her skin as she moved in the bed. Moist strands of hair fell into her eyes, stuck to her wet cheeks. 'I will not throw up. I will not.' The words stuck in the back of her throat as she blinked her way back from the nightmare.

The all too familiar nightmare.

Her fingers shook as she reached for the bedside lamp switch and flooded her bedroom with soft yellow light. Tossing the covers aside she put her feet on the floor and pushed up. Despite the heat-pump being on, the winter air was chilly on her feverish skin. But cold was good. It focused her. Brought her completely back from the nightmare and her guilt. Made her concentrate on the here and now, on today and not the past.

Tugging on a thick robe and slipping her feet into fluffy slippers she trudged out to the kitchen and plugged the kettle in to make a drink of herbal tea. Shivering, she stood staring into her pantry, unable to decide what flavour to have. Her eyes welled up as the floodgates opened, and she blindly reached for the nearest packet and plopped a tea bag into a mug.

The oven clock read 3:46. She'd had little more than three hours sleep before the nightmare hit, slamming into her head in full technicolour. Accusing. Debilitating. Painful. Reminding her that her position as head paediatrician at Nelson Hospital was, in her mind, as tenuous as whatever her next patient threw at her. Taunting she was a fraud and that it was only a matter of time before she made a dreadful mistake with someone's child that would expose her as incompetent.

She had to draw deep to find the belief she was a good doctor, a very good one. The ever expanding numbers of sick children coming to see her, not just from the top of the South Island but all over New Zealand, showed that. Unfortunately the nightmare always undermined her fragile belief in herself.

It also reinforced the truth about her not being mother material, how totally incompetent she'd be in that role. Not that she'd be contemplating that ever again.

Click. The kettle switched off. Boiling water splashed onto the counter as she filled her mug. Strawberry vapour rose to her nostrils. Taking the drink she crossed through the lounge to the wide, floor-to-ceiling window showcasing the lights of Rocks Road and the wharves of Nelson Harbour. Rain slashed through the night, falling in sheets to puddle on the surface ten storeys below.

Alex stood, shaking, clutching the hot mug in both hands, and staring down at the tugboats manoeuvring a freight ship through the narrow cut leading from Tasman Bay to the sheltered harbour. Day and night, boats came and went according to the tides. Now, in early June, they'd be loading the last of the kiwifruit destined for the other side of the world. Men looking like midgets worked ropes and machinery. A tough job. An honest job.

'Stop it.' There was nothing easy or dishonest about the work she did with sick children. 'You did not cause Jordan's death. The pathologist proved that, exonerated you.'

Tell that to Jordan's father.

Behind her eyes a steady pounding built in intensity. Alex cautiously sipped the steaming tea, her gaze still fixed on the wet scene below. Why had the nightmares returned tonight? Exhaustion? Or the nagging need to slot back into her role as head of paediatrics at Nelson Hospital as quickly and effortlessly as possible?

The job was more than a job—it was her whole life, a replacement for the family she wouldn't otherwise have. Lots of staff to mentor, harangue, watch over and care about. Oodles of children to care for in the only way she knew how—medically—and to love safely from the sidelines. Involved, yet not involved.

The fruity scent of her tea wafted in the air, sweet and relaxing. 'You shouldn't have taken the four-month sabbatical. It put you under pressure to again prove how good you are.'

But all those American hospitals and their savvy specialists showing how brilliant they were had actually boosted her confidence and made her understand once and for all she was up with the play, had joined the ranks of the best in the business of paediatrics. Everywhere she'd gone she'd been applauded for her paper on premature births. The job offers had been overwhelming. An awesome charge for her fragile ego. Even the nagging need to constantly prove to herself that she was good had taken a hike.

In San Francisco, when her old mentor from specialising days had offered her an incredible position at his new private paediatric clinic, she'd been beside herself with pride.

And that, she thought with grim satisfaction, should earn her stepfather's grudging respect. Except, of course, she'd turned it down.

Draining the mug Alex turned away from the window. Time to try for some more sleep. Jet lag, exhaustion from her hectic time in the States, the inability to relax while away from home. All reasons to explain why she ached with tiredness and her mind ran riot with yearnings for what seemed doomed forever. A family of her own to love and cherish.

Alexandra sighed through her throbbing headache as she dropped her handbag into the bottom drawer of her desk. Home, sweet home. Nelson Hospital Paediatric Department. The place she spent most of her life. Her stomach flip-flopped like a fish on dry sand. Nerves? Why? She was happy to be back. Wasn't she? Yes, but what if there'd been too many changes on the ward in her absence? Which regular patients had got well and left? Had any of them passed away?

She shivered. What was wrong with her this morning? To be feeling out of sorts was not the best way to start back on the job.

She'd been determined not to think too much about this job while she'd studied with the best of paediatricians in California and Washington, or when she'd presented her paper to countless meetings and conventions. During that time she'd pretended she wasn't worried about staffing levels and the ever increasing numbers of wee patients entering Nelson Hospital. Instead she'd tried to absorb all she could from her mentors and share her own experiences and knowledge. She'd been entertained, courted and tutored. And all she'd wanted to do was return here. Home. Where she felt safe.

She glanced around the familiar room at the paintings she'd bought at the annual summer art show in the Queen's Gardens downtown. They looked tired. Like her. Dusty. Not like her. She smiled reluctantly. It was great to be back—dust, or no dust.

Then reality crashed in on her. Her desk should be littered with stacks of files, notes, memos and all the other detritus that accumulated on a daily basis. Instead there was one small, neat pile in the centre of her desk. The acting HOD from London must've decided to give her a break on her first day back, despite having warned her during their Skype interview he'd be a better doctor than pen-pusher. 'Thanks, John. I owe you.'

Stepping closer she spied a note at the top of the pile and picked it up.

Miss Alexandra Prendergast. Welcome back. I've done the rosters for the next month, signed off the patient reports to date and answered all the mail apart from two letters regarding intern rotations you might like to deal with yourself. I hope you find everything in order.

The scrawled signature read something like Maria Forreel.

Who was Maria Forreel? And why was this woman working in her office? So much for thinking John had done all this. Forreel? What kind of name was that? Was it—? Her smile stretched into a grin. Seriously, was it for real? Alex peered closer. Forell? Forelli, that was it. Forelli. It made no difference. The name meant nothing to her.

Alex tugged the chair out from the desk and sank down on it. She had been excited about coming back and yet today felt like the first day at school—terrifying. Worse, she didn't even know why. 'Probably jet lag.' How many things could she blame on that?

'There you are. How was your trip? Did you do lots of shopping in all those swanky boutiques?' The charge nurse on her ward stood in the doorway with a wide, welcoming smile on her dear face.

'Kay, it's great to see you.' A welcome distraction. 'And yes, I found time to add to my wardrobe. A lot.'

'I'm so-o jealous.' Kay gave the most unjealous grin possible.

Alex reached into the drawer where she'd placed her handbag and pulled out a small package. 'I hope you like these.'

Kay gaped. 'You bought me something? Oh, you big softy. What is it?' The paper tore under her fingers. 'Oh, my gosh. They're beautiful.' She held up the silver earrings, turning them left and right so the light gleamed off the polished metal. 'I love them. Thank you so much. But you shouldn't have.'

Alex laughed. 'Of course I shouldn't. You'll have to work twice as hard now.' Like Kay could do that. She was already the hardest working nurse Alex had ever come across. She added, 'I'm glad you like them. When I saw them I immediately thought of you.' She had little trinkets for the rest of the staff too.

Kay slipped the hooks into her ears. 'Where's a mirror?' She took the one Alex handed her from the drawer. 'Wow, they're perfect.'

Alex rose, smoothed the skirt of her tailored suit and reached for her white coat hanging on the back of the door. 'So how's Darren? The kids?'

'Busy as ever. Why didn't I appreciate my single, peaceful life when I had it?' Kay grinned again.

'You wouldn't swap a thing.' *Whereas I would swap my amazing medical career for exactly what Kay's got.* Alex gulped. Her fingers faltered on the buttons they were doing up. What? *I'd love a Darren and some kids in my life? Okay, not exactly Darren but a loving, caring man who'd understand my eccentricities and forgive me my mistakes in a flash. I would? Since when?* Under her ribs her heart beat a heavy rhythm. Her shoulders drooped momentarily. As if a man like that existed for her. Pressing her fingers to her temples she breathed in slowly. This day was going all weird on her and it was only seven in the morning. Things had better start looking up soon.

'Alex? Are you all right?' Kay was at her elbow, her brow creased with concern.

'I'm fine.' She dropped her hands.

'Are you sure you should be starting back today? You only got back into the country yesterday, didn't you?'

Kay's concern would be her undoing if she let it. 'I'm fine. Raring to go, in fact.' Alex hauled her shoulders back into place and plastered a tight smile on her face, then reminded herself where she was. At work, in her comfort zone. She relaxed. A little. 'I'm a bit tired, nothing else. Rushing from one city to the next took its toll.'

Kay gave an exaggerated eye roll. 'My heart bleeds for you.'

Alex laughed, finally feeling secure with being back at work. Kay always kept her grounded when the going got rough, and today hadn't even started. 'I know I'm early but let's get the shift under way. What's been going on in my absence?'

Instantly Kay's demeanour turned serious. She

pointed to an envelope tucked half under the files lying on her desk. 'There's a message you need to deal with before anything else. I believe it explains everything.' She headed for the door. 'Umm, we've had some changes. Big ones.' Suddenly Kay was in an awful hurry to be gone. 'Good ones.'

Good changes? What was wrong with how things were before? She ran a well-organised and successful department. There wasn't any need to alter a thing. Her unease increased as she reached tentatively for the missive. 'Why? Has something happened?'

Beep, beep. The pager on her desk interrupted. Snatching it up she glanced at the message as she ran out of her office right behind Kay, who was racing for the ward. Then the loudspeaker crackled to life and told them what they needed to know. 'Cardiac arrest, room four.'

'Tommy Jenkins.' Kay shoved the fire door back so hard it hit the wall. 'It's so unfair.'

Alex ducked around the door as it swung back, and kept running. 'Who's Tommy Jenkins? Fill me in. Quickly.'

'He and his mother moved to Nelson to be closer to Tommy's grandparents last month after his father died in a fishing accident. Tommy has cystic fibrosis and was admitted five days ago with a massive chest infection that's not responding to any treatment.'

'What an awful time to shift the boy.'

'Tell me about it.' Kay scowled. 'He's missing his mates, and isn't happy about getting to know new medical staff.'

Room four was chaos. The boy lay with his head tipped back while a nurse, Rochelle, inflated his lungs with an Ambu bag. Jackson, an intern, crouched astride him, doing compressions on his chest.

'Hand me the tube,' a deep male voice Alex had never heard in her life ordered calmly. 'Now, please.'

'Here.' Kay obliged in an instant.

Alex pushed in beside Rochelle, ready to take over. She needed to be in control of this situation. Staring at the stranger, who admittedly seemed to know what he was doing, she demanded, 'Who, may I ask, are you?' He certainly wasn't the man she'd Skyped with about taking her place on the ward. This man she'd never forget. A strong jawline, a mouth that smiled as easily as breathing. Eyes that demanded attention.

'Mario Forelli.' He didn't look up, didn't falter in suctioning the boy's mouth. 'This lad's arrested.'

Since it didn't look like she'd be pushing this man out of the way any time soon and wanting something to do with her hands she reached for the drugs bag. 'What are you doing here?' Alex asked, feeling even more perplexed, while at the same time recognising the name on that note in her office. Not Maria, but Mario. Not a woman, but a well-muscled, broad-chested, dark-haired male.

'Mr Forelli, as in paediatric specialist,' Kay spoke from across the bed where she read the monitor keeping track of Tommy's status.

'Stop the compressions.' The stranger spoke clearly but quietly as he deftly inserted a tube down the boy's throat.

'How long has Tommy been down?' Alex asked while her brain tossed up distracting questions. Where had Mr Forelli come from? More importantly, what was he doing on her ward? And taking care of all her paperwork? Where was John Campbell? Big changes, Kay had said. Presumably this man was one of them. Alex forced herself to concentrate as she drew up the drugs in preparation to inserting them into Tommy's intravenous line. Right now this lad depended on her being focused on him, nothing or anyone else.

This Forelli character had no qualms about taking command as he asked Jackson to move aside so he could resume the chest massage. His hands were ludicrously large against the boy's thin, pale chest. He explained to the room in general, 'I found Tommy lying half out of bed a few minutes ago.'

'I'd popped out to get his meds only moments before.' Guilt laced Rochelle's voice as she glanced at Forelli, a disturbingly ingratiating look in her calf-like eyes.

'You mustn't blame yourself, Rochelle. No one could've predicted he'd go into cardiac arrest at that moment.'

Relief poured through the young nurse. 'Thank you, Mario,' she murmured.

Blimey. 'Just as well you were here, Mr Forelli,' Alex muttered, trying to ignore the flare of anger that there was a new doctor on *her* ward whom she knew nothing about. What was the point of being head of department if no one consulted her about something this important? Even if she hadn't been here, someone could've mentioned it in one of the many emails she'd been sent throughout her trip, supposedly keeping her up to date with staff gossip and scandal. She'd have preferred knowing about Forelli's arrival than Rochelle's cousin's car accident.

Forelli gave a quick flick of his dark head in her direction, a beautiful, winsome smile lightening a seriously good-looking face. 'You must be the marvellous Miss Prendergast I've been hearing so much about.'

There'd been no change in the rhythm of the compressions. Very smooth.

'I am,' she retorted. *Think you can charm me? Think again, buster.* So why the flutter in her tummy? Why the sense of something she couldn't quite fathom slipping past her fingertips? Her reaction had nothing to do with that sexy voice with a hint of an accent that made her melt inside. No, it had to be the fear of them losing Tommy. There was so much she needed to find out about.

After they'd saved the boy. According to the notes Tommy was fourteen years old. Too young to be in this situation. He hadn't even begun to experience life, and if his heart didn't start soon he'd never get the chance.

Squashing the distress flaring within her she focused on the monitors and pleaded for Tommy's weary heart to start pumping, itching to take over the compressions, feeling ridiculously useless as everyone worked well together.

The room went quiet as everyone concentrated on bringing Tommy back to life. More compressions, drugs and oxygen. Finally, Forelli sucked a lungful and commanded, 'Stop.' Everyone held their breath and watched the monitor's screen.

At last a rhythm appeared. A collective sigh of relief and a thankful 'Yes' resounded around the small room.

Alex fought to keep her shoulders from slumping. That had been too close. 'Is Tommy's mother in the hospital?' she asked Kay after she'd administered another dose of adrenaline.

'No. She usually comes in about nine and spends an hour or two with Tommy before going back home to work. She's still got her old job, working online. A tax lawyer for the government, I think. I'll phone her to come in early.'

'Thanks, Kay. I'll talk to Mrs Jenkins when she gets in. In the meantime I'd like to be brought up to date on everyone else on the ward.' Her eyes clashed with Forelli's pewter-coloured gaze. 'That includes you.'

He shrugged eloquently. 'No problem.'

'We'll talk after I've spoken to whoever's in charge of Tommy's case.'

Those eyes twinkled at her. 'That would be me. I've been taking care of this young man since he was admitted for the first time a month ago.' Before she knew what was happening Forelli put out his right hand to engulf hers in a warm, firm grip. 'We haven't had a chance to meet properly. Mario Forelli. Your new paediatrician.' He shook her hand, but didn't immediately let her go, holding her hand in an almost caress.

'Excuse me?' She tugged free, trying to ignore the spear of warmth zooming up her arm. 'Do you mind telling me how you fit in here?' Talk about being on the back foot in her own department.

'Certainly. Shall we each grab a coffee and go to your office, maybe after I've talked to Carla Jenkins?'

Her eyes locked on to Mario Forelli. Another charmer. The world seemed full of them. And yet his return gaze showed understanding and commiseration at her situation. Which rattled her further, cranking her stress levels dangerously high. Breathe deep, one, two, three. 'Thank you. I'd appreciate it.'

She headed for the nurses' station. Mr Forelli strode alongside her, towering above her, making her feel even shorter than usual. Strangely, that didn't bother her the way it usually did. Who was this guy? How did he so easily get under her skin? She spun around to get a better look at him and tripped over her own feet. She would've fallen flat on her face if *he* hadn't caught her elbow.

'Careful.'

'Thanks.' Again. Alex glared up at this disturbing man, and stretched onto the toes of her new Italian shoes from Los Angeles. Still way too short for level eye contact. For that she'd need a small ladder. Grr.

'Mario, can I get your signature on this letter?' Averill, Alex's secretary, stood in front of them, a dazzling smile on her face as she peered up at Mario.

'Sure.' He reached for the pad and pen being held out to him.

'Ah, hum. Excuse me.' Alex looked from Averill to Mario.

Her secretary finally dragged her eyes sideways and recognised Alex. 'Hi, Alex, you're back.'

'Yes, I'm back.' Since when did Averill come in so early? The starstruck look on the older woman's face held the answer. Since Mr Forelli had started working here. Alex continued watching the pair of them but had to admit the new doctor wasn't encouraging Averill in any way whatsoever.

Mario handed the pen and memo back, his signature scrawled across the bottom. 'There you go.'

As her secretary scuttled away Alex damped down the sudden fear brought on by her own stupid insecurities and rounded on Mr Forelli to demand some answers. The words dried on her tongue when her eyes clashed with his.

'Averill wasn't going over your head to get me to sign that. It was a letter from me to the board about my tenure.' When she again tried to speak he held his hand up. 'We'll talk as soon as we get our patients sorted. Okay?'

'Oh, fine, thanks.' What was she thanking him for? Flustered she looked away. If she went home and started her day again would it get any better? Another glance in his direction didn't clear anything up. Instead his open face and friendly eyes beguiled her. And his practical approach undermined her concerns, told her she had nothing to worry about.

'One hour.' He waved at her as he headed down the ward. 'Hopefully.'

Did she mention how he stole her breath away?

Kay stopped on her way past and joined her in watching Forelli's progress down the ward. 'Delectable, don't you think?'

'No, I don't.' *He's the most beautiful man I've ever met. Just standing in front of him makes me feel tiny and delicate.*

'You're the only woman on the ward to think so. He's charmed every female within miles.' Kay chuckled. 'He's got the staff falling over one another to help him out.'

Why am I not surprised? Those smiles alone would get him anything he wanted. But not from her. No, she was here to work, not play. Disappointment flared. Playing with Mr Forelli after hours might be fun, exciting even. 'How long's he been working here?'

When her head nurse didn't answer Alex turned around to see Kay quickly disappearing behind the nurses' station, her gaze intent on the file in her hand. Right. Alex followed, wondering how she could wait a whole hour to learn more about Mr Forelli.

Suddenly it dawned on her she was letting everything get out of control. She still hadn't caught up on the patients. Mr Forelli's presence had knocked her sideways. Since when did she let these things faze her?

*Come on. You worry too much. There were bound to
be some changes made during your absence. Hospitals
don't stand still.*

Little more than one hour back on the ward and she
was shattered. And she'd thought touring was hard
work.

'Welcome home, Alex,' she muttered. Would anyone
notice if she walked away, grabbed a flight to anywhere
and buried her head in the clouds for another day? Probably not if what she'd seen of Mr Forelli was anything to
go by. He was definitely in charge—of her department.

CHAPTER TWO

'SO THAT'S THE wonderful Miss Prendergast.' Mario's hands clenched and unclenched at his sides. Imperious despite being as confused as all be it. Did she honestly think the whole ward had been waiting, going nowhere, achieving nothing, until she returned to the helm?

She hadn't exactly rushed him with her enthusiasm at his presence. What she had done was disturb him deep inside where he hid his emotions. Right now that pool of feelings was swirling, putting him on high alert. If she could do this to him in such a short time she was dangerous to his equilibrium. Very dangerous. He needed to exercise caution. But how when just being near all that loveliness tied up in a mouth-watering package made him feel drunk. She was a neat package that reminded him of what he'd been missing out on for nearly a year, and what he did not have the time for now—a sex life.

His teeth ground hard as he cursed under his breath. He really enjoyed this job, but today it was shaping up to be a pain in the butt. Or a tickle in his hormone department.

Worse, like an ungainly teen, he'd struggled to stop ogling at her exquisite features: high cheekbones, pert nose, flawless skin. Not to mention that gleaming auburn hair locked up in a knot so tight not one strand could escape. 'She's so tiny. Yet her reputation is huge.' A powerhouse on heels.

As he continued to study her it dawned on him that he'd been expecting an Amazon woman to match the stories he'd heard about her—a demanding, punishing doctor who expected unsurpassed devotion towards the patients from each and every member of her staff, who accepted nothing but the finest care and treatment for every child entering this ward, and would do whatever it took to get it. Including, so he'd been told, reading stories to wee tots at all hours of the night and day. So he had that much in common with her. He'd also heard she cared a lot for her staff.

Those amazing green eyes, filled with angry questions, had sizzled at him, bursting with frustration because she didn't know what was going on in her domain. Never mind she'd been away a third of the year. Admittedly he fully understood her feelings. He'd be the same in a similar situation. *Scema.*

He'd expected it. Even in Italy he'd heard of Alexandra Prendergast and her groundbreaking theories on dealing with premature infants. He'd read the paper she'd written and had been keen to meet her, to work with her. Who hadn't?

Why hadn't she taken up a grand position in a large hospital overseas? Mistakes in her past? Something had rattled her in Tommy's room. There'd been a fear lurking in her eyes until the boy's heart restarted. Whatever caused it had tugged at his heartstrings, had made him want to wrap her up in a hug and protect her. As if she'd let him even try. As if he had time for another female, another broken soul, to look out for.

Because right now his focus had to be totally on Sophia. Which left no room in his life for anything, anyone, else. Sophia ruled everything including his heart. Getting his wee daughter's life back on track, making her happy and, hopefully, finally winning spontaneous smiles from her sweet cupid's mouth was paramount. Everything else was on hold for as long as it took and beyond.

He shrugged. Enough conjecturing. His first move would be to explain his presence without going into any personal details. Was it too much to hope she wouldn't notice the six-month gap in his CV? The CV the board's chairman insisted he show Alexandra, even though the job was his. Maybe he could forestall too many questions by talking about the reason for Liz's abrupt departure from the department.

Sighing, Mario finally managed to stop staring and instead called to her. 'Do you want to join me when I talk to Carla Jenkins?'

Her eyes lightened and that tautness in her shoulders relaxed. 'Yes. I should meet her.'

Just then a distressed woman in her thirties burst out of the lift and shot straight towards him, tears streaming down her cheeks. 'Mario, what's happened? Is Tommy all right?' Carla rushed at him. 'Kay told me to come in immediately. What's wrong?'

Mario looked into Carla's imploring eyes and had one of those moments when he hated his job. He understood her fears. Really understood them. He'd be absolutely terrified if Sophia's heart had stopped. 'Tommy's fine now but his heart stopped for a while.' He paused to let his words sink in. When Carla's eyes widened and her bottom lip trembled, he pressed her shoulder gently, and repeated, 'He's all right now.'

'I have to see him.' Fear and despair laced Carla's

voice. 'I shouldn't have moved here, but it was so hard dealing with this on my own after everything else.'

'Tommy's no worse off being here. His heart would've stopped if he'd been in Auckland.' Taking Carla's elbow Mario gently led her into a visitors' room. 'The nurses are staying with him and you can see him once I've explained what happened.'

Alexandra followed and shut the door firmly. Then she reiterated his first statement. 'Tommy's heart is beating fine now.'

'Who are you? Why did it stop? Are you sure he's all right?' Carla stopped the torrent of words and swallowed hard. Tears gleamed at the corners of her eyes as she stared at the door as though wishing Tommy would walk through and hug her. Her fingers were tightly interlaced against her stomach, her elbows taut and awkward at her sides. 'Sorry. I freaked when Kay phoned.'

'Take a seat, Carla.' Mario parked his backside on the edge of the small table. 'This is Miss Prendergast. You've heard about her and she'll be part of Tommy's medical team from now on. She's very experienced and Tommy couldn't be in better hands.' Hell, Tommy was getting excellent care in *his* hands.

Glancing around, he found Alexandra's eyebrows lifting ever so slightly as she listened to him, amusement blinking back at him from those emerald eyes. Had he gone overboard with his compliment? With a shrug, he got back to the main reason they were all shut in this airless room. 'Do you recall the conversation you and I had when Tommy was first admitted? About what to expect at this stage of Tommy's disease?'

'Yes, but I hoped you were wrong. No, I prayed you didn't know what you were talking about. They didn't put it so bluntly in Auckland. I'm sorry.' Carla sagged further.

Mario winced. There was nothing to be gained by keeping a patient's family in the dark. But then Carla and her son had been dealing with another tragedy, and anything else might've overwhelmed them at the time.

Alexandra took the empty seat beside the woman and reached for Carla's hands. So here was Miss Prendergast's softer side. 'It's very understandable for you to hope for better. I'd probably do the same thing if I was in your situation.' She shook Carla's hands gently. 'But as doctors we don't have that luxury. We have to be prepared for anything to happen so that we can do our very best for Tommy.'

Carla lifted her pain-filled eyes to Alexandra's face. 'Thank you.'

Mario watched as Alexandra talked softly, explaining the situation once again, having gone from confused to kind and compassionate in a flash. Amazing how her own priorities had been put aside for a suffering parent. He was impressed. This was the soft caramel specialist he'd heard about.

Alexandra said to Carla, 'What you can keep believing is that we're doing everything possible for Tommy.'

Carla's bottom lip trembled but she blinked hard and held herself very straight. 'I do, but I'm afraid of losing him.'

Mario murmured, '*Sì*. It is very hard for you. But Tommy's fighting hard. He won't give in. I've seen it in his eyes.'

He noted Alexandra listening as carefully as Carla. Sussing him out? Making sure he was up to speed on the job? That rankled. He'd worked in some of the best hospitals in England and Italy. He had an excellent reputation as a surgeon for the little ones. This hospital board had been more than happy to accept his qualifications. Miss Prendergast had to accept him, like it or not. Starting now.

He stood abruptly. The desperate need in Carla's eyes to see her son gave him the perfect excuse to cut this conversation short. Carla probably couldn't take in any more right now anyway. Taking her elbow he said, 'Come. We'll visit your son.'

He accompanied the woman to Tommy's room where he spent time checking the boy over again. Finally he stepped back and left Carla gripping Tommy's hand and talking soothing mother things while watching her precious son as though he was about to vaporise into thin air.

His heart stuttered. Sophia's mother had never been there for her child. Too busy having a good time to want to be tied down by her daughter. How the hell had she not loved sweet, lovable Sophia? What he wouldn't do to tell Lucy exactly what he thought of her.

As a father he connected with Carla's emotions. The two times Sophia had been severely ill he'd taken her hands in his and hung on for dear life, willing his own life source into her, urging her to come back to him. It had drained him completely, taken days to recover from, but he was her father and fathers gave their all to their bambinos. So should all mothers.

'Have you got time to join me on the ward round?' Alexandra spoke quietly from beside him. 'Or do you want to stay with those two a while longer? I don't mind waiting if you do.'

When he turned his head and looked down he met the direct but empathetic gaze of this enigmatic woman. 'They don't need me at the moment. Probably better off having time alone. Let's go over patient notes in Kay's cubbyhole she proudly calls her office. I'll bring you up to speed.'

'Right.'

Right. That's it? Did that mean she was accepting his presence? Did she realise he'd been doing her job while she was away? Not to mention filling in for Liz. 'Right,' he snapped back, suddenly tired of this, wanting to clear the air between them now, not after they'd completed their round. But the interns were waiting, grouped around the nurses' station, reading notes, and pestering the nurses. His teeth ground on a curse. He'd have to wait.

At Kay's door he stood back to allow Alexandra to enter first, and as she passed he drew a lungful of sweet spring air that reminded him of freesias. On a freezing winter's day? What was wrong with him? It was as though his brain had gone to hell in a wheelbarrow, leaving him delusional. It certainly wasn't because he was attracted to this woman. Absolutely not. He liked his women pliable and fun, not to mention tall and blonde. Fun especially didn't seem to fit Alexandra. Maybe he could show her some? Bah! Dumb idea. Perturbed at the direction his thoughts were heading he studied Alexandra from behind.

The shapeless white coat did not enhance her figure, but neither did it detract from her attributes. Her slim neck and cute ears poking from above the crinkled white collar appeared delicate. Nothing like the real Miss Prendergast at all.

'Hi, Mario. How's Sophia this morning?' Kay grinned at him.

'As quiet and good as ever.' Sadness struck as he thought of his daughter and her fear of doing something naughty. At times he almost wished she'd throw a tantrum or refuse to do what he asked of her, instead of her quiet sobs in the night and her need to behave perfectly so no one would growl at her. It wasn't normal to be so good. He'd probably never know everything that had happened to her before he'd come into her life. And for now it was more important to help her overcome the past, not make an issue of it. The only way he knew how to do that was to provide stability and loads of unconditional love, things she'd never experienced in her short and sad life.

'I found some of my boys' books and brought them in for Sophia. I hope they're not too young for her but I was thinking that as she's learning to read they'd be a good place to start.'

'I'm sure Sophia will enjoy them. She loves all sorts of books. Just like her dad.' His chest swelled, while at the same time he squashed a pang of annoyance. It was his place to provide everything Sophia needed. If he just had the time to go shopping.

Alexandra's eyes were flicking back and forth between him and Kay, puzzlement darkening the green to the colour of pine needles. 'Sophia's my daughter,' he informed her. Maybe telling her something personal would soften her attitude towards him. 'She's four years old.'

'She's gorgeous,' added Kay, making his heart swell more.

'Of course she's gorgeous.' *She's mine.*

Alexandra's eyes widened but she only said, 'Let's take a look at the patient files, shall we?'

'*Sì.*' Antagonising this woman wouldn't help anyone, least of all him. He had no intention of finding another specialist position in another city. Nelson was where he belonged, where Sophia now belonged. They were here to stay—forever.

So buying a ticket to Mars was not an option, even if, at this very moment with Alexandra eyeing him up like something the cat had dragged in, all that isolation seemed like bliss.

As Kay handed Alexandra the first file she said in an aside to him, 'I also brought in a chicken casserole for you to take home tonight. I made far too much for us to get through.'

'You're as transparent as glass.' Mario smiled. 'Thank you, but I really wish you wouldn't. I do cook for Sophia every day.' No need to admit that more often than not he heated up something from the freezer, or that often by the time he did have food ready Sophia had fallen asleep on the sofa in front of the TV.

'Just helping you out.' Kay winked, totally unperturbed by his annoyed tone. 'Don't forget to take the dinner home this time.'

Oops. So she'd noticed that the last meal sat in the staff fridge for days before he remembered it was there. Contrite, he smiled. 'I promise I won't.' Quickly scrawling a word on the palm of his hand he shoved his pen back into his pocket and looked up, straight into the amused look on Alexandra's face.

'You don't write memos on your hand?' he asked.

'No, I don't. I have an excellent memory.'

'Unfortunately.' Kay grinned. 'There are times when we all wish you could forget what you've told us to do.'

Startled, Alexandra looked away from this annoying man to gawp at Kay. 'Am I that much of a taskmaster?'

The nurse rolled her eyes and widened her grin. 'The only thing missing is the whip.'

Kay was teasing. Right? A little? What if the staff

did think she went too far with her demands of them? 'I can be difficult at times, yes, but I'm only thinking of my patients. I'm not a tyrant. Am I?' She'd been away too long. This was where she faced the world from, wrapping the ward and its inhabitants around her like a security blanket. Now worry gnawed at her. Because she'd found everyone falling over backwards to please Mr Forelli?

Kay chuckled. 'Your little patients adore you, their parents trust you and we all like working here. There, satisfied?'

Mario cleared his throat. 'The patient files?'

The files. Her head jerked up, turning in the direction of that voice that reminded her of red wine and crackers by the fire. Mario Forelli. To be going off on a self-pity tangent was so unlike her. She was tired, and the dregs of her headache still knocked at her skull, but they weren't good enough reasons for this ridiculous behaviour.

Kay tapped her shoulder. 'You're doing it again, going all pale on me.'

'Here.' Warm, strong fingers gripped her elbow, directed her to a chair. 'Take a seat. You must still be jet-lagged. It's a long flight from Los Angeles.' That voice was a balm to her stressed mind, tense muscles.

It also undermined her position as boss. But it was too late to argue. She already sat on the proffered chair. How had she got there so quickly, so effortlessly? Mario Forelli. That's how.

'Thank you. I'm fine, really.' But she stayed seated and reached for the first file. 'Tell me about Gemma Lewis.'

'Gemma has spina bifida. Her family moved here nearly a year ago. Her father is a district court judge.

When Gemma required surgery to realign her knees they came to see me rather than return to Wellington.' Forelli's confidence came through loud and clear.

Listening to Forelli explain the surgery he'd performed Alex tried to still the niggling sense of standing on the edge of a precipice. Of falling into a deep chasm she might never find her way back from. Who was Mario? Other than a paediatrician. In no time at all and with no knowledge of the man her thought processes had been hijacked in a totally distracting way. Not a good place to be. Especially, since he had a child, there was obviously a wife. Or a partner.

Or was he a widower? A million questions zapped around her skull, cranking up the throbbing behind her eyes. She should've taken a day at home to fully recover from her trip before facing all these changes.

'Anything you want to ask me about Gemma, Miss Prendergast?' Mario's voice cut through her confusion, and focused her on the job.

'I take it that you're a paediatric surgeon, Mr Forelli.'

His mouth tightened, and she waited for an angry retort.

He didn't disappoint. 'I am, yes. Which is why Judge Lewis was comfortable with letting me look after his daughter.'

'I see.' He hadn't really told her anything but this wasn't the right arena to be asking with other staff hanging on to his every word like he was a god.

'The next file is Tommy Jenkins's. You know about him so we'll move on.' He lifted the third file from her fingers. 'Amelia Saunders, ten years old, contracted dengue fever while on holiday in Fiji. Her liver took a pounding but with drugs her LFTs are slowly returning to normal and she's starting to feel a little better.

I'm thinking of letting her go home by the end of the week.' The file slapped down on top of Tommy's and another one was tugged from her light grip. 'Andrew Frost. Fractured femur after falling off a horse.' On and on went Mr Forelli. Completely in control. He answered all her questions without hesitation or referring to the patient notes. He knew his stuff. Very impressive.

Finally he said, 'Let's go and see these patients.'

'Of course.' Why was he in such a hurry? Did he want to get the upcoming conversation in her office done and dusted as much as she did? She pushed out of her chair. 'If you'd like to accompany me, Mr Forelli.' And she led the way out the door as Kay's phone rang.

'I'll be right with you,' Kay called after them.

Mario squashed down his annoyance with her. 'Can't you start by calling me Mario?' He gave her a charming grin that defied her to disagree. 'Everyone else does.'

'I think you'll find I'm not everyone else,' she retorted, her proud eyes little warmer than a glacier.

'How true.' He huffed an annoyed breath. 'You're head of paediatrics with a reputation that's the envy of all your peers.' He stopped and leaned oh-so-nonchalantly against the closed doors of the lift access, easing another wide smile across his mouth as he assessed her. Again. What was wrong with him today? Taking all this time to suss out a woman? A woman who clearly didn't want him here. Sure, he was tired after a sleepless night with Sophia but that was nothing new.

Then his mouth got further carried away with, 'You dress superbly.' Any woman would kill for that perfectly fitted navy blue suit and soft draping white blouse.

'Thank you.' Alexandra's tone was still sharp but her eyes were warming. Just.

He started walking. 'How long have you been working in Nelson?' *Where do you live? Who do you live with?*

'Three years.'

'And before that?' *Have you got bambinos running around somewhere? Though if you do, then why aren't you at home with them?* And why did he want to know these things? This was his boss. Her private life was of no interest to him whatsoever. *Just being friendly. And testing the temperature.*

'In San Francisco, specialising.' Alexandra tilted her head so she could glare up at him more thoroughly. 'I'm the one who should be asking questions. Such as, exactly how long have you been working here, Mr Forelli?'

So, not Mario, then. Not yet anyway. But give him time, he'd get there. 'Almost four months.'

Her eyebrows did that imperious rising motion, disappearing under her fringe as the implication of that sunk in. 'Four months?'

'Yes. I started a week after you left for your sabbatical.'

CHAPTER THREE

MARIO STOPPED AT the first door and ushered Alexandra ahead of him. Again freesias teased his nostrils as she passed. A sweet, beautiful fragrance. Hell, he didn't even like freesias.

Kay joined them, bringing Rochelle and Jackson with her. 'Hey, Lucas, how's your tummy now? All better?'

'It's still sore.' The boy barely lifted his head as he concentrated on the game on his console.

Mario tapped the eight-year-old on the knee. 'What are you playing today?'

Lucas grinned. 'I'm dragon-slaying, and I'm winning.'

'Good for you.' Mario turned to Alexandra and recalled the boy's details for her. 'Lucas presented with sudden severe abdominal pain three days ago. Peritonitis had set in, caused by his ruptured appendix.'

Kay held a thermometer up. 'Open up, Mr Dragon Slayer. Can't have you fighting dragons without making sure you're fit for battle, can we?'

'Mmm-mmm,' Lucas murmured around the thermometer, his fingers never missing a move on the keys.

Alexandra chuckled. 'You're not going to get in the way of his game, Kay.' She leaned around to watch the small screen. 'Hey, watch out, there's a dragon coming out from behind that tree. Yes, that's it.' She clapped her hands. 'Well done. Oops, there's another one.'

Mario gaped. This woman turned into marshmallow whenever she was around kids. As though she knew what kids liked. Did that mean she did have her own family? No one had mentioned one, but then he'd never thought to ask. Why would've he wanted to know? Perhaps he should borrow Lucas's console and play a game during his meeting with her. If he let her slay more dragons she just might begin to thaw with him.

Then Alexandra straightened and stepped across to the next cubicle. 'Hello, Amy. I hear you've been in for over a week this time.'

The twelve-year-old with nephrotic syndrome dropped the book she'd been pretending to read. 'Yeah, it sucks.'

Alexandra picked up the notes from the end of the bed and perused them. 'You've had more infections.'

'The same old thing. I wanted to go home yesterday but Mario said I had to wait a few more days.' She directed a conniving look at him from under her eyelashes.

'Sorry about that. I'm such a mean monster.' He grinned, totally unfazed by Amy's wish to manipulate him.

'But I can go tomorrow, can't I?' Amy asked.

He took the notes from Alexandra and scanned them. 'Keep this up and I can't see why not.'

'Cool. Mum's going to be happy about that. My uncle and aunt are coming to stay and she won't want to be stuck in here with me.' Her tone turned wistful. 'I want to see them too.'

As they finished the ward round Alexandra turned

to Kay. 'Dr Forelli and I will be in my office. We're not to be interrupted unless it's an emergency.'

Kay grimaced, glanced at him, then back to Alexandra. 'Of course.' And then she gave their boss a gentle smile. 'Welcome back to the real world.' Kay widened her smile. 'We're glad you're back, by the way.'

'I'm very happy to be back.' Alexandra returned the smile before turning away. That confusion had returned, lacing the glance she flicked him. Did she add 'I think' under her breath?

Alex sank down behind her desk and flicked through that small pile of paperwork she'd noted earlier. At the very bottom was an A4 envelope with 'Mr Mario Forelli, Paediatric Surgeon' typed across the middle. His credentials? She tapped the envelope corner against the desktop. Should she read it now? With Mario watching her?

Sitting opposite her, one long leg crossed over the other, his intent gaze disconcerted her, as if he saw right through all her carefully erected barriers. Yet at the same time he warmed her from the inside out, reminding her body of its sensuality.

Putting the envelope down Alex reached for the piping hot coffee Averill had just brought them. Then, pulling her shoulders back, she asked, 'What happened to John Campbell? He was meant to be here until the end of this week.'

Mario's mouth twisted left, then right. 'He was a no-show. Apparently he got a better offer in Perth where he stopped over on his way out to New Zealand.'

'The rotten so-and-so.' Anger gripped Alex as she recalled that Skype interview and how convincing Campbell had been. 'He sounded so excited to be coming here. Kept on about how New Zealand had been one of his dream destinations for most of his life and to work here would be wonderful.' He'd played her for a fool. 'Do you think he'd arranged an interview in Perth before leaving London?'

'Who would know? But I suspect so. He's never explained his actions to the board.'

Had she wanted the man to cover for her so badly that she'd overlooked something? It had been hectic back in those weeks leading up to her departure. The department had been undergoing renovations, patient numbers were way up. She'd been afraid she'd have to cancel her trip. Then Campbell made enquiries about a short-term position in Nelson. He had excellent credentials. It had been a no-brainer to take him on. 'Guess I didn't read him as well as I'd thought.'

Mario shrugged. 'Fairly hard to do in one interview, especially when it's done from opposite sides of the world.'

'So how did you come on the scene?' As she asked, more questions were popping up in her mind. Personal questions that had nothing to do with him working here. Nor were they any of her business. But for some inexplicable reason her interest was piqued.

Mario's gaze dropped briefly to the envelope on her desk before he answered. 'I walked into the department to speak to the HOD about the possibility of getting a position in the near future. Liz literally grabbed my arm and dragged me up to see the board chairman who all but locked me up until I signed a contract covering your leave.' He gave a wry laugh. 'He was frantic. I could've come with a kindergarten pass and got the job.'

She rolled her eyes. 'Sure. I'm supposed to believe that?'

Mario grinned with all the confidence of a man who knows his worth, then turned serious. 'About Liz.'

'How's she keeping? Her baby bump must be getting quite big now. Nearly seven months along, isn't she?' Lucky girl. A wee flare of envy twisted through her. The older she got, the harder her decision never to have a family was to accept. Her body clock ticking louder than her common sense? But one reminder of what had happened nine years earlier and the clock quietened.

'She's having problems with her pregnancy.'

'Ouch.' Alex winced. Guilt at her brief moment of envy was pushed aside by concern for Liz. 'That's so unfair after all the trouble it took for her to get pregnant.' Liz and her husband had taken more than a year for her to conceive. 'She must be really worried.'

Mario cleared his throat. 'She's beside herself with worry, which isn't helping. Her blood pressure is far too high, especially for twenty-nine weeks. And she's got mild oedema. Three weeks ago she was ordered to take complete bed rest for the remainder of her term.'

Alex felt her jaw drop. 'Is the baby going to be all right? How's Liz dealing with this? Why wasn't I told about this straightaway? It's not as though Kay and others didn't regularly keep in touch with me.'

'It was deliberate that you weren't told. When Liz first started having difficulties she didn't want you told, believing you'd be on the first plane home. Then when she had to stop working I had a talk with Jackson, Mathew and Linley. We agreed we could manage for three weeks. I'm sorry if you feel left out of the loop but we were backed by all the staff. Everyone said you should finish your time away. It might be hard to accept but your staff thinks the world of you and wanted to do the right thing by you, even if you'd have wished to be here.'

The understanding gleaming out at her from those pewter eyes stopped any retort she may have uttered. 'It must've been hard, one person down.'

'We coped,' he said, covering a yawn with one large hand.

'I can imagine how hard that was.' Studying him while trying to grapple with Liz's news she suddenly noticed dark shadows below his eyes, strain lines at the corners of that beautiful mouth. Exhaustion came off him in waves. 'Looks like you've worn yourself out.'

'Ahh, I can't blame Liz for that. I have a four-year-old who doesn't know the meaning of sleeping at night.' Worry clouded his eyes, darkened the pewter to charcoal. 'Too many shadows in the night even for me to vanquish.'

Alex felt her heart squeeze for this unknown little girl. To be afraid of anything was awful, and sad, especially for such a young child. 'Kiddy monsters.'

'Something like that, yes.' Uncrossing his legs he sat up straighter. End of that line of talk.

That was okay. She still had plenty of other questions. 'Where have you been working before turning up on our doorstep? Did you train in New Zealand?'

Around another yawn he told her, 'I did my medical degree in Christchurch, specialised in London with paediatric surgery being my area of expertise. After that I moved to Florence where I ran the paediatric department in one of their hospitals for four years.'

'Florence?' Mario was Italian? 'That explains the cadence in your voice.' When his eyes widened heat shimmered in her cheeks. She'd just given herself away. Big-time. So what? The guy had a sexy accent. She wouldn't have been the first to notice or comment. It didn't mean she wanted to climb into bed with him. Did it? Shifting in her chair she looked everywhere but at the disturbing Mario, waiting impatiently for the colour to fade from her face.

Thankfully he chose not to pick up on her blunder, instead explaining, 'I'm a born and bred Kiwi, went to the boys' college across the road.' He nodded towards her window. 'My parents grew tomatoes in the Wood, along with other Italian families in the district.'

'So why Italy?' As long as he wanted to talk about himself she was ready to listen.

'My grandparents came out here from Florence when they were first married. All my life I've wanted to know my relatives over there so the job was perfectly placed.'

'You've still got family here?' Italians had large families, didn't they? Lots of siblings, cousins, aunts and uncles, to have fun with, to support one another, to share life's ups and downs. Family. The one thing lacking in her life. The one huge thing. But she didn't deserve family, especially children. No, even her dogs were fictitious, bounding across the pages of the children's books she wrote and illustrated. She focused on Mario, away from her own problems.

That appealing grin was back. 'Sort of. Mamma and Babbo went over to Italy at the beginning of the year and don't look like coming home any time soon. Two of my sisters are married to Italian nationals, and one sister lives here.'

'Is your wife Italian?'

The grin slowly disappeared and he studied his hands with intensity, a frown creasing his brow. 'Sophia's mother was a Kiwi. Unfortunately she died in a diving accident two years ago.'

Gasp. No wonder the little girl had trouble sleeping at night. She'd be missing her mother. Hard to understand at that age why Mummy wasn't there for her. This also explained the moments of sadness she saw in Mario's face when he didn't think anyone was looking. 'I'm very sorry to hear that. It must be very hard for you bringing up your daughter on your own.' And working long hours, often six and seven days a week.

Suddenly he looked up and clashed gazes with her, a huge 'don't go there' flashing out at her. 'We're getting off track. With Liz on indefinite leave I've been given a permanent position in your department.' His eyes burned into hers, daring her to argue with the situation.

How could she? She might be miffed that the board hadn't waited to talk the situation over with her but she wasn't stupid. With Liz gone the department was down to two full-time paediatricians and one trainee. Highly qualified paediatricians didn't regularly waltz in the door looking for work. 'I'm glad you came along. As you've already learned we put in some long hours as it is without being short of staff.'

Relief poured into those piercing eyes and he relaxed back in his chair. 'Jackson is shaping up to be a good paediatrician.'

'Yes, he is.'

How did Mario juggle work and a child? She couldn't begin to imagine what that was like for him. Why hadn't he stayed in Italy if that's where his parents were? His sisters too. Families. They never seemed to work out the way anyone expected. Look at hers. A stepfather who resented her for loving her dad; a mother who couldn't care two cents about her. She'd had a lonely, solitary upbringing after Dad died. Sent to boarding school so that Mum and George could swan off all over the world where the inclination took them. When she married and became pregnant she'd really thought that she'd found her own family. Talk about a misconception. Jonty couldn't wait to leave her after everything went horribly wrong. Don't go there. Not now when she was being scrutinised from the other side of her desk. Mario had already proved how good he was at mind-reading.

She reached for the envelope, slid her finger under the flap.

And Mario stood. 'I'll leave you to read that while I go and check up on Tommy again.'

She stared at the closing door. Now what brought about that hurried departure? The CV in her hand? Unfolding the pages she read quickly. Wow, the guy was a megastar of paediatrics. Warmth stole through her. They could make an awesome team if they worked well together.

But this was her domain, the place she felt in control—of herself and of everything around her. Would Mario try to take away her security by insisting on making changes? Only one way to find out—spend as much time on the ward with him. Without smothering him. He didn't need her hanging over his shoulder watching everything he did.

Excitement trickled along her veins. This could turn out to be fun having a colleague as experienced as Mario. They'd be able to bounce ideas off each other, discuss new treatments.

Her smile slowly disappeared. That was fun? It might be the best she'd had in a long time but it wasn't up to scratch in the enjoyment stakes. Real fun would be being held in those strong arms and kissed by that beautiful mouth. Fun would be a walk on the beach out at her cottage in Ruby Bay, hand in hand with Mario, kicking the sand, watching the gulls swooping and soaring, laughing over silly, pointless things.

Yeah, right. She'd better get a full night's sleep tonight. Otherwise sign up for the loony bin. Because something was desperately wrong with her mind, tossing up crazy dreams like holding hands with a man whom until first thing that morning she hadn't known existed.

Mario shivered when icy wind whipped under his jacket and got through to his skin as he crossed the staff car park at the end of the day. June was the pits. Winter was the pits. Though if he had to live through winter Nelson was the best place to be. The forecast for later on in the week hinted at snow. Maybe on Saturday he'd take Sophia and Gina's boys up to Mount Arthur car park so they could build a snowman and throw snowballs.

Sliding in behind the steering wheel of his family wagon Mario slammed the door and leaned his head back on the headrest to stare up at the dark interior. 'What a horrendous day. Thankfully Tommy survived his cardiac arrest, but he's got problems racing towards him, for sure.'

And then there was Miss Alexandra Prendergast. Annoying, intriguing, worrying. Especially worrying. She'd sparked his libido into life big-time. The last complication he needed right now. Not that he'd turn down an evening in bed with a stunning-looking woman—if he had a babysitter on hand. But a quick romp with his boss was not on. Somehow he doubted Alexandra would be into one-night flings. She was deep, thoughtful and not quite into fun. He cracked his knuckles. So suck it up and forget all about getting naked with the woman. Keep everything strictly professional; ignore the wary looks she gave him when she thought he wasn't looking. Forget that you don't have a private life apart from one messed-up daughter. Sophia is your life now, and she's not getting enough of your attention as it is.

The car rocked as another blast of wind slammed against it. Mario looked around the car park, his gaze following a paper cup as it flew through the air to bang into the sports car parked two slots away. Obviously owned by someone who didn't have a brood of kids to run around the place.

Twisting the key in the ignition Mario groaned when the engine raced but didn't start. 'Not again. Not to-night.'

Last week he'd had trouble starting the engine but he'd cleaned the spark plugs and hey, presto, it had gone like a dream since.

He turned the key again, and again. The whining sound of the engine spoke volumes. Slapping the steering wheel he tugged at the catch to release the bonnet and pushed out into the cold. With a torch in one hand he lifted the bonnet and stood studying the wires, the battery and the spark plugs. Everything appeared to be in order. Huh. Like he knew what he was looking for. Topping up the water and oil had been sufficient until now. He pushed and poked everything, shook some wires that meant absolutely nothing to him, went around to try the ignition again. Nothing but that squealing sound.

Definitely time he took the car in for a service. His fingers pushed through his hair. Damn it. Why did cars break down right when you needed them? He had to get home before the nanny did her usual sulky thing. If only he had a few hours to find another, more obliging girl to take care of Sophia when he was at work.

'Problem?' One word and Alexandra made it sound so sweet. Not to mention irritating.

He spun around, stared down into the dark pits of her eyes. It was probably just as well he couldn't see her expression clearly in the half-light of the street lamps. No doubt she'd be laughing fit to bust. 'My car's packed a sad.'

'Bad timing, right?' When she waved her keys in the air the locks on the sports car popped.

Of course that red racy thing would be Alexandra's. It suited her. Small, compact and sexy. He might be abstaining but his hormones had taken a hit today. They still knew a great package when they saw one. Working with her just got a whole lot more difficult.

'Very bad timing. I need to get home quickly.' Hint, hint. Would she offer him a lift? Though being squeezed into that sardine can with her might prove to be the hardest thing he'd done all day. Even ten minutes rubbing shoulders would only make him crankier than he already was. But he'd do anything for Sophia, right? So he'd accept a lift.

But she shocked him. 'What exactly is the problem?'

What? You think you're a mechanic now? Are you teasing me? 'I turn the key and all I get is a noise. The engine's not firing.'

'But it sounds like it wants to?'

He was gaping at her, his mouth half open. Not his best look, for sure, but what the hell was this woman on? She was a paediatrician, not a grease monkey. 'Yes, it keeps up a steady noise but doesn't even hint at catching.' He reached for the bonnet, began to push it down. If Alexandra wasn't forthcoming with an offer of a ride, then he had to get cracking with finding a taxi. Sophia needed to be in bed within the next half-hour.

'Wait. Don't close that yet.' She placed her handbag inside her to-die-for car and came over to peer under the bonnet of his people-mover. Make that children-mover. Taking a hot date, namely Alexandra, out in it would be a novelty. For her, at least. Reaching in, she pulled a spark plug and blew on it. 'Looks okay.'

'I cleaned them a few days ago.'

She checked the rest of the plugs anyway. Under his collar his neck grew warm. Didn't she believe him? Then she moved around to the driver's door. 'Can I?'

He could only nod. Was she trying to make him look a bigger idiot than she obviously already thought him? If so, she was succeeding.

She hopped in and planted her foot hard on the accelerator. 'This might be a bit noisy.' Her fingers twisted the key and flicked it on.

A bit noisy? A screaming banshee wouldn't have been heard over this. 'Okay, okay, stop it, will you? You're going to cook the motor and then you'll have to lend me your car.' An image of Sophia strapped into that tiny vehicle brought a reluctant smile to his lips.

Of course Alexandra couldn't hear him. A cloud of black smoke spewed from the vicinity of the muffler, and still she kept the key in the on position and that tiny foot firmly pressed to the pedal. In the half-light from the car's interior her face looked determined, confident. Her mouth moved. Had she just said, 'Come on'?

Then unbelievably his engine started. It ran rough, coughing, soaring, quietening. The woman behind the wheel eased off on the juice, lifting her foot slowly until the motor ran quietly and sweetly.

Mario's jaw dropped—again. 'Well, damn me, if she hasn't fixed it.'

When Alexandra clambered out and stood in front

of him looking oh-so-smug he hurriedly swallowed his astonishment and tried for a look that said he was totally used to women fixing his car. 'What was that all about, then?'

'A build-up of carbon, I'd say.'

'Can't trust that carbon, can you?' Time to get out of here, away from this extraordinary woman before *he* blew a gasket.

Surprisingly she burst out laughing. 'Don't worry. I'm not a car nerd. Years ago as a teenager in defiance of my stepfather I bought a car without getting it checked over. It turned out to be a bit of a wreck but rather than selling it and proving George right I went to a night school class to learn basic mechanics. I have to admit those lessons have often come in handy.'

He liked it when she laughed. Her eyes lit up and that upright stance softened a little. 'Not with that sports car, I'll bet.'

'You'd be surprised. It's a bit of a prima donna at times.' Her eyes were full of warmth. For a car?

'You and your stepfather had issues?'

The laughter switched off in a flash. 'Among other things.' Stepping past him she headed for her vehicle. 'I'd better get going. My fish and chips will be ready.'

'So you didn't take a cooking class, then?' The words were out before his brain kicked into gear. She'd probably think he was criticising her.

Looking over her shoulder she threw him a small smile. 'Yes, I did actually. Cooking's good when there's someone to share it with, but plain boring when I'm the only one sitting down to the end result.'

So she lived alone. No partner or children. How lonely that must be. And yet his heart lifted at the thought. 'Hey,' he called as she began to close herself inside her can of a car. 'Thanks for sorting me out. I do appreciate it.' *Even if I'd have preferred it to have been Jackson who'd shown me up.* Hell, even Kay would've been okay, but not Alexandra, who seemed to be more than good at absolutely every damned thing. Miss Perfect? Nah, couldn't be. No one got to be liked as much as Alexandra was on the ward if they were that good.

'See you tomorrow.' She waved and turned her key. Of course her damned car started instantly.

CHAPTER FOUR

'IS YOUR CAR starting all right these mornings?' Alex asked Mario a week later as they settled into chairs in her office.

Averill placed mugs of coffee on the desk and closed the door on her way out, taking all the breathable air with her.

From the annoyed expression that briefly flitted across Mario's face Alex figured he wasn't happy with her. Because she'd got his car going? Had that dented his male pride? Then he should learn some basic mechanics.

'*Sì*. Runs like a dream.' He winced. Then his head lifted and his eyes met hers, sending heat darting through her tummy. 'Thanks again. It would've cost a bundle to get the mechanic to come out at that hour.'

Alex grinned at his discomfort. 'Why do men have to think they've got a monopoly on engines, fishing and driving tractors?'

Those come-to-bed eyes widened, then the room filled with laughter, catching her unawares, curling her toes in a delicious way. 'It's in our genes. We're expected to know how to change a flat tyre, put out the rubbish and paint the roof. And when we don't there's hell to pay. Our egos suffer, our mates rib us mercilessly and women feel let down.'

'We do? Oh, I see. You're not including me in that statement because I know how to do those things.' Her grin faltered. Wasn't she feminine enough? Is that why men inevitably turned away after a short time into a relationship with her?

'You know how to do *all* those things?' Mario was still laughing.

'I hate fishing. They stink, and as for the bait, yuck. And I've never painted a roof.' Did that win her any feminine points? Her insecurities were ramping up today.

'Phew, for a moment there I thought you were superwoman.'

And that would definitely be a turn-off. 'I try not to wear my cape at work.'

'You don't need to. Everyone knows how good you are with the little ones.' His laughter had stopped and a serious expression settled over his face and in his eyes. He held his hands out, palms up, and lifted his shoulders. 'Over the months you've been a hard act to follow at times. "Alex this, Alex that."'

Stunned, she stared back. 'But you've got an awesome reputation yourself. This morning in theatre everyone talked about the fabulous Dr Forelli and his skills.' There'd been a few giggles and queries as to what his skills outside work might be like but no one had any answers. It seemed Mario wasn't rushing round dating all the available females, apparently happy to be charming them into bringing meals for him to take home. When he wasn't at work no one heard a peep from him.

Mario nodded. 'I am good. Paediatrics is a passion which makes it easier to do a great job, to learn everything necessary for my patients.'

Not shy about patting his own back either. But then why should he be? His CV was awesome. 'Nelson's children are in good hands, then.' And she relaxed further, adding, 'In two pairs of good hands.'

Mario chuckled. 'We'd better get on with the real work. Discussing patients.' He reached down for a file from the top of a stack he'd dropped on the floor by his chair minutes earlier.

'Before we do that I wanted to ask about the six-month gap from when you left Florence and started here. Care to comment?' The gap didn't tie in with Sophia's mother dying two years ago.

The chuckle died. His pewter eyes became frosty steel. 'No.'

'Is there something I should know that might reflect on your work, previous or current?' She hated secrets, especially at work. It didn't do anyone any favours.

'No. It's personal.' He didn't look away. Nor did that steel lighten.

Making a rapid decision Alex let it go and moved on. 'Fair enough. Who's file is top of that pile?' Maybe some time in the future when they knew each other better he might explain. Or he might not. She doubted he'd be hiding anything important that affected his career, and if the chairman was happy with his work history, then so was she.

Mario didn't even blink. 'Tommy Jenkins. There's no change with that infection. Better than getting worse, I suppose.'

'He wouldn't survive worse.'

Those solid, mouth-watering shoulders shrugged eloquently. 'I talked to Tommy's previous specialist in Auckland yesterday. We agreed it's time to register Tommy's details with the organ donor centre.'

When had she developed a shoulder fetish? Since she'd met this guy. That first night, when trying to go to sleep after an awful first day back, she'd had a sudden mental picture of Mario above her, those shoulders bare and so close she could run her fingers up and over them.

'Alexandra? Hello?'

Hello yourself. Get back in the picture. You're at work, discussing—? Her mind fished around. What had they been discussing? Tommy Jenkins. That's right. 'All we can do for Tommy in the meantime is keep a close watch over him and try to lower the risk of further infections.' Which would be hard. The lad needed people around him at the moment, and yet they could be detrimental to his health.

Mario placed the file on her desk and reached for the next one, hopefully unaware of the fantasies spinning through her head. 'Caleb Kernan, tonsillectomy and adenoidectomy. Previous glue ear and repeated throat infections. Taking too long to recover from surgery. I'm running more tests looking for an underlying cause of his lethargy.'

'Why did you change the admission process for our non-urgent patients? It worked the way it was.'

His head jerked up. 'It works even better this way.'

Loud knocking on the door interrupted anything else Mario might've said. A nurse Alex recognised from ED burst into the room. 'Mario, you've got to come. Now. Sophia's in PICU with a silent chest.'

Mario's chair smacked against the wall as the man moved incredibly fast for someone so big. All the colour drained from his face. His eyes filled with fear. 'How long's she been here?' he demanded as he charged after the nurse.

Nurse Epping, wasn't it? Gina Epping. That's it. How

did she fit into the picture? His new wife? Girlfriend? Gina could be an Italian name. So?

Alex automatically chased after Mario. This was an emergency. On her ward. The patient was his daughter, which meant Mario couldn't treat her.

Compassion tightened Alex's chest. Parents found watching their children suffering incredibly difficult. Every parent she'd met, and there were many, would've given their soul to swap places with their desperately ill children.

Her feet tripped over each other.

She'd have swapped places with Jordan. If she'd been given the opportunity.

Her precious baby boy had never had the chance to open his eyes and see the light of day, had never known her love, or turned to her for answers to life's questions. All the things she'd been so excited about sharing with him. Loving her child, giving him everything he needed, sheltering him, guarding him like a lioness, showing him how the world worked. They'd have been a family—her, Jordan and Jonty. Instead she'd been left behind to put the shattered pieces of her life together into a different shape than it had been before. Her heart jerked under her rib cage. It had been many years since she'd laid her son to rest, yet it seemed like yesterday. No, it seemed like today.

Concentrate. This situation was not about her. But it was odd how she'd suddenly started having these moments again. The nightmare, the unrealistic dreams of happy-ever-after scenarios, wondering what it would be like getting up close and naked with Mario.

Maybe the job was taking more out of her than she realised. After one week back? Get real. Another oddball idea waltzed across her brain. What if she did cut back on her hours? But that was plain crazy. The board wouldn't allow it, the ward couldn't manage, and she'd go bonkers trying to fill in the hours.

It's not supposed to be about filling in time, rather about getting a life beyond this place.

Yes, right. Another day, perhaps. In the dim, dark future.

Mario thought his chest would explode with fear. Unbelievable pain ripped him apart. His baby couldn't breathe. 'Does she know I'm coming?' he yelled at Gina. 'Hang in there, Sophia. Daddy's coming. Daddy loves you. Keep breathing. I know it's hard, darling, but do it for me, for you, for us. Keep breathing.'

Gina snatched at his hand. 'She'll be all right, Mario, I promise.'

'Don't make promises like that.' She was tempting fate to intervene and turn the outcome into something too horrible to contemplate. The PICU appeared ahead, the corridor kilometres long. And his baby needed him. 'What happened?' he roared.

'Bridget said she was talking to a friend on her cell phone for a few minutes and when she finished Sophia was gone.'

'A few minutes? More like hours. That phone's attached to her ear. Wait till I see her.'

Gina hadn't finished her explanation. 'Sophia was hiding and when Bridget finally found her she was barely conscious.'

Mario's eyes shut for a brief moment. Hiding again. His little Sophia was still afraid of her own shadow. Anything could send her scuttling into the back of the wardrobe or sneaking out into the garden shed.

Gina was still yapping in his ear. 'It could be time to

find a new nanny, Mario. One who loves children more than her phone. Maybe one who'd be happy to live in.'

'The first thing I'm going to do when my little one's safe again.' He kept up his race along the ward. To hell with the rules. They were allowed to run for an emergency and this was definitely an emergency. 'She must've been showing signs of an impending attack most of the morning.'

'She'd been coughing and wheezing, but Bridget thought the wheezing had started getting a lot better.'

'Not better at all.' Sophia's lungs would've been tightening, thereby reducing the wheezing. A warning sign of worse to come. A warning sign he'd drummed into Bridget's peanut brain a hundred times.

Gina grimaced. 'She's a nanny, not a nurse or a doctor, Mario. Give her a break.'

'I know that but she could try to pay attention.' Was he expecting too much? All he asked was that the girl call him any time she thought Sophia was unwell. A quick text message would've worked. But, on a deep, heavy breath, he acknowledged his guilt. At the end of the day Sophia was his responsibility. His alone.

His shoes skidded, screeched on the floor, as he spun into PICU. Then he was there, standing at the end of the bed, hands on hips, huge gasps filling his lungs with oxygen, staring down at the adorable bundle that was his daughter. Only right now the sight was terrifying. Her eyes were closed, her little chest barely rising and falling. The oxygen mask covering so much of her face isolated her from him.

Mario slipped around the bed to reach for her tiny hand lying on her tummy, curled into a fist. From the very first moment he'd set eyes on Sophia he'd fallen in love with her. Her big, wary, brown eyes had sucked

him in and locked his heart around her. At three years
old she hadn't trusted a soul, couldn't rely on any adult
to always be there for her. Nearly a year later they hadn't
made as much progress rectifying that as he'd have
liked. It was going to take him a very long time to prove
he would never leave her.

'Jackson, what else have you given Sophia other than
oxygen?' Alexandra asked in a calm, no-nonsense voice
from the opposite side of the bed.

Mario lurched. Obviously Alexandra had followed
him. Now she was focused entirely on his daughter, listening carefully as Jackson told her the dosage of Beta 2
agonist he'd set up for Sophia to inhale. She can't have
hesitated when Gina had barged into her office, obviously as quick to respond as he'd been. Mario felt gratitude on top of his fear. Not that Alexandra wouldn't
have come, but still. He was glad she was here.

'Did you apply a spacer, Jackson?' Alexandra asked
quietly. 'What else have you done?' Her calm voice settled Mario a little. If one of the best paediatricians in the
country was on the case, then Sophia was in good hands.

The intern glanced across to Mario, his nervousness
apparent as he hesitated, and when he spoke it was to
Mario, not Alexandra. 'We've only had her for ten minutes. Gina brought her straight to us from ED.' He drew
a breath. 'I haven't done a peak flow yet. Thought it best
to start treatment immediately I'd established this was
a severe asthma attack.'

'You did the right thing,' Mario murmured, crossing his fingers it was enough. How many times was he
going to have to go through this agony? Watching and
tearing apart inside as his child did the one thing he
could not do for her—fight to live.

Alexandra supported him. 'That's right, Jackson. In

severe asthma attacks always treat the patient first, get them breathing.' She took Sophia's wrist, felt for her pulse. 'But the obs need to be done now.'

Mario watched her lips moving as she counted, her eyes fixed on her watch. When she'd finished she ever so carefully replaced Sophia's arm on the bed. Her eyes clashed with his, sympathy flowing towards him. 'One hundred and thirty.'

The knot in his stomach tightened painfully at the abnormal result. An acute attack. His eyes fixed on Alexandra's forefinger running a gentle track down the back of Sophia's hand, as though she was willing his girl to pull through.

Then Alexandra asked, 'Has Sophia had many severe attacks?'

'One's too many,' he snapped. The sympathy in those eyes would undo him as much as the frightening sight of his beautiful girl. If he let it.

Gina's fingers dug into his shoulder as she answered for him. 'Sophia's been having asthma attacks for as long as we've known her, but this is the worst yet.'

Even as Alexandra's eyes widened at this information he was acknowledging this was definitely the worst Sophia had suffered. Damn it, what sort of doctor was he if he couldn't take care of his own daughter, couldn't prevent these terrifying events? What sort of father left his precious child with a nanny all day? A scatterbrained one at that.

He'd thought working at this hospital only minutes up the road from home would be a better option than flying across to Wellington for days at a time. Days when he'd left Sophia with Gina and her boys, and the nanny. As if Gina didn't have her hands full with her three boys and a broken marriage to sort out. He hated that he'd had to rely on her to help him out. Worse had been the days when he hadn't got home to kiss Sophia goodnight, to read her a story, to feed her dinner. Those things had made him question whether he was any better at parenting than Sophia's mother had been. He'd really believed returning to New Zealand had been the best option for them both. But now? Looking down at his reason for living he asked silently, *Do I promise the gods that I'll give up my career if they save Sophia?* He got no answer.

Alexandra continued talking with Jackson, asking about what he'd do next, encouraging him to run through his treatment and the reasons for it, quietly but firmly underlining the necessity of waiting twenty minutes after the initial treatment before giving another dose. As she talked, Mario felt some of his tension ease off. Forget asking the gods to look out for his daughter. He and Sophia had Alexandra Prendergast on their side.

Not to mention Jackson, Kay and Rochelle, all working together to save Sophia.

He went back to watching and waiting, Sophia's tiny hand still tucked into his. She would make it. As a doctor he believed that. As a dad? Twenty minutes was a lifetime to wait to see if the treatment was working. 'Come on, little one. I'm here for you. No one's going to hurt you again. Nor am I going to abandon you. You're mine, a Forelli, and Forellis look out for their own.' Even if he wasn't doing such a good job at it all of the time.

Alexandra asked, 'Is there anyone else you want here with you, Mario?'

'No.' Oh, hell. 'Sorry. I mean, there's only us here. On my side anyway, and Sophia doesn't have any relatives on her mother's side.' This woman was already learning more about him than anyone else had in the past year since he'd first begun his search for Sophia. From the day he'd found out he was a father his sole purpose in life had been to track down his daughter and bring her home. He hadn't wasted any time on small talk, only speaking to those who might be able to help him in his search. Even when he'd finally found Sophia he'd not eased up on his reticence to share what Sophia's mother had done to her. It had been too huge, too unimaginable, not to mention life-changing, to share. And yet slowly, one by one, he was letting out details to Alexandra. They may not add up to much yet, but if he kept on this way she'd one day have a complete picture.

Thankfully Kay changed the subject. 'That reminds me. Mario's got surgery at two.'

Alexandra beat him to a reply. 'I'll need to go over the cases with you, Mario, but otherwise leave everything with me. I'll get Averill to bring the files in here so you won't have to leave Sophia's side. At least until you know she's going to be all right.'

All right? Sophia had years to go before then. First she had to learn what love was, how unconditional it could be. She had to stop getting distressed and run-down so that her asthma didn't keep getting increasingly serious with each new attack. But Alexandra was talking about now, today. She didn't know Sophia's history but she was supporting him—as a father, and as a colleague, which showed she'd gone some way to accepting he worked with her. 'Thank you.' He met her steady gaze, and nodded, repeated, 'Thanks, I appreciate it. I'll be spending the night here.'

Alex watched Mario sitting with his wee daughter, his eyes filled with such love and tenderness, with fear and worry, that her heart swelled. There was no doubt about his devotion. It struck her hard. He'd be just as loving and loyal to the woman he married. Despite what he'd said he seemed to balance family and work well. He would never be remote or too busy for his family.

She glanced at his hands. Big, capable and oh-so-tender when they touched, soothed, Sophia.

Turning to Gina she tried to work out where they fitted into each other's lives. There was little family likeness, Gina being blond and slight. 'So you two are related?'

Gina and Mario looked startled, as though they thought everyone knew that, then both grinned identical grins. 'For our sins, yes.' Gina gently slapped Mario's back. 'My brother was the spoilt one. He had me and our sisters running around after him from the moment we could walk.'

'Yeah, yeah, you were so hard done by. I never had a moment's peace with you lot.'

'Sometimes we'd find Mario reading with a torch in the wardrobe. He used to say it was to get away from us but we knew he was hiding so he didn't have to pick the tomatoes.'

Mario rolled his eyes. 'As if.'

There was something about the easy banter between Mario and his sister that sent a splinter of envy twisting through Alex, further underlining her solitary state. *Oh, get over yourself.* But it wasn't easy, especially when she watched Mario with his daughter and sister. She sighed away the mood and got back onto safe ground the only way she knew how, asking Kay, 'Are Sophia's obs improving?'

'Barely.' Kay handed her the page she'd written results on. 'I'll put Rochelle on to special her.'

'Jackson, I'd like you to continue to keep an eye on Sophia too. If you have any concerns call on Matthew. I'll get Linley to run my diabetic clinic while I take over Mario's surgical list.' As she mentally ran through the doctors and nurses available she studied the little girl's breathing. 'You might want to measure Sophia's peak flow now.'

Alex was reluctant to leave. Mario, despite his sister's presence, looked very alone. Just like other parents she'd observed over the years. No one could quite feel the pain and fear he was feeling right now. That was his alone. She leaned against the end of the bed. 'Mario, is there anything I can get you? Do for you?'

His head came up slowly, as though he couldn't bear to tear his sight away from his little girl as she laboured to breathe, almost as if he was breathing for her. But when Alex could look into his eyes she saw surprise, and gratitude. 'Not at the moment, Alexandra. But I'm glad you offered.'

She held her breath. There was a connection there between them. Something had gone down, yet she didn't know what it was. But it felt right, life-changing even. Then she shook her head. Who was she fooling? She was letting the moment get to her. It wasn't as though she'd at last found a man she might like to get to know well.

Even if she had it wasn't going anywhere. She wasn't meant to be a part of a family, remember? Oh, she remembered all right, but right now she'd happily forget the past tragedies and take another chance. Which went to show how those beautiful grey eyes had hoodwinked her. She would not, could not, be a part of this family. The price was too high, to them and to her.

Her father's death when she was twelve had devastated her, and left her stranded in a lonely life where her mother barely acknowledged her and her stepfather thought no more of her than a pesky fly hovering around him. It had taken numerous knockbacks for her to accept not all fathers were fun to be with. She'd believed she'd fixed her life when she and Jonty married and got pregnant with Jordan. But once again she'd been left behind, bewildered, grief-stricken and alone.

So no matter the sense of longing Mario evoked in her nothing was going to happen between them. She had to look out for her heart.

Alex leaned back as far as possible in her chair, tipped her head back and closed her eyes. It was after eight o'clock in the evening and she should be heading home. Instead she concentrated on straightening out the kinks in her spine after six hours in theatre by rolling her shoulders left, then right, did the same with her hips. Click, click, went her spine, but the headache behind her eyes continued throbbing. Her back seemed more reluctant than ever to put up with the bending required to perform surgery.

'Hey, there, you look exhausted.'

She snapped forward, sending the headache from a low throb to a pounding. 'Mario. I was about to come over to PICU. How's Sophia doing?'

Without waiting for an invitation he dropped into a chair and put his feet up on her desk, crossing his ankles. 'Sleeping. Breathing normally with a little help. We seem to have got through this attack intact.' He scrubbed his hands down his cheeks. 'Until next time.'

'How do you manage this all on your own?' Why hadn't he stayed in Florence where he'd have help?

Mario put his hands behind his head and stared up

at the ceiling. 'There is the nanny, though for how long I'm not sure. And then Gina helps a lot, though she's bringing up three boys on her own since her husband decided he liked single twenty-year-olds without stretch marks on their stomachs. We share Bridget whenever Gina's at work. In the weekends if I'm working Gina tries to fit Sophia in with her lot, and when I'm not here I try to take the boys out. All these kids are why I own that wagon you got going for me. I seem to spend my spare time transporting noisy, boisterous Forellis from one side of town to the other and back.'

'The Italian way.' Certainly not her family's way.

'Isn't it every family's way?' Those steely eyes were scrutinising her. 'Guess I got lucky, huh?'

'You have no idea.'

'Alexandra?' His voice was soft, caressing in its query. 'Are you all right?'

'Of course I am,' she growled. Quickly shaking away the envy she redirected the conversation onto safer ground. 'Who's sitting with Sophia?'

'Jackson offered to hang around while I took a break. I think he's hoping Gina will pop in.' His hand dragged over his light stubble. 'Poor guy. I should warn him he's got a long wait. Gina's still so angry at her ex. But she's mesmerised Jackson.'

'So the charm thing runs in the family.' Mario had certainly got more than a smattering of that gene.

He grinned, a long, slow, heart-melting grin. 'Me a charmer? Where did you get that idea?'

She'd been battling it for days now. Try as she might to keep this sexy, intriguing man at a distance as she wrenched back control of her department, he'd managed to worm his way in under her fiercely protected cover. Not liking to admit that, she detoured the conversation again. 'You were working in Florence when Sophia was born?'

Instantly Mario tensed. 'Yes.'

Did the explanation to those missing months in his CV have anything to do with Sophia? Obviously something terrible had happened if Mario thought his daughter needed to come to New Zealand. Had her mother hurt her? Had he taken Sophia away from her mother before she died?

His gaze drilled into her, the granite shade turned charcoal. His cheek twitched. His chest rose as he drew breath. 'Lucy drowned in a scuba-diving accident up in the Bay of Islands.'

No wonder Sophia had her nighttime demons. 'That's terrible. I'm sorry. You must be devastated.'

He hadn't heard. 'I couldn't take Sophia back to Italy, not to all my family when she'd never met them.' He shook his head. 'It was bewildering enough for a little one.'

'I'd say unimaginable.' Probably equally distressing for Mario too. Though he hadn't looked too rocked when mentioning his partner's death. Had she missed something?

His feet hit the floor with a bang and he stood in one smooth movement. For a big man he was graceful. 'Guess you wouldn't want to share some chicken and mushroom casserole?'

Her eyebrows rose. 'Sounds delicious. You been cooking late at night?'

'No, Kay again. She spoils me. Come on, then.' He reached a hand as though to take hers, hesitated and withdrew, quickly turning for the door.

Alex slipped her jacket on. Heck, he'd changed the subject from Sophia to dinner so effortlessly she'd fallen for it. So he didn't like talking about his past. Fair enough, nor did she. She called after him, 'I'd like to check up on Sophia first.'

'She's my very next stop. She might be okay with Jackson but she's still very frightened. I don't want to leave her for long.'

Yet he'd come to find her. To talk to her. 'You're still sleeping over tonight, then?'

'Of course. Thanks for coming to see Sophia. Jackson has been superb, by the way. He'll make a wonderful paediatrician if he goes ahead and specialises. But—' Mario gave an eloquent roll of his shoulders '—I'm pulling strings and asking for you to look over the notes and see for yourself that my girl's fine. Speaking as a parent, you understand.'

Alex smiled, a full smile that lifted her cheeks and warmed her on the inside. 'Of course I understand.' He was a paediatrician himself and yet he'd asked her to see his precious daughter. She felt warmer and warmer.

And her hormones went from a slow two-step to a racing tango.

CHAPTER FIVE

Mario watched carefully as Alexandra checked Sophia thoroughly, looking for a sharp intake of breath or the tightening of her fingers on her pen, signs that would tell him Sophia wasn't getting over the attack. So far all was well. But as he watched her gentleness with his girl, something deep inside him split wide open, letting her in. Immediately he squashed done on the warmth permeating his body.

Forget it, Mario. She might be stunningly attractive, intelligent, caring and whatever else I haven't discovered yet, but I ain't going there. I'm not interested. His gut knotted in disagreement and disappointment. *No, really, I haven't got a spare minute in my life now so how could I fit in a demanding woman? There will be no kisses, no lovemaking, no candlelit dinners, for a very long time to come. Especially not with this woman.* Just working with Alexandra would be more than he could deal with at times. But being focused on Sophia hadn't prevented Alexandra sneaking under his skin like an annoying itch. She was impossible to ignore.

Already she'd dented his resolve to remain unattached, yet he'd swear she wasn't out to snare him. Completely the opposite. Not once had she made a suggestive move or looked as though she wanted to jump his bones.

Which he admitted with regret was unusual. Losing his touch?

He should be grateful but his ego was taking a hit here. Didn't Alexandra think of him in any other way than as a doctor? And maybe as a father?

Sadness pulled at him, turning his heart over. A rare loneliness filled him. He'd always wanted a family of his own, and he now had one. But he'd presumed there'd also be a wife to love and cherish. Children should have two parents as well as siblings to rely on and share things with. Once he'd have given anything for that.

Sì. But that was before Lucy. Lucinda Blake had hurt him, sticking the knife in and turning it. Yet that was nothing compared to what she'd done to her daughter. Bile soured his mouth. At least he'd found Sophia and given her a loving home, away from the welfare system, away from an adoption by strangers. Sophia was his family. That was it in a nutshell. There was no room or energy for anyone else. Stunning human dynamo on heels or not.

He hunkered down beside the bed and reached for his girl's hand. 'Sophia, love, it's Babbo.'

Small brown eyes opened, stared at him as they watered up. 'Daddy, it hurts.'

Leaning over he kissed her forehead. 'I know, sweetheart. But you're getting better every minute.'

Then Alex sat on the other side of the bed and picked up Sophia's wrist. 'Hi, Sophia. I'm Alex. Can I count the beats in your arm?'

Mario struggled not to snatch Alexandra's hand away. For sure Sophia would turn in on herself again. Strangers worried and frightened her. A stranger touching her could send her screaming for a corner to hide in. But wonder of wonders his girl was studying this particular newcomer from under lowered eyelids without getting upset. Slowly she pressed a thumb into her mouth and nodded.

Alex continued, not at all disturbed by the heavy silence from his daughter or him. 'I'm a doctor like your daddy. I'm here to make you better. See?' She held up Sophia's arm. 'My finger's making sure you're all right on the inside.'

The thumb slid out. 'Alex?'

A smile softened Alexandra's face. 'Yes, Sophia?'

'Pretty.' The thumb slid back into her mouth.

Mario stared around, trying not to look at Alexandra. Sophia was wrong. Alexandra was not pretty, she was distractingly beautiful. And right now, when his eyes did finally rest on her, she looked even more ravishing as embarrassment flickered in her eyes, across her face and reddened her cheeks.

He had to get out of here. 'Rochelle, I'm going to the kitchen but I won't be long. Press that button if Sophia suddenly goes downhill.' Then stupidly threw over his shoulder, 'Coming, Alexandra?'

Stepping through the doorway he headed for the kitchenette, not waiting to see if Alexandra followed.

Alexandra did join him, trotting along, her short legs stretching out to keep up with him. 'What's the hurry?'

'The sooner I eat, the sooner I'll be back with Sophia.'

'Want me to organise the meal and call you when it's ready?'

A good idea, but everyone ran around after him and he just wasn't ready to let Alexandra do the same. 'Not at all. You asked if I cooked, now I get to show you.'

Her laughter tinkled between them. 'By heating a precooked casserole?'

'It's all in the way I heat it.'

'Right.'

Mario took her elbow and guided her into the tiny annexe the ward staff used for making hot drinks and heating meals. Under his fingers she shivered, and when he glanced down at her he saw confusion gleaming back at him. Suddenly he wanted to know things about her. 'Where did you grow up?'

'Auckland.' The word was flat. A big stop sign shadowed her eyes. Family problems?

'Sit.' He held a chair out for her at the table, then turned to the stove top. 'Any siblings?'

A sigh oozed across her lips. 'Persistent, aren't you?' Her hesitation dragged his attention from the pot he'd placed on an element to her face. All sorts of emotions scudded across her face, not one of them happy. 'No siblings. Dad died when I was twelve. Mother's a socialite who's very good raising horrendous amounts of money for charities. My stepfather is a stockbroker.' She sat and crossed her arms under her splendid breasts.

Mario's mouth dried as he stared at her. *Bella.* She might be tiny but she had all the necessary curves in the right places. That amazing auburn hair had started falling out of its restraints, shining where the light caught it. He itched to unhook the clip and splay those tresses across her shoulders, to burrow his fingers into the silkiness. When Alexandra wasn't annoying the hell out of him by trying to remind him she was in charge she was shoving him sideways with her physical attributes.

Jeez, Sophia's emergency must've rocked him more than he realised. He was not interested in Alexandra's physical attributes. *Liar.*

'You'll burn the casserole.' She nodded towards the cook top.

Spinning around he snatched up the pot and carefully stirred the contents before returning it to the ring, the gas turned low. What had she been saying about her family? 'That's good what your mother does. There's no shortage of people in need of help from charities.'

'Charity should begin at home.' Her fingers picked at non-existent fluff on her navy skirt.

Facing her again, he leaned against the bench, his hands lightly gripping the bench at each side of his hips. Her voice had been barely more than a whisper but he was sure he'd heard correctly. Why was the woman who liked to remain totally in control telling him this? Any moment now she'd wake up to what she'd said and back-pedal so damned fast she'd pass herself on the way. 'Are you saying you missed out on love and attention as you grew up?' As regret filled those beautiful eyes he knew he was right, and added softly, 'How can that be?' If parents weren't there for you, who was?

'I'm sorry. I don't know what came over me to be blathering on like that.' She was off the chair, heading towards the door. 'You know what? I'm not hungry after all.'

Mario reached the door first. Catching her arm, he turned her around and drew her back to the little table. 'Sit down,' he ordered quietly. 'You don't want to insult Kay by not eating her dinner, do you?'

Alexandra did not sit. She looked everywhere but at him. 'I don't think Kay meant for me to share it in the first place.'

The tension in her muscles under the palm of his hand tightened further. His fingers curled with the need to caress her. How would her skin feel under his fingertips? Taste as his tongue stroked her palm? He dropped her arm. This was off-the-page stuff.

Her chin moved as she swallowed. She glanced across at the pot, her nostrils sniffing the air like a retriever. 'It is hard to walk away from that delicious aroma.'

'Knew you'd see reason.' Hell, he should be yelling at her to go, leave him be. She annoyed him beyond comprehension when he just wanted peace and quiet to think about Sophia's latest asthma attack and what could be done about finding a better nanny.

'But I'm strong. I can resist,' and she was gone.

His jaw dropped as he stared at the empty doorway. God, the woman was definitely irritating. Not to mention downright difficult. Now he'd got the peace he craved. But his stomach soured at the realisation that the last thing he wanted was to eat alone.

At a little after six the next morning Alex popped her head around the door of Sophia's room and gasped at the sight of Mario sprawled full stretch on the bed, taking over most of the space, his daughter's thin arms wound around his chest and her head squashed into his shoulder. Alex felt hot tears prick the backs of her eyelids. This is what a father did. Protected, sheltered, cherished his precious child. A long-buried memory of her dad soothing her when she was feverish with measles rose before her eyes. Another of crying with a stubbed toe and Dad reading to her to calm her. Dad kissing her forehead. Mario seemed to know instinctively what Sophia needed from him. Probably learned it from his own father.

With a man like that at her side even she might manage to become an acceptable mother. Huh? Where'd that come from? There weren't going to be any children in her life. She'd had her chance and blown it. But an intangible something had her dreaming dreams that had long ago been dashed. Dreams of a loving husband, children, a house with a yard, real dogs to play with. Blast Mario. He'd unsettled her more than anything or anyone had since her baby died.

In sleep Mario's mouth had lost that jokey facade that he presented to everyone—except her. To her he always came up looking confident and with a 'don't fool with me, I'm as good as you' expression. Now he appeared vulnerable, sad even. But she suspected if his eyes were to pop open right now he'd instantly show nothing but a benign outlook on the world. It would be laced with his inner strength which came through in everything he did.

Except when he slept. This was an oddly intimate moment. Her feet took her closer to the bed. Slowly, carefully, she reached out. The back of her hand lightly grazed the stubble on his chin. A thrill of yearning and tenderness flooded her. A reminder of what she didn't have in her life. What she wanted.

Snatching her hand back she stepped away, and quietly placed a Harry and Bella book on the bedside cabinet. But still she was unable to tear her eyes away from Mario. Her finger tapped her bottom teeth. He seemed hell-bent on stirring up her days by not totally relinquishing his hold on her department and staff. At the same time he twisted and squeezed her heart so that an alien pull towards him caught her at the most unlikely times. Like in the middle of a patient appraisal. Like when she had to discuss meds with Kay. Like now.

Sprawled out as if he owned all the space, his long legs reached the end of the bed, his powerful thighs pushing into the mattress. Her teeth snapped shut on her fingertip. Those thighs sent heat waves rolling through her, thawing the cold corners of her heart, waking up that muscle-tightening need right at her core that had been dormant for far too long.

Dragging her gaze upwards over the masculine bump at the apex of those thighs to the flat plain of his stomach, the wide chest Sophia clung to. What would it be like to make love with Mario Forelli? Possibly life-changing. Definitely exciting. She imagined those thighs against hers, that chest pressing her breasts.

Oh, get over yourself. Nothing is going to happen with this man. He may be the most alluring male specimen she'd ever met but so what? He was firstly a colleague, secondly a colleague. End of story.

Backing quietly out of the room Alex bumped into someone and whipped around. 'Jenny, so sorry. I didn't want to wake Mario and Sophia.'

The night shift head nurse murmured, 'Sophia kept her dad awake most of the night.'

Heading down the ward Alex asked, 'Any other problems during the night?'

'No emergencies, but some patients didn't settle. Just enough to keep us on our toes and out of our cots,' Jenny replied.

'I'll leave Sophia until she wakes.' If Mario had had a sleepless night he wouldn't thank her later for disturbing either of them. 'I can sit with her while Mario grabs some breakfast.'

'You can tell Sophia one of your stories.'

'I brought in a book for her. Do you think she'll like it?'

Jenny stared at her. 'Every kid I've met loves hearing about Bella and Harry. Why wouldn't Sophia?'

'Why wouldn't Sophia what?' Mario appeared in the doorway to the nurses' office, looking dishevelled and grumpy. Stubble darkened his chin and dark curls fell into his eyes. 'Is there something I haven't been told?'

Alex felt her heart swell. Gone was the swagger, the sharp suit, the charming manner. This was a man who'd had little sleep. He looked good enough to eat. Not to mention very worried. 'Nothing's wrong with Sophia. We were talking about books. I was wondering if Sophia would like a copy of *Harry and Bella Go Fishing.*'

A cute smile lifted his tired mouth. His eyes twinkled wearily back at her. 'Stinky stuff? I didn't think she was ready to learn how to fish, but if you think so, then I guess I should be buying her a rod and reel.'

She chuckled. 'It's a children's storybook.'

'I figured as much. Written by the renowned Lexi Gast, I'll bet.'

'You know about my books?' Tongues had been wagging.

'First thing I heard about you when I started here. Everyone's so proud of what you've achieved with your stories. Apparently being a superb paediatrician doesn't compare. They're a dollar a dozen.'

'Everyone—' she waggled her forefingers in the air '—talks too much.' But she liked that they thought enough of her other career to endorse it so well.

'When do you find time to write and illustrate books?'

'During the weekends when I go out to my beach cottage. Or late at night when I can't sleep.'

'You obviously don't sleep much at all, then, if you've found the time to draw all those amazing illustrations.' Mario grinned. 'Yes, I've seen one of your books when Kay lent it to a little girl with bronchitis.'

This was embarrassing. It was one thing to receive

a compliment but quite another to have Mario raving on. 'I left a book by Sophia's bed.'

'Why don't you stop by and read it to her? When you're not busy being a doctor, that is.'

'Hopefully she'll be asleep that late at night.' Why did she get so sharp with him? It wasn't his fault she needed to deny her attraction for him. She tried for a softer tone. 'Though if you want a break for food or a shower I can sit with Sophia. If you're okay with that?'

'I definitely need to freshen up.' He rubbed his stomach, drawing her eyes to that part of his anatomy, making her mouth water. 'And eat something. So Sophia's all yours.' Then his eyes darkened. 'Maybe I should wait. She gets very upset if strangers are there when she wakes up.'

'She seemed okay with me last night. Let's try it. I can page you if you're needed.' Suddenly it seemed imperative that she be able to stay with Sophia, to be there when she woke. Like a test. *Can I get on with children other than as a doctor? Would I've been a good mother to Jordan?* Sophia hadn't turned away from her when she was frightened and stressed to the max, so it was possible she'd accept her presence this morning. And there were the dogs to talk about if things got a bit tense. 'Please.' She nearly reached out and gripped Mario's arm in her need to do this, but at the last moment kept her hand tight at her side.

Mario swallowed hard, nodded slowly. 'I'll go and have a shower first. If I haven't heard a peep from you, then I'll head down to the canteen for breakfast.'

Relief and something akin to happiness surged through Alex, making her almost dizzy. 'We'll be fine. You'll see.' She headed for Sophia's room before he could change his mind but hesitated inside the doorway.

'Oh, my gosh. Isn't she gorgeous?' Alex gazed down at the sleeping tot with her thumb jammed in her mouth and her dark curls falling across her brow.

'She's gorgeous because she's asleep and quiet and not panicking about anything.' Mario's voice was soft but Alex still spun around so fast it made her giddy.

She hadn't heard him following her. Two quick breaths. 'You're supposed to be heading to the showers.' *You're not supposed to have overheard me talking about your girl.*

'On my way.' But he didn't move, kept watching Sophia. A deep, slow sigh spilled across his bottom lip. 'She's going to be all right.'

Convincing himself? 'With you there for her how can she not be?'

'As long as she learns to forget the past. It's a terrible burden for one so little.'

'Want to tell me?' Alex whispered, afraid he might stop talking about this if he thought about where he was, who he was with.

With his hands jammed deep into his trouser pockets he continued watching Sophia as though she was the most precious child in the whole wide world. Which she was to him. 'I didn't know she existed until a year ago. Can you believe that?' Pain lined his words.

Shocked, Alex was stuck for words. How cruel could someone be? But of course she didn't know all the facts.

'Daddy?' Sophia's eyes flew open. 'Babbo,' she shrieked.

Instantly Mario was at his daughter's side, pulling her body against him. 'Hey, hey, little one, Daddy's here.'

Sophia curled into him and stuffed her thumb back

in her mouth. Her big brown eyes stared out at Alex as Mario's hand rubbed her back.

Alex picked up the chart to read the night's obs. 'I can see you're getting better, Sophia.' Guess she was wrong to think Sophia would be okay waking up to find her there.

The girl continued staring at her in that unnerving manner. Alex felt as though she was floundering. What did she say to a child, this child? No one had taught her how to behave around children. She managed fine with them as a doctor but now the right words or actions wouldn't come when she wanted to be more for this little one. She wanted to be a friend because the child had obviously missed out on so much in her short life. So what did she say? Or do? Her mind just would not come up with anything that wasn't trite. Was she more like her mother than she'd thought? Oh, no. Please no. She wanted to be loving, caring and fun, not remote and frigid. Like her dad, not her mother.

Mario kissed the head of curls tucked under his chin. 'She usually comes right fairly quickly, though she'll probably sleep a lot today.'

'We'll keep her in for a while yet. Unless you want to take her home and spend the day with her?' Alex asked.

'No, she's better off here. And I can carry on with my duties. I can't leave another round of surgery for you to deal with. I know you've got an oncology clinic this morning.'

'A small one, thank goodness.' Small meant fewer children with cancer on her turf.

'Dealing with those cases knocks you about a bit, doesn't it?'

A sigh huffed over Alex's bottom lip. 'Sometimes I wonder why I chose such a distressing specialty.'

'Because you want to help. Because you care.' Mario kissed Sophia's cheek. 'Hey, pumpkin, Alexandra's going to sit with you while Daddy's having a wash. Is that okay?'

Big brown eyes impaled Alex, full of caution but also recognition. 'Okay.'

Alex felt as though she'd been bestowed a huge honour. 'I've got a story to read you. Do you like dogs, Sophia?'

The little head didn't move.

Slipping her butt onto the bed Alex picked up the book and, opening on the first page, showed Sophia the drawing of two black schnauzers carrying fishing rods and a basket of bones. 'That's Harry.' She pointed to the slightly bigger dog.

'Harry,' Sophia repeated. 'Who's that?'

'Bella. She's carrying lunch. Leftover bones from the family's dinner.'

'I like chop bones.'

'Me too.' Alex settled closer and, bending her head nearer Sophia, began to read.

I could get to enjoy this. The book shook in her hands, her voice wobbled. *I could? Darned right, I could.*

Mario's feet were glued to the floor. He knew he should be grabbing the opportunity to shower and put on clean clothes, but he was riveted by the sight of Sophia snuggling up to Alexandra.

Sophia didn't do snuggling very often and certainly not with just anyone. Especially not with aloof dynamos. She had to have known them for a while first.

Bet Alexandra didn't nestle into a bed with a young child too often either. Who did she snuggle into bed with? Something akin to jealousy unfurled deep inside. What? He didn't like the idea of Alexandra in bed with another man? Since when? With her tiny frame and worry-filled eyes she did bring out the protective instinct within him but that had nothing to do with not wanting to imagine her with someone else.

Something was going on. Hell, he'd nearly told her about Lucy and the horrendous pain she'd caused, and that said something about his state of mind. Because—his shoulders rose and fell—because he didn't tell anyone what had happened. Apart from his family. He'd hardly have got away with turning up with a very young daughter and no explanation. It had been a year since he'd informed Mamma and Babbo that they had a granddaughter, and that little Sophia was going to need all the love they could give her plus some. The first months Sophia had been in his care had been excruciating. In the numerous phone calls back and forth between Nelson and Florence none of them talked about Lucy and why she'd done what she did. Especially not him, shutting anyone down who tried to raise the subject.

Yet now he blathered on to Alexandra about it. He'd barely started the sorry story but that was loads more than he'd ever let out before. His gaze stuck on her. Again he wanted to finger that hair. It shouldn't be pulled back off her face. Lying free over her shoulders would be much more delectable. But that wouldn't become the position of HOD. This woman tried hard to keep her distance from her staff, to make them remember every moment of the day she was in charge. And thankfully failed. Everyone knew their boss was marshmallow.

Mario wished the sweet smile she gave Sophia could be directed at him. Just then she raised one hand and scooped Sophia's curls back off her forehead and Sophia turned her cute little face and thanked Alexandra with her own sunny smile.

Mario's stomach crunched. Wow. For the first time since he'd known his daughter he'd seen her turn to another person who wasn't family, a person she'd only met the night before under frightening circumstances. Warmth slid through him, relaxed that part of him that constantly worried about Sophia. Who'd have believed it would be Alexandra who'd get through to his daughter? Two lost souls recognising something in each other?

What he didn't get was why Alexandra should be so lost. Everything she did seemed to turn to success.

'I don't believe it,' Gina whispered over his shoulder.

Raising his finger to his lips, Mario tipped his head in the direction of the nurses' station. 'Come on,' he whispered. 'We'll leave them to Harry and Bella.'

'Alex's reading her the dog story? But Sophia's afraid of dogs. Even seeing them on TV sends her screaming to you.' Gina sounded as perplexed as he felt.

'Apparently paper dogs are okay.' Did everyone know about Alexandra's books? Then the tantalising smell of warm cheese distracted him. 'Is that my breakfast?' He pointed to the bundle she carried in one hand.

Gina handed him the cloth-wrapped parcel. 'Straight from the oven. The boys wanted chocolate muffins for their lunch boxes so I threw in a batch of cheese ones for you.'

'Did I tell you you're the best sister?' Gina might have a load of her own problems but she still came through for him all the time. It might be selfish of him but he was grateful she hadn't followed the rest of the family to Italy.

'How many times have I heard you say that to any one of us?' Gina grinned at him.

A vision of Alexandra, her eyes brimming with longing for a close-knit family, snapped on in his head. She really didn't know what it was like to have people there for her. Even if she hadn't said as much it had been blatantly obvious in those sad eyes. He used to take his family for granted, but not since Sophia's arrival. With her fears about being left again stabbing at his heart he'd quickly realised how lucky he and his sisters were. Not once in their lives had they even thought they weren't special to their parents or their siblings.

'Hey.' He slung an arm around Gina and hauled her in against him. 'Thanks. For everything.'

Squeezing him back she pulled free. 'No problemo.'

See? Gina knew exactly what he'd been on about without any explanation needed. They were close, understood each other at a glance. That was family. That was the most important thing in life. Maybe Alexandra didn't have that. Nor would she be getting it from him or his.

Then Gina blew him apart. 'You should try to get to know Alex better, bring her close. She'd be perfect for you.'

Shock exploded through Mario at this traitorous statement from his sister. She should know better. She did know better. 'No,' he bellowed. 'No way.'

Gina smiled that infuriating know-it-all sister smile at him. 'Shh, you're disturbing the ward.'

'Stuff the ward. Where did you get that half-baked idea? Huh?'

'By watching you whenever Alex is within touching distance. You only have to hear her voice and you're on alert. And look at you. You never shout, especially at work, but what have you just done?'

'I am not shouting,' he shouted.

Kay popped her head out of her office. 'Everything all right here?'

Mario glared at Gina, then at Kay. 'Why wouldn't it be?'

He spun around and strode past both meddling women, intent on having breakfast, but as he passed, Kay quipped cheerfully, 'Gina's right. Alex is behaving the same way.'

Bollocks. Nothing, no one, in this world could distract that fierce woman from whatever held her attention at any given time. His shoes screeched when he whipped around to stare Kay down, put her in her place. 'I'm sure you have more important duties than delving into my personal life.'

Kay didn't even blanch. No, damn it, she winked, first at him, then at Gina, who laughed.

'You are so screwed, brother.'

'You— You—' He spluttered to a stop, threw his hands in the air. An image of Alexandra slapped against his mind. Alexandra walking with her head high and her back ramrod-straight, that mass of hair he had yet to see spilling free down her back plaited tight into her head, yet another whiter than white blouse a stark contrast to yet another navy suit. Deep inside him something further gave way, letting warmth into places that had been iced over since Lucy did the dirty to him. No!

Jerking his head around, his eyes clashed with his sister's knowing look. 'You're wrong,' he told her. *You have to be.*

He'd met Alexandra far too late to give her what she needed. He didn't have spare hours to wine and dine her. Sophia wasn't ready for siblings. His heart thumped once. In disappointment? Nah, couldn't be. He wasn't interested. *Trying to convince yourself? Trying too hard to prove Alexandra hasn't got under your skin? Into your psyche?*

Mario turned away, closed his eyes, concentrated on bringing up a picture of Sophia and only saw a small, auburn-haired firecracker of a woman standing glaring at him, daring him to step outside his comfort zone.

Hell. No way. He stormed down toward the staff bathroom, trying to outrun his mind, outrun that delectable, annoying image. Except already he was getting used to her, getting used to the fact that she didn't roll over to have her tummy scratched like every other female he came in contact with.

His steps slowed. Alexandra was being wonderful with his daughter, giving selflessly as she did with everyone. More importantly, Sophia hadn't spurned Alex. He'd never have believed that if he hadn't just seen the way they were cuddled up together. Perhaps Sophia was a better judge of character than her father. Maybe he'd got it all wrong. It wouldn't be the first time.

Lucy had told him she loved him, promised to marry him, then disappeared out of his life one night, never to return. The only thing she'd left behind was a note to say she'd couldn't live with him any more, that he never had enough time for her and that his family completely overwhelmed her.

She hadn't told him she was pregnant with his baby.

She didn't tell him she'd given Sophia up to the welfare system.

She'd been proof of how bad he was at reading women.

CHAPTER SIX

'HEY, AMELIA, HOW's that maths homework going? Solve those pesky problems?' Mario asked as he lifted the girl's notes from the end of her bed.

The redhead wrinkled her nose in disgust at him as only ten-year-olds could. 'It's too easy. I bet I get one hundred per cent.'

'Are you any good at chess?' Mario grinned at Amelia, while sadness gripped him for this kid who knew nothing about playing on the back lawn with a bat and ball. Seemed her parents were driven to make her a scholar, obviously missing the point that there was more to life than classrooms and lessons. Even their trip to Fiji had been to learn about the local flora and fauna, not to lie on the beach or swim with the fishes for fun. Unfortunately Amelia had found out the hard way about mosquitoes and the diseases they carried.

'The best. I beat Dr Linley yesterday.'

For a ten-year-old that seemed the wrong answer to Mario. But, 'You should ask Jackson to play against you. He's good.'

'I will.' Amelia stretched upright against her pillow. 'My temperature's still too high, but I got through the night without any convulsions, so I must be improving. Another blood test to check my CBC today?'

Mario grinned at this precocious child. 'You should be almost better by now. And yes, I'll arrange for the lab to take a sample this morning.' Replacing the notes he stepped around the bed. 'But first I have to check your lymph nodes.'

'They've gone down a lot since yesterday,' his patient informed him.

Feeling under her chin and then around her armpits, Mario had to agree. 'Okay, missy, any nausea after breakfast?'

She shook her head at him. 'No, only disgust at what they gave me.'

Alexandra stepped over from the next bed, shaking her head in amusement. 'Seriously, Amelia, if you're going to be a doctor you'll have to get used to hospital food.' She lifted gut-twisting eyes to him. 'Are you still giving her acetaminophen?'

'Fluids and drugs for today at least. Then if the CBC has returned to near normal I'll dispense with both and think about sending Amelia home.'

'Do I have to go?' Rank disappointment contorted Amelia's face. 'My parents will make me go back to school straightaway.'

'I thought you liked school,' Mario said.

'Not really.' Her mouth screwed up. 'It's kind of lonely. I wish I could do correspondence school.'

And that wouldn't be lonely? 'How about I give you a note to stay at home until after the school holidays. No point going back for one week.' Mario wanted to cut this girl some slack, to make her life a little easier. But in reality there was little or nothing he could do for her once she left his care, which, he reminded himself, was only medical.

Amelia nodded. 'That would work. Thank you, Mario.'

'Jeez,' Alexandra whispered as they turned away. 'I bet she's the school nerd.'

'Yep, and all because her parents have an agenda that doesn't include being a normal kid,' Mario replied quietly as they moved toward the next patient.

'I hate it when parents push their needs onto their children. It's so unfair. What if Amelia wants to be a carpenter?' Her words were underlined with knowledge.

'Is that what you wanted to be?' Mario smiled at the thought of this tiny woman wielding a hammer, and knew she was perfectly capable of it, or anything she set her mind to.

'No, a cabaret singer. My father and I used to push the furniture back against the walls and dance up and down the lounge, singing at the top of our lungs. Mother hated the racket and was forever telling Dad off for encouraging me. She thought I should be studying hard to keep ahead of the crowd. Dad ignored her most of the time, though I did sometimes overhear fierce arguments about it late at night when they thought I was asleep.'

'So you can sing too?' He didn't keep the astonishment out of his voice.

She grinned, a happy, totally unfazed grin. 'I'm tone deaf.'

He laughed with relief. She wasn't perfect after all. 'There ended your cabaret aspirations.'

'No way. It was huge fun.'

'What about the dancing? Do a good Moulin Rouge dancer impersonation by any chance?'

She blinked endearingly at him. 'With legs shorter than a chicken's? I don't think so.'

His gaze dropped to those shapely pins. Nothing

chicken-like about them. His mouth dried as he imagined them wrapped around his waist. What was going on here? When he raised his eyes to her face she was grinning, oblivious to his thoughts.

'But I do squawk in the shower sometimes, just for the hell of it.'

'Remind me not to visit when you're in the shower, then.' The words spewed off his tongue with no help from his brain. If he didn't know better he'd have said he was flirting with her, but he wasn't. He couldn't be. No way.

She tripped over her tiny feet as her head flipped further back and her focus clashed with his. 'I can't imagine why you'd be visiting me at all. Let alone me being in the shower at the time.' The words trailed off as her face turned scarlet and her tongue slipped across her bottom lip.

Catching her arm to steady her, Mario's fingertips burned as though touching a hotplate. She *was* a hotplate. A darned hot lady in a tiny, and hot, package. Jerking away he stepped sideways, putting space, air, something, between them.

She stared at him from enormous eyes. 'Oh. Right. Sorry, slip of the tongue.'

Could her brain be as fried as his? Miss Cool turned Miss Hot? He'd swear she wasn't playing games, doubted she knew how to. But she'd managed to fire up the dormant hormones from every corner of his body. Including south of his belt. Especially south of his belt.

He wanted her. Badly.

He couldn't have her. Not now, not ever.

Tell that to his body.

Shut down or take a cold shower.

The threat didn't work.

Mario spun around, charged into the next room and snatched up Gemma Lewis's file to stare blindly at the words and figures dancing before him. Figures. As in numbers, not in a small, compact feminine frame on heels that brought the top of her head to little past his chest. Chest. Breasts. Those sumptuous curves that filled out the front of her blouse drove him crazy with desire whenever he looked at them. Which was why he didn't look. Yeah? Okay, not often.

'Hey, Mario, I'm glad you dropped by while I'm here. I've got some questions for you about Gemma's bowel problems.'

What? Who? His neck cracked as he jerked his head up. Ahh. Judge Lewis. 'Brandon. No court session this morning?' *Concentrate, boyo, or you're in deep doo-doos. This is one man you can't fool with medical burble while you're getting everything else back under control.*

'Ten-thirty is my first showdown. Court staff are holding a meeting at the moment regarding pay rates so I grabbed the opportunity to see Gemma.' Brandon stood and shrugged his expensive suit jacket into a more comfortable position. The guy would look more at ease in gumboots and jeans, but Mario wasn't fooled. Brandon had a reputation for being tough on offenders and no one liked coming up on trial in his court. He also spent every spare moment he had here with his daughter, reading stories, playing games. An all-round good guy.

'Fire away with your concerns about Gemma.'

As Mario delved into a conversation about Gemma's continual health issues the heat slowly dissipated from his muscles. The gripping sexual tension eased off enough to stop distracting him. When he'd finished answering Brandon's numerous questions he headed for the coffee maker and a moment's solitude.

Away from the temptation of Alexandra Prendergast. Despite all his rehashing of his previous relationship with Lucy his body—and his brain—refused to ignore Alexandra.

Infuriating. Sexy. Beguiling.

Alex curled up on the couch, her hands clamped around a steaming mug of strawberry tea. Wind-driven rain pelted the windows. Down below streetlights looked all skewed through the torrential downpour which was also putting her off going out to get something for dinner. It would have to be eggs on toast—if there were any eggs in the fridge. Who knew? She hadn't made it to the supermarket all week.

Sipping the fruity tea she wondered where the days had gone. They'd flashed past in a flurry of patients, emergencies, staffing problems and the new specialist. Not to mention his little girl. It seemed only yesterday that she'd returned to the hospital, and been hit with the presence of Mario Forelli.

The buzz of her intercom was loud in the quiet apartment. Puzzled she went to answer it. 'Hello.'

And got the shock of her life. 'Alexandra, it's Mario. Can I come up?'

Blink. Mario? Here? Why? 'Sure.' At least she wasn't singing in the shower. She pressed the button to let him into the building. Her watch showed nine-thirty. Late to be calling on someone, especially someone he didn't know outside of work. Did he want to clear the air over that ridiculous moment on the ward? She'd prefer he didn't bother. Less said the better.

Her heart sank. Maybe there was a different, worse

explanation. Something might have happened to Sophia. Another attack? But she'd been fine two hours ago when Alex had left. Mario had intended taking her home when he finished up for the day. Anyway, he wouldn't be here if Sophia had become seriously ill again.

Her doorbell rang at the exact moment Alex looked down at her trackpants and sloppy sweatshirt. 'Oh, heck. He can't see me looking like this. He'll be laughing for weeks.'

Buzz, buzz. 'Alexandra?'

'Why can't he call me Alex?' Admittedly, when Mario said 'Alexandra' it rolled off his tongue like melted chocolate to make her think of sweet treats and hot kisses. Which was bad, bad, bad. She certainly wasn't about to be anything sweet for Mr Forelli, despite the image of a shower and them both naked under the steaming jets of water. He certainly wouldn't want to spend any more time with her than he had to so to heck with her appearance.

But when she opened the door and Mario stepped past her without blinking she decided she could've been decked out in a Madonna bra and he wouldn't have noticed.

Odd how exasperating that was.

Then he handed her a bottle of cabernet merlot. 'Thank you for spending so much time with Sophia in hospital, and for the book you gave her. She's smitten with Harry and Bella. They now sleep under her pillow.' He held out a plastic container in his other hand. 'Another casserole. This time from Averill.'

'Th-thanks. I think.' Alex took the wine and the container from his outstretched hands.

Without being asked Mario slipped out of his coat

and hung it on the coat rack, removing a packet of rice from a pocket. 'I thought we could share the food. Have you eaten?'

'Not yet. I was trying to decide what to order from my favourite restaurant over the road. Hard to dredge up enthusiasm when I'd have to go out in that weather to get it. Anyway, it seems too late to bother now.'

He shook his head like a cat shakes its paws after walking through a puddle and droplets of water flew through the air. 'The casserole will fill the gaps. Right, so where you keep your glasses?'

Make yourself at home, why don't you? Alex headed for her designer kitchen that was mostly used to boil water for tea or coffee.

'Sorry, am I being too forward?' Mario was so close behind her he must be almost stepping on her heels. She could sense him, smell his aftershave, feel his breath as he talked. And he read minds. Hers, at least. 'If you want me to disappear, then you've only got to say so. But—'

When he didn't finish the sentence she turned to face him and leaned against the bench for strength as he grinned a slow-burn kind of grin. The sort of grin that had probably got him anything and everything he'd wanted throughout his life. Continuing in a low drawl that reached inside her to tease and twist her nerve endings and spin her blood along her veins at a break-neck speed, he told her, 'But I really don't want to go out in that rain again just yet. Not until I've had a taste of that wine.'

'Here I was thinking you'd brought it for me.' When his mouth curved further upward she moved her head from side to side, trying to negate the sudden warmth swamping her. When that didn't work she abruptly changed the conversation to something less provocative. 'What was so important to tell me that brought you out in the rain?' Stepping sideways she endeavoured to put some space between them, backing across the kitchen.

He stepped into the space. 'I really did want to thank you for being so good with Sophia. You have no idea how wonderful it was to see her relax with someone who was a virtual stranger only a couple of days ago.'

Back two more steps. 'You could've told me all that at work any time of the day.'

He filled the space again. 'Too little effort. You might've thought me a bit offhand.'

'Never.' The next backward step brought her up against the centre counter. Watching Mario as he studied her in return her mouth dried. Deep inside her muscles rolled like an ocean swell. This man was something else. And he knew it. But for once that didn't bother her. He was open and honest. What she saw she suspected would be what she got.

Huh? Like she was going there? This man was a colleague, not a hot date. He'd come to thank her for a small kindness, not to strip her clothes off in a passionate frenzy. He'd brought wine and casserole, not champagne and lobster.

'Alexandra.' He towered above her, his chin almost touching his chest as he looked down at her.

Whipping sideways, she managed to avoid touching him anywhere on that mouth-watering body. 'Why don't you call me Alex like everyone else?' *And don't you dare say you're not like everyone else.*

'You have a pretty name. Why not use it?'

'Only my family uses my full name.' And then it never sounds pretty—or hot.

'Is that why you don't like me doing it?' Could he see

right into her head with those eyes that at the moment were the colour of polished pewter, eyes that saw everything, and made her knees knock in a very unladylike manner? Did he know the turmoil going on inside her usually calm body? He probably did. He'd be experienced with women, would be able to read their every nuance. Whereas her? When it came to reading men she was still at kindergarten.

Then he added, 'Alex isn't as feminine as Alexandra.' Slowly his gaze slid off her and he peered around the kitchen. 'You could cook up a storm in here. I'm drooling just thinking about it.'

Feminine. Drooling. The bottle she'd forgotten she held clanked on the marble centre bench. In her other hand the container of food suddenly felt very heavy. For the first time she noticed how wide Mario's mouth was, how full his lips. Bet his kisses were magic.

Bang. The heavy container slid from her lifeless fingers, slammed onto the bench, slid towards the edge. They both reached for it at the same instant. Their hands met, grabbed and saved the meal. Alex tugged free immediately, shaking away the heat that had just poured through her fingers, up her arm, turning her neck red, her insides liquid.

Mario hurriedly stepped away, his chest rising and falling rapidly. When she dared look at him he had thrust his hands deep in his trouser pockets and turned to stare out the window into the black night.

Her tongue licked her lips while her brain tried to get past that stupid mistake of dropping the container, then trying to snatch it up again. A mistake that shouldn't mean anything, shouldn't have her heart thumping like a dog's wagging tail on the floor, shouldn't have her suddenly wishing Mario had come to visit her as a woman he might like to get to know and not as a colleague he had to thank for going that little bit extra with his daughter.

Suddenly she needed wine, not strawberry tea. The cupboard door thwacked back as she reached for two red wine glasses.

'Here, let me.' Mario saved the glasses from her trembling fingers and placed them on the bench.

He seemed so calm, so unperturbed by that touch. But of course he would be. Experienced, remember? She must've imagined his quick breaths a moment ago, while *her* body hadn't returned to its normal half-dead slumber. Her heart rate hadn't quietened down to its usual pace, nor had her knees suddenly found their supportive strength. *Guess if you haven't been running at all and then you try a marathon this is how your body would react—completely out of sorts with itself.* And face it, she hadn't been running, or kissing, for a very long time.

The crack and twist of the bottle top sounded loud between them. The heady scent of a full-bodied red wafted through the air as he poured the nectar into the glasses. And her body remained out of sorts with itself.

Handing her a glass Mario raised his. *'Salute.'*

'Cheers,' and moistening her parched mouth, she savoured the flavour of sun-kissed vines and dark grapes on her tongue. It still didn't fix what ailed her body. Only an hour in her bed with Mario would do that.

Heading for the lounge she sank onto the couch, while Mario followed and crossed to the big windows. Peering out and down, he noted, 'Not much of a view tonight. I wonder how much snow is being dumped up on Mount Arthur right now.'

'Enough to make the hills look pretty tomorrow

when the sun pushes through. I can never get enough of gazing at the snow-clad mountains and hills. My first winter here was a novelty. Still is.' Verbal diarrhoea now? 'I wasn't so keen on the frosty mornings when the washing froze solid on the line. Don't do a lot of hanging washing these days, living in an apartment.' Definitely driveling!

'Ever been up the mountain to play in the snow?' Mario crossed to sit on the other end of the couch.

'No, I've never ventured up there.' Not a place to go alone. Who would she throw snowballs at?

'If Sophia hadn't taken sick I'd planned on taking her and her cousins up there for some snow fights this weekend.'

'Sounds like fun.' The wistful thread in her tone embarrassed her but before she could redress it Mario was talking again.

'Heaps of fun. The kids have a fabulous time.'

She loved how when he talked of something he enjoyed his eyes widened and the pewter colour gleamed out at the world. His generous mouth twitched and she had to restrain from reaching to run a finger over his lips. Gulp. Had she reverted to a teenager sometime over this past week? Or had it happened en route from the States, this strange change in her? Since when did she want to touch a man she worked with? Not just touch him, but caress him intimately, to get up close and very personal.

When Alexandra remembered to relax as she talked her face lit up, her eyes shone and her soft mouth curved into a delicious smile lifting her cheeks. She was lovely when she forgot to be serious, when she didn't recall that a lot of tiny Nelsonians relied on her to make them better. *She's lovely all the time. Even in a snitch, when her eyes screw up tight and her mouth flatlines.*

She was telling him, 'I dropped in to see Liz after work, hoping to catch up, but she wasn't home. I hope everything's all right.'

'She and Kevin probably went out for a meal.'

'Guess you're right. Making the most of the time they've got left before junior makes his or her appearance.' Again that wistful tone coloured her voice.

So Miss Prendergast would like kids of her own? Why wouldn't she? Any woman who was as good as she was with her young patients must yearn to be a parent herself. A fleeting image of a string of gorgeous little Alexandras stopped his hand holding the glass inches from his mouth. His tongue stuck to the roof of his mouth. Oh, hell.

She was taking a sip of wine, rolling the liquid across her tongue, savouring the ripe, rich flavour. 'This is good. Thank you, though it wasn't necessary.'

She unfolded her legs from under her butt and stood, stretching onto her toes. Doing more damage to his overenthused hormones. Pink trackpants and sweatshirt. Who'd have believed it? Miss Power-dresser with her array of fitted suits and crisp white blouses did ultra-casual and shapeless?

Forget shapeless. Definitely not shapeless. What the clothes didn't have her curvy body more than made up for. Her pert breasts shaped the front of her sweatshirt perfectly, pushing out the fabric in an enticing manner that had him longing to touch them. Her thighs were taut under the clinging fabric of her pants, sending his blood southward. Again.

This was so not a good look. He needed to go, get away from her before he did something dumb like make a pass at her. How would that go down? Actually, he knew the answer to that. He might as well hand her the axe to take his head off right now. Imagine turning up on the ward on Monday if he'd made a move on her. Frosty would feel warm compared to how she'd treat him then.

Why had he come? It had to be one of the dumbest things he'd done in a very long time.

No, it wasn't. He'd come because she was the first person who wasn't family to get through to Sophia so he'd wanted to thank her personally in a personal setting. Not on the ward, surrounded by sick children and busy nurses and doctors. A film played across his mind. Sophia gripping *Harry and Bella Go Fishing* in her tiny fist, refusing to let go of the book even in sleep. Sophia refusing to lie down until he'd read that story twice more. This was why he'd come to the lion's den. And now he realised he'd made a mistake. He should've stayed away.

'I guess at this late hour you're past wanting to eat?' She sounded hesitant.

Hello? He was thinking sex and she was talking food? A laugh tore through him. Miss Prendergast was so grounding. She might even be good for him. 'I'm never past eating.'

Maybe he hadn't made a mistake. Maybe this was the way to finally knock away those last few barriers Alexandra kept firmly in place between them. He stood and headed for the kitchen. 'Which is the pot drawer?'

Alex rubbed her very full tummy. 'What a delicious dinner. In the past week I've discovered I work with at least two very good cooks.' They'd eaten all the beef casserole, right down to the last delicious scrape of sauce, and every grain of rice Mario had steamed.

The wine had long gone, and now they were back sitting side by side on her couch, their shoulders almost but not quite touching. Empty coffee cups sat on the low table in front of them. The rain had stopped beating at her window, letting the lights below shine through.

'I'm glad you didn't chuck me out when I took over your kitchen.' Mario's hand rubbed lightly down his thigh, drawing her eyes to follow the movement. Right down from the top of his leg to his knee.

'You're more than welcome to it. I hardly get the bench dirty.'

'And thank you for an adult evening. Talk that's got nothing to do with learning to tie shoelaces, a drink that's about enjoyment and a dining companion who's not picking through everything on her plate looking for hidden nasties.'

'Sophia's not a good eater?'

'We're getting there. When I first brought her home I could count on one hand what food she liked, none of it healthy.' His fingers began to play a slow beat on his knee.

Alex stirred, straightening away from his warmth and biting down on the urge to cover those fingers with hers, to lift his hand and place soft butterfly kisses on his palm. His hand was large, would easily cup her cheek and chin. If he did that would he rub his thumb across her hungry lips? Swallow. There'd be no stopping her taking his thumb into her mouth if he did.

'Alexandra.' His voice was almost a whisper, caressing and seductive.

If you touch me, caress me with your fingers as your

voice is already doing, then there'll be no such thing as
quiet. I'll combust, noisily.

'Look at me, Alexandra.' Her name rolled off his
tongue, sending shivers of need through her body, goos-
ing her skin.

Twisting around on her bottom she slowly looked
up into his strong face and met his opaque gaze, saw
desire flickering back at her. Her own need expanded,
reached every place in her body, became sweet heat at
her centre. She began leaning forward, closer to the
source of this desire, closer to the body that had held
her fascinated since she'd first set eyes on him. Nearer
and nearer to the man who'd woken her up from a long
drought of feeling anything close to desire. These sensations rippling through her body were like flames following an oxygen source. 'Mario,' she murmured through
parched lips.

She spread her hands on that marvellous, expansive
chest filling her vision. Felt the hard muscle underneath his shirt, knew the moment he quivered. Tipped
her head back. All the better to see him. He was unbelievably beautiful.

His hands slipped up her arms, and he caught her elbows to draw her even nearer so that her breasts brushed
against him. She tugged her hands from between them,
placed them on his waist. Felt his pager begin to vibrate.

Simultaneously her cell phone rang.

They sprang apart like guilty teens, Mario mutter-
ing, 'Great timing.'

'Something must be going down on our ward. Hello?'
Alex jammed the phone against her ear and turned away
to hide the deep blush staining her cheeks. If the phone
had rung moments later they mightn't have had the
strength to stop and answer it.

Whoa. She should be grateful. She had so very nearly kissed Mario Forelli. And that surely would've been the biggest mistake of her career. No, not quite, but right up there.

'Alex, it's Jenny. You're needed in PICU. Liz is having her baby.'

'Emergency in PICU,' Mario read from his pager simultaneously.

Alex's head whirled. 'But she's not due for weeks, months.' No wonder Liz hadn't been at home. 'We're on our way,' she told Jenny, her skin lifting in chilly bumps.

Alex snapped her phone shut. 'Liz is in labour.' Rushing to her bedroom she grabbed a warm jacket and track shoes, then returned to the lounge to find Mario had switched off lights and was checking the gas was off. 'I'll meet you there. Poor Liz must be beside herself with worry. This is awful.'

'Come with me. I'll drop you home later.' His eyes were full of concern and something else she didn't understand.

Alex slipped her hand into the crook of his arm. 'Let's go.'

CHAPTER SEVEN

'LIZ, GO TAKE a shower and grab some sleep.' Alex draped an arm around her friend's waist. 'I'll stay here with Chloe until you get back. That's a promise.'

'She's so little. How can she possibly survive?' Liz remained still, her voice wooden as she stared down at her fifteen-hour-old daughter in the humidicrib. Tubes and lines snaked in every direction, supplying oxygen, fluids and antibiotics. Monitors blinked and beeped. Bili lights to help lower the high bilirubin making Chloe's skin yellow, eerily highlighted the wee girl's predicament. The patch protecting her eyes added to the terrifying picture.

On Liz's other side Kevin looked as stunned and disbelieving as his wife sounded. 'She has to, Lizzie. She has to.'

Alex stepped around the incubator and checked the oxygen flow. 'Liz, on a medical level you know she can. And yes, I know.' She sucked in an unsteady breath and ignored the fear for these two now making itself known in her chest. 'You're fully aware of all the things that can go wrong. I'm sure your heads are crammed with every scenario imaginable. Today you two are Mum and Dad, not doctors.' It must be dreadful for them. That precious little bundle held their hearts in her tiny,

tiny hands. 'Hang on to the fact that babies thirty-two weeks premature do survive, more often than not with great outcomes.'

The eyes Liz turned on her were bleak. 'Gosh, Alex, how do we do that? It's so different standing on this side of the equation. You have no idea.'

Alex's mouth soured. Her eyes misted. *Oh, yes, I do. More than you can imagine. Worse, I know how it is when your baby dies.* But Chloe wasn't going to die. No way was Liz going to know the anguish of losing her child. *Not on my watch.* Her hands were shaking. She stuffed them deep into the pockets of her white coat, at the same time thrusting away a mental picture of holding Jordan swathed in a tiny blanket as she pleaded for him to start breathing. *Come on, get a grip. This is about Liz and Kevin and their daughter, not you and your son.*

She sucked in air and winced as it touched the hole in her molar. 'I'm Chloe's doctor, sure, not her mum, so I'm not going through what you are. But believe me, I'll be doing everything within my power to help her.'

'As will I,' said a familiar, deep voice from somewhere above her shoulder. 'Chloe's got the A-team on her side.'

'Besides, Chloe's already shown us she's a fighter.' Alex risked a quick glance up at Mario and instantly wished she hadn't. He was watching her with a disturbing intensity that seemed to bore right inside to the place she kept her innermost secrets. She dropped her head, blinking away the telltale moisture at the corners of her eyes. Hopefully Mario hadn't noticed that. But somehow she knew he had. The man never missed anything.

Kevin cleared his throat. 'What about RDS? That's always a possibility with her underdeveloped lungs.'

Alex had answered questions from Kevin and Liz about respiratory distress syndrome during the night, knew that they were well aware of the facts behind this condition common in prem babies. But they were beside themselves with worry and would ask the same questions again and again over the coming days and weeks. 'We're giving Chloe surfactant to help her lungs cope. As you know it keeps the air sacs open and allows better oxygen and carbon dioxide exchange.'

'I want to cuddle her to me,' Liz cried. 'It's not right that she can't be held by her mum and dad. She must be so lonely in there after all these months growing inside me.'

A shudder rocked Alex. That cry from Liz's heart was something she understood all too well. A hand touched hers briefly. Mario.

Kevin pulled Liz into his arms and rocked her, whispering into her ear, his face filled with distress.

Alex stepped aside, busying herself with checking monitors again, trying to ignore the ache in her own heart. Mario also moved away and joined her, flicking through Chloe's charts.

'Are you all right?' he murmured close to her ear.

Alex snapped straight. 'Of course. Why shouldn't I be? Apart from hurting for my friends, that is.' *Please don't ask me anything personal right now.*

His eyes met hers, locked gazes. 'You seem rattled.'

I am. Very. Think of something to say to divert that compassionate voice. Mario could so easily be the undoing of her carefully put-together life if she made a wrong move, said the wrong thing. 'Just as Liz and Kevin are struggling with being parents and not doctors with Chloe, I'm struggling with treating their child compared to a total stranger's baby. Not that I'll do anything different or with more effort, but I feel as though this case is different. I want Liz and Kevin to walk out of here one day with Chloe in their arms, heading for a bright future.'

Those pewter eyes didn't look away. But Mario's mouth softened into the warmest of smiles. 'I know exactly what you mean. It is harder when you know the patient's family personally. It shouldn't be but that's the way of it.'

Phew. She'd got away with shifting Mario's focus off her. Not that she hadn't been telling the truth, just not all the truth. 'Right, let's see if we can get these two to take a wee break and freshen themselves up.'

Mario headed for Sophia's room. Why did he get the feeling Alexandra was hiding something from him? From all of them? Was it to do with that sadness that often crept into her eyes when she thought no one was watching? He'd seen it a few times since they'd raced in here last night to work with Chloe. Back there when she'd told Liz she'd do anything possible for Chloe it had been as though she felt something more than a doctor did, felt a connection with Chloe's parents. Or did she just want—or was it need?—to prove she could save Chloe? Save Chloe unscathed from all the things that could go wrong?

'Hi, Daddy. Look what Alex gave me.' Sophia held up a different Harry and Bella book to the first one she'd received.

'Who's a lucky girl?'

'Me. Where's Alex?' Sophia leaned sideways in the bed to peer past him. 'Isn't she coming to see me?'

Mario chuckled. He'd thought Sophia would be thrilled so see him, but seems Alex ranked higher in the popularity stakes. 'Alexandra's looking after a very sick baby, but I'm sure she'll say hello later on. Do you want me to read you the new book?'

Sophia's head swung left, then right, left, then right, her eyes very solemn. 'Nope.'

Oh, okay. 'What about a game of snakes and ladders? Bet you can't beat me.'

'Course I can. Where's the board gone?' She leaned so far over the edge of the bed looking for it Mario grabbed her before she fell headfirst onto the floor.

'Careful, munchkins.' Mario settled down to entertain his daughter but his mind stayed with Alexandra and what might've upset her earlier.

Five games later he was none the wiser, but at least Sophia had settled down to rest. Her obs were good and if he hadn't needed to stay on overnight for Chloe he'd have taken her home. But Sophia was better off being here where he could spend time with her than going to Gina's and being trailed around rugby fields getting cold and tired. Besides, it was unfair to ask Gina to look after his child yet again.

Mario ran the back of his hand down his cheek. If only he had time to take the boys off her hands for a whole weekend and send her away to her girlfriend's for a night. But he barely managed to cope with his own hectic schedule. Which reminded him he needed to get to the supermarket or he and Sophia would be doing a starve when they got home. Maybe he could squeeze that in first thing tomorrow morning.

'Alex.' Sophia sat up, her eyes wide with excitement. 'Have you come to read me a story?'

'If that's what you want, little one.' Alex sat on the opposite side of the bed to him and smiled sweetly at his girl.

He didn't know whether to be amused or grateful that Sophia seemed to have taken such a shine to Alex. Not even with him had she been so accepting so fast. He'd never heard her ask anyone else to do something for her. Not even Gina. 'Blimey,' he muttered. Hopefully this wouldn't cause problems further down the track.

A warm hand covered his. 'You're her dad—you get to do all the hard work. I'm a novelty at the moment, probably because of the stories I write and she loves to hear.' Alexandra's fingers curled over his hand, squeezed lightly, then were withdrawn.

So she read his mind now? Scary thought. He'd have to be careful to only think about work when she was near. Looking at her, he found her smile now directed in his direction. 'So I'm not obsolete?' he asked in jest.

Instantly she turned serious. 'Your daughter adores you. She frets when she hasn't seen you for half an hour. She's always talking about you to anyone who'll listen.' An impish glint filtered into those fascinating eyes. 'Not that any of us stand around listening to all that nonsense.'

'It's good having my own cheerleader.'

Her gaze dipped. 'It must be.'

So she wasn't happy being alone. What was her history? She'd not mentioned a husband or children in any of their conversations. Not that Alexandra was good at talking about herself. Far from it. She lived alone now but had she ever been married? Did she have a family that now lived with an ex-partner? He knew so little about her and yet felt so at ease with her that he'd even spilled the beans about Sophia and Lucy.

'Daddy, are you going to listen to the story with us?' Sophia's high-pitched voice reminded him who was meant to be the centre of attention here.

Heat stole into Alexandra's cheeks. 'I think your daddy's got things to do.'

'Like lick my wounds after being thrashed at snakes and ladders.' Mario stood reluctantly. He'd love to stay and watch over Sophia and Alexandra, but he'd only make Alexandra uncomfortable. 'I'm going to look in on Chloe. I'll be back soon, sweetheart.'

'Okay, Daddy.'

Mario strode briskly out of the room trying to work out which of those two females he was calling sweetheart.

'How many times has Chloe stopped breathing?' Alexandra asked.

Mario read back to Jackson the measure of drug he was about to administer to his tiny patient, then turned to her. 'She's having regular apnoeic episodes, hence the methylanthine drug.'

'And I thought she was doing so well.' Alexandra stared down at the very small baby. 'Any sign of brady-cardia with the apnoea?'

'Unfortunately, yes. And hypoxia.'

Alexandra's mouth tightened. 'Liz and Kevin must be beside themselves.'

Kay told her, 'It took some persuasion from Mario to get them to go downstairs for a coffee break together. They need time out.'

Mario expanded, 'They're exhausted. But who can blame them for wanting to be with Chloe every minute of the day and night. I know I wouldn't be able to leave her if she was mine.'

Jackson's pager interrupted. 'Looks like I'm needed elsewhere. I'll be back as soon as possible.'

Alexandra told him, 'Take a break when you can. I'll stay with Chloe for a while.'

'Me too,' Mario added, and settled on a chair by the humidicrib to take yet another reading of Chloe's respiration movements, heart rate and pulse oximetry.

Sadness tugged at him for this girl and her parents. He thought he had problems with Sophia but at least she was healthy most of the time, except for the asthma. One day she'd overcome her past and then hopefully her ailment would clear up—a little at least.

Alexandra stood on the other side of the humidicrib, gazing at Chloe. 'It's so frightening how fragile life is.'

'Chloe's not giving up though.' The resp movements were slow.

'Amazing how hard these babies fight to survive. As though they understand what they have to do.' Alexandra sighed. 'I guess parents never really expect something like this to happen to their child.'

He filled in Chloe's chart and hooked it on the end of the crib. 'We're all optimists. Then again, I never knew I was going to be a dad so no worrying for me.' His lungs filled on a long intake of air. 'What about you? Ever think about having children?'

Her hands slipped into her coat pockets, her face clouded and those green eyes turned the shade of a forest. Still watching Chloe her chest rose and fell. 'No, I'm never having a family. I'm single for starters.'

'You wouldn't have one on your own?' Why was he pressing her? What made him want to know when they could never be more than friends at the most?

'I don't think that's fair on a kid. Anyway, I'm too involved in my career to give a child all the attention it needs, with or without a partner. I've got goals to attain.' But the eyes that finally met his didn't look so positive about that being a great idea.

If Alexandra thought she'd convinced him her career was all important she could think again. He was reluctant to ask any more though. She'd likely tell him to mind his own business. One thing he had learned was to approach her slowly, slowly. But the devil in him just had to add, 'Never say never. I can see you with a brood of your own, reading bedtime stories about dogs and dancing in the lounge to off-key singing.'

She shrugged. 'You really haven't heard my—' she waggled her forefingers in the air '—singing.'

He laughed. 'Apparently that's a good thing.' At least she hadn't bitten his head off. If only he knew how to banish that longing lurking in her eyes every time she looked at Chloe. Not for a second did he believe she didn't want children. Her career was an excuse. Every time he learned something new about Alexandra he found another brick wall to knock down.

Mathew stood in the doorway of Chloe's room as though blocking entrance to Mario and Alex. 'Go, the pair of you. Get some sleep. We've got it covered here.'

'Yes, and take Sophia out for some fun.' Jenny added her two cents' worth.

Alex looked at Mario and chuckled. 'Guess we've got our marching orders, then.' It was two weeks since Chloe's sudden and early birth and the tiny girl was doing well. Mathew had stepped in when needed to give them a break over that time.

Mario shrugged those wide shoulders that drove her to distraction. 'You are the boss.'

'You know what? I'm happy to step aside for a few hours.' And she had an idea of how to fill in her afternoon. She'd go out to her beach cottage and walk along the water's edge for an hour or so. But as she studied the man who'd kept her lying awake most of the few hours she'd got to spend in bed since that Friday two weeks ago when they'd nearly kissed, loneliness caught at her. That unforgettable near kiss had rattled her. If the hospital hadn't phoned at that moment would they've only kissed? Or would they've ended up in her enormous bed making hot love?

Sometime since then Alex had come to her senses. She worked with Mario. She was his HOD and had to keep the upper hand with him for those times that would arise when she had to speak sharply to him. Besides, he already had a messed-up child to sort out. He didn't need a messed-up woman as well.

So, no hot kisses, no lovemaking. Which didn't make her happy at all. No, now she felt deprived of something special, wonderful, exciting. Heaven knew there wasn't a lot of excitement in her life these days. Only medical emergencies and they left her drained and worried, not light and happy, or exhilarated.

Today in body-snug jeans and a thick navy jersey covered by a woodsman jacket he was still as mouth-watering as he had been in dress trousers and shirt that night. Face it, Mario Forelli was a turn-on, and probably would be even if he appeared in Spiderman's costume.

She heard him asking, 'What do you think you'll do with your enforced time off?'

Hide out at the cottage and try to find the Alex of a few weeks ago. The one who remained in control of her emotions no matter what. The one who definitely did not get excited over a man. Not any man. This man. Her mind and body could do with some quiet time. Her mouth had other ideas. 'Going for a walk on the beach. Want to join me?'

'I'd have to bring Sophia.'

'I expect you to.' Sophia's presence would act as a buffer between them. Just in case things heated up again. Which they mustn't.

'So where are we going? Tahunanui Beach or further afield?'

'Ruby Bay.' When Mario's eyes scrunched in question she enlightened him. 'I've got a cottage right on the beach that I inherited from my father. It's where we all came every summer for a month over Christmas and New Year.' It's where she learned to swim. Where dad used to take her fishing in his small alloy boat or put out a net overnight. The place where, weather permitting, all meals were outdoors and all the neighbours gathered round at the end of the day to share a barbecue.

Her mother had been against her inheriting the cottage but Alex had stood up to her mother, fighting for what she wanted. In a way her dad was still there for her, sometimes making her smile, sometimes causing her to weep.

'Bet you have lots of wonderful memories from then,' Mario said.

'Absolutely. It's my favourite place in the whole wide world for that reason.' It had also been her bolthole over the years. It was the place she'd grieved after losing her son. This was where she'd tried to come to terms with Jonty's defection. The cottage and the beach were filled with sweet and harsh memories. Those memories were what her life was made of. The good and the bad. The losses. The things that had crushed her heart so badly she'd never risk sharing it again—no matter how tempting a man like Mario was. No one was worth that intense, excruciating pain. She'd never survive the relentless, burning agony another time. No point even considering it could be different next time. She'd thought that once and learned how wrong she could be. All her life she'd lost those she loved—one way or another.

'Then you're lucky to have such a place.'

Mario stood at the bay window, breathing in the relaxing atmosphere of Alexandra's special place. Surprising that she'd invited him here, really. This was showing him more about her than any conversation had so far in their relationship.

You don't have a relationship with Alexandra. Other than a working one. And one meal and an almost kiss at her apartment.

On the beach young boys kicked a ball along the wet sand, shouting as though the world was deaf, and having a wonderful time. If only Sophia felt confident enough to join in but as usual she'd stayed glued to his side when they'd ventured to the bottom of the lawn. Now she was sitting at the table reading a Harry and Bella book. Whatever, she was happy and so was he. 'This is so magical.' He sighed. 'I feel like I've been transported to another planet. The hospital and all those sick youngsters seem a long way away.'

Alexandra paused her lunch preparations and came to stand beside him, instantly distracting him with the scent of the outdoors overlaid with pine smoke from her woodchippy that burned in the corner of the room. 'It has that effect on me too.'

Turning slightly he watched, fascinated, as her mouth curved into a gentle smile. Without thought he leaned closer, traced a finger along that smile, felt her lips stretch wider and open slightly under his finger-tip, drawing him into her heat. Her tongue touched, licked. He tried backing away, couldn't, his feet apparently nailed to the floor.

That unfinished kiss lay between them. It was in her shy glances when she didn't think he was watching her, in her guarded smiles. It fizzed along his veins, fried his brain. It would not be denied any longer. So tilting her head up with his hand under her chin he lowered his mouth to hers. Where this would take them he didn't know, didn't question. He just had to have his fill of her. Now. He tasted her. And couldn't get enough. His tongue pressed into her mouth, further, deeper. Savouring, exploring. The world spun away, leaving him alone with Alexandra. Nothing, no one else, mattered.

Her hands laced at the back of his neck, pulled him down to her level, brought him closer to her warm body. Her return kiss was fierce, laden with sweetness, passion, desire. For him. He breathed her in—her feminineness, her hair, her skin, her heated body.

He had to touch that skin, to feel her under his palms. A quick tug freed her shirt from her trousers. Sliding his hands underneath the soft fabric he touched her silky skin. Hot. Smooth. Tormenting.

She moaned against his mouth.

He hardened instantly. A fast takeoff. They'd only moments ago been talking, not kissing. And now he was ready. Throbbing. For Alexandra. He needed to sink into her. To know all of her.

His mouth still possessing hers, Mario lifted Alexandra up against him, pressed her body the length of his. His arousal pushed against her stomach.

Another moan escaped her lips. He opened his eyes to watch the emotions flickering across her face. Desire matching his had turned the green of her eyes deeper, darker, so that he felt he was tipping into bottomless pools.

Alexandra turned her head, and stilled. 'Mario,' she whispered.

His mouth followed hers, intent on furthering the kiss. *Don't interrupt me. Not now. I can't bear to stop.*

'Mario.' Her tone became insistent.

His eyes nearly disappeared as he struggled to look around while continuing to kiss this goddess. All those dreams since that night in her apartment hadn't come close to the real thing. Kissing Alexandra was now his favourite pastime.

'We have an audience.'

Blink. Who? Slowly he pulled his mouth away from those delicious lips. Great. The boys with the ball were now lined up at the edge of the lawn, laughing and pointing up to him and Alexandra. 'Go away,' he muttered without rancour. Sliding Alexandra down his body he settled her on her feet, wishing he never had to let her go again. Which was a very good reason to drop his hands to his sides.

Alexandra's laugh was rough, filled with tension and wonder as she turned away. 'I'd better finish getting lunch ready before Sophia starts wanting food.'

How did she do that? Walk away from that kiss? Wasn't she burning up inside? He was. He'd swear she felt the same.

'Mario, where's Sophia?'

'What?' A bucket of icy water poured over his head wouldn't have dampened his ardour as quickly. 'Sophia?' He spun to gape at the empty chair at the table. 'Sophia.'

'It's all right. She won't have gone far.'

He shook Alexandra's hand from his arm. 'She's probably hiding. It's what she does when no one's looking. And then she has an asthma attack.' What if she'd witnessed him kissing Alexandra? That would send her crawling into a dark corner to avoid him.

'Mario,' Alexandra spoke sharply. 'Calm down. We'll find her. She can't have gone far in that time.'

Alex watched Mario stride across to the door leading outside, tossing angry words over his shoulder at her. 'Easy for you to say. You don't what it's like to lose your child.'

'Yes, I do,' she whispered. Pain laced her words. Gone was the desire from moments ago. Replaced with a hideous memory. *Yes, Mario, I know exactly what it's like to lose your child, to hold them close when there's no hope. To scream silently with pain, with despair, longing. To be filled with love and words that you can no longer give. To fall into an abyss where pain was shelved until you peeked out into reality again. I know the reality more than you do.*

Outside Mario yelled at the top of his lungs, 'Sophia, where are you?'

Alex watched him go, saw him peering down the beach, left, then right, left, then right, undecided on which direction to take. Thank goodness he hadn't heard her secret. They might be getting close, too close, but no way did she want to share Jordan with him.

'Sophia, stop hiding and come to Daddy.'

Mario's urgency snapped Alex out of her own pain. 'I'll search inside the cottage first.'

Again he didn't hear her, but she made sure he heard her a minute later when she ran to the door and yelled, 'Mario, it's all right. Sophia's inside.'

He spun around to race back to the cottage. 'Where? Is she safe?' Mario sped past her, his eyes wild with worry. 'Where's my girl? I need to see her, to make sure nothing's wrong.'

'She's having fun.'

Reaching for his hand Alex pulled him to a halt. 'She's as happy as any child can be.' She put her finger to her lips. 'Shh. Come quietly.' And she led him down the hall to her studio.

At the doorway she stopped and pushed Mario through so he could see Sophia. The little girl had climbed up onto the stool in front of the artist's pad where a nearly completed page for a new Harry and Bella book was pinned to a board. She was leaning forward, her little face scrunched up as her finger traced along the words she was trying to enunciate.

'"Bella is hiding Harry's far—"' She leaned so close she surely couldn't see the word. 'Bella is hiding something.' Lifting her head she used her forefinger to carefully outline the pencilled picture of Bella digging a hole under a lemon tree.

Mario turned back to Alex. Relief glittered out at her. 'I'm sorry. I guess I overreacted but—' He stopped, swiped a hand through his hair. 'She terrifies me whenever she disappears. I don't know what's going on in her mind. She underlines the fact I haven't a clue what happened in the years she wasn't mine that makes her do this.'

'Stay with her, read the words aloud.' She wanted to reach out and hold him, smooth away that pain twisting his mouth, staining his eyes. She even took a step towards him, stopped when he tensed up, as unyielding as a concrete wall. Despite what he'd just told her he didn't want her touch, wouldn't let her share the burden.

Well, that was something she understood, something they had in common. 'I'll get you a coffee.'

'Her mother didn't want her.' His eyes filled with fury and agony. 'How could any woman not want her child? Lucy carried Sophia in her belly for nine months. Wouldn't she have formed a bond with her baby in that time?'

Yes. Definitely. Alex opened her mouth in response, but closed it as his flood of words continued.

'I never would've believed Lucy incapable of loving Sophia. She wasn't always affectionate or outwardly loving with me but I thought that was because of a fairly loveless upbringing. But shouldn't that have made her try harder? Then when she chose not to bring Sophia up shouldn't she have brought my daughter to me? She never gave me a chance.'

'She still didn't tell you even when Sophia was born?'

'Nope. Not a word. One day we were living in Florence, planning for our wedding, the next she'd gone. It wasn't until I bumped into a colleague from our training days in London and was shunned that I finally learned I'd apparently tossed Lucy out when she became pregnant to me, and that Lucy had died. I immediately began searching for my child.'

'The six missing months in your CV.'

'No.' Mario turned to head down the hall. Getting away from little ears? 'Those happened once I'd found her in foster care about to be adopted by her most recent carers. She'd been through the mill—her mother's desertion, three different foster families, the asthma, nightmares about God knows what. All by the time she was three.'

A quick glance at Sophia showed her still totally engrossed in Harry and Bella so Alex followed Mario, quietly, letting him vent, barely able to comprehend Sophia's life. Totally unable to understand the girl's mother. What Lucy'd done was unforgivable. In the kitchen she reached for the coffee maker and spooned in grinds.

Mario had plonked his butt down on a bar stool by the kitchen island. 'I met Lucy while specialising in London. She'd gone over there to study at Oxford and we were at the same party one night. Hit it off immediately. But when I moved to Florence things started going awry. Lucy swore my family didn't like her and that they made her life difficult whenever she came to stay with me.' Lifting a glass of water he drank deeply. 'She might've had a point. There are a lot of Forellis, and we can be full-on, especially when you're an only child from small-town New Zealand.'

Alex gulped. She'd do well to remember that. Just in case she ever got to meet any of Mario's family. 'I would've said it could be daunting for an only child from the middle of anywhere.'

'You're probably right.' His smile flicked on, then off. 'I still believed we were in love and getting married once she'd finished her degree, until the day she sent me a note saying she was going to the Caribbean and I wasn't invited. Oh, and that she wouldn't be back. End of engagement.'

'That's harsh.' And cruel. Mario must've been devastated. If the way he was with Sophia was anything to go by he loved deeply, and having Lucy dump him so carelessly would've been dreadful for him.

'To say the least.' His throat worked as he swallowed more water. 'Then one day I learned Lucy had been pregnant and I began tracking her down, only to find she'd died while scuba diving and that there was a child back in England. Finally after a lot of door knocking, welfare desk thumping and a DNA test I found Sophia.'

'It's unbelievable. I don't understand why Lucy wouldn't tell you about your daughter. Especially as it seems she didn't want her. She'd have known your family would've taken Sophia in, surely?' Mind-boggling, to say the least. Alex shook her head. She'd never have deserted her child, no matter what the situation.

'Probably payback for how she perceived they'd treated her. Looking back I can see that Lucy was very selfish. She did tell me she wasn't ready to have a family but I thought she'd get past that when we were married. Seems I was wrong. But I have to take some of the blame, I guess. I was working all hours, putting my career before all else.'

'Sophia's lucky you found her. You might think she's got a way to go but she loves you so much. That's a huge step forward considering everything she must've been through.'

'I quit my job in Florence and spent months living near to Sophia, letting her get used to me before I pulled her out of her foster home she'd got used to and brought her halfway around the world to start yet again.'

'She's very lucky you found her,' Alex repeated.

'Yeah,' he sighed. Suddenly out of words? 'Yeah. I hope so.'

'Give yourself time.'

'Now you know why my life is totally dedicated to Sophia. I could've returned to Florence and my relatives but she'd have had to learn Italian and that wasn't fair when she was barely coping with almost everything going on in her life. Also I had a fantastic childhood here and wanted that for my child. It seemed the right thing to do, still does most of the time.' His smile was ironic. 'That's why I'm living and working in Nelson. And why I'm living the life of a monk.'

Alex felt her eyebrows rising. Too much information? Or a warning? 'So monks kiss, then?'

That beautiful mouth twitched, then a full-on laugh rumbled over his bottom lip. 'Touché.'

CHAPTER EIGHT

ALEX FINISHED HER last patient round and handed over to the night shift. 'Hope you have a quiet night,' she told Jenny, barely swallowing a yawn. Chloe had taken a backward step at two in the morning and Alex hadn't been home since.

'Not a chance.' The nurse dropped files into a tray. 'Mario's still in theatre operating on the little girl with post meningitis complications.'

Alex winced. 'He's amputating Bee Harvey's legs now? I thought that was scheduled for this morning.' It should've been done and the child back on the ward by now.

'Theatre got taken over with an emergency. An MVA with multiple casualties which threw the operating list into complete disarray. Mario opted to operate late rather than put the girl's parents through any more distress waiting for it to happen another day.' Jenny dropped onto her chair. 'Not that they're going to feel any better about the operation's outcome. Their beloved little girl is still going to have to learn to walk all over again.'

Alex nibbled her lip. 'Absolutely ghastly for them all. I can't even begin to imagine what they must be going through.' But she did know how Mario would be feeling when he finally finished his hideous task and spoke to the parents. He'd be gutted, sad and, being a dad, terrified of something similar ever happening to Sophia. 'So who's looking after Sophia, do you know?'

'Mario left her in the hospital day care centre until Gina could pick her up when she finished her shift. How those two manage their families is beyond me. Which reminds me, there's pasta in the fridge for Mario to take home that one of the ED nurses dropped in.'

A smile broke through Alex's gloom. 'That guy doesn't know how lucky he is with all of you running around after him.'

'Who wouldn't want to spoil that gorgeous little girl?' When Alex raised her eyebrows at that Jenny laughed. 'Yeah, all right. He's so hot no one's going to let him go hungry. In more ways than one—except he's not obliging any of the girls in that way.'

At least she'd had his kisses. And so far hadn't paid for it with food. 'Call me if anything crops up, especially if Chloe's condition changes. I'm not expecting trouble. Which is a very silly thing to have said. I'll drop in to check on her later tonight.' She crossed her fingers against her thigh. 'And leave Mario alone tonight unless it's about his patient.'

'Will do, though I think he's sleeping over anyway to be here for Bee.' Jenny made a note for the staff and then lifted the ringing phone.

Alex's next stop was her office. Except she didn't know why. Unless she could blame this strange restlessness gripping her, making her feel as though she'd been blindfolded and turned around and around until she was dizzy. Right now she should be driving home, stopping to get something for dinner on the way. Not sitting in her office staring round like she'd never seen this room before. Another ward round before she left? Looking for Mario? Seeing if he'd finished in theatre yet?

Go home, Alex. Be sensible.

It was the 'be sensible' that did it, sending her delving into the phone book and looking up a restaurant to order an appropriate dinner for two to eat in a staff kitchenette off the ward at whatever hour Mario felt it safe to leave his wee patient.

The 'be sensible' tolling in her head had her warring with herself about how it was time to stop being sensible about absolutely everything in her life. It was all very well to play life safe, not endanger her heart, nor leap into a relationship without checking the water, but sometimes, just sometimes, it was very tempting to step outside the boundaries she'd erected around her life.

Define *sometimes*.

I've never done it before.

Umm, what about that very short fling last year?

A blip on an otherwise clean and clear lifestyle.

Boring.

What's to say Mario won't turn out to be a similar blip?

Because I don't want him to.

Alex gasped at her own honesty. But unfortunately Mario had pretty much said there was no room for anyone else in his life while he concentrated on getting Sophia through to adulthood.

'Asian Gardens Restaurant. How can I help?'

Alex gave up arguing with herself and ordered dinner for two to be ready for her to collect in an hour's time. She was no different to all the other females working in the hospital.

* * *

Mario rolled his shoulders, stretched his back, then tossed his cap into the basket, and patted his rumbling stomach. 'Quiet.'

Bee Harvey lay in recovery, slowly being brought round to a drug controlled, semi-comatose state. It was too soon for reality.

Reality: a world where her legs below her knees were gone. At six years old it seemed preposterous what she was facing. She'd already been through hell. The meningitis had taken its toll, leaving her thin, fragile and at risk of more rampant infections. What he'd done to her, for her, broke his heart. Right now he loathed his job. All very well to say someone had to do it. He hadn't met a doctor yet who'd say they were happy to amputate a child's legs—no matter what the circumstances.

Wandering into recovery he stood for a quiet moment, watching over Bee as she fought waking up. He wanted her to stay asleep, unaware of her future. Realistically, at her age it would take some time for the full force of her operation to hit home. But it would hit hard one day. No avoiding that. Especially once she was ready to join her friends, return to school, to go to birthday parties, play sport. At least she had good, caring parents to help her through it all. With a bit of luck thrown in her head space wouldn't be screwed.

'Her obs are good,' the nurse assigned to Bee told him.

He nodded, resisting the urge to lean over and kiss the child's forehead. Just. An image slipped into his mind of Sophia looking totally bewildered when he first took her away from her foster home. Instantly he wanted to be at home, holding his girl.

But there'd be no going home tonight. He was staying here, ready at a moment's notice if something went wrong for Bee. He might lie down on the hard cot and close his eyes, he might even doze off, but he'd be on full alert if he was needed.

Slowly he headed for the washroom where he tossed his soiled scrubs into a laundry basket and pulled on a clean set. He wrenched a tap on full force, splashed cold water over his face, trying to sluice the ache and grit from his eyes and mouth. Shaking his head he leaned forward, his hands gripping the basin, and stared into the mirror before him.

A weary man stared back. A man with a million questions about his life zipping out of those cool, cloudy eyes. Almost a stranger. When had he got so exhausted, so unsure of what he was doing with his life? Bringing Sophia home had been the right thing to do and he didn't regret that at all.

In doing so he'd dropped his ambition to be at the top of the world of paediatrics and surprisingly that hadn't been as hard as he'd expected. The career he'd always dreamt of, had worked hard for. The career that had destroyed his relationship with Lucy, and what he'd wanted more than anything up until a year ago when he'd learned he was a father.

He'd also given up any hope of more family of his own, of a wife or partner to share the highs and lows with. At least he had until Alexandra Prendergast arrived in his life.

All his certainty turned to dust in his mouth. Now he glimpsed something he might want to grab for the future, to hold on to and cherish. A life, a family, a woman who tipped him upside down with a word. With a kiss.

Cupping his hands, he filled them with water to pour

over his head, letting it trickle down his cheeks, his neck, into his clothes. It didn't take away the fog in his skull, didn't provide answers to all the questions pestering him non-stop. Pulling in a lungful of air he headed for the ward.

'How did Bee's surgery go?' Alex looked up from the nurses' computer as Mario approached. Heck, the guy's eyes were dull with exhaustion. His shoulders had dropped and his walk was slow. He needed taking care of. Someone to prepare him a hot bath and give him a massage. Make a meal and pour a glass of his favourite red wine.

'Straightforward. Poor little tyke.' A yawn stretched that delicious mouth.

Alex gulped at the closeness of that wide chest. If she leaned ever so slightly sideways she could lay her cheek against it and hear his heart beating and know his strength. She jerked the other way, and nearly tipped off the chair.

'Easy.' Mario caught her arm, helped her regain her balance.

Blushing profusely she straightened her back, looked along the ward to avoid meeting his all-seeing gaze. 'Thanks,' she muttered, and rapidly changed the subject. 'You could ask me to sleep over.' Heat flamed in her cheeks. Not what she meant at all.

His fingers slashed through his wet hair. 'I could.' Then he smiled. '*Grazie*. But I'm fine, really.'

Standing, Alex touched his arm lightly. 'Come with me.'

'What now? Another patient you want me to see? Chloe?'

Shaking her head, she repeated, 'Come with me,'

and headed towards the kitchenette. If only she had an oven in her office, then this could've been a more intimate moment.

He didn't immediately follow her. *Do I have to grab him and haul his body down the ward? Or should I bring the meal to him at the nurses' station?* Suddenly her certainty that she'd been doing the right thing for Mario evaporated. Doubt at her ability to read men and their needs reared up. Why couldn't he just have done as she'd asked?

'Where are you taking me?' Mario spoke from directly behind her.

Phew. Her mouth relaxed into a wide smile. 'Wait and see.' When she turned into the kitchenette she glanced over her shoulder and saw relief fill his eyes. 'Relax, this isn't about a patient.'

Mario closed the door behind them. Shutting work out for a short while? His shoulder leaned into the wall, his feet crossed at the ankles. And he sniffed the air. 'Please tell me you've got food in here.'

Placing plates and cutlery on the table Alex said, 'I hope you like Thai.'

'Bring it on.' He stared at her, his mouth relaxing at last. 'You're serious, aren't you?'

She began removing containers from a heated bag and opening lids. 'Phad Thai, chicken green curry, prawn fried rice, beef salad, fish cakes.'

'This is a banquet. Who else is joining us?' He pushed off the wall and held a chair out for her.

'I tried to cover all the options.' Looking at the mountain of food on the tiny table she shook her head. She'd gone overboard, as bad as the girls who brought in casseroles for him. 'I guess the night shift will make short work of what we don't eat.'

Mario took a seat beside her. Not opposite, but next to her. Picking up a spoon he hesitated and looked at her. 'Thank you. I need this. The food, the distraction from Bee, your company.'

'I know.' At least she knew about the first two, but her company? That was a surprise. 'It's been a grim day for you.'

Leaning closer his mouth brushed her lips. 'Yeah, but it's looking up.'

Warmth stole through her and she pressed her mouth against his. His lips curved tantalisingly against hers before he pulled away.

'At the risk of insulting you I think I'd better eat. If I continue that kiss, then this food will get cold. And anyone could barge in on us at any moment. I don't think you'd like your staff seeing you kiss one of your specialists.' The smile didn't falter, and the warmth in his eyes grew, letting her know he wasn't trying to avoid her, just keeping their places at work in order.

Picking up a fork Alex began filling her plate with a little bit of everything. She really would've liked more of that kiss. Even here at work where they could be interrupted. She'd have dealt with it. Surprise caught her. Yes, she would've. Definitely stepping outside her safety net.

The first mouthful of curry sent exotic flavours bursting through her mouth. 'Oh, yes, that's so delicious.' When she glanced at Mario he was staring at her, a smile on his beautiful mouth. 'What?'

He swallowed. Leaned over and kissed her cheek. 'This is great.' Then he concentrated on eating, filling his plate twice.

Voices, hurrying footsteps, laughter from the ward, filtered through into the kitchen, wrapping round them, making it unnecessary to talk, letting them be comfortable with each other.

Alex had no idea where this was going, or if there even was anything between her and Mario, but she didn't care. For once she was happy to let whatever it was play out in its own good time.

Except she'd give an arm to kiss Mario again. Just thinking it made the air sizzle. She'd swear she heard the crackle of sparks as she watched this intriguing man doing something as simple as enjoying a meal. Except it wasn't simple. Every time they were together without the benefit of other people to keep them on the straight and narrow Alex knew this deep pull in her belly. A longing, a need, that would not be denied. No matter how crazy the notion might seem to her 'sensible' side she wanted Mario. Not just his kiss but all of him—his skin against her body, his hands stroking, exploring her. His arousal pressing into her, entering her.

The door opened and Jenny sauntered in. 'Nice for some.' She nodded at the remaining food, carefully avoiding looking at Alex's hand near Mario's. 'Mario, Bee is back in her room. Her temp is slightly elevated, and she's restless.'

Shoving his chair back, Mario unwound his frame and stood. 'I'll be right there.' He began clearing the table, rinsing his plate in the sink. 'I'll give her more pain relief and keep her sedated for the night.'

'Leave those.' Alex took a container out of his hands. 'Go and see to your patient. Jenny, tell everyone to help themselves to what's left.'

At the door Mario turned back. 'Go home and take a break, Alexandra. The ward doesn't need both of us dropping with exhaustion.'

'Yes, sir.' But she smiled. And went home.

* * *

Mario turned off the motor and sat for a moment, letting the cold night air sharpen his mind. Was he about to make a huge mistake? Through the windscreen he studied the stars but they had no answers for him. He'd have to rely on his gut instinct.

And that said, *Run*.

But he'd never been a coward.

Out on the roadside he hesitated again. When Alexandra had brought dinner in for him two nights ago he'd had to admit he'd been humbled at her thoughtfulness. Since then he'd tormented himself with questions about why she'd done that. Because she was a kind woman? Because she was treating him specially? The second idea suited him better. And fitted in with that sizzling moment that would've led to another hot kiss if Jenny hadn't burst in on them.

He looked up at the apartment block towering above him. Lights from Alexandra's lounge shone bright against the dark of the rest of the building. Unable to sleep? It was past midnight and she should be tucked up in dreamland.

So should he. But the dreams he'd have would be X-rated and only serve to wind him ever tighter. And he'd only shared a kiss with her. Alexandra was something else. Which was a problem because he couldn't imagine not getting to know her better—in every way possible.

He tossed the keys in the air, caught them, tossed them, caught them. Pushed them into his pocket and strode to the entrance of the apartment building. Lifting the speaker phone he pressed the button.

'Hello?' Wariness croaked out at him.

'Alexandra, it's me, Mario. I know it's late but I

would like to see you.' *I'd like to hold you, kiss you, make love to you.* Swallowing hard in a hopeless attempt to squash down the lump of need blocking his throat he waited. Surely she'd tell him to get lost. At this hour who could blame her?

Buzz. The lock clicked. One quick push and he was inside, striding for the lift, which took him to the top floor all too quickly.

And there she was, standing in her doorway, wearing another shapeless tracksuit, her feet covered with fluffy socks, her hair floating around her shoulders.

It was the hair that did it. He'd spent days and nights wondering how that thick auburn hair would look when set free of its usual constraints. Shining waves tumbled around her face, highlighting her elfin features, framing those pull-him-in eyes.

Words deserted him. His fingers slid down her hair, then through the curls, lifting strands, inhaling the lemony scent of her shampoo. Heat pooled in his gut. Expanded his chest. Sent his blood south.

'Mario?' Alexandra whispered.

'Shh.' His arms encompassed her, brought her lithe frame against his bigger one. So delicate, yet not fragile. Lifting her against him he stepped into her apartment and kicked the door shut with a resounding clunk.

Those big green eyes got bigger as they filled with desire. For him. That sensual mouth curved wickedly, tantalisingly. Dainty hands slid around his neck and fixed her body firmly to his. Any last shred of restraint disappeared.

How had they got down the hall to the dining room so quickly? Dining room? They needed a bedroom. The woman in his arms stood on the tops of his shoes and stretched as tall as she could to fix her lips to his. Sweet hell, she tasted of—woman. Hot woman. Alexandra. A groan ripped through him, across his lips into their kiss.

Bedroom. Now. Dining room? Table. Ah-ha. He walked them across the carpet up to the enormous, highly polished Rimu table. Backing Alexandra against the edge he held her tight while his mouth devoured hers. Her tongue darted across his bottom lip. His belly cramped as the desire increased, winding tighter and tighter until he was about to explode.

Alexandra shuffled her bottom against the table. Her fingers were working his belt and buckle, his zip. And then his manhood was free, sliding against the warm flesh of her palms. Jerking his mouth away from hers he tried to gain some control. His chest rose and fell sharply as he hauled air into his lungs. 'Alex? We need to slow down.'

She blinked, smiled fast and hot and so sexy. 'We do?'

'Okay, maybe not,' he croaked. 'You're sure about this?' If she wasn't he was in big trouble.

'Yes.' That beautiful mouth kissed a trail over his chin, around his neck to his ear. Her teeth bit his ear-lobe, sending him past stopping. Reaching between them he was stunned to find her lower half already naked. When had that happened?

In his arms Alexandra was turning her back to him, bending so that her buttocks pushed back against his erection. Leaning forward over the table her hands searching between his legs, finding him, squeezing gently, rolling his balls carefully between finger and thumb.

'Wait,' he managed to gasp. 'Condom.' He groped in his pocket for his wallet, hoping the condom hadn't fallen out over the months since he'd put it there. Haste made getting it on difficult but finally he managed and reached for her moist nub, rubbed long and slow.

Almost instantly her back arched as she shuddered against his hand. Quick, sharp pants and she was guiding him into her. Mario gasped at the wet heat enveloping his shaft. And then the sensations blasting through him took over and he ascended the pinnacle to fall over the edge. With Alexandra.

Alex twisted her head on the pillow and in the weak light from the hallway she studied the man lying next to her as warmth and laughter bubbled along her veins. Amazing. The man was amazing. So big, yet incredibly tender. 'Hey,' she whispered. 'How're you doing over there?'

'Couldn't be better.' He rolled onto his side and draped an arm over her waist, pulled her closer, kissed the top of her head, making her feel unusually cherished.

Snuggling closer, her lips tracked a line down his chest to his bellybutton where her tongue made slick circles. She'd made love with Mario. Twice. And each time had been better than she could've ever imagined. Not because it had been a while, but because he'd made her feel like a goddess in the way he touched her body with his hands, his tongue, his eyes.

Tension squeezed her. Thank goodness that in the heat of the moment she hadn't tossed her sweatshirt off in the full glare of the dining room lights. Then she'd be answering some difficult questions right about now. Just as well that in here the sheets covered her stomach and breasts. When Mario had tried to tug them away from her she played shy. Guilt at that was fleeting. Tonight was not the time to be telling Mario her life story. That time might never come. It was hard to show anyone her vulnerable side, especially after Jonty hadn't taken her seriously, had accused her of dramatising everything.

'Hello, Alexandra, where've you gone?' His fingers stroked her spine. 'You've left me.'

Perceptive, huh? 'Just languishing in the afterglow.'

Deep in his chest she heard the rumble of his laugh begin. 'I'm not a rocket.'

'You certainly take off on a hurry.'

'That—' he tapped her nose with a forefinger '—is your fault for being so desirable. It would've been a sin to have ignored you.' His lips brushed her forehead. 'You're one hot lady, Alexandra Prendergast.'

As her name slid off his tongue like warm syrup Alex stretched her legs towards the bottom of the bed, luxuriating in being so close to him, in the feel of a man beside her, his hip touching hers, his thigh against her leg. This was something she didn't have in her life, and until now hadn't realised was missing. With the few other men she'd slept with over the years she'd always wanted her bed back to herself once they'd finished having sex. But tonight she wanted to tie Mario to the mattress, keep him there to have her wicked way with him whenever the fancy grabbed her. Even better would be to wake up beside him in the morning. Scary.

As though he'd read her mind he sat up and swung his legs over the edge of the bed. 'I'd better be going home. It wouldn't do for someone from work seeing me leaving here in the morning.'

Disappointment throbbed loud in her ears. She hadn't finished with him. Would she ever be? 'The odds on that happening are small.'

'You want to risk it? Really? I know I don't.'

Feeling at a disadvantage lying flat on her back while

Mario gazed down at her she hurriedly slid up the bed to lean against the headboard, making sure the sheet didn't slip below her breasts. 'I guess that depends on where this is going.'

'Which brings us to why I turned up here tonight. Let me get my clothes first.'

Watching him stride out of her bedroom a sinking feeling of impending loss overtook all other emotions, dampening the warmth of sexual release, shutting down her hope that she and Mario might find a way to have a relationship and still work well together. Not wanting to hear him say this had been a mistake, especially while she lay in her rumpled bed that he'd help destroy, she leapt out of bed and grabbed her robe. Slipping into it she followed him down the hall.

Tugging his shirt over his head and smoothing it down that broad expanse of chest he looked thoughtful. Too thoughtful.

The thumping of her heart slowed. Two hours ago she hadn't believed there was a hope in hell she'd ever make love with Mario. Now she didn't want to lose the opportunity to do it again. The words to stall him, hold off whatever he was about to say, snagged around the lump in her throat. Her hands twined the belt of her robe round and round, wove it through her fingers.

Mario stepped in front of her, reached for her hands. 'I'd like to have an affair with you.'

CHAPTER NINE

As ALEXANDRA'S EYES widened in surprise Mario cursed under his breath. How was that for finesse? Blunt didn't begin to describe it. But he'd been nervous. So totally out of character. But this was Alexandra and she did strange things to him. He kept holding her hands, could feel her trembling. 'I'm sorry. That didn't come out how I wanted it to.'

'You d-don't want an affair?' Her cheeks paled.

Hope rose through the mess in his head. '*Sì*, I do.' He couldn't resist placing a tender kiss on her mouth. 'Definitely.' Then quickly withdrew before he tossed her over his shoulder and headed back to her bedroom.

Her stance softened as relief flowed through her. 'Good.'

'Good? That's it?' His knuckles dragged down his face. He'd thought he'd have to spend hours convincing her and she just said good?

'Definitely good.' A smile twitched at the corners of her sweet mouth. 'I haven't had enough of you yet.'

'Alexandra.' Mario stepped further away, strode to the big window overlooking the harbour, spun back to lock gazes with her. 'I have to explain. It can only be an affair. Nothing else. I have Sophia's future to think about and I've already sworn to put her first in my life.

At least until she's totally settled into her new life and the way that's going it could be years.'

Looking somewhere beyond his shoulder she replied, 'I'm not looking for a long-term relationship either. Just a little fun until it doesn't work for us any more. Until the heat burns out.'

'Then we understand each other.' Too well. So why did his heart ache? Why had his gut suddenly turned sour? He should be swinging from the light fittings. He was going to have a fling with this beautiful woman who turned him on with a look. Alexandra had brought him alive tonight, reminding him of what he'd been missing out on, of what certain parts of his body were for. He'd have the affair he wanted and in return intended giving Alexandra a wonderful experience. Yet it seemed all wrong.

Why had Alexandra agreed to this? He'd have sworn she'd want the full works: the shared house, the wedding, babies. Despite saying he'd put Sophia first and not bring anyone else into her messed-up life, yet he could no longer pretend he was happy with that edict. He wanted it all. He was thirty-five after all. If he'd listened to Mamma he'd already be married with a brood of kids rushing around his house. Of course all the girls she'd paraded past him hadn't snagged his attention. Not one of them had been anything like Alexandra.

Stop being greedy. Sophia's an angel. Alexandra's amazing, beautiful, sexy. Not to mention being his boss. He shrugged. So what? It wouldn't be the first time the boss had a fling with a colleague.

Shyly Alexandra asked, 'I guess this is to be kept quiet? No sneaking out my front door first thing in the morning?'

'I'm afraid so. Firstly, I need to go home to Sophia.

The new nanny is a gem and having her live in Monday to Saturday is a bonus, but I still have to be there for my daughter. Secondly, I don't think it's a good idea that our colleagues know about this, do you?' He'd turned that question back on her, testing to see how far she was prepared to go in letting the world know about their arrangement.

'I guess not.' Her perfectly white teeth nibbled her bottom lip. 'So no hiding away in the ward's linen cupboard or locking my office door while we kiss each other senseless?'

Squelching the questions buzzing around his head he reached for this fabulous woman, wrapped her in his arms and held her tight. His chin rested on the top of her head, and he sniffed in the scent of her hair. 'We could press the fire alarm first, clear the place out.'

Alex wandered into work the next morning, late and in a daze. Mario's touch was imprinted on her skin giving her a sense of joy and excitement. How was she going to concentrate on little patients without vivid pictures of last night getting in the way?

And there he was. Talking to Jenny and Kay at handover, looking as though nothing out of the ordinary had happened. Maybe for him it hadn't. Maybe he was used to brain-melting, body-burning sex. Just then he raised his head and looked down the ward, directly at her.

Under her ribs her heart rolled over and put its feet in the air, waiting to be tickled. Yeah, right. Brain melt still in charge. But that man had to be the most handsome, sexy, gorgeous male on earth. Did she mention sexy? She wanted him. Now. Here. Anywhere. Anyhow. Where was the closest fire alarm? Cripes, as far as flings went this one was going to be stellar.

'Morning, Alexandra.' That honeyed voice rolled down the corridor straight to her tummy, turning her knees hopelessly weak.

'Mario.' She dipped her head, running her tongue across her lip. Then, afraid the nurses would notice something amiss, added, 'Morning, Kay, Jenny. No disasters or major problems I need to know about?'

'A quiet night apart from wee Bee shrieking every now and then.' Jenny handed a file to Mario. 'When Jackson couldn't get hold of you he talked to Mathew about upping the painkillers. That seemed to work. She settled down quickly.'

Guilt flickered through Mario's eyes. 'Sorry, I must've turned my phone off by mistake. It won't happen again, I promise.'

'No.' Alex almost screamed the word. 'You're not on call 24/7, Mario. None of us are.' This could put a stop to their affair before it really got going.

A loving look caressed her. 'It's okay. We both know that's not true. Being available at all hours comes with the job description of paediatrician. But—' his shoulders rolled eloquently '—occasionally we miss a call and the staff will call on others.' His eyelid dropped ever so slightly. A near wink. 'That's good for Jackson and the other doctors. Keeps them on their toes knowing they have to think about the patients without us breathing down their necks all the time.'

Phew. The affair was still on, then. And her patients were still in the best of care because Mario was right. They had a very good team here, a team that consisted of more than just her and Mario. 'You're right.'

The phone on the nurses' desk rang. 'For you.' Jenny

handed it to Mario, who took it and wandered out of hearing. But not out of sight.

'I need Mario to take a look at Bee. Something's not right with her breathing.'

Alex almost leapt off the floor at Jackson's loud voice behind her. 'Mario's busy. I'll come.' Turning, she stared at the intern as though she'd never seen him before. Looking past him she noticed the sunlight falling on the floor at the far end of the ward. Did it always do that? Or just today?

'Bee's coughing badly, and her temp is creeping up again.' Jackson rattled off more details, totally unaware of the way Alex was seeing the world this morning. 'I'm worried.'

A quick shake of her head got her back on track. Until Mario gave her another semi-wink as he listened to his caller, and her heart did that roll-over movement again. This was so much harder than she'd have thought it would be. Right now all she wanted to do was drag him into the nearest cupboard and have her wicked way with him. Which was so unprofessional it shocked her into the real world and had her moving fast towards Bee's room.

'I'm right with you.'

Rochelle was wiping Bee's face and talking sweet nothings to the distressed child.

'You'll make a great mum one day,' Alex told her as she reached for Bee's charts and was astonished at the fiery red stain creeping up Rochelle's neck. Uh-oh. Was she about to lose another staff member to pregnancy?

One day it will be your turn.

The chart clattered to the floor. What? She glanced around the room to see who'd said that but everyone was totally focused on Bee. So her brain was playing cruel tricks on her now. Well, newsflash. She might be embarking on an affair with Mario but nothing else had changed. No children, ever.

Snatching up the charts Alex quickly perused all the obs from throughout the night. 'Take bloods for a CBC, ESR, LFTs and cardiac enzymes. That infection's still not responding to the drugs, and I need to know why.' Moving around the bed she squatted down and spoke softly. 'Bee, is your chest hurting today?'

Alex didn't like the grey pallor of the child's face. Immediately she reached for Bee's wrist, felt for a pulse. More erratic than normal, and far too fast.

'Hurts here.' Bee tapped the centre of her chest. 'And here.' Her small fingers walked over her upper body as she struggled to drag air into her lungs. 'Mummy.' Her lips wobbled and tears spilled down her face into the pillow. 'I want Mummy.'

Just then Jill Sawyer slid into the room and hovered in the background, her face as pale as her daughter's, her arms folded under her breasts with her hands gripping her elbows. 'What's going on? Is Bee all right?'

'I'm giving her a thorough check over, Jill.' No, Bee was not all right, at all. She was in danger of a cardiac arrest. 'Jackson, the defibrilator. Now. Grab Mario while you're at it.' She spoke softly, calmly, in direct opposite to the panic making her own heart race and blood pound. Jackson understood the urgency instantly and dashed off to get the crash cart. No need to hit the emergency button, she had on hand all the staff she needed. 'Rochelle, I need a BP reading.' *Please don't arrest. Please don't. I hate this. I know I can save you if it's at all possible—but what if I don't? What if I fail?* She flicked a fast glance at Jill, saw the terror in her face.

Digging deep within Alex focused entirely on Bee

and her obs, watching, waiting, begging whatever and whoever to keep this child safe. Where was that crash cart?

Jackson burst into the room, the trolley with him. Mario ran beside him, quickly followed by Kay. Within moments they had the pads stuck on Bee's chest, the cables snaking over the white sheets to the machine that'd monitor her for as long as it took for her heart to settle back into a more normal state. The machine began printing the graph on her heart rhythm.

Mario called calmly, 'She's gone flat. She's arresting.'

Immediately Alex was on the bed, her interlaced hands pressing down, lifting, pressing, lifting, pressing. Alex didn't take her eyes off the monitor, pleading with it to show a heartbeat. 'Come on, Bee, you can do this. You have to do this,' she whispered, more to herself than the child.

Beside her Mario drew up the drug that would hopefully stimulate Bee's heart, checked it with Jackson before plunging the needle into the girl.

'Bee,' Jill shrieked. 'Beatrice.'

Alex chilled, but she didn't stop the compressions. Her stomach knotted, but her eyes were glued to the screen. *Come on, kid, come on.*

'We've got something,' Rochelle spoke into the tense silence.

'Stop compressions, Alexandra.' Mario tapped the back of her hands.

She knew to do that. But the need to keep this wee heart beating was strong. Slowly, reluctantly, she lifted her hands away from Bee's tiny chest. But she couldn't move too far away. She had to be ready for an instant replay if that little heart stopped again.

A hand on her shoulder, familiar fingers pressing her gently. 'That was amazing. You undoubtedly saved Bee's life.' Mario's voice was full of admiration.

Shudders wracked her. They'd been lucky. This time. They'd done their job and this time there'd been the best outcome possible. She could relax.

'Alexandra?' The admiration had changed to concern.

Straightening her shoulders she shrugged his hand away and stood up on wobbly knees. 'I'm fine.' She mightn't have been able to save her son, but she'd saved Jill's daughter.

Jackson was staring at her. 'That was amazing. How did you know Bee's heart was about to stop?'

'I'll run through my observations with you in a minute.' She turned to the woman standing dumbstruck at the end of the bed, her eyes popping out of their sockets as she stared at her beloved daughter. 'Jill, Bee's doing okay. Her heart stopped briefly but it's beating just fine now.' Thank goodness.

Still Jill didn't move. The bed rail was in danger of bending under the pressure of her grip. Alex suspected it was the only thing keeping her upright.

Moving to drape an arm around the woman's thin shoulders, she squeezed her into a hug. 'Bee's still very sick, Jill, but she's breathing, living. We're going to help her with that breathing problem next.'

Under her arm Jill moved slowly, turned and peered into Alex's eyes. 'It's never-ending. Every time I dare to think she might be recovering she has another setback. It's so hard.'

'I know.' Jill's pain, anguish, even fury at what was happening to her precious child, tore at her. 'Hug her, Jill.'

She didn't need to add 'carefully.' Since Bee had

contracted meningitis Jill had had a crash course how to hold her daughter without interfering with the pads, wires and mask that cluttered Bee's body in times like this.

Leaving Mario with Bee, Alex headed to Kay's office and signed off some letters Averill had left for her. Then she went to see Chloe. 'Hey, gorgeous, how're you doing?'

Chloe blinked up at her, her eyes enormous in her small face.

'Good to see you're not so yellow any more. And I hear Mummy's been feeding you. How good is that?'

Sprawled in the chair beside the crib Kevin snored quietly, his exhaustion less obvious in his relaxed state. Chloe might be out of immediate danger now but her parents still took it in turns to be with her every hour, day and night. Things could go wrong even now. But Kevin had gone back to work part-time while Liz had no intention of gracing the paediatric ward for a very long time.

'Chloe's coming along just fine, isn't she?' Mario's arm nudged her, then remained plastered the length of hers.

Warmth stole through Alex at this small intimacy. It made her feel special, alive even. It made her hope and dream that maybe there was someone in this world for her. Someone who'd love and cherish her the way she'd love and cherish him. 'She's coming on in leaps and bounds now. Kevin and Liz are finally starting to relax about the future.'

'It's been a nightmare for them.'

A sigh slipped across her lips. 'Babies really make a family, don't they?'

'*Sì*. Without bambinos you're only a couple, not a family.' Mario's hand turned, his fingers brushed her palm in a gentle gesture. 'Though what that makes a solo dad and one child I'm not sure.'

'You're still a family.' Then found a grin and told him, 'A little lopsided though.'

A low chuckle and, 'Thanks for that.' Then, softly added, 'What about you? Still adamant you don't want children mucking up your life?'

'Of course I am.' But was she? Watching Liz and Kevin willing their daughter to overcome the odds and win had made her wonder if she was wrong to think she'd never get a second chance. Seeing Mario and Sophia together, loving and sharing despite their rocky start, reiterated her doubts. Mario had shown a mixed-up little girl her place in life, in his life, with kindness, patience and, most of all, bucket loads of love. There'd been a time when family had been the most important thing to Alex, but the deaths of her father and her baby had changed all that. She'd begun to believe she wasn't meant to have her own family, that she was meant to help other families, just not hers. And nothing in her life since had altered her thinking, until recently. Until Mario and his little girl.

'You can have both,' Mario continued quietly. 'I do. Most of us do. Though whether I'm a good dad is up for debate.'

Her neck cricked as she looked up at him. 'Hey, you're doing a fabulous job. Sophia's not unhappy. And she's getting all the physical comforts from you any child should have.'

'Apart from all the donated meals, you mean.' The wry smile he gave her showed how incapable he felt.

Her finger traced the smile. 'You wouldn't look good

in a red and blue suit with a cape. Take everyone's kind-nesses with the grace they're given.'

The tip of his tongue licked her finger, and a wicked glint lightened that pewter gaze. 'How come you get it so right for me but so wrong for you?'

'That's where you're wrong. I have it exactly right for me. I know the consequences of believing I should have a family.' With that she stepped back, putting a little air between them so he wouldn't feel the shaking of her muscles as she wondered if she'd made a mistake. Wondered if she could have the impossible dream after all—with Mario.

CHAPTER TEN

'ALEXANDRA PRENDERGAST, HOW do you plead? Guilty…?'
The judge paused.

Her heart squeezed with pain. *Not again. Please
don't do this to me.*

'Or not guilty?'

She couldn't swallow around her dry tongue. The
tears oozed from her eyes, slicked down her cheeks to
drip off her chin. 'Guilty,' she tried to whisper. *Guilty,
guilty, guilty,* her brain yelled, the word reverberating
around her skull.

'No, Alexandra, wrong. You're not guilty. You're
innocent, remember?' The man standing on the opposite side of the operating theatre table watched her
from friendly pewter eyes. 'You would not deliberately
let a child die. You'd do everything in your power to
save him.'

'How do you know that?'

'Because I know you. You're a very clever doctor.
You care, Alexandra. You care. You saved Bee. You've
saved plenty of others. Trust me.'

'I want to so much. But—'

'Trust me, Alexandra.' The honeyed tones sounded
so familiar. So sure.

Alex's eyes blinked open. Where was she? She stared

around the dark room, recognised the quirky black and silver fabric of her bedroom chair, the silver shine from the bedside lamp stand. She gasped. Mario was here? He'd just spoken to her. She fumbled with the bedside light, finally clicked the switch, bringing in soft light to brighten the dark corners. She peered around but she was alone. In her apartment. Her heart slowed.

Mario wasn't here. But he'd just spoken to her, told her he believed in her. He had to be somewhere in the apartment.

Rubbing her forehead her hand came away wet. Oh. She'd had the nightmare.

But what did that have to do with Mario? He's never been in it before, the voice in her head argued.

It was though he wouldn't believe the judge in her nightmare. Mario seemed think she was a good doctor. What if he was right? What if she really couldn't have done a thing to prevent what happened to Jordan?

Yeah, but he didn't know about Jordan.

Sliding out of bed Alex picked up her robe and headed for the kitchen and a mug of lemon ginger tea. Her hands were surprisingly steady and her stomach calm, considering the nightmare. But it had been different tonight.

The lemon ginger flavours freshened her mouth, soothed her soul. In the lounge she curled up in an armchair beside the big picture window and gazed down on the quiet harbour. Her eyes followed the headlight on the lone forklift moving meticulously yet quickly between ship and pen, carrying logs that were on the way to China.

To think she'd spent all these years keeping the facts surrounding Jordan's stillbirth hidden in that dark place inside her, not telling people she met that she'd even had a baby. She felt as though she'd cracked wide open and in doing so had reconstructed the facts into a more tolerable scenario. Not that her guilt had vanished. It probably never would, but suddenly she knew she could live with it.

She drained her mug and headed to the smallest bedroom in her apartment. On the art board Harry and Bella were in the middle of a go-kart race, Bella nudging Harry's cart to shove him off the track. Settling comfortably before the board Alex picked up a red pencil and began outlining the 'finish' flag.

Next, with a dark blue shade, she added into the background a small version of a large man with a heart-melting smile. Added his little dark-haired daughter. Then put in another child, a wee boy. Hers and Mario's? The pencil snapped in her fingers. Crazy. She did not, must not, think of having a child with Mario.

But she could continue to enjoy their affair.

Mario felt little fingers poking his cheek and groaned. 'Sophia, Daddy's asleep, darling.'

'No, he's not. He's talking to me.' A giggle followed. 'Come on, Daddy, get up. I'm hungry.'

He made a snoring noise and more giggles filled the room, then little fingers tickled his chin and neck. *Let me catch up on the hours of sleep I missed while making out with Alexandra.*

'Get up, lazybones.' The bedcovers were lifted and a freezing cold foot slid down Mario's belly.

No rest for the wicked or overworked fathers. 'Ahhhh,' he cried, and sat up, scooping his wriggling daughter into his arms. 'Where have you had those feet, missy? In the deep freeze?'

Thank goodness he'd remembered to pull on some

pyjama bottoms after Alexandra left in the wee hours. A yawn ripped his mouth wide. When was the last time he'd had so much exercise? Every muscle he had ached or twanged when he moved. But damn, he felt good. The weeks since they'd agreed to an affair had flown by.

'No, Daddy, that's silly. You told me never to open the freezer in case the lid goes bang on my head.'

'So I did. Now what do you want for breakfast, little Miss Muffet? Toast?'

Sophia moved her head slowly from side to side.

'Cereal?'

More sideways moves.

'Eggs?'

'No.'

Mario gave a deliberately big sigh. 'I'm all out of ideas.'

'Daddy, you aren't. There's one more.'

He scratched his chin. 'Umm, let me think. I suppose I could make pancakes with maple syrup.'

'Yes, Daddy, yes, yes, yes.' Sophia clapped her hands so close to his face his nose was in danger of being squashed. Then she leaned forward and placed a sloppy kiss on his jaw. 'I love you, Daddy.'

His eyes misted as his heart slowed and a sweet warmth stole from his head to his toes. '*Sì*, I love you too, sweetheart.' This was what made parenting so special and made up for the frightening moments.

This was why he could only have an affair with Alexandra. There wasn't room for two all-consuming females in his life.

But as he poured batter into the hot pan coated with sizzling butter he wondered if he was being hasty with that decision. Could he have Sophia *and* Alexandra? And more bambinos? Little Alexandra lookalikes running around the backyard? Sophia being the big sister would be squabbling with them. He could hear the racket now. Italian noise, Alexandra would call it.

And despite the number of times he used to hide from his sisters for some peace and quiet as they were growing up, he knew deep down he really wanted this. There wouldn't be much time for paediatrics. Families were all-consuming, especially of time and attention.

But there'd be two paediatricians in the household. They could job share.

Steady up, boyo. You're getting way ahead of yourself. Alexandra has categorically denied wanting to get involved on a deeper level. Not once has she admitted to wanting a child of her own. Though he never quite believed her on that score.

She was so loving, caring. Look how good she was with the little ones on the ward. Didn't mean she'd be keen on being a mother though. But she was great with Sophia. What about those books written and illustrated for children? Surely anyone who did all that wanted to be a mum? She'd loved her father a lot, still felt the pain of losing him. Maybe that was why she didn't want to settle down? Nah, not a good enough reason. A lot of people lost a parent when they were young and went on to have their own family.

He flipped the pancake. If only she'd talk about her past, open up to him. Trust him.

'Daddy, the pancake stinks.' Sophia stood at his elbow.

Yuk. Rancid burnt butter was not a great start to the day. 'Okay, kiddo, Daddy needs to start again.' And needs to stop daydreaming the impossible dream.

Which is?

A more permanent relationship with Alexandra. *Be-*

cause I can't see I'll ever let her go. I can't get enough of her. She's amazing, and fun, and serious, and so, so addictive.

Alex stretched her toes towards the end of the bed, her arms above her head. 'I feel so good. You manage to make my body ache in the most delicious ways in places I'd forgotten I had.'

Mario smiled a slow, lazy smile filled with wickedness and a hint of arrogance. 'Glad to know I haven't lost my touch,' he purred.

'Your ego certainly doesn't need boosting.'

They'd come back to her apartment at the end of a particularly gruelling day on the ward with the intention of having a meal. Except neither of them had been anywhere near the kitchen in the hour they'd been here. The moment her door lock clicked shut behind them Mario had hauled her into his arms and carried her to the bedroom. Alex had nuzzled in against his chest, her lips trailing kisses up his neck to his ear where her teeth nipped his earlobe, sending Mario into a hot frenzy.

It had been another beautiful, exciting lovemaking session. Almost as though they couldn't have enough of each other, no matter how often they got together. The storm was not abating.

Mario reached for the bedside light, and golden light flooded the room.

Alex snatched at the sheet to tug it over her body, but most of it was tucked beneath Mario and didn't come free. 'Hey, roll over, let me have the sheet back.' She nudged him with an elbow. 'Come on, Mario, move.' She had to cover up. Now. Before he saw. Her heart began to speed up and she breathed quick, short gasps. 'Please.'

'Why? You never let me see you fully naked. We've made love in all sorts of positions and yet you're shy of showing me your beautiful body. I don't understand.' Mario raised himself onto an elbow and looked at her, his gaze sliding down her throat to her breasts, down her stomach to the triangle at the junction of her legs.

Alex held her breath. Maybe he hadn't noticed. Please.

His eyes moved down her legs.

She tugged at the sheet again. 'Please, you're making me feel uncomfortable.' In any other situation that languid gaze would've turned her on instantly. But not now. She made to flip onto her tummy.

He reached a hand to stop her, spread his fingers over her belly, his forefinger tracing the telltale lines marring her skin. 'You've got stretch marks.'

Her lip hurt when she bit down. Staring at Mario she willed him to look away, or meet her eyes full-on so he could see the warning to stop right there. 'Yes,' she whispered.

'You've had a baby.' His hand jerked away from her as though she burnt him and finally he looked directly at her. What Alex saw in those usually sparkling grey eyes turned her cold. Fury, disappointment, hurt—all lashed at her.

Unable to face him from this position she shot out of bed and hauled on the robe lying over the chair. Then she sat on the chair, tucking her feet beneath her. 'Yes, I have.'

'When?'

'Almost ten years ago. When I was twenty-four.'

He latched on to one thing. 'Ten years ago? That's an excuse for not telling me?' He stood and shoved his legs into his trousers, tugged the zip up with such force it was a wonder it didn't jam. His hands slapped onto his hips. 'Were you ever going to mention this? What else haven't you told me?'

Anger at his unforgiving attitude stiffened her spine, tugged her shoulders back. 'We're having an affair, not making a lifelong commitment. That means we don't share all the details of our pasts. Anyway, when we're together we're too busy making love to be talking about all the minutiae surrounding ourselves.'

'Aren't I entitled to know the real Alexandra?' Hurt won over the other emotions darkening his eyes, but he still snapped at her, 'Where is your child? With its father? In Nelson? Or have you left it in another city?'

As Lucy had done. He didn't have to enunciate the words, they were there, hanging in the air between them. The ache in Alex's chest tightened, made breathing difficult as he continued berating her over something that had absolutely nothing to do with him. It was in the past. Her past.

Finally he shut up and she snapped back, 'Thanks for the vote of confidence. You're pretty quick to think the worst of me.'

'Not once have you mentioned visiting a child.' His fingers were white where they gripped his hips. 'Did you have a boy or a girl, Alexandra?'

'A boy, Jordan.' At the mention of her baby's name pain lanced her, sliced her up inside. It didn't matter how long ago it had happened because at times like this it felt like yesterday.

'And?'

She did not want to talk about Jordan. Not now when he was so angry. Definitely not when he believed she was capable of the appalling act of deserting her baby. Not even his history with Lucy was an excuse. Besides, why tell Mario when they weren't in this for the long haul? Judging by his anger their affair was already over anyway.

'Didn't you love Jordan enough to keep him? Did you hand him over to his father and get on with your amazing career?'

She had to say it, shout it at him so he heard her correctly. 'I am not Lucy. I would never, ever hand my child over to someone else to raise. Not even his father. If I'd had to quit med school and work in a supermarket to support Jordan I'd have done it.' She leapt off the chair and marched over to him, stabbed his chest hard with a finger as the dam burst and the words she'd buried so long ago spewed forth. 'I would've done absolutely anything for my baby.' Stab. 'But—' stab '—I didn't get the chance.' Stab. 'He died. Stillborn.'

She saw the shock jolt through him. 'Alexandra.' He hesitated. Remorseful? 'I'm so sorry. I never expected that, but if you'd told me I'd not have put my foot in it.'

Definitely not remorseful enough. And now that she'd started talking about Jordan she couldn't stop. Mario would get what he wanted—all the details. 'Jordan never once heard my voice. Or got to know my touch. Or to open his eyes and see me. He never felt my love.' She ignored the tears pouring down her cheeks as she bounced on her toes, impaling him with her anger at his criticism. 'I loved my baby. I love him still. I live with this every single day. I see boys of nine and wonder what Jordan would look like now, what he'd be up to, would he love me as much as I love him. I wonder what he wants to be when he grows up. Will he be short like me or tall like his father?' The breaths over her lips were hot, short.

Her hands clenched as she struggled for control.

Sinking down onto her heels she took a long, shaky breath and said quietly, 'There you have it. I don't talk about him—to anyone. He's mine.'

Then she turned and walked out of the room, leaving Mario standing in the middle of her bedroom staring after her. She was done with him. For good. There was no place in her life, in her heart, for a man who didn't listen first, speak second.

In the kitchen she plugged in the kettle and dropped a tea bag into a mug. Her hands shook, her stomach churned and the tears continued.

'Alexandra.' Mario's shirt hung out over his trousers, his jacket crushed in his hand. 'I'm very sorry about your loss. I can't begin to know what you've been through.'

When she didn't say a word, didn't turn around, he said, 'I'll see myself out.'

It seemed forever before the door quietly clicked shut behind him. Alex dropped her chin onto her chest and let go the huge sobs pushing to be freed. Her lungs hurt and her throat ached as her body was wracked with the familiar pain and anger. Only this time the anger was directed at Mario. Blast the man for his accusations. He worked with sick children day in, day out. Why hadn't it occurred to him there might be a very good reason she didn't have her child growing up with her? How could he have thought so little of her?

Just as well she'd learned how judgemental he could be before she made some stupid mistake like thinking their affair could become something more, could flower into the love she'd been starting to hope for. Her hands gripped the edge of the bench to hold her upright. Why did the pain of losing Jordan never lessen? Why tonight did it seem even worse than usual?

Because Mario had accused her of being a bad mother. She might think that but he had no right to. How could he even consider it? Just because that Lucy woman had done something terrible to him and Sophia didn't mean every woman he came in contact with would deliberately mislead him.

Didn't he understand how hard it was for her to talk about Jordan? Her family and friends had known what happened. Those friends had been there for her as she fell apart after Jordan died. They'd supported her when Jonty left. They were the ones to help her get herself back together into someone barely resembling the girl she'd used to be. Nowadays those friends either didn't recognise her or said she'd changed so much they didn't connect with her any more. Why wouldn't she have? Who stayed whole and fun-loving and exuberant when their heart had been chopped out? She'd lost more than her son. She'd lost her husband, friendships, her sense of achievement. She'd become driven, always trying to prove to herself and everyone else she could succeed at everything she tried. Except keep her baby alive.

And now Mario had the pip because she hadn't told him. No wonder she stayed single. If a man couldn't give her unconditional understanding, then she was better off without him. Mind-blowing sex or not.

Love him or not.

Mario drove slowly through the quiet streets trying to absorb what had happened back at Alexandra's. Not once had he suspected she was hiding something from him. Not once. When she'd covered her body during their lovemaking he'd put it down to unexpected shyness.

Those few stretch marks had tipped him upside

down, shocked him. A trillion questions had rampaged through his skull, all needing immediate answers. Yet he'd failed her in his approach, stamping into the fray like an irate elephant.

How had she coped with the loss? Not very well if the way she slowly dissolved into heart-wrenching tears earlier was anything to go. She'd looked so lost. In agony. Those silent tears streaming down her face as she poked his chest broke him up inside. He'd wanted to haul her into his arms and kiss her better. But he knew how impossible that was. There was no making the situation better. He needed complete and utter trust in a relationship. He needed all the facts laid out right from the beginning. He loathed unexpected surprises.

He turned into his driveway and parked. Next door Gina's house was in darkness. Half an hour of idle chatter would've distracted him. Maybe instead he'd go inside and lift Sophia out of bed and into his arms to hug her close. Just because he could. Too bad that the nanny would growl at him. Because Sophia was the world to him and the reason he hadn't been able to take Alexandra in his arms after her revelation.

So what if he'd been getting closer to Alexandra? Thinking they might take the relationship further into something permanent? He'd been making a mistake and this had been a wake-up call.

Pushing out of the car he headed inside, still pondering why Alexandra hadn't told him about Jordan. She'd had the perfect opportunity when he'd talked about Lucy's treachery, or when he'd asked if she wanted children. It didn't matter to him that Alexandra had had a baby, just that she hadn't told him. She knew how hard it was for him to trust a woman.

Inside he peeked in on Sophia, resisting hugging

her, then headed for the liquor cabinet to pour a heavy slug of whiskey. Adding a splash of water he took a deep swallow, let the fire water burn down his throat. Then he sprawled over the couch. It was going to be a long night.

He'd had a few of those lately—with Alexandra. Hot, sexy nights; fun, sleepless nights. Now the affair was over. He could see his sister's disappointment already. She'd thought he might be getting serious about that lovely paediatrician who wrote those beautiful books about the dogs that Sophia adored.

'Tough. This is me looking out for my heart.'

Which didn't seem so clever right this moment.

CHAPTER ELEVEN

WHEN ALEX GOT a break between surgery and the diabetes clinic she popped along to see her favourite patient.

'Hello, Chloe, how's things with you today?'

'I'm doing just fine, thanks,' Liz answered in a cheeky voice.

'Hey, I thought you'd gone home.' Alex crossed to give Liz a hug.

'It's missy's lunchtime. Or should that be second lunch? Now she's started breast feeding there's no stopping her. She's constantly hungry.' Liz looked thoroughly pleased with her daughter.

'You're looking so much more relaxed these days. Positively smug at times.' Motherhood was suiting her friend, especially now that Chloe was improving every day.

Liz's smile slipped, showing how precarious her newfound happiness really was. 'I still wake up at night terrified Chloe's going to develop more problems. I can't believe how lucky we've been.' Another hug. 'You've been wonderful. You and Mario are the best. Best paeds, best friends. I'm meant to wait until Kevin's here to ask this but I can't. We want you two to be Chloe's godparents.'

A lump blocked Alex's throat preventing her from replying. All she could do was nod, and slash at the tears blurring her vision. What an honour. Did Liz know what she was asking? Her, Alexandra Prendergast, to be a godmother to their precious daughter? What if history kicked in? Took Chloe away? She'd never cope with that. Alex wandered to the crib, stared down at the tiny but growing, pink-skinned girl who'd been born fighting. Not once had she given up, no matter what nature had thrown at her. A wacky heart, high bilirubin, lung infection after lung infection, no hugs and kisses from her mum or dad for weeks. A tough cookie who wasn't letting anything stop her from growing and getting healthy.

Learn from her, Alex. Learn from your goddaughter.

'Alex, say something. Have I asked too much of you?' Liz sounded perplexed, as well she might.

Turning, Alex grasped her friend's hands. 'No, you haven't. I'm thrilled, really thrilled. And I swear I'm going to do everything within my power to be the best godmother on the planet.' The tears spilled and poured down her face, and she didn't care. Liz and Kevin believed in her, so why shouldn't she begin to believe she was capable of what they'd asked her to do?

'I've watched you with Sophia. You're so good, so understanding of her. You're a natural with children.'

Hadn't Mario told her the same thing a few days ago when they were still on good terms? Her spine clicked when she straightened her shoulders. Time to start believing everyone and put the past behind her.

Liz asked, 'Is Mario staying in Wellington tonight? I know Kevin's going to want to ask him to be godfather now that I've spilled the beans with you.'

'I think he's flying back as soon as the conference winds up. He doesn't like to be away from Sophia any longer than necessary.' Since their bust-up she'd spent her days trying to avoid Mario on the ward, only getting together to discuss patients and then usually with other staff members close by. But today when she could relax knowing he was out of town she found herself looking for him at every turn. She missed him. Face it, she missed him even when he was here. It was his embraces, his kisses, quick wit and laughter that she missed. Now all she got was a grim countenance.

'Mario probably won't come in here tonight. Kevin might have to pay him a visit at home. If he's not interrupting anything between you, of course.' Liz's wink went straight to Alex's tummy, twisting like a sharp knife.

If only there was something to interrupt. 'Not a problem. I'll be at my apartment.' Where not even Harry and Bella's antics were a distraction any more.

'Is something wrong, Alex? I've just realised you haven't been as cheerful these past days. I'm sorry, I've been so tied up in my own problems.'

Alex's pager squawked. Saved. Snatching the pager from her belt she read the message with a sinking heart. 'I'm really sorry, Liz. I've got to go.'

She tore down the ward to the newest patient. Her heart pounded hard and heavy against her ribs. Her hands were clammy. A dull ache set up behind her eyes. She fired questions at anyone who'd answer them. 'What's happened? How did Sophia break her collarbone and arm? Has Mario been told? Is her asthma under control?'

'Mario's cell phone is switched off,' Jackson replied. 'Not sure if that means he's already flying home or still in the auditorium. Probably the latter. I think his flight leaves Wellington around five. I left a brief message which hopefully won't freak him out.'

'Sophia fell out of a tree,' Kay told her. 'X-ray shows greenstick fractures of the left ulna and clavicle.'

'Sophia's wheezing is mild to moderate but is getting worse as her distress grows. She needs Mario right now, not in a few hours.' Jackson strode along beside her, ushering her into a side room where she heard loud shrieks coming from. 'In here.'

Alex felt her heart squeeze tight when she saw Sophia, white with pain, her eyes wide and filled with fear while fat tears slid down her face. When she drew a breath the wheeze was obvious. Alex hurried to the bed and sat down. 'Hey, Sophia, I'm here to make you better, sweetheart.' She reached for Sophia, carefully wrapping an arm around her waist, avoiding causing any more pain. 'Shh, sweetheart. It's all right. I'm here.' She kissed the damp curls, rubbed Sophia's back.

'Wh-where's Daddy? I want my daddy.'

'I know you do. Daddy's coming as soon as the aeroplane can get him here.' Mentally she crossed her fingers. 'Do you want me to stay with you?'

The biggest, saddest eyes studied Alex, wrenching her heart again. 'Yes. And Daddy.'

Another kiss and Alex asked Kay, 'Is Gina in the hospital?'

'She's had to go pick up her boys from school. One of them got into a fight,' Kay told her.

Jackson grimaced. 'The youngest has been getting bullied lately so I imagine one of his brothers has stuck up for him again. As if Gina hasn't got enough to deal with.'

So it was true Jackson was seeing Gina out of work. 'Did Gina bypass ED when she brought Sophia in?'

'Hope you don't mind? She figured Sophia would be more comfortable with us than strangers.' Alex liked the protectiveness for Gina sparking back at her from Jackson's eyes.

'I'd have been upset if she hadn't. How long since you put a cast on?'

'Last year during my ED rotation.'

'Right, let's sort out pain control and get our girl fixed up. That shoulder will hurt but hopefully with a soft strapping Sophia won't move it around too much while it heals.'

Jackson's eyes rolled. 'This is a child you're talking about.'

'Wishful thinking, huh?'

'Definitely.' Jackson chuckled. 'Her cousins don't stop moving even in their sleep.'

'I think those boys probably don't have half of Sophia's hang-ups.'

Jackson shook his head at her. 'Their biggest hang-up is when the next meal is due.'

Alex smiled for the first time in days. She'd always got on with Jackson. Maybe because he'd started his medical training in his mid-twenties so didn't have all those hang-ups the junior doctors usually had. 'Sophia, I'm going to give you something to make your arm stop hurting, sweetheart.'

'Where's Daddy?'

'Coming, sweetheart.' She might've spent the past ten days avoiding him but she'd do anything to have him walk through the door right now. 'How about you sit on my knees while Jackson and Kay fix you up?'

Sophia nodded slowly, her thumb back in her mouth.

Half an hour later Sophia's arm was in plaster, her shoulder strapped and her breathing settling down with the aid of her inhaler. She lay curled up on her good side, a thumb in her mouth, and sound asleep.

Beside her bed Gina kept watch over her niece. 'I can't believe she's so settled. Nothing like her last admittance, is it?'

'A fracture isn't as frightening as not being able to breathe.' Alex ran a hand over Sophia's curls.

'More like something to do with her doctor.' Gina grinned. 'She's always at ease around you.'

Alex could feel her chest expanding. Mother material after all?

Gina scowled at her. 'What's up with you and that numbskull brother of mine? He's such a grouch at the moment.'

The air oozed out of her lungs. 'He'll come right. I'm sure it's only a temporary aberration.' But he wouldn't be coming around to her apartment any more.

Gina's scowl softened. 'Don't let him push you around. He's so used to females doing his bidding that if you've stood up to him he'll be in shock.'

'I'll remember that.' Not that she'd have the chance to stand up to him again. At least not in their personal life.

Thankfully Gina let the subject drop. 'I'll have to leave at five to pick up the boys from my neighbour. Think Sophia will be all right on her own?'

Alex smiled. 'I'll sit with her until Mario gets here.' One look at the gorgeous sleeping bundle beside her and she knew wild horses couldn't keep her away.

Gina looked thoughtful. 'Have you heard the weather forecast? Apparently it's snowing in Wellington and the airport has been closed for an hour. Mario might not get back until tomorrow.'

'If that happens we'll keep Sophia in so we can monitor that asthma. I'll sit with her through the night.'

'Mario will love you for that.'

Alex's face tightened as she tried not to look too upset. Not likely. He might be grateful, but he wouldn't love her. And that's how it should be. She did not want his love. Right. Tell that to anyone who'd listen. *If you don't want Mario to love you, then why the sleepless nights? Why the churning tummy 24/7? Why the feeling you've let the most important thing ever to happen to you get away?* Spinning away from his sister's all-seeing gaze she muttered, 'I'll be back as soon as possible.'

She headed for her diabetes clinic with more questions than answers popping up in her brain. *Do I really love him? Is that why I feel sick every time I see him first thing in the mornings? Last thing at night? Not to mention all the minutes in between. I love Mario?*

Yes, I think I do.

No. I know I do.

Her head spun and she leaned against the wall to stay upright. *I've missed him ever since he left my apartment that disastrous night but does that mean I love him?*

Yep. Absolutely.

Great. Now I'm in love with a man who'll never look at me again except to wish I'd vanish in a puff of smoke.

A man who strode through her life every day with patient files in his hands, little lives depending on him. A man who had helped her discover her sexuality on a whole new level to anything she'd previously known.

A man she wanted to have children with, spend her life with, to see out the golden years beside. The man who'd helped banish her insecurities over Jordan.

'Alex, are you all right?'

Mario? She opened her eyes to find Jackson hovering beside her, concern for her in his eyes. Not Mario, then. Disappointed, she dragged herself straight and continued to the lift. 'I'm fine, thank you.'

Jackson wisely kept his mouth shut until they were down at the day ward and settling into their clinic, then he talked about the patients they were about to see which gave Alex the opportunity to get back on track and focus on what mattered—her patients.

At the doorway into Sophia's hospital room Mario stopped his mad dash to his daughter's side. The air whooshed out of his lungs at the beautiful sight in front of him. The tranquil sight.

He'd been in a state of panic for the past six and a half hours as he'd struggled to get home. When he'd learned there'd be no flights out of Wellington before dawn he'd taken a horrendously rough ferry crossing to Picton where he'd hired a car and driven for two hours in pelting rain and buffeting wind, finally reaching Nelson a few minutes before midnight.

Now here he was and there wasn't a sign of chaos or distress. Quite the opposite. His heart rate slowed and his breathing settled to something near normal. Sophia lay sleeping, her thumb jammed in her mouth. Her other hand poked out from the edge of a plaster cast and was tucked carefully into Alexandra's hand.

Alexandra also slept, her head resting on the pillow beside Sophia, her fair hair a sharp contrast to his daughter's dark locks. *Bella.* Lovely. The book they'd been reading lay open on her lap. Both looked completely at ease with each other. The deep lines that had appeared on Alexandra's face these past few days were smoothed out in sleep. Her mouth had softened, her body relaxed.

As for Sophia—who knew what trauma, stress, she'd

been through today? It certainly didn't show at the moment. Thanks to Alexandra? Definitely thanks to Alexandra. Sophia didn't cope with being surrounded with strangers at the best of times. Being in hospital and hurting didn't come close to the best of times.

Crossing the room quietly so as not to wake either of his girls, he picked up a chair and placed it on the opposite side of the bed to Alexandra.

He liked that Alexandra had taken care of his daughter while he was out of town. She had in spades what it took to look after Sophia. She only had to read a Harry and Bella story and Sophia was putty in her hand.

Stretching his legs out he tipped his head back and waited for the night to pass. Waited for the questions to stop buzzing through his skull, the 'I told you so's' to stop laughing at him.

He'd made a mistake with Alexandra. She was perfect for him and his daughter. Except for not letting him in, not sharing her past as he had with her.

Like he'd been entirely up front with her from the beginning? He'd explained why Lucy had struggled to fit in with his Italian family in Florence, hadn't he? How he'd never been there for her, to support her, because he'd been too busy furthering his own interests? He hadn't been fair to Alexandra. Not at all. Would she ever let him make it up to her? Would she forgive him? And if she did, where to from there?

The ceiling blurred before his eyes.

The next thing he knew a nurse was taking Sophia's obs and his neck hurt like hell where it had cricked while he slept. And Alexandra was nowhere to be seen.

'Daddy,' Sophia shrieked, no doubt waking the whole hospital. 'You're here.'

'Hey, gorgeous, how's my girl?' He reached for her

warm little body and hugged gently, careful not to bump the damaged shoulder or arm.

'I fell out of the tree in Auntie Gina's yard. The ground broke my arm.' She proudly held up the plaster-encased limb. 'See, Daddy? Alex wrote her name on it. And those are kisses there.' She touched the inky Xs. 'Alex read me a story, a Harry and Bella story so I could fall asleep.' Sophia looked around the room. 'Where is she?'

'She's probably gone home, *amore mio*.' His heart was heavy. 'It's Saturday and Alexandra doesn't always work all day during the weekend.' She'd gone quietly some time while he'd been dozing. Didn't want to wake him? Because she couldn't abide their cold war? It wasn't a war but it sure felt like it at times. Over the past week he'd missed their easy camaraderie on the ward or at their discussions about difficult patient diagnoses or treatment. He'd missed their intimate evenings, stolen hours from hectic lives.

Better get used to it. Nothing has changed. He still couldn't trust Alexandra to tell him the important things in her life.

'Daddy?'

'Yes, sweetheart.'

'Why haven't I got a mummy? Everyone else has.'

So much for thinking he had all the answers.

The storm that had forced Mario to find another way back from Wellington the night before had passed through and the morning sparkled in the early-spring sun.

Dressed in her one pair of jeans, a sky-blue shirt and a thick navy blue jacket Alex strolled through the Saturday market buying fresh salad vegetables. She bumped and jostled with other shoppers, enjoying the slow meander through the crowd. It seemed the fine weather had brought out half the population of Nelson and, though it was nearing midday, the stall holders were still doing a brisk trade.

Daffodils. Her favourite flower. The yellow heads, bright and cheerful, filled rows of plastic buckets at many stalls. She bought six bunches and continued down the row to stop at a stall selling local cheeses where she selected a havarti and a blue. Next to the cheese vendor was the fresh bread man. Choosing a ciabatta loaf she paid and slipped it into her grocery bag along with her other purchases and headed for her car. Hopefully her taste buds would be tempted. Her clothes were beginning to look baggy.

Driving around the waterfront she noted that the clouds had pulled back from Mount Arthur leaving its snow-covered peak glistening where the sun kissed it. 'An absolutely beautiful day.' Amazing how the weather never let her down on this particular day of the year, not once over the past nine years.

Half an hour later she pulled up outside her beach house and turned the engine off. As the roar died away she just sat, gazing down the lawn, over the sand and across the water. The sea was tossing up tiny whitecaps as it did a jittery dance across the bay. Still rough from the storm but not intimidating. Perfect.

'Hello, Jordan,' she whispered. And sat, looking, seeing, remembering.

Finally she pushed open the door and scrambled out, gathered up her purchases and the bag she'd brought from home and went inside. It felt oppressive in there so she left everything on the table and went to open the French doors wide, letting the warmth in. Stepping onto the patio she drew a deep breath. And felt him. Remembered holding her baby in her arms. 'Happy birthday, Jordan, love.'

Her feet dragged as she headed down the lawn to the beach where she crossed to the lapping water's edge. She had no idea how long she stood there. The water covered her shoes, soaked the bottom of her jeans, and still she didn't move. Just stood and let her few memories of Jordan flow into her mind. His beautiful little face, his ten fingers and toes, perfectly formed feet. The wrinkled new skin. The baby smell.

Only when she began shivering from the chill in her feet did she walk back up the beach to sit on the sand, her knees drawn up under her chin, her arms wrapped around her legs. And reran the memories. Again and again. It was cathartic.

Gulls swooped and soared, filling the air with their high-pitched cries, fighting over treasures of food they found on the beach. An old fish skeleton, dead cockles, an apple. It was survival of the fittest—or the meanest. Life at its most basic level.

Alex smiled. Despite what day it was. She loved this spot. Her favourite place in the whole wide world, not that she'd seen a lot of the world, but she just knew nowhere would speak to her like this beach where she'd lived through some of the most important, exciting and harrowing times of her life.

She sensed him before she saw or heard him. She didn't turn to look for him, just carried on watching her piece of beach. He squatted beside her, his hands hanging between his knees. He was so big beside her, so strong. But loving? Wishing for it didn't make it real.

She told him, 'I scattered Jordan's ashes here.' It had

been the right thing to do at the time and she'd never once regretted it.

'That first time I was here I noticed how you kept glancing across the lawn to the beach as though looking for someone.'

Sensitive? 'Today's his birthday. He'd have been ten.'

They remained quiet for a while, absorbing the sounds of nature, relaxed together for the first time in a while.

Then Mario said quietly, 'You're amazing. It's a hell of a tragedy to cope with.' He sat down on the damp sand beside her, took one of her hands and held it between both his. Caring?

'Sometimes I thought I was going insane with the grief.'

'That's understandable. Can I ask what happened to Jordan's father?'

'He left me within a month of Jordan's birth. It was dreadful during the days leading up to Jonty's abrupt departure. He had to blame someone for Jordan's death, and he picked me for that role. I guess Jonty couldn't handle the whole situation but I didn't see it like that at the time. I thought no loved me enough to stay around.' She shivered. 'Two years to the day I received the divorce papers.'

With her free hand Alex scooped up sand, let the grains slip through her fingers. 'We were teenage sweethearts. Met here one summer when he came to stay with relatives. When we were back in Auckland we kept in touch, eventually married and got pregnant.' End of story.

'So you had no one special to help you through your loss.' His thumb rubbed light circles on the back of her hand.

'My mother and stepfather tried, but we'd never had a close relationship and we just couldn't find a connection. I came here for a while because this is where I was happiest with my dad. I'd take long walks along the beach talking to him, crying at the injustice of it all, wishing Jordan back in my arms. I was crazed. It's a wonder the locals didn't have me locked up.'

'They knew you, understood you.'

How did he know that? Because that's how he'd have thought if he'd witnessed a friend going through what she had. He knew stuff like that. She whispered, 'I wish I'd known you back then.'

'You know me now.' Mario slipped an arm around her shoulders and tugged her close, and said nothing. He'd obviously recognised there really wasn't anything more to say.

Loving?

CHAPTER TWELVE

'BIRTHDAYS ARE MEANT to be celebrated. Even Jordan's.' Mario spoke softly, afraid Alexandra might misinterpret his intentions and think he was making light of the situation while all he wanted was to help her through this, to turn the tide against her grief.

Her hand jerked in his grasp. 'No one's ever said that to me before.'

He held his breath.

Scooping up another handful of sand with her free hand she opened her fingers to let the grains dribble through. 'I bought cheese and bread at the market. There's a bottle of wine in the fridge.'

'Then let's have a picnic down here.' Mario stood and reached to pull her to her feet. 'Preferably with chairs so my backside can dry out.'

'Toughen up.' She smiled up at him, sending his heart rate out of kilter. Maybe there was hope of reconciliation.

How could I have believed I could walk away from her? To have accused her of being as cavalier as Lucy was very wrong. He'd hurt her badly. It had showed in her eyes every time they'd been together at work. He'd had no right to expect her to bare her soul just because they were sharing a bed. There was intimacy and there was intimacy. They hadn't been at the stage where Alexandra felt totally at ease with him. He should've recognised that instead of going off in a funk like a spoilt child. He'd growl at Sophia if she behaved as badly.

Now he understood why Alexandra reacted as she had. That Jonty was a prize bastard. No one deserved to be treated so badly, even if he was also suffering the loss of his son. He should've been sticking to his wife like glue.

As they strolled up the lawn he kept her hand in his, not wanting her to pull away. This was her day and he'd remain with her for as long as she needed him, be strong for her. Did she need him? She definitely needed someone by her side for her son's birthday. Whether he fitted the role was up to her. There was so much love in his heart for her, but he wasn't about to risk the moment telling her. Nor would he apologise for his mistakes. This was her day, not his, not theirs. Right now he was happy to show how much he cared for her.

'Where's Sophia?' she asked suddenly. 'Still in hospital?'

'At home with Gina and the boys. She's not at all distressed about her fall or injuries. Amazing.' Because this woman had formed a bond with Sophia that made her hospital visit a whole lot easier. Sophia liked and trusted Alexandra and he'd do well to follow his daughter's example.

'She feels safe with you now which means the world isn't such a bad place any more.'

Alexandra's certainty unravelled another knot in his gut. He determined to try even harder to make this day work for Alexandra.

Mario put together the picnic while Alexandra went to change out of her wet jeans into a pair of those trackpants she seemed so fond of. He grinned. She was hardly a fashion statement when she shucked off those power suits she wore to work but he wouldn't change that for all the exquisitely dressed women in the world. He loved that she felt comfortable enough in her own skin to dress as she liked, not how she thought the world would want her to.

Sitting on a plastic chair down on the beach Alexandra raised her glass to tap his. 'Thank you. I haven't been on a picnic since I don't know when. Probably right here as a kid with Dad.'

'You've been missing out on so much fun.' Everyone went on picnics. Didn't they?

'My mother and stepfather never had time for such frivolity.'

'Having fun with your children is frivolity?'

'For them it was. Fun was studying music or taking extra lessons so I could top the science class every exam. Not playing.' Her voice petered away and she studied the inside of her glass. 'But I think now that Mother didn't know how to have fun either. Her parents were austere, strict and never laughed.'

'Nothing like you, then. Where did Harry and Bella come from? They certainly know how to have fun.'

She swilled the wine around the glass, then took a sip. 'I loved art at school. Dad always encouraged me—probably easier on his ears than my singing. In the beginning the stories were my fantasies. They began after Dad died. I guess I was trying to find what I'd lost. Fun, laughter. I'd always wanted a brother or sister to be naughty with, family stuff, you know. Also the dog stories were something that couldn't suddenly be taken from me.'

'Where did your passion for medicine come from?'

This was great, learning more about Alexandra in one morning than he had in weeks.

'Dad was a GP and I always wanted to be the same, except I found I loved paediatrics more. Then after Jordan died it became a penance.' She gulped a mouthful of her wine. Swallowing she stared out to sea, seeing who knew what.

'Alexandra, you can't blame yourself for what happened to Jordan.'

'Why not? Jonty did. Jordan was inside me, in my care. No one else's.' She raised a hand, palm out. 'Oh, I know the medical facts, know stillbirth happens. But believe me, that counts for nothing when you're the mother.'

'I can see why you'd think that. I really can.' The desolation in her voice had cut him in two. Sometimes his family were overbearing and a right pain in the butt. Sometimes he'd even wished for a quieter life but he'd always known they were all there for him as he was there for them. Alexandra hadn't had that. He refilled her glass and raised it to her lips. 'Thank you for telling me your story.'

'You listened. That's special.' Those beautiful emerald eyes glistened with unshed tears, breaking his heart. 'Since meeting you, seeing you with Sophia, even sharing some time with her, I've started to put my anger and grief aside. I'll always love Jordan, and wish for a different outcome, but I accept now that I can't change that. I'm also beginning to think I might be entitled to a second chance.'

'Of course you are. You deserve it, *tesoro.*' *With me, I hope.* Leaning close he kissed her forehead, her cheeks and finally her lips. Then he pulled back. Now was not the time to take this any further.

Silence fell between them. A comfortable silence nudged occasionally by an errant shrieking gull. The air cooled as the sun descended behind Mount Arthur. The tide began pulling back from its high line.

'Mario, would you stay with me tonight? Here? I need you.' Her cheeks coloured, but her eyes were filled with sadness. And entreaty.

Pushing out of the chair he lifted his Alexandra into his arms and carried her up to the cottage. Tonight he'd look after her, feed her body and soul, make love to her, hold her all night. Today, tonight, forever, he was hers.

Alex woke slowly, opening one eye at a time. She'd slept most of the night. That was a first after a day at the beach with Jordan's memories. Stretching her legs and arms in starfish fashion across the bed she felt the sheets rumpled from making love with Mario, but she didn't come up against the solid warmth of the man who'd chased her bad dreams away.

'Please don't go home. Not yet. Though I did only ask you to stay the night I'm not ready for you to go again.' Staring up at the ceiling where sunlight made patterns from around the edges of her curtains, she smiled.

Last night Mario had been so tender, so generous. His lovemaking had been exquisite. Earlier in the day he'd been caring and sharing and loving. As though he'd forgotten his anger with her, had forgiven her and at the same time accepted he'd been out of line. He'd apologised yesterday. Not with words, but in the hours he'd sat listening to her without trying to suggest she might've got some things wrong, in celebrating Jordan's birthday, and in sharing the night with her.

She needed to hug him, thank him. She needed to

tell him she loved him. If he didn't like it, then she'd accept that too. At least she'll have been honest with him.

And nothing ventured, nothing gained. Right?

Mario snapped his phone shut just as Alexandra entered the kitchen, her nose sniffing the air like a retriever. 'Hey, sleepyhead. Thought you'd never wake up.'

'I haven't slept so well in forever.' She headed to the stove top. 'Hot, strong coffee. You're a sweetheart. Exactly what I'm after.' The grin she gave him was big and friendly and happy. 'But first I need you.' Wrapping her arms around his neck she stretched up to plant her mouth on his and as she kissed him she murmured, 'Thank you for everything you did, for being you. You made my day special.'

'I'm glad you let me share it with you. Now, *amore mio*, before you get too cosy I'd better warn you that we are about to be inundated.'

Her eyes popped. 'With Italians?'

'*Sì*, Sophia is fretting a little so I suggested Gina bring her and the boys out here for a few hours. I think Jackson's coming too. Seems he spent the night at Gina's. Sorry to take liberties with your place.'

Alexandra was shaking her head in that sage way she had as she poured coffee into the two mugs he had ready. 'How long have we got alone?'

'Long enough for a shower, not long enough for what you're thinking.' More's the pity.

'Think you're capable of reading my mind now, do you?'

He took the mug she handed him. 'Hell, no. It's shambolic in there. It's the "I want to get laid" look in your eyes that kind of gives you away. You're insatiable.'

Alexandra flicked a tea towel at him, cracking it on

his thigh. 'Insatiable, huh? Don't tell me you're complaining.'

'Ouch, and no, definitely not.' Seems their argument was a thing of the past. 'Brunch is coming with the family. Thank goodness, because I've checked out your cupboards and fridge. A man could starve around here, especially after all the exercise I've had. At least the coffee tastes good, even if I say so.'

'I'm taking mine to the bathroom. I'm not greeting all your family in my dressing gown.'

'Or with *I've just had sex* written all over your face.' He laughed as she flicked the tea towel again. 'Careful. I might have to put you over my knee and spank you.'

'Kinky.' Then Alex sucked a lungful. 'Mario, there's something I need to tell you.'

Instantly the laughter died from his eyes, his mouth. 'Yes?'

'I love you.' When he didn't say anything she burbled on. 'I don't know how or when it happened but it's true. I love you. With all my heart. With all me. With—'

His forefinger on her lips stopped the torrent. 'Thank you, *amore mio*. And I love you. I've been busting to tell you. Wanting to shout it out across the beach. But this is your weekend, yours and Jordan's. I didn't want to encroach. But bottom line is I love you.'

Alex thought she'd implode with the love and warmth and excitement and everything she felt for this wonderful man. Her hands met around his neck and she pulled his mouth down to hers. 'To hell with the family. Let's celebrate,' and she tugged him towards the bedroom.

Two hours later Alex stared around her cottage in amazement. Not for a very long time had there been so many people squeezed in here and yet it felt right somehow. Gina and her boys had swarmed in and made themselves totally at home, putting up enough food to feed an orphanage, all laughing and chattering at once so that no one could hear anyone else. Jackson had trailed behind, a bewildered yet happy expression on his face. He was now chasing the boys and Sophia around the lawn accompanied with ear-splitting shrieks filling the bay.

Gina and Mario kicked Alex out of her own kitchen. 'Set the table up on the lawn where it doesn't matter if the bambinos make a mess.'

Gina banged a pan down on a gas ring. 'Oh, and don't forget glasses for the champagne Mario demanded we bring.'

'He did?'

Beside her a deep sexy voice told her, 'What's brunch without champagne?'

'A dry argument?'

'No more arguing for you and me,' he murmured against her neck as his tongue did a little lick thing on her oversensitive skin.

Turning, she slid a hand behind his neck. 'You're right. Been there, done that, and didn't like the consequences. So we're definitely okay again?'

Mario's eyes smouldered back at her, granite coloured. His tongue flicked over his bottom lip. Under her hand he trembled briefly. 'Come with me,' he growled before grabbing her hand and hauling her outside and down to the beach without giving her a chance to answer.

'What happened to you and me cooking brunch?' Gina called after them.

Mario looked around. 'Jackson, you're wanted in the kitchen.'

At the water's edge Mario stopped and turned Alex to look at him, his hands on her waist, a very serious expression on his face. His Adam's apple bobbed. 'Alexandra.' Her name slid off his tongue in her favourite way. Another swallow. 'Alexandra, I screwed up badly. I had no right to demand you tell me such private things about your baby. Not even what Lucy did lets me off the hook. I am very, very sorry for getting so angry.'

'You showed me that yesterday. No one has ever turned Jordan's birthday into a celebration before. That was unbelievably special.' And now she could dream about having more children. But first she had to catch her man. 'Mario—'

His finger pressed her lips. 'Shh. Let me finish. I know I'm rushing things but today seems the perfect day with family here and the cold bottles of champagne waiting to be popped open.' Another swallow and he was saying in his heart-melting voice, 'Alexandra, I love you with all my heart and I want to marry you, have bambinos with you, even retire and race mobility scooters with you in the distant future.'

Laughter vied with tears as she reached her hands to his face to pull him down and kiss him. 'Yes, yes, yes. I love you so much I'd do anything to be with you for the rest of our lives. Even fine-tune your engine.'

'You certainly know how to keep that running.'

'Right.' She covered his mouth with hers, then pulled back. 'I think I've loved you from the moment you strode through my ward looking like it was yours.' Then before he could argue she kissed him, long and hard.

Cheers and clapping broke their kiss. Alex found herself torn from Mario's arms and embraced by Gina. 'Welcome to the Forelli mob,' her soon-to-be sister-in-law said.

Jackson handed round glasses of champagne to the adults and lemonade to the kids.

'To my beautiful Alexandra, *tesoro*.' Mario held his glass high.

'Daddy, what's happened? Why's everyone laughing?' Sophia appeared at Mario's side and tugged at his hand. 'Why's Alex crying?'

Alex dropped to her knees in the sand and reached a hand to the sweetest little girl she'd ever encountered. 'Sophia, Daddy's asked me to marry him. Is that all right with you?'

Big brown eyes studied her in the sudden silence. 'Are you going to be my mummy?'

'Is that what you want?' Her heart thudded in her ears, because if Sophia said no, then she wasn't marrying Mario. This child had first dibs on him.

'Yes, please, Alex.'

And suddenly Alex was being squashed in a cuddle with her fiancé and daughter-to-be, and more cheers were deafening her as her glass tipped in her hand and spilled its contents over her feet.

Mario whispered, 'Think of all those bambinos we can make.'

Gulp. Her own children. 'Ahh, could we start with just one?'

'Not a problem. I know when you hold our first baby you'll be begging me for more.' His eyes twinkled at her, warming her heart, curling her toes.

'How many grandchildren do your parents think they can handle?'

'Lots.' Mario grinned. 'Be warned. There are days with my family that you'll want to hide in the back of a wardrobe with a torch and a good book.'

'Trying to talk me out of this now?' She couldn't

stop smiling, she felt so alive and happy. She had a future to look forward to.

'No, you'll find I'm already in there. I'll bring the cheese and bread, you bring the champagne.'

One year on...

Alex lay back against the pillows on her hospital bed. Her left arm cuddled baby Forelli, female. Her right arm cuddled baby Forelli, male. Age two hours twenty minutes.

Her face ached from her permanent smile. Her heart throbbed with pride, joy and relief.

Mario and Sophia sat on the end of the bed arguing over the babies' names.

Sophia wanted to call them Harry and Bella.

Mario wanted to call them Alexander and Alexandra.

Alexandra just wanted to hug them all forever. This was her family. Loud, noisy, beautiful.

* * * * *

A sneaky peek at next month...

Medical Romance™

CAPTIVATING MEDICAL DRAMA—WITH HEART

My wish list for next month's titles...

In stores from 3rd May 2013:

☐ NYC Angels: Flirting with Danger — Tina Beckett

& NYC Angels: Tempting Nurse Scarlet
  — Wendy S. Marcus

☐ One Baby Step at a Time — Meredith Webber

& P.S. You're a Daddy! — Dianne Drake

☐ Return of the Rebel Doctor — Joanna Neil

& One Life Changing Moment — Lucy Clark

Available at WHSmith, Tesco, Asda, Eason, Amazon and Apple

Just can't wait?

Visit us Online

You can buy our books online a month before they hit the shops! **www.millsandboon.co.uk**

0413/03

Join the NYC Angels online community...

Get all the gossip straight from the hospital on our NYC Angels Facebook app...

- Read exclusive bonus material from each story
- Enter our NYC Angels competition
- Introduce yourself to our Medical authors

You can find the app at our Facebook page

Facebook.com/romancehq

(Once on Facebook, simply click on the NYC Angels logo to visit the app!)

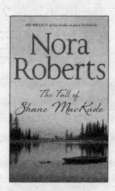

Mills & Boon® Online

Discover more romance at
www.millsandboon.co.uk

 FREE online reads

🌹 **Books** up to one
month before shops

🌹 **Browse our books**
before you buy

...and much more!

For exclusive competitions and instant updates:

 Like us on **facebook.com/romancehq**

 Follow us on **twitter.com/millsandboonuk**

🌹 Join us on **community.millsandboon.co.uk**

Visit us Online | Sign up for our FREE eNewsletter at **www.millsandboon.co.uk**